CHARLES HARREL

THE
DAY AFTER
ALWAYS

THE NOVEL

BY

CHARLES EARL HARREL

DEDICATION

To Laura Lee,
my beloved wife and
co-laborer in the harvest:

Thank you!

Without your support, editing, and encouragement,
this novel would not have been written.

To Teresa, friends, and family who helped with the book,
believed in it, and prayed for it to make a difference:

"I thank my God upon every remembrance of you" (Philippians
1:3).

MAP OF CENTRAL HEAVEN

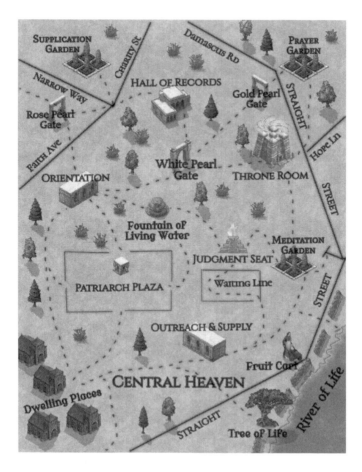

The locations and landmarks in Central Heaven are speculative. Notwithstanding, several are based on Scripture, others inspired by tradition.

"But as it is written, Eye hath not seen, nor ear heard, neither have entered into the heart of man, the things which God hath prepared for them that love him" (1 Corinthians 2:9).

Till the sea runs dry, till the moon don't shine, till the rain clouds are all left behind. Till the wind don't blow, till the stars don't show, I'll praise His name till the day after always.

—Song lyrics by Paul Dee Allen (1988)

CHAPTER 1
THE ARRIVAL

Heaven was not exactly what Jesse Walt expected. Taking inventory, he paced around the room they assigned him. His living quarters were modest. The place contained a comfortable bed, a hardwood writing desk with four-legged stool, and a chest of drawers. It had no windows, no bathroom, and only one entry door, which Jesse kept propped open. All the units on his floor and throughout the entire housing complex were much the same.

The events from the last few days, if one can call them days, filled his thoughts. He had hoped things would be different here in heaven. In many ways they were, but former emotions and feelings of insecurity were still a part of him. Those hadn't changed at all, nor had his memories: some nice, others disconcerting. No doubt, there were reasons for that. Perhaps such understanding would come with time. *Time, hmm, interesting concept,* half-chuckling to himself, *it's perpetual now. What am I supposed to do for all eternity?*

As he continued his walkthrough, an individual popped into the middle of his room. It was Seth again, the blond-haired teenager who lived across the hallway in the adjacent unit. Jesse had met him right after the Arrival. "Hey dude, are you going to the lecture? It's starting soon, and I heard it's gonna be packed. We better book it if we want to find a seat in the front."

Jesse scratched his chin, trying to think of an excuse to forgo the meeting. Being new, one of the many who had just come up in the Rapture, he was still settling into this unique environment. "Sorry Seth. Think I'll stay in my place and rest. You go ahead without me."

"No, man, you don't wanna do that. It'll be radical. Even better than the lecture Moses gave. Abraham is the main speaker for this one. He's gonna tell his life story. You gotta come."

Seth usually didn't take no for an answer. "Where are they holding the gathering?"

"At Patriarch Plaza, next to the fountain, below the main pearl gate entry."

"Alright, I'll meet you there, except I'm walking." Jesse preferred the old way of getting somewhere—using streets and pathways. This popping in and out of places wasn't for him, not yet anyway.

"Well, don't be late. I'll save a place for you. I have two friends you might want to meet. They're going to the lecture, too." Seth gave a thumbs-up, then vanished, disappearing right through the wall.

Jesse waited an additional moment or two and then exited his apartment, closing the door behind him. He followed the crowds. Apparently, everyone in the heavenly city had chosen to attend the lecture tonight. *Tonight, no nights here either. Guess I'll need to make that adjustment as well.*

As he walked, angels soared overhead, followed by hundreds more—all heading toward the plaza. As soon as Jesse arrived, he began hunting for Seth. He was about to abandon the search when he heard his voice: "Dude, over this way, over this way!" The teen was wearing blue jeans and a tan hoodie, not the white robes most of the new arrivals wore. He would ask Seth about clothing options later.

While waiting for the meeting to start, Seth introduced his friends. He pointed to a man over seven-foot tall with a chiseled jaw. "This big fella is Maximus Gallius. He served as a Roman soldier. Max has a tough-guy persona, you know, like that cyborg dude in those old earth movies, except he's really a cool person. He's been in heaven a long time." Maximus trooped over and gave him a hardy slap on the back, which Jesse assumed was his way of greeting folks.

"And this nice lady over here is Annabelle Altshuler. We call her Anna. She has a prophetic gifting and sings chill songs.

She came up in the Rapture with you." Annabelle smiled at Jesse and nodded respectfully. Before Seth could finish the introductions, Gabriel, the messenger of God, took the podium and introduced Abraham. Those who were already seated stood to their feet and joined the audience clapping their hands. Shouts of shalom filled the plaza.

Abraham looked well aged and shorter than Jesse had imagined. The patriarch stepped onto the platform and adjusted the sash around his Bedouin outfit, pulling it snug. His garments were dazzling white, almost reflective. He removed the mantle from his head and wrapped it around his shoulders. A tall wooden staff, which he held in his right hand, was propped upon a nearby bench. Abraham cut short the applause and motioned for the group to retake their seats.

"Welcome saints, including all you newcomers. Blessings! May you have an ear to hear . . ." and so he began. Since time was no longer an issue, Abraham spoke for what seemed like hours. Jesse's mind wandered during the speech until he heard Abraham say, "Some of you may be asked to do as I did, to leave the familiar, the safety of your abodes, and journey to an unknown place to carry out God's purposes. You and I were not redeemed simply to enter paradise and have an eternal vacation but to further God's outreach to lost worlds, wherever they may exist."

"One day, the Lord asked me to relocate, and by faith I obeyed Him, not knowing where I was going. I said my goodbyes and left my country, my people, and my father's household to travel to a land of promise." He paused, scanned the crowd for a couple moments, and then bent over to grab his staff. "Well, I'm sure y'all know the rest of the story."

"And now, today, if you will hear His voice and open your hearts, I believe you'll understand His call as I did. Heaven hopes you are listening." With that, Abraham closed the lecture, dismissed the crowds, skipped down the plaza steps like a young man, and in an instant, disappeared.

After the meeting ended, Jesse told the new acquaintances he would catch them later and departed, heading to his room. When he cleared the plaza, he started to run. Jogging was an activity he did on earth if he wanted to be alone and think.

Usually, he tired quickly and needed to slow down. Having a stiff, injured knee didn't help the situation; now however, he had no pain at all. He wasn't even winded, so he increased the pace, then switched to a sprint. The footpaths led to streets. At the end of one, another materialized, appearing out of nowhere.

Up ahead, a small stand with a rainbow-patterned canopy came into view. As Jesse drew closer, he determined it was actually a mobile food cart, similar to the ones used at the Saturday market near his hometown of Dayton. A vendor stood behind it, arranging his wares. Jesse stopped. "Your produce sure looks tasty."

"It is, and fresh too." The vendor reached into the cart, pulled out a purple-skinned fruit and handed it Jesse. "Try this one, it's my favorite."

The fruit had the shape of a mango, although somewhat larger and rounder. As Jesse bit into it, the juice trickled down his chin. "You're right, it's delicious. Thanks! You know, I haven't eaten anything since I arrived."

"You'll find that eating or drinking is optional." The vendor grinned, enjoying how Jesse devoured the fruit. "Toss the pit into the seed holder when you're finished." He pointed to a bowl containing several dried pits. "All things in heaven have a purpose, even an old seed."

"Makes sense. No doubt, I've got much to learn about your eternal kingdom."

"Most do at first." The vendor's eyes glistened as he spoke. "Here, take one more with you for later."

Jesse turned the fruit around in his hand, inspecting it, feeling the smooth skin. "Is there a cost or something?"

"No, they're free, like everything in heaven."

He glanced around to see if anyone else was listening to their conversation. The crowds seemed to have moved on or transported to another location. "What about advice?"

"Yep, that's free too. What do you want to know?"

Jesse wiped the juice from his face using his sleeve. "This for one thing." He tugged on the collar of his robe. "I noticed people in various wardrobes at the meeting, not just these white gowns. My neighbor, Seth, wore what appeared to be a pair of Levis. And Max, his buddy, dressed as a Roman soldier."

"Ah, you must be one of the recent arrivals. Good to make your acquaintance." The vendor put out his hand so Jesse could shake it. "Sure, you can wear different clothes in heaven. Check with Orientation. It's near Faith Avenue. They have a wide selection of heaven-appropriate clothing."

"Good deal, much appreciated. I'll check it out." Jesse tucked the extra fruit into his robe and took off running again.

About ten strides later, he heard the vendor yell, "So, what did you think of Abraham's message?"

He peered over his shoulder, but the vendor was gone, fruit stand and all. The sudden disappearance didn't bother him. The question did, however.

CHAPTER 2
EXPLORING HEAVEN

Maybe I should have paid closer attention to *Abraham's message, something about leaving the familiar, wasn't it?* Jesse had a habit of muttering to himself; it seemed to help him sort out his thoughts. As a former police officer, mulling over the details of an investigation uncovered leads and resolved cases. He decided to rehash the patriarch's lecture later. Right now, though, he wanted to explore more of heaven.

Jesse started running again, seeing folks everywhere along the way. Most smiled as he raced by, some waved. Everyone seemed happy, carefree. The roads leading out of Central Heaven branched off in all directions. The one he traveled down was called Straight Street. Jesse wasn't sure how he knew this name since there were no signposts. Somehow, the designation popped into his mind when he wondered about it. He stopped for a moment and pounded on the pavement with the heel of his leather sandal. *Seems solid enough and has a golden appearance. The Bible sure nailed that description.*

As he trekked across the outlying areas, Jesse encountered large pillars, pearl gates of various colors, jeweled walls and structures, parklands, and lush gardens. Overhead, the skyline shimmered with white glowing beams. Not a cloud in sight. No sunlight or shady areas either. Jesse wondered what additional secrets heaven held. On the left, he passed what looked like horse stables. Thinking back, he remembered reading about four horses mentioned in Revelation. *Perhaps this place has other animals, too.* Since he had all of eternity, he would return later and investigate.

Jesse had been following a large river, which meandered through the heavenscape. It flowed wide in spots; the waters clear as crystal. Leaf-filled trees and flowery bushes flourished along the riverbanks. All the scenery appeared alive, vibrant, with unique colors and designs. *Wow, if people only knew.*

Somewhere along the line, the crowds thinned out and Jesse found himself alone. Although he didn't feel lost or tired, he'd seen enough for a while and wanted to return to his room. Since he wasn't ready to try the transporting thing, he kept traveling until he came to a fork in the road. He slowed to a walk, considered his options, and chose the route turning left.

A short distance away, the roadway merged into a small T-intersection. From there, a winding path led to a solitary place with white marble benches, small fountains, hedges, and trees of all kinds. Jesse recognized a few species; others were unknown types, exotic, and strangely beautiful. He followed the cobblestone path until it ended. On one of the benches sat an older man, his eyes closed, his head bowed.

The man glanced up at Jesse and rubbed his eyes. They appeared swollen and puffy. *Had the old man been crying?* "Oh, I'm sorry to have disturbed you, sir. You probably want to be alone."

"No, not at all, laddie." The man stood, adjusted his coat, and tucked an item into his pocket. "Merely doing a little reading."

"Do they have a library up here?"

"Not exactly, but we do have a scroll room inside the Hall of Records."

"Any books?"

"Naw, just scrolls, a whole chamber of them: Scripture, history, prophecy. In fact, the archives contain a record on all matters said or done. Those, however, are not for general viewing. Only high-ranked angels have access to such information, and of course, God."

"I can tell by your questions you're one of the new arrivals, therefore, let me introduce myself. I'm Reverend Lundy MacBain." Lundy tipped his tartan-patterned cap, showing respect to Jesse.

"Good to meet you, sir. My name is Jesse Walt." He put his hand out and gave Lundy a firm handshake. "What do they call this place?"

"It's the Garden of Meditation, one of many prayer gardens in heaven. I was meditating and reading a Scripture scroll when you walked over." Lundy pulled the rolled parchment out his pocket, showed it to Jesse, and then tucked it into his boot.

"You know, laddie, I've been a minister all my life. Lived in Scotland 400 years ago, earth time I reckon. One day I encountered a mob of agnostics who didn't care for my preaching. Everyone's a critic, I guess. At any rate, they pulled knives and did me in. Been in heaven ever since. Aye, not a bad place for an extremely long, unending day."

"Yeah, I know. I'm still trying to figure out how this no night and endless-day situation works."

"So, what about you Brother Walt? What's your story?"

Jesse shuffled his feet, staring at the stone pathway, trying to think of what and how much to tell the preacher. "After high school, I enlisted in the Navy, became an MP. When I got out of the service, I took a position as a small-town police chief, but it didn't work out as planned. Clerked in a convenience store for a while. I've done a little writing and journaling, nothing published."

Lundy plopped down on the bench, removed his cap and stuffed it into his empty pocket. "Aye, sounds like a dandy life to me."

He knew that wasn't the case but chose not to correct the older gentleman. Pondering what to say next, Jesse sat on the bench by Lundy, leaned back and stretched out his legs. "Since you've been here for a while, Reverend, what do you think about heaven?"

"It's a wonderful place. Me thinks, however, there should be more to do . . . well . . . enough conjecture."

"I hear ya. I'm also wondering about my purpose here."

"Mine is ministry or was. It's what I was called to do. Please don't take this wrong, laddie," Lundy continued. "For me, heaven is not what I expected, not thus far anyway."

Jesse simply nodded, hoping to avoid a discussion about

his own views or feelings, especially with a new acquaintance.

"Ah, I gotta go." Lundy stood and extended his right hand for a farewell shake. "It's been nice talking with you. So, have you learned to transport? It's the quickest way to get around."

"No, not really sure how to do that."

"Just think where you want to be and you're . . ." In a flash, Lundy vanished, leaving before he finished the sentence.

"Okay, time I learned to fly or transport or whatever this method is." Still seated on the bench, Jesse closed his eyes and thought of his room. And zap, he was there, standing in the doorway. It didn't take long either, a few seconds or what he used to consider as seconds. Next time he encountered a long-term resident, he'd ask how one accounts for the passage of time in eternity.

Jesse wandered over to his writing desk and opened the top. Inside he retrieved a blank scroll, a quill pen, and a brass inkwell. He put the ink container into a round slot on top of the table and dipped his pen in. At the same moment, a craving for a bite to eat hit him, so he put the pen aside and grabbed the extra fruit the vendor gave him. Devoured it in three bites. Remembering what the vendor said—that everything in heaven has a purpose and nothing is wasted—he placed the leftover pit on the tabletop.

He unrolled the scroll, dipped his quill pen into the inkwell again, then paused for a moment while considering his first line. *Ironic,* he thought to himself, *one would think newer instruments would be available. Quill and bottled ink seem quaint. No doubt, it goes with the décor. No books, either just scrolls.* He needed to ask the management about writing materials, and if possible, requisition a journal made with actual pages and a hard cover.

Since heaven has no nights, only daylight, and no passage of time in the normal sense, Jesse picked his starting date as entry one:

Entry One

No changing of days, or nights, or light from the sun. Normal time continues on earth, I think. Here, it's basically one, long, everlasting day. Therefore, I'm calling this eternal era "the day after always," a day that goes on forever and ever.

He stopped writing to contemplate his rationale. That

would be the perfect title for his journal. Jesse decided to use it on the cover if he can get one. For now, this rolled-up piece of paper will have to suffice.

I have not seen any little children or babies, only teens, who I would estimate to be around thirteen years old. A book I read once said people in heaven would be in their prime, yet I see a ton of older individuals, like Abraham, who looks to be the age described in the Bible. There are all ages here, just no little ones. If all the saints were thirty years old, it might feel like a cult or something. I plan on asking someone in the know about these matters. As for me, I look the same age I was before I arrived, except I don't need eyeglasses anymore or have a sore knee. And I feel strong and energetic.

Jesse rerolled the scroll, leaving it on top of the desk; the pen and ink he placed inside. He moved over to the bed, sat on the edge and patted the mattress. *Not bad.* Deciding a little break would be nice, he laid back and adjusted his feather pillow. Not feeling sleepy, he stared at the decorative white ceiling, interested in the swirling patterns. Within the designs, he noticed several symbols: ꓤ Y ꓤ Z . He didn't remember seeing them before. As he studied the markings, he drifted off into a deep sleep. An assortment of images and scenes flashed through his mind, some familiar, others strange and disturbing:

Car crash, pain pills, injured knee, police badge

Lady with long braided hair, temple ruins, man with tarnished crown, hidden cave

Violence, hatred, deception, fields ablaze, poison, mysterious fruit

After the dream sequence ended, he shook himself awake and peered at the ceiling. The strange markings had disappeared. *That's odd!* He swung his feet over the bed and sat up. As he pondered the missing symbols and images in his dream, he heard footsteps nearby. When he cranked his neck around to see, a tall individual stepped into the open doorway, his head almost touching the top header. Jesse jumped off the bed as if it was on fire.

CHAPTER 3
Meeting elChesed

Jesse froze in place, watching the visitor move closer. The person wore a bright white robe that touched the top of his leather sandals. A deep blue sash rounded his waist, which he had tied into a knot on his left side. The fringes hung down to his knee. His hand rested upon a sheathed sword attached to his sash on the right side. He stood at least a foot taller than Jesse's height of six-foot one. "So, what did you think about Abraham's message?"

"You know, you're the second person to ask me this question," Jesse replied. "Is there some reason why everybody I meet wants to know my answer?"

"I'm sure it's not everyone, but we can discuss that later. First, allow me to introduce myself. I am not a person. I'm an angel of God. No doubt, you have already made this determination by looking at my sword. In heaven, only angels carry them. What you may not know, however, is that I'm your guardian angel. My given name is elChesed. It means mercy of God. Most fellow servants call me Chesedel."

Relieved, Jesse relaxed his shoulders and unclenched his fists. "Then you've been with me through thick and thin?"

"Indeed, during your time on earth, I stood by your side, whispered God's messages, and encouraged your faith. Since you reside in heaven now, I wonder if you have questions about this place."

"Yeah, a few. Do they have books here? I'm interested in starting a journal. When I lived on earth, I wrote police case logs and kept a personal diary. Writing things down helped me organize my thoughts."

"Sorry, Jesse, there are no books in heaven, just scrolls. It's what we have used since the beginning, but I have an idea. Perhaps I can make you one by cutting several blank pages and binding them into a small workable journal. Give me what you have written thus far, and I'll add your entries to the first page."

"Great, much appreciated." Jesse slipped over to his writing table, retrieved the scroll, and handed it to Chesedel who tucked it into his sash.

"I'll drop off your journal after everything is put together. Is there anything else you desire to know?"

"Um, yeah, I haven't seen little children or babies. If they're around, where are they?"

"That's a spiritual maturity issue and a practical one." Chesedel moved over and leaned against the back wall, making himself comfortable while he pondered how best to explain the answer. "We consider thirteen the age of accountability, a time when children have understanding about responsibility. Judaism believes a boy reaches adulthood when he turns thirteen and a girl at twelve. Other belief systems have similar rationales. In heaven, all these younger individuals emerge as teenagers and are considered adults. On the practical side, it wouldn't be wise to have babies or little children crawling around the celestial streets."

"Okay, makes sense. What about remembrances? I mean certain memories, feelings, and events."

"All emotions and feelings, whether beneficial or contrary, are expedient. They have a divine purpose and God allows them. However, certain events, known as former things, are forgotten. For example, heaven would not be blissful if you remembered for all eternity those who were lost or left behind. Therefore, God hides such remembrances until He feels the time is right to reveal them."

"Sounds reasonable."

"Any additional concerns?"

"This one's kind of dumb. I had a couple days stubble before this rapture thing, and I still have it." Jesse ran his fingers across his chin and neck to make his point. "Can I shave up here or do I have to keep this facial hair for all eternity?"

"Whichever you prefer. Check with Orientation for guidelines. They usually carry starter kits with grooming materials."

"Good to know. Maybe I'll grab a comb, too. What about a person's age?"

The angel moved away from the wall, walked over to Jesse's writing desk and sat on the stool. "We get this question a lot." He paused for a moment before continuing with his answer. "With the exception of the young children I already mentioned, deceased or raptured saints retain their same-age appearance. Your friend Seth looks like a teenager because he was one. Moses and Abraham appear as older men, same reason. When the rich man saw Abraham in paradise, he recognized him as being aged. Likewise, when Saul talked with a deceased Samuel, he appeared as an older prophet. Regardless of age at entry, all saints will have the endurance, stamina, and strength of a younger person—as you experienced yourself. I realize it's a lot of information to digest."

"Well, I asked. I believe I've gotten enough answers for now."

"Don't worry; most new arrivals have the same questions. Glad to be of help. If you have more, please ask me. You'll get the hang of things in time."

Time? Jesse decided to save that question for later. He didn't want the angel to think he was conducting an investigation.

Chesedel stood and pushed the stool underneath the writing desk. "Jesse, as your guardian angel, I can hear most of your thoughts and all of your prayers. It goes with the job. Regarding the flow of *time* in eternity, let's discuss the concept at a future date." Before leaving, he handed him a written invitation from Uzziel:

Favored One, you and several other saints are invited to a gathering at the Fountain of Living Water. I will meet you there. Maranatha, Uzziel

"Who is this Uzziel?" Jesse asked.

"He is a cherubim angel whose name means strength of God."

"A gathering about . . ."

"It concerns Abraham and the message he gave at Patriarch Plaza." Chesedel bowed, took one step backwards and vanished.

CHAPTER 4
DECISION TIME

The area around the Fountain of Living Water was often crowded but not at this moment. Only four individuals were present. Two sat on marble benches visiting, a third paced around the perimeter holding a scroll, and the fourth knelt in prayer. The fountain lay between Patriarch Plaza and the Judgment Seat. It was a popular heavenmark where residents enjoyed drinking from the living waters or wading in the shallows of the pool. Uzziel and elChesed stood across from the fountain, facing one another, speaking in quiet tones.

"Did you contact everybody in the group?" Uzziel asked.

"Yes, they're on their way right now."

Uzziel's long golden hair waved in the gentle breeze as he scanned the garden with a watchful eye. His celestial wings were folded behind his back. His flaming sword, usually gripped in his left hand, remained in its scabbard. Even sheathed, it still glowed, sending out rays of white fiery light. "Do they understand what is being asked of them and the sacrifice involved?"

"I hope so. Perhaps Abraham's message helped open their hearts."

"Perhaps . . ." Uzziel, lost in his thoughts, glanced over at the Tree of Life, which could be seen almost anywhere in Central Heaven. His eyes narrowed, revealing apprehension. "As you recall, Chesedel, I was present that day in Eden. God had sent me to block the way to the garden, but the damage from Satan's meddling occurred beforehand."

"Was the Lord caught unaware?"

"No, He knew what Satan planned." Uzziel checked his sword again, giving a tug to the reddish sash around his waist that secured the scabbard to his side. "The Lord allowed it for a purpose."

"What purpose would justify the damage?"

"We will know that in the Lord's time, which brings me to the situation in Eskaonus. It has become grave. Corruption is spreading and soon it will reach the southern province. Do you remember what happened on earth, where the thoughts and intentions of people were evil continually? Our concern here as well. Time is running out to avert a similar disaster."

As the angels talked, the invitees began to appear. Seth Cahir materialized first, then Holley Rossie, followed by Annabelle Altshuler. Lundy MacBain had walked over earlier and was reading a Scripture scroll. Maximus Gallius strode up next—he didn't care for this popping in and out thing—marching was more his style. Jesse Walt arrived last. The assembled saints took seats on a front bench near the fountain and waited. Jesse analyzed facial expressions for tells, hoping they might reveal the purpose of their summons.

"I'm glad everyone made it," Chesedel said. "Please feel free to get a drink from the fountain before we start. It's always refreshing." He waited for them to drink from one of many water outlets streaming from the fountain. After they were reseated, he continued, "If you haven't met Uzziel yet, let me introduce him. He is one of the highest-ranking angels in heaven. We call him *the Cherubim*."

Uzziel thanked his fellow servant for the introduction and then offered greetings to their six guests. He unsheathed his sword and held it high over his head. Bursts of light flamed everywhere. "This is the blade I used in Eden when the Lord sent me to guard the garden. That mission was important, as is the one I will give you now." With their attention procured, he placed his sword back into his scabbard.

"God created all things, not just the heavens and earth you are familiar with, but everything, in every place and every dimension. They are His worlds without end. One of those, called Eskaonus, is in danger of being destroyed by wickedness."

Their eyes widened as they listened. Several from the group fidgeted in their seats. Reverend Lundy leaned forward, elbows on his legs, knuckles propping up his chin.

"An unknown evil stalks the land," Chesedel added, "and worst of all, the knowledge of God and His ways have been diluted, corrupted long ago, and unviable. Unless this can be remedied, their world could be lost forever."

"So here is our invitation and appeal," Uzziel said. "We need you to travel to this distant world, scope out the situation, identify the problem, and try to resolve it. Because of the urgency, you must portal there as soon as possible, immediately in fact. Moreover, we are asking you to leave your immortality behind, to become mortal again, much like the Lord did when He took on the earthly form of Jesus. In Eskaonus, you will be human, not spirit beings. Nonetheless, you'll still retain your eternal souls. This change will be a major sacrifice, as the Lord would know, and it carries risks: possible jeopardy to your lives and the lives of others."

The fidgeting stopped; each person sat motionless, eyes straight ahead, pondering the dire implications.

"Whether yea or nay, you all have the freedom of choice in this matter. There is no condemnation in heaven. However, you must choose, as time is running out for the inhabitants of Eskaonus."

When the Cherubim finished speaking, Chesedel gathered the little band together in a circle. "I think it would be a good time to pray. Please join hands. And Jesse, since you will be the assigned leader, please lead us in a prayer for wisdom."

Jesse looked down at his feet, took a deep breath, exhaled, and hesitated. All of them felt the awkwardness, the silence. "Maybe somebody else could—"

Annabelle jumped right in. "Thank you, Yeshua, for bringing us together. We believe there is a reason You redeemed us and have selected us for this critical outreach ministry. We all have different talents and gifts to offer. Precious Mashiach, as disciples, we want to serve as best we can, so please guide our decisions. Amen!"

"May the Lord bless you and keep you." Uzziel waved his hand over them, releasing an unseen anointing. "And now, Dear

Ones, we leave you to discuss the situation among yourselves and to make your final decisions." The angels turned and started toward the Throne Room.

"Excuse me, Chesedel, before you leave," Jesse asked, "can I see you on a personal matter?"

"Sure, step over here." They moved to the Waiting Line since it was not being used at the moment. "What is your concern?"

"You asked me to be team leader. Maybe you should have recruited the Reverend or Maximus?" Jesse checked to see if any of his colleagues were close enough to hear the conversation before he continued. Speaking in a soft whisper, he added, "I assume you know I was fired from my position as police chief and about the DUI injury accident?"

"Yes, I do, both circumstances, and as I mentioned before," Chesedel put his hand on Jesse's shoulder, "I've always stood by you, offering strength and support."

"What about the others, do they know I messed up?"

"No, they don't. Perhaps when the time is right you can share your heart. Now is not that time. I assume this is why you hesitated in prayer?"

"Um, partly. There's—"

"Listen, Jesse, heaven is a place of second chances. And while we can't guarantee what will happen on Eskaonus or if you will be successful, we believe you are the one to lead this endeavor. God does as well. You have our blessing and support. Nonetheless, you're free to decline because serving is always a choice. I hope you'll say yes for the sake of your companions and the residents of Eskaonus. Either way, there's no condemnation here."

Chesedel rejoined Uzziel who had been waiting, and together, side-by-side, they walked to the Throne Room, greeting saints along the way. Jesse returned to the fountain.

After a lengthy debate and spirited discussion, Jesse, now the accepted leader, asked for their decisions. Annabelle spoke first. "Beloved, how can we not help these individuals? We must! They need us, and I believe we need them as well. Perhaps like Esther in the Bible, we have been chosen for such a time as this. So yes, Jess, I am willing to go to Eskaonus." Anna closed her eyes, lifted her hands, and began to hum a tune. Then she added words: "Trust in the LORD with all thine heart; and lean not unto thine own understanding. In all thy ways acknowledge him, and he shall direct thy paths." The song sounded amazing, even angelic.

"Aye, Annabel, it's a dandy melody for sure, especially the words, verses 5 and 6 from Proverbs 3 as I recall." Anna smiled, responding to Lundy's encouragement. "You know, laddies, this assignment is right down me alley. Redemptive ministry is what's expedient. Sign me up. I'm going too."

Max gave a hefty pound across his chest with his fist. "Sir, it's my honor to serve."

"His salute is a soldier thing," Seth said. "Well, dudes, it seems we're agreed. Let's do this gig." He glanced over at Holley and asked, "What about your—" Before he could finish his question, she vanished before his eyes.

Later, when the angels returned, they confirmed Holley had decided to pass on the invitation. "She had her reasons," the Cherubim said. "Therefore, she won't be joining the team. I assume the rest of you have decided to go?" The five remaining shook their heads yes. "Good! Any questions?"

"How will we understand the jargon on an unfamiliar world?" inquired Seth. "Will the people or whoever these dudes are be able to recognize our rap?"

"Yes, it has already been arranged," Uzziel replied. "Similar to what happened on the Day of Pentecost, the Holy Spirit will make it possible for you to understand them, and they, you, all except a few local terms and names you'll have to learn."

"Aye, makes perfect sense to me. In Acts 2:6, the crowd heard them speak in their own language. That'll be a tidy miracle, almost like being part of the same clan."

"Are we considered emissaries or missionaries?" Jesse asked for clarification.

"A little of both. The Eskaonites, though, will believe you are distant travelers to their land, at least at first. Some will welcome you, others will not."

"Anything else?" Uzziel waited for more questions or comments, but the party of five remained silent. "Okay, we must get you off-heaven as soon as possible. World-appropriate clothing is already in your rooms. Change into them and head over to Outreach & Supply. You will be allowed to take one item with you from Supply. Use wisdom in your choices. We will meet you at the White Pearl Gate."

In a flash, the fountain plaza emptied . . .

CHAPTER 5
GETTING OUTFITTED

Jesse returned to his room and found a book and cloth bag on top of his desk. The book had leather binding with a title carved on the front that read *The Day After Always*. Excited, he opened the journal and found his first entry already bound in with the blank pages. He also noticed a second entry:

Entry Two

Hope you enjoy the book. I made you a waterproof satchel to carry it in. Your pen is inside, full of ink, and ready to go. Take the journal with you. It may come in handy. I also recycled the old fruit pit I found on your desktop. Everything has a purpose here. Godspeed, elChesed

A new set of clothing lay organized on his bed. He changed out of his white robe and put on a pair of khaki-styled cargo pants with wide pockets down the legs. *They'll be handy for carrying things.* He slipped into a tan, long-sleeved shirt with pale yellow strips and buttoned it. Strange looking buttons, almost square, but they worked fine. Next, he removed his heaven-issued sandals, leaving them on the bed, and pulled up a pair of laceless leather boots. *Nice fit.* He donned a heavy fur-lined coat with more of those square fasteners. *Must get cold there.* Lastly, Jesse placed his journal back inside its carrying case. Since it had a shoulder strap, he swung the satchel over his head and adjusted it at his side. *Well, that's it.* He paused for a moment to look around his room and then popped over to Outreach & Supply to join the others.

The building was located between Patriarch Plaza and Straight Street. He had passed by it on his exploration run but didn't realize its purpose. After he entered the facility, he saw endless shelves holding everything imaginable. Max stood at the front counter; three members in the group were in line behind him, waiting their turn. Jesse joined them.

"What's your preference?" the angelic clerk asked.

Maximus spoke first. "Sir, can I requisition a sword? Not just any sword, I prefer one I'm familiar with. Do you have any Roman blades?"

"Let me check." The angel floated to the top shelf in the armament section and grabbed a sword, sheathed in a leather scabbard, and returned to the counter. "I think this one might be exactly what you're looking for. It's a double-edged, sharp-pointed Gladius, suitable for cutting, chopping, or fighting. This weapon, however, is superior to any made on earth since it never needs sharpening and is practically unbreakable."

Max grabbed the scabbard, holding it almost reverently. He drew the sword out and listened as the blade made a high-pitched noise, sounding like a fiddler pulling his bow across a violin string. He smiled to himself, pleased with the selection.

"Who's next?"

"Me I guess." Annabelle moved forward to the counter. "Shalom to you, Precious One," bowing her head in respect as she spoke. "I'm interested in a musical instrument, if any are available."

"Thank you for honoring me, but remember, only God is truly precious. Concerning music makers, we carry many types, and I have the perfect one for you." The clerk slipped over to the next aisle and returned. "Here's an eight-stringed instrument, half guitar, half harp, our most popular model, very anointed, and it comes with a shoulder strap, handy for the traveling minstrel. And the glifstring never requires tuning. Most individuals love the rosewood pattern."

Anna gave it a strum and sweet music filled the room. "I love it." She slung it over her shoulder, allowing it to settle on her back. "May Yeshua bless you."

"He always does. Next?"

Lundy stepped forward. "Do you have a Gospel of John?

A decent book of Scripture it is, and my favorite."

"Indeed, we do. We stock a pocket-sized, pre-folded scroll, ideal for reading on the go. Moreover, this version is unique because the text miraculously translates into one's own dialect. And it's autographed by John himself." Reaching under the counter, the angel handed it to him. After examining it, Lundy stuffed it into his boot for safekeeping.

"How about you, young man, what do you need?"

Seth stepped up to the counter. "I was thinking a climbing rope might be cool."

"I got just what you want." The angel opened an adjacent display case and pulled out a beige-colored line. "This little cord-sized rope is thin in diameter yet strong. It will hold the weight of ten people, maybe more, and amazingly, it will never lose its length, even if you cut off pieces. We call it a *tikvah*, a cord of hope and possibilities."

"Hey man, this is mint, thanks." Seth wrapped it around his waist a couple times and tied it on like a cincture.

"Next customer?"

"That would be me, except I already have an item, my journal."

"Oh yes, you're the person who requested a book instead of a scroll. Chesedel told me about you. I suppose I'll have to stock journals for everyone in heaven now. At any rate, the Cherubim told me to supply all team members with one item for the journey. So, what will it be? Any ideas?"

"No, none I can think of. I had assumed it would only be my journal."

"Well then, allow me to make a suggestion. I have a portable light, called a candle lamp, which will fit into your traveling satchel. You'll be able see what you write on those dark nights ahead. This lamp has a few extra benefits: It never runs out of oil, is self-lighting, and it gives off a little warmth. Nice fragrance too. Here, take it." After thanking the clerk, Jesse slid the candle lamp into one of the strapped pockets inside his satchel and joined his party at the front door.

All outfitted, the group walked out and headed for the portal, their spirits high, their hearts hopeful. Uzziel and Chesedel greeted them as they arrived at the White Pearl Gate.

The angels took turns embracing each person, whispering words of encouragement. Their hugs were mixed with tears. Jesse couldn't determine if they were tears of appreciation or sadness. Soon they were all misty-eyed.

Uzziel gave the emissaries their final charge: "Hold hands when you pass through the gateway, so you stay together. Remember what you have learned here in heaven, acknowledge God no matter what, use wisdom, don't quit or lose heart, and most of all, trust the Holy Spirit to guide your paths."

Chesedel added, "And we wish you Godspeed. All of heaven will be praying for you."

As the five *Abrahams* walked single file past the gate's two white pillars, a bright light flashed, thunder sounded, and they were gone.

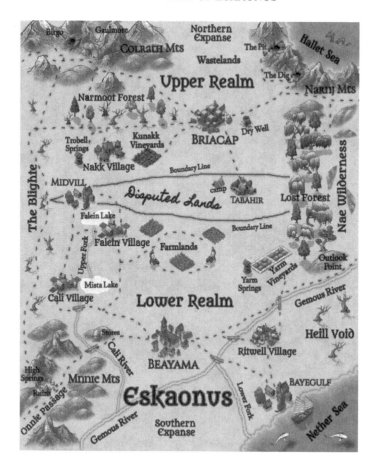

Eskaonus is a fictional world or place. However, all tangible worlds and places, whether known or unknown, were made by God.

"Through faith we understand that the worlds were framed by the word of God, so that things which are seen were not made of things which do appear" (Hebrews 11:3).

CHAPTER 6
ARRIVING IN ESKAONUS

Like waking suddenly from a frightening dream, the group found themselves disorientated, dizzy, and somewhat nauseated. "Oh man, what a ride, wild!" Seth checked all his limbs to make sure none were missing. "I assume we're in Eskaonus, right JW?"

Jesse shrugged his shoulders and looked around. At first glance, the landscape appeared earthlike. The longer he studied it, the more he noticed several major differences. The plants were huge as if fertilized with steroids, and the trees, a type of evergreen pine with oak-shaped leaves on their branches instead of needles, towered skyward, three hundred feet or higher. Jesse leaned back to view the horizon, trying to locate the sun. There was none, just an aurora borealis glow with wide yellowish bands. "Yeah, Seth, I hope—"

Interrupting their conversation, Max shouted, "Sir, has anybody seen Reverend MacBain?" Jesse stopped what he was doing and scanned the immediate area. The others did likewise, yet Lundy was nowhere in sight.

"Hey, Lundy where are you?" Jesse waited, then called out again. No movement, no reply, just silence.

Anna shook her head, almost crying. "I might be the reason he's missing. During our transport here, I lost his grip. I tried to hang on, but one by one his fingers slipped off. Oh no! The angel warned us to hold hands, so we all arrived together. I'm sorry, guys. It's my fault." She fell to her knees, palms covering her face, sobbing.

Jesse rushed over and put his hand on her shoulder trying to console her. It didn't seem to help. "What a minute, Annie, he may have simply landed elsewhere, perhaps close by. I think we should split up and do a quick search. Let's meet back here in a half hour or so." Jesse marveled how he had already converted to tracking time by earth standards. Without waiting for further instructions, the party scattered in every direction.

Jesse stayed at the arrival site in case Lundy reappeared. While waiting for the three searchers to return, he felt a cool breeze rise, sending chills across his neck. He buttoned his coat, pulling the fur-lined hood over his head. The strange light glow had waned by the time the crew straggled in from searching. Each person frowned, shaking their heads in frustration. "Well, we can try again in the daylight. Right now, we should probably get a shelter built. Feels like it's gonna be a cold night ahead."

"Seth and I can work on constructing a lean-to," Max offered. "I see a secluded area over there by those pines. The trees are similar to the Stone Pine umbrella trees from my homeland in Rome. They should make a decent shelter."

"And I can hunt for edibles." Anna leaned her glifstring against a boulder and headed down what appeared to be a crude footpath. "I'm sure this leads somewhere."

"Okay, be careful. We don't want to lose anyone else." Jesse bit his lower lip, a habit he did unconsciously when he worried. "I'll hike over to the ridge and see if I can find a stream or water source. Since we're mortal again, we will need nourishment to survive, and I'm already feeling a tad thirsty."

"Let's try these." Maximus pointed to half dozen low hanging limbs. Pulling his Gladius from the scabbard, he slashed through the tree branches as if slicing butter. Seth stacked them into piles where they fell.

"Hey Maximum, don't you think we have enough already. We're only building a shelter, not a house."

"Hold out your rope, recruit, and I will cut a few sections for lashing these poles together. We'll soon find out if it retains its original shape." Whack, chop, whack—pieces fell everywhere—but Seth's rope remained the same length as before.

"Watch it big guy! Your last swing almost took off my fingers. I hope you're not trying to terminate me like that dude in those sci-fi flicks." Since Max and Seth were friends, they enjoyed the playful banter.

"No, merely demonstrating your first lesson: Always expect the unexpected. Staying focused may keep you alive." Max turned around, hiding the half-grin on his face. He finished stripping the branches and began assembling a crude frame. "Okay, recruit, start lashing these poles together. Watch close, here's how you tie a clove hitch."

"Nifty. So, bro, how many poles do you want me to lash?"

"All of them."

"Right, I figured you'd say that." Working together, Seth and Max finished the frame. They weaved small branches together in between the poles to cover the sides and roof. The leftover leaves worked as chinking.

Meanwhile, Anna searched for something to eat. She descended the winding path, which led her to series of vineyards. Each section held rows of bushy vines covered with dark pink berries about the size of small grapes. She assumed they were edible since someone had planted them in cultivated rows. She popped two into her month and crunched down on them. The flavor exploded, sweet and tart at the same time. "These are delicious. I'm sure our team will savor them." Hunger had begun to gnaw at her stomach. No doubt, her partners felt the same cravings—or soon would. She picked enough for dinner and gathered them into the folds of her long dress to carry back to the camp. She hoped the farmers or whoever planted them, were benevolent people who wouldn't mind sparing a few berries for starving travelers.

Jesse discovered a river on the far side of the ridge. Ironically, the water flowed uphill. He followed it to the crest where the river changed course to run downhill until it reached the next rise where it again climbed the slope. *Odd place, so much for normal gravity.* He bent over and palmed a sip of water to his lips. *Silty with a bitter aftertaste. It'll have to do.* Jesse pulled the journal from his satchel and stuffed it into his front leg pocket. The candle lamp fit into the opposite pocket. He dipped his satchel into the river, filled it with the liquid, and then returned to camp.

He found everyone standing around the finished shelter discussing the design. Jesse walked over and gave the lean-to a quick inspection, shaking the support poles to test the lashings. "I see you placed leaves on the ground for insulation. Good idea. It will help keep us warm tonight. Nice job guys!" Still admiring the shelter, he stepped aside and pointed to a rock formation. "I located a river about a half mile past that ridge. The water is silty with a strong mineral taste but drinkable." Jesse handed his satchel to Anna first, who consumed a small amount. She passed it to the next person. They all took turns sipping water until the satchel was empty. "Annie, did you find any food? I'm sure were all famished by now."

"I sure did, and these berries are delightful. I picked enough for everybody." As she related the story of finding the vineyards, she offered fifteen berries to each individual.

Max only ate a couple berries. "I assume you didn't find any real food like chickens, rabbits, or venison. I'm not really much of a fruit eater." He handed the rest of his share to Seth.

With their hunger eased and their thirst quenched, they settled inside the shelter. Jesse hung his wet satchel on a corner support to dry out. The group watched as the last glows of light faded. Soon the cold winds arose, howling through the tree limbs, rustling the leaves. The team huddled together for warmth, tired from all the exertion.

"Since there's not much else to do this evening, let's get to know one another better." Jesse hoped getting their minds focused elsewhere would lift their spirits. "How about you, Annabelle, can you tell a little about yourself?"

"Not much to tell. I was born in a place called Ghana. When my parents died, a nice Jewish family in England adopted me. I attended their synagogue, and later, a messianic fellowship where I had a charismatic experience that changed my life. Soon thereafter, God started giving me prophetic dreams and spiritual songs, which certain folks in the congregation didn't appreciate. They asked me to keep those revelations and songs to myself or leave. After praying for wisdom, I decided to move on. Then the Rapture happened. I've always enjoyed composing worship music and singing. Wish I could have—"

"Do a tune for us?" Seth blurted out. "It would be chill." The other two members encouraged her as well.

"A short one perhaps." She pulled out her glifstring, bowed her head, closed her eyes, and began: "O God, thou *art* my God; early will I seek thee: my soul thirsteth for thee, my flesh longeth for thee in a dry and thirsty land, where no water is." When Anna finished, she told them the words came from the opening verse of Psalm 63.

Anna's voice was soft, almost a whisper, her picking on the stringed instrument, mesmerizing, lifting their spirits as she played. The lyrics seemed appropriate for their new circumstances, and although they couldn't see it, a misty cloud hovered over the top of the shelter, gradually dissipating after she laid her glifstring aside.

When the twilight phase ended, an eerie darkness spread across the landscape. Max, Seth and Anna decided to retire for the night. Jesse stayed awake a while longer, watching the pitch-black sky, pondering their circumstances. *No stars out yet; maybe they don't have them in this place.* Then he remembered his journal and pulled it out of his pocket. He retrieved the candle lamp, unlatched its top, and watched as a small flame burst forth, radiating light. Able to see better in the darkness, Jesse opened his journal and took out the pen to write:

Entry Three
Made it to Eskaonus. Rev. Lundy is missing. He didn't

arrive with the rest of us. I'm getting a bit worried. We'll search for him in the morning. Built a shelter and made camp for the night. We are all feeling tired. Annie says she's a little sick to her stomach. Probably nerves. Hope things are better tomorrow. Will try to make contact with the Eskaonites and do some investigating. I don't want to give away our purpose, not until I know who's friend or foe.

Since his satchel had dried out, he placed his journal, pen, and candle lamp inside and secured the flap. He lay down in his cramped sleeping spot, hoping things would be better in the morning.

They weren't.

During the night, their stomachs started aching. By morning, dark pink rashes had developed over their bodies. Puss oozed out from open sores. Jesse strained to sit up straight but couldn't. As he dropped backwards, he cranked his head to look at his companions. No one moved; they all appeared unconscious or dead. He tried calling for help. No voice, nothing, not even a mutter came forth. He could barely breathe through his swollen throat. Moments later, he passed out.

CHAPTER 7
SAEPHIRA'S DREAM

Saephira tossed and turned all darkout long, unable to find restful sleep. Strange dreams plagued her mind. First, she was a young girl in her parent's home. Next, she confronted an ancient wickedness and battled raiders from the north. Then a man with a tarnished crown caused a fire that destroyed everything in its path, including people, farms, livestock, even the lakes burned. Some of the images felt familiar, though distorted. Lastly, she saw a small group of vagabonds lost in a great wilderness, a huge river, a deserted void, an overlook vista, and vineyards. One of the travelers, who appeared hurt or in danger, tried to call out for help but couldn't speak. So, she screamed for him, "Help me! Help!" She awoke in a daze, her nightwear soaked with perspiration. Saephira sat up on the bed, trying to remember all the images. *Had she been yelling in the dream or later after she awoke?*

Narleen was passing by Saephira's room in Residential Hall when she heard a muffled scream coming from the bedchamber. She threw the door open. "My Lady, are you alright?" As Saephira's trusted lady-in-waiting, she never needed permission to enter her private quarters unless she was escorting others. "Do you require assistance? I will call for our militia."

"Just help me get dressed. I feel a little shaky right now." She stood and shuffled around her room, trying to settle her nerves and focus her thoughts. "Then yes, please summon Waubush and Melmandus." Narleen went to walk-in closet, picked out Saephira's normal court apparel, and laid them on the bed.

"I'm sorry, Narleen, not those. I'll need my riding clothes this cycle." Narleen returned the garments and replaced them with her traveling outfit. Since Saephira appeared more at ease, Narleen curtsied and left, closing the door behind her. After Saephira slipped into her riding attire and braided her long, brunette hair, she heard three quiet knocks outside her chambers. She assumed it was her lady-in-waiting with the militia officers. "You may enter."

Narleen walked in first, followed by Waubush and Melmandus, who rushed forward and bowed. "Good dayrise, my Lady, how may we be of service?"

"Good dayrise to you, my captains. Thank you for getting here right off. I know you are busy with training, but I have a mission of utmost urgency. And I'll be accompanying you. Please ready three kacks. We ride immediately." The men bowed their heads and departed. Saephira gave Narleen a hug to thank her for helping and followed her captains out. On the way, she stopped by the kitchen to break her fast. *Good, no one's here. No questions either.* She grabbed a slice of yestercycle's kin to munch on, poured a cup of yarm, which she downed in two gulps, and hurried out the main entry, sprinting toward the stables.

Her trusted captains were waiting. Melmandus, Captain of the Militia, busied himself sorting out rations and supplies for the day, while Waubush, Captain of the Safeguards, readied Saephira's favorite white-striped kack. Her animal was strong, a good runner, even though it measured two hands shorter than the captain's mounts, whose heights marked eighteen hands at the withers.

"Where are we riding to this time, my Lady?" Waubush asked, as if such outings were now common occurrences with their leader.

"East, toward the wilderness regions. I've had another premonition. I'm getting more of these lately, and as you well know, they often come true. The last ten cycles, my dreams have become more foreboding. However, this one is different. It concerns several distressed wayfarers who recently entered our realm, and if it proves true, their location is near Outlook Point between the Heill Void and the Nae Wilderness."

"Do you think they migrated through the Nae? I've heard rumors about settlements on the eastern side. As far as I know, no one has successfully trekked across the Wilderness or the Void."

"That may be so. Still, I sense these sojourners have come from even farther way."

Melmandus had finished tying side carriers on their rides and began packing their gear. "Shall we bring weapons?"

"No, I don't expect any raids this far south. Just bring a mender kit, three torches in case we don't make it back by nightrise, and a haversack of rations. Better throw in a couple sets of tie cords as well."

The search party rode their mounts at a gallop, hanging on to their long fluffy manes for stability, steering the kacks by using gentle leg movements and touching their necks on the right or left to make turns. They covered the two leagues between Beayama and the Nae before midcycle. Up ahead, underneath a grove of cottlepine trees, they discovered a crudely built shelter with four individuals inside sprawled out on the ground, either dead or dying.

Saephira stopped first, jumped off her ride, and ran over to the shelter. She covered her mouth with her hands, shocked to what she saw. "These people have yarm poisoning. I've never seen symptoms so severe. Grab the mender bag and bring it to me."

"Yes, my Lady. Unfortunately, we didn't pack any antidotes," Melmandus replied. "All we have are wraps, stitching materials for wounds, herbs for pain, and a little healing salve."

"Shouldn't adults be immune?" asked Waubush.

"They should be." Melmandus handed the mender bag to Saephira. "I thought only children and newborns had those reactions until their immunity developed."

"My assumption as well." Saephira quickly checked each body, finding weak pulses and shallow breathing. "Nonetheless, this group has overdosed on yarm berries, probably from our vineyards below the ridge. For some reason, however, their bodies are reacting like newborns with no immunity. Strange." She rifled through the aid kit and found a half container of

Helixzon. Not nearly enough salve. "There's not much we can do here. Best to get them to Beayama where the mender can treat them."

They placed the woman on Lady Saephira's mount, straddling her across the animal's withers on her stomach, using a set of tie cords to secure her. The man and adolescent were loaded on the larger gray-furred kacks and likewise secured. Although Saephira and the captains had tried, they couldn't lift the fourth injured person high enough to attach to a side carrier.

"This guy with the sword must weigh six stones," Melmandus said. "He's huge, wide as a kack and tall as a cottlepine."

"More like eight stones," Waubush countered. "Maybe we should leave him for now and return next cycle with more militiamen to help us transport him."

Saephira considered his suggestion. "We could also tear their lodging apart and make a litter to haul him behind us."

"I'll walk!" The three of them turned about to see Max wobbling to his feet, standing upright.

"It's two leagues to the city, sir. How are you going hike that far?" Melmandus asked. "You can barely stand, and a quarter span ago you were out cold on the ground."

"Been injured worse. I'll walk."

"Well, we can't stay here and argue all cycle." Saephira glanced at Max and then at her captains. "Let's give him the benefit of the doubt. Besides, it will be nightrise soon. We better leave before the darkness comes." Waubush gathered the traveler's belongings from inside their shelter: satchel, instrument, and corded rope—and packed them into his side carrier. After a quick check to see if they missed anything, they climbed on their mounts and started down the path for home. Since the injured people were unconscious, the riders moved slowly so as to not cause further discomfort. Max trudged on behind them, looking determined, not saying a word.

The party stopped at the river to water their mounts, rehydrate themselves, and eat dried rations from their supplies. Max sat on a nearby rock to rest, sipped the water they offered him but ate nothing. Saephira inspected his rashes, which seemed to be fading, and applied what healing salve they had in the mender bag. "You seem to be faring better than your companions."

Max inspected his arm. "Only ate couple."

"You mean yarm berries." Max nodded. "I have a few questions. Do you feel like talking?" she asked. Max shook his head and tapped his throat. "Okay, I understand, talking hurts right now. I can't do anything about the rawness in your throat or mouth until be we get you to the mender's, so she can administer the antidote."

Max pointed in the direction of his three unconscious friends. "Others?"

"They're not doing too well. They need the antidote before nightrise ends or they may not survive."

Max frowned, stood, adjusted his sword, and began marching ahead, quickening his pace the best he could.

Saephira raced back to her ride and checked on the woman. A squeeze on Anna's leg brought a muffled moan yet no movement. "Let's hurry if we can." She mounted up. The captains did the same. They continued following the trail, riding single file, urging their animals to a faster clip.

Melmandus turned his head to watch Max march behind him. "I wouldn't mind having ten like him in my militia. The raiders would probably think twice about attacking us or stealing our stores."

Waubush agreed. "A soldier, no doubt. I wonder where he hails from."

"I have no idea. I'm sure we will find out more about him and his associates after the mender helps them recover." Melmandus looked over at Saephira to see if she had something to add to the conversation, but she was studying the horizon, watching the daylight fade.

They pulled out their torches as nightrise began. By the time they reached Beayama, complete darkness prevailed. Seeing them approach, the gateman signaled for the group to enter the city. Max followed, walking past the watchtower where he fell on his face in the dirt, exhausted, unable to take another step.

Five gatemen jumped into service, dragging Max onto a stretcher and carrying him to Ottaar's home. Saephira and her captains followed behind, avoiding the spectators who had gathered to watch the commotion. Several of the bystanders helped retrieve the injured from their kacks and haul them upstairs, gently placing them into beds. Ottaar, the city mender, gave each person a quick examination and recognized their symptoms—yarm poisoning—the first case she had seen in yarns. She immediately started brewing the antidote, a thick tea made from Utondra leaves. When it cooled, she would try to get her patients to drink a cup. If they remained comatose, she'd pour a dose into their mouths every span until the antidote took effect or they succumbed. In the meantime, she removed their clothes and applied Helixzon healing salve to all their rashes.

As Saephira watched Ottaar tend to her patients, she inquired, "Will they recover?"

The mender replied, "Dayrise will bring what it brings. We shall see. Go home and rest, my Lady. I will send you word."

CHAPTER 8
LUCIFER'S EVIL PLAN

Osalawn appeared out of nowhere, taking on human form. Fear reflected in his yellow eyes. "Why did you summon me, O Lucifer?"

"I don't need a reason. In this case, though, I want you to call a gathering of all the angels who are favorable to my cause."

"And what cause is that, your Lordship?"

"Rebellion! I plan to overthrow God." Satan smiled with delight, rubbing his hands together. "I hate Him, I hate Him, and everything He represents!"

"What has you so riled this dawn, O Son of the Morning?"

"Watch your mouth, Osalawn." Satan pounded his fits together, screaming, "Do you know what God did to me and what really transpired in Eden?"

"I'm somewhat aware."

"I suggest you pay closer attention then." Satan cursed, unsheathing his sword, ready to strike Osalawn down. "While you were playing good angel and cuddling up to God, He cursed me in front of every immortal being, not to mention Adam and Eve, and then kicked me out of the garden. It was embarrassing and beneath my dignity. He told me I would have to crawl on my belly from now on. Well, I ain't gonna, never, nor use that serpent gig again. I'll simply transform into one of my amazing disguises. I have hundreds of them, you know."

Osalawn nodded. "Master, I'm not so—"

"Shut up you fool and listen. God sent Uzziel, along with a group of cherubim, to block the way into the garden with their stupid flaming swords. However, before those cherubs arrived, I swiped one of the fruits from the tree of the knowledge of good and evil. Here, take a look." Satan pulled out a whitish-skinned fruit from his robe, sliced it in half with his talon-shaped finger, and showed it to Osalawn. "Although God forbade humanity from eating this fruit, lest they die, I convinced them otherwise. It's sweet beyond measure and consuming it, even a single bite, can make one wise as a god."

"Perhaps you should eat some yourself."

"You idiot, it doesn't work on us immortals."

Osalawn took ahold of the half slice and inspected it. "The fruit resembles a pomegranate. This piece could have a hundred seeds inside."

"Probably more." Satan grabbed it out of his hand and stuffed it back into his robe. "Here's my plan: I will plant these knowledge seeds in other created worlds, enlist corrupt individuals to consume its fruit, and after their eyes are opened, wickedness will prevail. When this occurred on earth, people's thoughts were only evil continually, so God decided to terminate humanity. I believe choosing evil knowledge over good will follow the same pattern in those places as well, thereby forcing God to destroy them because of their sins, just like He planned to do before Noah embraced religion and ruined my ruse. But if for some reason God won't judge sinners for their guilt and penalize them, then I will. I plan to hurt God for all eternity, punish Him for punishing me."

"He's the Almighty. Is that a wise—"

"Enough! Get out of my face, Osalawn. Do what I commanded. Assemble our supporters for a heaven-wide rebellion. My time is short."

"Are you talking about the bottomless pit prediction?" No answer came. Satan had vanished. Relieved, Osalawn glanced around to make sure, then popped away, disappearing into the unseen realm.

Satan streaked through the heavens, unhindered by time,

space, or dimension, and arrived in Eskaonus, one of God's many created worlds. It was his first stop. There would be others, many others.

Staying hidden, Lucifer surveyed three mountainous locations, deciding upon an old cave in the Colrath range. He flew deep into the cavern and found the perfect spot, an open area with a high rocky ceiling. He dug a hole with his foot, placed one seed inside, and kicked a little dirt on top to cover it. Instantly, the ground cracked open, and a shoot sprung forth. Moments later, it grew to full size, almost touching the ceiling. The tree branches spread out and whitish fruit appeared on each limb, bending them downward under the weight. *Yes, an exact duplicate of the knowledge tree from Eden.* Overwhelmed with hideous glee, Satan danced a jig around the tree, singing repeatedly, "I've done it, I've done it, and sorry You'll be." On the fourth refrain, he stopped mid-verse, sporting a foul grin on his face. After taking one more look at the tree, he flew out of the cave's entrance. Using his angelic powers, he sent a blast of wind, causing a massive rockslide, which sealed the cave under boulders, shale, and debris.

Next, he popped unseen into the archive hall at Briacap and left a sealed scroll on the reading table. Written in an ancient language, the scroll mentioned a treasure of great power and gave clues on where to locate it. Finally, he slipped into Eddnok's bedchamber, leaned over his face, and whispered into his ear as he slept. With everything in place, Lucifer smiled one last time, knowing his malicious plans would soon unfold. No longer caring if anyone saw him, he started singing again, "I've done it, I've done it, and sorry You'll be." The tune jarred Eddnok from a deep sleep. Lucifer let the leader of the northern realm catch a glimpse of him before he disappeared through the bedroom wall, his vile laughter echoing behind him.

CHAPTER 9
LUNDY CAPTURED

Lundy sat on a boulder, trying to clear his head, feeling a tad dizzy. The last thing he remembered was entering the White Pearl Gate holding on to Annabel's hand. *Did she let go or did he?* Either way, he lost his grip. The people he departed heaven with were not here, assuming here is Eskaonus.

He stood, feeling a little steadier on his feet and scanned the area. Steep barren mountains rose behind him. No plant life or trees were visible, just rust-colored shale everyplace he looked. Making matters worse, the heat of the day would soon become an issue since there were no shady or sheltered areas. His throat already felt as dry as a slice of jerky. Shielding his eyes from the sunless glare, he continued to scrutinize his surroundings and spotted several walled structures, probably ten or more miles away. He decided to head downhill toward them and what he hoped was civilization. Perhaps he would find his companions there—and some water.

After what seemed like hours of walking, he stumbled across a water source. Licking his lips in anticipation of soothing his parched throat with a cool drink, Lundy lowered a wood-slatted pail connected to a rusty chain into the cistern, shook the chain a couple times to fill the bucket with precious liquid, and then cranked the lever to bring it back up. Peering inside he discovered a handful of dirt and small rocks. *That's just dandy.* Exhausted from hiking and the heat, which felt like a hundred degrees, he slid down the side of the well's circular base, landing hard on the rocky dirt. He no longer possessed the youthful endurance he'd experienced in heaven. Sitting with his legs sprawled out, he wiped a few drops of sweat that had dripped onto his brow and rubbed it over his cracked lips. "Lord, if I don't locate water right off, I'm a goner."

"There he is, Commander Bolgog, over by the dry well." A small attachment of guards approached Lundy, all holding spears. One of them sat atop a large horse-like animal. "Who are you and what are you doing here? Are you spying on us?"

"No, no. I simply got separated from my crew." Lundy realized he'd made an error by indicating he was part of a group. "What I mean is—"

"What crew? Are you here with others?"

"Not anymore."

"What does that mean?"

"I don't know. I'm just rambling, delirious from the lack of water. Can I please have something to drink?"

"Sure, give him your waterskin." Senior Commander Bolgog pointed to one of his men who quickly untied the skin from his belt and tossed it to Lundy. "It's only got a sip or two, so you'll have to wait until we reach Briacap to get more." Lundy gulped down its contents, squeezing the skin to eke out the last drop. Not waiting for him to finish, two of the guards pulled him off the ground and mounted him behind Bolgog on his kack. The patrol turned around and headed for their fortress city.

At the entry gate, Bolgog yelled up at the tower, "I found this guy outside our city." He pushed Lundy off his kack, who tumbled to the ground, landing on his back. "Take him off my hands. I need to report to Lord Eddnok." A sentinel rushed out of the exit, arrested Lundy on the spot, bound him with ropes, and took him to the holding area.

Another person, a warder, with stern face and gruff voice interrogated Lundy, asking endless questions but receiving few replies. "Better talk if you know what's good for ya."

"I'm saying diddly until you give me a swig of water and a morsel of scran. It's the least you can do for a prisoner, of which I ain't. And I demand an audience with this Eddnok chap."

"You'll get more water when you start talking. Concerning Lord Eddnok, he's probably on the way now." The warder slammed the cell door and locked it behind him.

"Yes Commander Bolgog, what is it?" Eddnok reclined in his lounger while one veiled individual rubbed his shoulders and the other massaged his feet.

"Lord Eddnok, excuse me for the interruption. My patrol captured a stranger by the old well. I think he's traveling with companions, perhaps spies from the Lower Realm. He's being cautious, though, not saying much."

"Where is he?"

"In the holding cell at the east tower."

"I'll go pay him a visit and play the friend scenario after I'm finished here. Better send a homing flyer to our agent in the south in case she knows anything. And bar the stupid door when you leave! I want privacy." Bolgog bowed and rushed out, heading toward the message tower. A span later, Eddnok dismissed his two concubines and strolled over to the sentry tower.

The warder peeked into the small, barred window in the holding cell and hollered, "Step away from the door. Someone's here to see ya."

A short, stocky, balding man walked in. "Good dayrise to you, sir. I am Eddnok, lord of this place and faithful leader of the Upper Realm." Lundy said nothing in reply. "I believe we've had an unfortunate misunderstanding and I have come to apologize."

"Delightful, I'm glad somebody figured out I'm not the enemy here."

"Sorry for the inconvenience. One cannot be too careful with southland traitors always seeking to get the advantage. Their spies are everywhere. At any rate, arrangements have been made to place you in our best room as my guest, down the hall from my own chambers." Turning to the guard standing in the entry, Eddnok said, "Remove those restraints, take this man to his room, and get him settled in." Staring back at Lundy, he continued, "I will check on you at firstlight. Again, sorry for the misunderstandings." Eddnok bowed, left the cell, grinning at his performance.

"Time to go old fella. Follow me. And just so you know, you may be his honored guest, but you're not mine." He dragged Lundy across several dirt streets, past a fortified barrack, and into a great hall. The guard pushed Lundy down a dark passageway to his room. "I'm sure a servant will be in shortly to bring you nourishment." As he slammed the door shut, he said, "See you later . . . maybe."

Lundy heard the bolt slip into place. He rushed over and tried the door, only to find it locked. He paced around his quarters, thinking, *I'm in a wee bit of trouble if this is an honored guest room.* Lundy pulled up a bench and sat by the table. "Hey laddie," he shouted in frustration, hoping the guard heard him through the closed door. "Where's the dang water? This ain't hospitality!"

About an hour later, he heard the door unbolt and a scantily clad woman entered the room, carrying a tray with dried mushrooms, a crust of orangish-brown bread, and a tall copper pitcher, which he hoped held water. "My name is Flissae. I've been asked to serve you. Here's a beverage to refresh yourself." She poured him a full cup and offered it.

"What's that?"

"We call it kunakk. It's what we serve our honored guests."

Lundy held the cup, smelled it, took a sip and spit it out. It burned his mouth with a taste similar to strong liquor. "I would prefer water."

"Water is in fairly short supply here in these arid northlands. Perhaps the kitchen has extra in their holding barrels. I'll check. In the meantime, sip the kunakk slowly, it is an acquired taste and will quench your thirst better than the water. Hope you enjoy the kin and dallups. Let me know how we can make your stay more comfortable." She curtsied and departed, locking the door.

"Did he drink any?" asked Eddnok, who had been waiting outside in the hall for an update.

"No, I think he realized our ploy to intoxicate him and loosen his tongue. I will bring him the water he requested and try a different approach." Knowing what she had in mind, he winked his approval.

Again the bolt slid open and Flissae entered, carrying a full waterskin. "I hope this is more to your liking." She handed it to Lundy but let it slip from her fingers before he could grasp it. It fell to the floor. "Sorry, sir. I'll get it." She bent over, hiking her dress over her rear thighs, revealing her long slender legs. Smiling seductively, she asked, "Is there anything else you need? You have my services until dayrise, courtesy of Lord Eddnok."

"No thank ye. You're a bonnie lass for sure. However, that scheme ain't gonna work neither."

"Too bad." She dropped the waterskin on the table. "It might have been nice. I'll be outside if you change your mind. Knock twice." She strutted out, slowly her swaying hips. The door slammed shut behind her.

He listened for a while, expecting Flissae to barge in again. The latch never moved. Feeling more at ease, he propped his feet on the table to stretch out his aching legs. He consumed all the mushrooms, hoping they weren't toadstools, nibbled on the stale crust of bread, and drank most of the mineral-laced water from the skin. The kunakk he left alone. Lundy watched as darkness slowly replaced the light in the barred window. Finally, exhausted beyond measure, he lay on the bed and fell sound asleep. Early the next morning, a familiar creaking noise from the sliding deadbolt woke him, causing him to spring out of bed. "I'm not interested I said!" Instead of Flissae, Lord Eddnok entered.

"Hope you slept well. We regret our methods from last cycle. I assumed you wouldn't tell us much without a little motivation. Let's begin anew, more honestly this time. Please explain how you ended up in our province."

"Aye, that's more like it. Here's the deal. Me and four companions were traveling your land and got separated. Can you help find them?"

"We can send out homing flyers to our local magistrates and organize a search party. I'll let you know what turns." Eddnok stalked around the room, looking at what Lundy had eaten, scrutinizing the clothes he wore. "So where do you hail, from the eastern wastelands? We've always assumed there are settlements on the far side of the Nae and in additional places our scouts haven't charted, like the Blighte."

"I come from one of those unmapped locations."

"Alright, I'll accept your answer for now. Can you tell me something more substantial?"

"Sure, my name is Lundy MacBain. I am educator and linguist by profession." Lundy didn't feel he should divulge information about being a minister or coming from heaven, not until he knew more about this lordship person and his realm.

"A linguist? Does this mean you can translate different languages?"

"Why do you ask?"

"We recently discovered an ancient scroll in our archives. It's written in an unknown text. Would you be willing to examine it, perhaps translate it for us? It would mean a lot to me."

"Not sure till I see the document." Lundy walked over to the table, grabbed the waterskin, and drained the last of it. Holding up the empty skin, he added, "Before I do any translating, I'll require more of this."

"Okay, I'll bring another waterskin and drop off our scroll later. In the meantime, you are free to leave your room and wander the city limits. For your protection, though, we still need to secure your door at nightrise. The southern province has unscrupulous people who may seek to harm you. Over the yarns, they have taken our flocks, stolen our lands, and drained precious water supplies. I'm sure you understand my concern for your safety."

"Well, if you say so. You seem like an honest chap." *More like a sly jackal.*

"I am, I am, loved by many here. Good dayrise to you, Master Lundy." Then Eddnok shuffled out the entryway, leaving the door unbarred.

As the cycles passed, Eddnok allowed Lundy to roam the grounds during dayrise but locked him in his room at nightrise. In truth, Lundy was little more than a prisoner of the Upper Realm.

CHAPTER 10
QUESTIONS AND ANSWERS

Ottaar, the city mender, sat at a makeshift desk, rubbing her tired eyes, reviewing scrolls and taking inventory of herbs and healing remedies. She had just poured a cup of steaming hot yarm berry tea when Jesse stepped through the hallway. "How are we feeling this dayrise?"

"Much better," answered Jesse as he walked over and plopped onto a settee by her dining table. "Are you the one who saved us?"

"No, a search party did. They found you near the edge of the Nae Wilderness. I only treated you after they carried you back to Beayama, barely alive I might add. You and your companions were infected with yarm disease, the worse cases I've ever seen, and I'm eighty yarns old."

"All from eating a few pink berries?"

"I would guess it was more than a few. For some reason, though, your bodies didn't exhibit the normal adult immunity. Yarm berries are deliciously sweet, nutritious, but toxic, so we dilute any products made with them until one's immunity develops, which usually takes two yarns in children. Whereas in your cases because of the high dosage you consumed, you may have already built up a tolerance to the berry's harmful effects." Ottaar went over to her cupboard, retrieved an extra cup and handed it to Jesse. "At firstlight, I brewed a fresh batch of yarm tea. Let me pour you a tad. It's been diluted."

"I'll pass on the tea." Jesse flipped his cup over and set it on the tabletop next to her desk. "I never want to see another yarm berry the rest of my life."

"I understand your hesitancy, but I wouldn't forgo them forever. Yarm berries are in most things we eat or drink. And if you haven't noticed already, the water here has a strong mineral taste. Although drinkable, most people prefer the sweet tartness of the yarm berry."

"Think I'll stick with water for now." Jesse bit his lower lip as he scanned the room. "So, doctor, how are the others in my group doing?"

"The big guy rose early, devoured a half loaf of baked kin, and headed over to watch our militia train. He appeared normal, no rash or lingering side effects. According to him, he only ate a couple berries. It's probably the reason he responded to treatment better than the rest of you."

"The big guy's name is Maximus. What about Annabelle?"

"Ah yes, the woman in your little collective. She consumed many berries, a lethal dose I feared. Almost lost her. She is doing much better, sleeping, and her rashes have mostly faded. I'll wake her by midcycle and get her up and moving."

"What's the word on Seth?"

"The teenager, hmm, he had a difficult time. He was delirious during most of darkout, mumbling strange words or phrases like gnarly surf, shark, and need a bigger board. High fevers like his can sometimes cause incoherent rambling. Come firstlight, he was up, hungry, ate a quarter loaf of kin, and asked to see his friend Maximus. Being fully recovered, I released him."

"I don't know how to say . . ."

"A thank you is not required. I do what I do because I can. Others don't have the knowledge or experience in mender methods."

"I have a bunch of questions about this province. Who do you suggest I talk with?"

"Lady Saephira. She led the search party that rescued you. I already sent her word about your recoveries. I assume she wants to chat with you as well. Try a little kin while you wait. I baked it early this dayrise." Ottaar grinned as she watched Jesse scarf down a four slices—glad her patient's appetite had returned—always a positive sign.

"How is the good mender this fine day?" Saephira asked as she bounded up the steps and through the open entry door.

Ottaar turned around and curtsied, "Good dayrise, my Lady." Jesse stood to his feet, bowed, and gave the same odd greeting, assuming dayrise meant good morning.

"The same to you Ottaar." Saephira walked over and gave the mender a tender hug, then turned to face Jesse. "And you sir, may I inquire as to your name?"

"I'm Jesse Walt, your Highness."

"Good dayrise to you, Jesse Walt. Nice to finally greet you. However, I am not a queen, merely a noblewoman our citizens look to for provision and protection. If you're feeling sufficiently recovered, let me show you our beautiful city, and as we walk around, perhaps we can visit a bit."

"Works for me." After the latest setbacks, this is exactly what Jesse had hoped for. As a former detective, he needed to get his investigation going and solve the case heaven assigned him. He felt motivated, excited to be on the hunt for clues. "Give me a moment please. I want to bring my journal along to take notes." Jesse dashed upstairs, stopping first by Anna's room. She was still sleeping. Peering in, he whispered, "You're gonna be okay, Annie, just rest." He grabbed his satchel from his room and rejoined Saephira who was waiting on the street.

As they strolled through the city, Jesse didn't focus on the tour. Although he nodded his approval and glanced at all the places Saephira indicated, he had a different agenda on his mind: dig out the facts, which according to his police training were best done by listening to a suspect before analyzing his or her demeanor. He assumed the queries would come next. They did.

"I have questions, Jesse Walt, and I'm sure you have several yourself, but let me ask the three most pertinent to me. Who are you, where do you hail, and why are you here in Lower Realm?"

Jesse wasn't sure he should answer those inquiries until he knew a little more about this Saephira person and her situation. He decided to stall. "Well . . . I'm . . . sort of a . . . ."

"I see I've caught you off guard. I'm sorry. When you're

ready, I'm sure you'll feel more comfortable addressing my concerns. I can wait a cycle. Now it's your turn, what are your questions?"

Like being handed the crucial interview at a briefing, Jesse jumped right in. "You said you're not a queen, yet everyone treats you as if you are one, calling you my Lady and such. What is your position in this city?"

"I am the magistrate of Beayama and leader of the Lower Realm. Fifteen yarns ago, my parents died, and I inherited their leadership roles."

"Died?"

"Our citizens believe they were assassinated."

"By whom?"

"Assailants from the Upper Realm."

He stopped, shaking his head in disgust. "I apologize, Lady Saephira, I didn't mean for our talk to become an interrogation. I've forgotten my place." *Watch it Jesse, you're not a policeman anymore.* He paused his rapid-fire questioning for a moment before he continued, hoping he sounded a little less confrontational. "What can you tell me about your two realms?"

"I appreciate your exuberance. Facts are important, determining the rationale even more so." She looked at him with such understanding it melted his heart. "The northern and southern realms have been at war for ages. Some say it was a religious war of sorts. No one really knows. The hostility between our provinces continues unabated."

"Why all the ill will?"

"As a teenager, my parents betrothed me to Eddnok, the current ruler of the Upper Realm. They hoped to join the provinces together with an alliance. Before the wedding, I discovered Eddnok only desired me as one of his concubines, so I declined the arrangement. Ever since, he has burned with hatred towards me."

"This Eddnok fellow sounds like a real evil guy."

"No, not at first. I actually fell in love with him. Many considered him handsome. Even with his short stature, maybe fifteen hands, he maintained a muscular build. He was a respectful person, a skilled tracker, and people trusted him. Sadly, he changed after the Event."

"What event?"

"Ten yarns ago, a burning rock hit Eskaonus. The southern lands grew colder yet remained fertile. The northern lands, however, dried up: farms, rivers, lakes, almost everything. As the temperatures increased, the climate changed, turning it into a hot, arid wasteland. The only water they have comes from seasonal wells and one flowing spring. Eddnok believes I used magic or sorcery to cause those calamities."

"Did you?"

"No, I don't endorse or practice such arts, but I do have the ability to discern things, mostly in dreams. In a cottlepine shell, that's it. He blames me for rejecting the betrothal and for the climate changes to his lands. He hates me and anything to do with the southern province."

Jesse pondered it all. "I'm beginning to get the picture. May I ask if—"

"Our archives might help explain the rest of our history. It's over this way." She indicated an isolated rear alley. "It's a shortcut."

"Archives, what kind of . . ." Jesse paused, hearing the familiar sound of air being displaced. Two knives whistled by them. One aimed at Saephira, the other at him. The first one missed and stuck into a wall with a loud clunk, the second dropped short. When they turned to see who threw them, another knife whizzed by and nicked Jesse's lower arm. It ricocheted off and slid under the walkway. Blood trickled down his shirtsleeve.

Two assailants rushed forth, followed by a third one. The men had been waiting in open doorways on adjacent sides of the ally. As the closest one approached, Jesse reached for his service revolver, an automatic reflex, immediately realizing he didn't have one. Instead, he clutched the arm of the attacker, ducked his head low and flipped the guy over his shoulder. The man spun a half circle in the air and tumbled backwards to the ground. He rose slowly, stunned, pulled a small dagger, and charged again. Jesse removed the satchel from his shoulder, holding it by the strap, and waited for the thug to get closer. Before he could thrust his blade for a killing blow, Jesse swung his carry bag at the man's hand, knocking the dagger loose. It landed a couple feet away. When the guy leaned over to grasp it, Jesse smashed him right between the eyes with a back swing of his satchel, sending his attacker stumbling to the ground again, this time holding his face, bleeding from a deep gash across his forehead. Having disabled him, Jesse kicked the man's dagger out of reach.

The remaining scoundrels advanced on Saephira and began circling around her. "Stay away from them," Jesse yelled. "I'll be right there."

One of circling assailants said in a sneering voice, "It's over, Saephira," and he sprung toward her with his throwing knife held backhanded, ready to cut her throat. She waited until he lashed out with his blade and then kicked him in the groin. Surprised by the maneuver, the man bent over and grabbed between his legs, moaning in agony. "You little tramp, you're gonna pay for that."

Before the stunned aggressor could straighten himself, Jesse tackled him from the backside. Both of them crashed to the ground. They wrestled with each other, struggling for control. Jesse finally gained the upper hand and pried the knife from the man's hand. Gripping the handle tight, he rolled over and plunged the blade into the guy's side. He wanted to incapacitate, not kill him.

The third assailant, who had been hanging back in reserve, drew his dagger and rushed at Saephira. At the last minute, Jesse stuck out his foot and tripped him. He stumbled to the ground, dropping his weapon. Saephira retrieved the dagger and held it at arm's length, aiming it at his chest. "Move a quarter pace and your life ends. Stay put and you'll live."

The man ignored her advice, stood and bolted away. Anticipating his actions, Jesse raced forward, seized the guy from behind, and slipped him into a headlock. He pushed on his neck until the man yelled, "Okay, okay, stop, you're breaking my neck." Jesse knew he wasn't, but he also knew better than to release his grip.

He glanced over at Saephira, who was still holding the dagger, and asked, "Are you hurt?" She shook her head no. As Jesse held his adversary captive, Saephira moved over and inspected the one bleeding from his side. She put pressure on his stab wound, trying to slow the blood loss. The person Jesse had subdued with his satchel seemed content to lie on the ground, holding his bloody face and moaning.

While Jesse and Saephira contended with the three assailants, a squad of militia approached, galloping up the alley. Captain Melmandus jumped off his animal and rushed over to Saephira. He snapped his fingers at the nearest militiaman and pointed at the downed man. "Take over for Lady Saephira and see to this fool's wounds." To his militia, he yelled, "Arrest these traitors and take them to the stockade." Next, he addressed Jesse, who continued to restrain his hostage with a neck hold. "We haven't properly been introduced. I am Melmandus, captain of our militia. You weren't faring too well last time I saw you. Yarm disease they say. Glad you recovered. It appears you saved Lady Saephira's life and for your heroic actions, I owe you my bond. If you don't mind me asking, sir, by what name do you hail by?"

"Jesse Walt. Actually, she may have saved my life." As Jesse interacted with Melmandus, the hostage saw his chance and tried to wiggle free. Jesse countered by applying more pressure to the hold. He only released the headlock after the militiaman finished binding the prisoner's hands. "Who were these guys?"

"Assassins from the Upper Realm would be my guess. No doubt, we will get to the bottom of it after we interrogate them. My men will take it from here. I need to get our Lady to safety." Turning to Saephira, he said, "My Lady, please take a mount and follow the militia escort to your residence. I will get Jesse Walt to the mender's house as soon as I finish here."

Before she mounted the kack, Saephira turned to face Jesse and curtsied, her eyes were filled with gratitude. "You are invited to a banquet in our Great Hall at nightrise. Perhaps we can finish the conversation about our local history. We also have ancient ruins nearby, which I would enjoy telling you about, or better yet, showing you. I will arrange for an expedition. And at the dinner, I'll introduce you to my trusted advisors. All your companions are invited." She smiled, leaped on the kack and galloped away, following her escort down the street.

A span later, Melmandus dropped Jesse off at the mender's place. "Sir Jesse, I would appreciate having a discussion on what happened here. Right now, however, I have duties to attend. I'll see you at the banquet where we'll have more time to visit." And off he rode.

Jesse entered the mender's home and found Anna, Max, and Seth sitting around a table, drinking yarm tea. "I sure hope it's diluted."

"Ottaar assured us it was safe," Anna replied. "She's out running mender errands to restock her medical supplies. She mentioned we all have a change of clothes in our rooms and a tray of grooming items, including shavers, combs, and cutters. There's a washbasin too."

"Good to know, thanks. I'm glad everybody recovered from eating yarm berries, especially you Anna. You sure had a time of it. I guess we all did." Feeling it was safe to talk privately since they were the only ones present, Jesse relayed what he knew about recent events, the attack, and what he discovered about Eskaonus. "Oh yeah, we are all invited to dinner tonight, which is being held in their meeting facility. City officials will be there, so I want us to mingle and find out what we can. I'll meet you in an hour. I'm going upstairs now to change into those fresh clothes. Mine are a mess, torn and bloody. Think I'll shave, too. I haven't done that in a while."

"Hey JW, you better bandage that nasty cut as well."

"Thanks Seth, I will." Jesse climbed the steps to his room, washed up, and changed out of his dirty clothes. He tried out the straightedge razor on his beard. Only nicked his chin once. Afterwards, he pulled his journal and pen from the satchel and started writing:

Entry Four

Interesting couple days. Everyone poisoned by yarm berries. We had no immunity. Search party from the southern lands found us and took us to local medic for treatment. Almost lost Annie. Attacked by assailants this afternoon. Not sure why.

Concerning the evil, I haven't determined much. I think it concerns Eddnok and the northern lands. Big dinner tonight. Hope to find out more.

Returning everything to his satchel, he threw it over his shoulder and descended the stairs, finding the group still gathered at the table, drinking tea and chatting.

"Take a chair, Jess. Seth has been telling us about his life on earth." Anna pointed to an empty seat by Seth.

"Sure, for a few minutes. Remember, we have a banquet to attend."

"I'll cut to the chase. As I said, I loved all outdoor sports, rock climbing, surfing, whatever. One day, the surf was high in Malibu. I was floating past the breakwater, waiting for one of those wicked ten-footers, when a shark took a bite out of my short board. He started to circle, looking to chomp me. Great white I think."

"Is that how you died, Seth?"

"Nope, I made it to shore, swimming like crazy, but the shark chased me all the way in. His dorsal fin was huge. Afterwards, I swore I'd never enter the water again, any water. I couldn't even watch those shark movies, you know, like *Jaws*. Then one day during a bike ride, I got run over by some dude, a drunk driver the police said. He never even stopped to check on me." The hit and run part of the story troubled Jesse. He started fidgeting in his chair, hoping no one noticed.

"So, you died in an accident?"

"Nope, just got paralyzed from the waist down. Ended up in a wheelchair." Now beyond uncomfortable, Jesse sat motionless, staring at the floor, trying to avoid direct eye contact with Seth. Images from his own DUI accident flashed through his mind.

"Later, the doctors discovered brain cancer, a big tumor, the kind teenagers get. When they tried to remove it, I started hemorrhaging. I never made out it of surgery."

"That's really sad, Seth."

"No, it was cool, Annie. I awoke in heaven, and one of the first saints I met was the big guy over there. You should hear Max's story. His is a sad one."

"Maybe another time," Jesse interjected. "We need to head

over to the Great Hall for this welcome dinner thing, and it's almost evening . . . I mean nightrise." Moments later, they arrived at the hall and were escorted to their seats near the front table by Saephira. Militia guards stood watch in the doorways, eyeing the four strangers, scrutinizing their every move.

CHAPTER 11
THE DINNER

Preaverca, the Postal Overseer for Beayama and surrounding areas, raced around the mail tower trying to finish her duties. She was running late for the banquet Lady Saephira scheduled at the last moment. All city officials, including her, were expected to attend and welcome the newcomers. Preaverca had just walked out the door when she heard the bell ring, indicating the arrival of a homing flyer. With transitional vision, these flyers can navigate day or night, even during darkouts. She rushed over and pulled a rolled message from the small leather carrier strapped to the bird's back. The message came from Lord Eddnok in Briacap:

Any strangers arrived your area? Need immediate reply.
—E

Preaverca wrote out a quick response and sent it on a fresh flyer to Briacap:

Yes, 4 persons: 3 men, 1 woman. What are your orders?
—P

She tore up the message from Eddnok, burned it, and then hurried off to the hall. By the time she arrived, the introductions were almost finished. "And this here is Menarbat, the Tracker, our faithful scout," announced Saephira. "He also oversees all provisions for our province and is one of my most trusted confidants." The attendees clapped as Menarbat rose to speak.

"Much appreciated. Since we are all hungry, I will keep this short by simply saying it's an honor to serve our fine realm." Menarbat gave a flippant half-salute toward the guest table. "I will be leading an expedition come dayrise to show these special travelers the ancient ruins at Onnie Passage, as ordered by Lady Saephira." Staring at Jesse with unblinking eyes, he curtly added, "We need to discuss our itinerary. Stop by my table during the feast." Because Jesse didn't care for the tone of his voice or being ordered around, he acknowledged with a mock navy salute of his own, thinking *aye, aye, sir.*

"Ahh, there you are, Preaverca." Saephira pointed in her direction as she entered the dining area. "And this is our trusted overseer of correspondence sent by homing flyers." As she drew closer, Saephira asked, "Have any important messages delayed you?" Preaverca shook her head no. She offered a quick curtsy to the vice-leader and slipped into her spot at the front table, smiling at the four visitors already seated. "Since my guests have now met our family of province officials, let's serve the meal." Saephira motioned to the kitchen staff to begin. "Oh, and one more reminder, please don't share your yarm berry drinks with our esteemed friends." The hall broke out in rolling laughter. By now, every resident in the city knew what had happened to the recent wayfarers.

The dinner consisted of entrees of fish that tasted like tuna, dishes of stuffed eel, and several trays of sliced meat, which the group later discovered was antaloop roast. The servers brought out baked loaves of kin, platters of odd-looking vegetables mixed with nuts and mushrooms, plates of orangish-red squash, various bowls of fruit salad, and pitchers of slightly fermented yarm berry drinks, none of which were served to the newcomers. Instead, they were each handed tiny cups with a dark, frothy liquid.

"What is this?" Jesse asked, holding up his cup.

The server replied, "It's kunakk. Since you and your friends have immunity issues with yarm berries, the mender suggested this refreshment. It's a distilled liquor produced in the northern lands and imported from Midvill. We serve it at celebrations with water added. Even diluted, the drink is potent, so it's best to sip it slowly. Enjoy!"

After everyone had eaten their fill of entrees, most served cold and seasoned with exotic flavors, Jesse stood and nodded to his companions. That was their signal to spread out into the hall, mingle with people, and try to glean information without appearing too anxious or obvious.

Max and Seth met with Captain Waubush, along with several of his safeguards. They listened to the men share old war stories, rehash recent conflicts, and complain about province matters.

Anna walked over to Saephira's table. "Shalom and happiness to you, Lady Saephira. I enjoyed the wonderful dinner. I'd love to have the recipe for your vegetable platter. Where I come from, individuals who prefer plant-based foods are called vegetarians."

"Interesting word. Where is it you hail?" Anna realized she had made innocent error. Going forward, she would need to use wisdom on what information she shared.

"From the high country. My mind, though, is still a little fuzzy about details after consuming all those yarm berries." She felt her answer was truthful on both counts.

"I see. Well, I'm sure you'll feel better in a couple cycles. Why don't you visit with Narleen while I make the rounds to see a few friends. If you're like Jesse, you probably have questions."

When Saephira left, Anna turned to Narleen and curtsied. "Shalom and joy to you, Lady Narleen."

"Thank you for those honors, but I am not a royal, just Saephira's lady-in-waiting. In Beayama, it's a title given to a leader's personal assistant. Concerning questions, what would you care to know?"

"Who is this Lord Eddnok of the Upper Realm?"

"He is not much of a lord, more like scoundrel. He envies our fertile farmlands and abundant water supplies. Eddnok is self-centered, cunning, helps those who are faithful to him, and turns on those who are not. Many fear him. I don't trust him. And now it's my turn for a question."

"I guess that's only fair."

"Is the person you call Maximus, a soldier?"

"I believe he was at one time."

"He looks so muscular and carries a sword at his side. I assume he's attached."

"Attached?"

"I mean betrothed to someone in your high-country province."

"No, I don't believe so. Why?"

"Oh, just wondering."

Anna grinned to herself. *I guess people are the same everywhere.* Their conversation continued, mostly with small talk, until Narleen excused herself to check on the kitchen staff. Anna then moved over and joined a circle of women, involved in lively discussion about their children.

Jesse steered a path to Captain Melmandus' table to follow up on their earlier conversation. Before reaching it, Menarbat cut him off. "Do you have a moment sir? I want to discuss the expedition to the ruins."

"Sure, go ahead."

"Since we will be riding kacks, you and your friends should arrive at the stables beforehand, so I can give you a quick lesson on how to steer your mounts."

"Can do. We'll be there bright and early. Anything else?"

"No, not really, other than giving you the schedule. The ruins are a two-cycle trip, one cycle there, stay overnight, and return the next."

"Sounds great, thanks." Jesse started to walk away, only to stop mid-step and turn around. "What are these ruins?"

"You mean Lady Saephira didn't tell you? She thinks the structures were part of an abandoned temple, destroyed eons ago."

With his interest sparked, Jesse asked for clarification. "Do you mean a religious temple?"

"No, we have no religion here or other useless beliefs. Maybe at one time they did, not anymore. All fables as far as I'm concerned. Regarding the ruins, they're nothing but an old forgotten settlement." He huffed and raised his eyebrows to show his disdain and skepticism.

"Remember, we're leaving promptly at dayrise. As the head tracker and scout, I will lead the expedition. We will have escorts for Lady Saephira and Narleen, her handmaiden . . . I mean, personal assistant. Captain Melmandus and his militiamen will handle the security part. I will see you on the morrow." Before Menarbat departed, he made one last inquiry, pretending it was an afterthought. "Where did you say your party hails from? Lady Saephira thinks you traveled from the eastern lands past the Nae Wilderness."

Jesse recognized a shakedown when he saw one. Choosing not to respond to his question or reveal their mission, he replied, "Can we talk in the morning? I'm extremely tired right now. After today's events, the attack on your Lady and myself, and almost dying from yarm berry disease, I'm wiped. I hope to get some needed sleep before we leave."

"Alright, I'll expect you at firstlight. Enjoy your rest." And Menarbat stomped off.

With the banquet concluded, Preaverca stopped by the mail tower to send off another message to Lord Eddnok:

Lady S taking strangers to Onnie ruins at dayrise. —P

No sooner had the first homing flyer darted off, than a second came in. She retrieved and unrolled the message. It was marked urgent and had come from the northern fishing village:

Falein Village raided, food stores taken, people hurt, send help. —F

She folded the dispatch and tucked it into her sash. She would give it Menarbat at firstlight and let him handle it. She decided to wait a few spans to see if she received a reply from Eddnok before she retired to her quarters. Sleepy, she dosed in her chair until the flyer bell woke her. It was Eddnok's reply:

Ambush arranged at Onnie Passage, 2 cycles, tell the Tracker. —E

She would give that one to Menarbat as well.

As the darkness spread throughout the landscape, Jesse and his band returned to the mender's home. Beayama's vice-leader, Lady Yhmim, had supplied them with torches and striking stones. In Eskaonus, torches were necessary to see during nightrise and darkouts, which occurred around midnight and continued until firstlight.

Once they arrived at Ottaar's place, Jesse called for a meeting in his room. He put his candle lamp on the dresser and flipped the lid open. A light burst forth, even the room felt warmer. Anna, Seth, and Max took turns sharing the information they had gathered. Jesse paced back and forth, listening as they offered assumptions and debated conclusions. When his turn came, he relayed what Menarbat had said during their brief encounter and about his earlier conversation with Saephira. "She recommends we visit these ancient ruins and scheduled the trip for tomorrow. I think she knows more than she lets on, but either way, we can snoop around the site and see what we can turn up. Perhaps we can get to the bottom of things."

"And the skinny of it," Seth offered.

"The kid means the whole truth."

"Thanks Max. I assumed it was an expression from the 70s. Seth is right, though. The full story is critical." Jesse glanced around the room, seeing a bunch of droopy eyes. "Unless there are additional comments, I think we're finished here. Remember, the expedition leaves early in the morning. Let's meet at the stables at firstlight and learn how to ride these horses of theirs."

"If it's okay with you guys, I would like to play my glifstring before bed."

"Sure, not a problem. We all enjoy your music. Good nightrise, everybody." They returned the saying, smiling at Jesse, realizing they had begun using the local vocabulary in their speech. One by one, they headed to their rooms. Anna quietly strummed her instrument. It seemed to have a calming effect and soon the group drifted off to sleep, all except Jesse. He grabbed his satchel, pulled out his journal, and began writing:

Entry Five

Dinner went OK. Gathered good intel. Expedition planned for tomorrow to see some old ruins. They may provide clues to what happened here and why there's no knowledge of God or belief system. Saephira thinks it may be an ancient temple. If so, why was it destroyed or abandoned? Need more facts. The leader has discerning dreams and seems open to spiritual matters. Not yet sure what evil lurks here on Eskaonus. Something, however, isn't right. We're all really tried. It's been a day. Praying for a restful sleep.

CHAPTER 12
LORD EDDNOK

Eddnok left the mail tower after sending his second message to Preaverca. Since it was almost darkout, he assumed she had already received it and notified Menarbat. His concubines waited anxiously for him to return to his private quarters, but when he climbed into bed, his mind drifted to other matters. The timeframe for the ambush bothered him. He arose and called to the guard stationed outside his chamber door. "Go wake Commander Gelr and have him report to me immediately. I will be waiting at my headquarters."

Gelr had just retired for the night and wasn't happy to be summoned at this late span. However, saying no Eddnok was not an option, not a healthy one anyway. He threw on his clothes, attached a curved, single-bladed sword to his belt, and moments later knocked at Lord Eddnok's door.

"Enter, it's unlocked."

Gelr stepped in and bowed. "Yes, my Lord, how can I be of service to you this nightrise?"

"I have a mission for you and your raiders. It can't wait till firstlight. You need to be at Onnie Passage before two cycles."

"The Passage? It's too many leagues to ride in such a short period of time."

"You will ride day and night, starting now!" Eddnok's face turned stern, his eyes glared.

"Through the darkouts, isn't that dangerous?"

"Don't question me. Yes, both darkouts if necessary. You must arrive by dayrise the following cycle. If you lose kacks or

64

men along the way, leave them and keep going. Take extra torches, supplies, ride your animals into exhaustion, if necessary, but get there on time."

"Which route do you recommend?" Gelr moved over and studied the map laid out on Eddnok's writing table.

"This one." Eddnok ran his finger across the map. "Take the old trail past the Narmoot Forest, then down the leading edge of the Blighte until you reach the Mnnie Mountains."

"That's the long way around." Using his stubbed, misshapen index finger, Gelr pointed to a different trail along the Cali River. "It's shorter, faster."

"No, take my route. I want to avoid Lower Realm entanglements."

"Right. And when we get there?"

"You'll arrange an ambush. Make it appear as an accident. A rockslide along the pass would be perfect."

"Who or what are we ambushing?"

"An expedition. Lady Saephira is taking four strangers to see the old ruins. We cannot let them snoop around and discover what actually happened there. Disrupt their endeavor. If some of them die, so be it. Watch for a signal from Menarbat, the Tracker. He's working for us. Gather your best men. Mount up and ride."

"Yes, my Lord, as you command." After he left the room, Gelr cursed under his breath, "the pompous little chump," yet he did as Eddnok ordered. In a span, they were on their way, their mounts stumbling along in the night. During darkout, Gelr kept the pace, pushing their rides at a full run.

Eddnok stayed at his headquarters and poured himself a cup of kunakk, pleased with the possibilities of his ambush, especially if it hurts Saephira. He sat back in his settee and watched the dark fade into the dawn of a new cycle.

Over at the main entry gate, a sentinel yelled out, "Riders coming in."

Senior Commander Bolgog peered into the lingering

shadows of darkout and identified five riders, each leading a kack laden with bundles. "Looks like Brappt returning from the raid at Falein. Pass him on through, and if those are spoils, assign a squad of guards to unload them."

As the raiding party drew closer, Bolgog called out, "Hey, sub-commander, it appears your little outing found success. My men will help offload the loot. You better scoot over and give Lord Eddnok an update. You know how he is about getting timely reports. Saw him enter his headquarters during nightrise. I think he's still there."

While the plundered goods were being sorted and stored, Brappt rushed over to Lord Eddnok's office. Since the door was open, he entered and found Eddnok dozing in his settee. "Lord . . . excuse me . . . Lord. I don't mean to disturb you. I'm here to make my report about the Falein Village raid."

Eddnok sat up and cracked his eyelids open. "Well, get on with it, how did it go?"

"We confiscated most of their stored provisions and all their dried fish from last season, which we loaded on five kacks. The pack animals belonged to them. Now they're ours."

"Good, good, any casualties?"

"Not on our part. They had a few losses, though. A group of elders tried to resist us. We had to cut 'em down. Bloodied our swords a bit. Most were either dead or dying when we left."

"Is that why you're late? You should have arrived last cycle."

"Sorry about the delay. I rewarded my men by letting them relax, drink kunakk, and have their way with several of the village women. It took slightly longer than expected."

"All in a day's work, I guess. Next time, bring the women with you. It'll save time. Besides, I might be interested in adding to my assortment." While Brappt smirked, Eddnok enjoyed a bout of hearty laughter. "Give your men a portion of the plunder for their efforts and take a double portion for yourself. You are dismissed." Brappt bowed and left. A few moments later, Eddnok walked out, still laughing "Aha, firstlight already. Time to let this Lundy fellow out of his cage."

When Lundy heard the bolt slide open, he quickly folded the Gospel of John scroll and tucked it back into his boot. "So, lassie, the hour has come for me temporary release, eh?"

Eddnok strolled through the opened door. "No, not Flissae this time, Master Lundy, only me. She's busy with, shall we say, other priorities. Therefore, I offered to drop off the ancient scroll and update you about your missing companions."

Lundy moved over to the table and sat on his bench. Eddnok settled into the adjacent seat and handed Lundy the scroll. "I'll take a gander at it, but first tell me about my friends."

"Alas, I believe they were either captured by southern rebels or died in an unfortunate accident."

"Do you have credible information or are ya just speculating?"

"A little of both. Our scouts continue to search for them. No sign yet of their whereabouts. Concerning accidents, I received a report concerning a rockslide near Onnie Passage. We sent a squad to investigate. I'll let you know more as soon as they return. What about my scroll, can you translate it?"

Lundy unrolled it and examined the text. "It could be a type of Hebrew or Aramaic."

"Which means?"

"It means I can probably decipher the document for ya, except it will take time, and I'll require writing materials to make notes."

"Yes, yes, I can get those for you."

"And I request one more thing."

Eddnok leaned forward on the bench, trying to intimidate Lundy. "What else could you possibly want?"

"To leave the city limits and explore the countryside."

"It might be arranged. I'll expect you to take an escort with you. Can't allow you to be harmed in anyway or fall prey to rebels. The supervision is for your safety, of course."

"Of course it is, laddie, I figured as much."

"Let's celebrate our agreement. I see you have a full

pitcher of kunakk." Eddnok poured two cups and offered one to Lundy. "Let's toast our collaboration."

"No thank ye, I'll pass on the booze."

"If you're not going to drink it, I will." He emptied his cup in two gulps, then reached over and grabbed Lundy's. He guzzled the second one down even faster.

Lundy watched as the intoxicating properties took effect. Feeling tipsy, Eddnok began slurring his words. Ironically, he had schemed to get Lundy drunk to loosen his tongue. Instead, his own tongue loosened, and he started complaining about the Lower Realm. "Their leader, Saephira, she's a witch or sorceress. People say she can see the future. Used dark magic against us, destroyed our northern lands. Temperatures are now almost unbearable."

"How did she do that?" Lundy asked, egging him on.

"Not sure exactly. About ten yarns ago, she conjured up a fireball and sent it crashing into the mountains of our eastern territory."

"Sounds like an asteroid."

"I have no idea what that is. All I know is what happened after it hit. The rivers and lakes dried up, as did our farmlands. It scalded the entire Upper Realm of Eskaonus, turning it into hot, dry wasteland."

"No water at all, eh?"

"We maintain a couple wells and underground springs. However, everything else on the surface evaporated except the sea water, which is too alkaline to drink. Of course, the Lower Realm remained unaffected, their water supply still abundant, lakes full of fish, and their farmlands fertile and productive. She's a kack, and I hate her!"

"Keep the heid, laddie, I think you've had enough to drink."

"I'll decide when I've had enough." He emptied the last of the pitcher into his cup and finished it off. "The little temptress even had the gall to decline my sincere marriage proposal." Eddnok pounded his fist on the table. "To blazes with her!" He rose to his feet, unsteady, teetering to one side, and staggered toward the door.

"Are you fit, sir? You look a wee bit scunnered. I can give

you a shoulder to lean on."

"No, I'm fine, merely tired. Stayed awake all nightrise worrying about your lost friends. We'll get them, one way or another, you can count on it."

A bunch of malarkey. "So you'll hasten back with any news."

"Yes, yes, of course. Right now, though, I'm headed to my chambers for some much-needed sleep. Let me know how the translation goes. Good riseday to you, Master Undy . . . I mean Lundy." Eddnok turned and shuffled out of the room, half-chuckling to himself about all the lies he told.

Dizzy from drinking too much kunakk, not to mention being exhausted from staying up all nightrise, he stumbled into his private chambers, undressed, tossed his clothes on the floor, and toppled into bed. Eddnok's two favorite concubines covered him with a kack-furred blanket, then removed their face veils and slipped under the covers beside him.

CHAPTER 13
THE RUINS

The group arrived early at the stables as requested by Menarbat, but Anna, Seth, and Jesse could not master the leg techniques required for steering the kacks. Max did much better. His experience riding horses in the Roman army gave him a learning advantage.

"You three will have to ride double," Menarbat decided. "Let's see, hmm . . . Anna, you ride with Captain Melmandus. Jesse you go with Lady Saephira. And Seth you can—"

"I'm riding with my pal, Maximus," replied Seth. Menarbat gave a disheartened nod, turned around, and continued loading supplies and provisions for the expedition.

Max trotted his mount over to Seth. "Here kid, let me give you a hand." He reached down and slung Seth upon the kack behind him as easily as lifting a ten-pound sack of potatoes. "Okay recruit, let's give this overgrown horse a test run." He kicked the hindquarters and the kack took off at a full gallop.

"Hey dude, I hope you know how to steer this half-mammoth creature?"

"I learned to ride when I was your age, and once you learn you never forget. The size or type of animal doesn't matter." Max raced the kack about a hundred yards down the trail and then pulled on its mane to bring his mount to a sliding stop. "I wish I had one of these back in the day." He jumped off, leaving Seth sitting alone. He patted the animal's neck. "Good job old girl, ya done well." He turned his kack around, facing it toward the stables.

"Bro, what are you doing?"

"Worried, are you?"

"A little bit."

"Would you say you're afraid?"

"Yah think." Seth looked for a way to jump off without falling and breaking his neck.

"Good! Hope you recall your first lesson: always expect the unexpected. Here's the second one: face your fears to overcome them." Without further comment, Max slapped the rear of the kack, causing it to bolt off at a dead run. Seth hung onto its mane to keep from falling off, while Max jogged along behind them, taking in the scenery as if he didn't have a care in the world.

"Halt, whoa, stay, somebody stop this crazy thing!" The kack, however, kept running until it approached the stables where it slowed to a gentle finish. Jesse helped a wide-eyed Seth dismount, noticing all the color had drained from his face. As Max drew near, Seth sneered at him. "Not cool, man. I sure hope there isn't a third lesson."

Sporting a big grin, "No, not today, recruit, but just so you know, I have many lessons. The same ones my elders taught me. If you learn 'em and apply 'em, they'll help keep you safe. Your friends too."

"Alright you guys, quit messing around. We gotta get going." Jesse shook his head in mock disgust even though he enjoyed watching their comradery.

Before they got underway, Preaverca rushed over from the Postal Tower and passed a message to Menarbat. Actually, she held two messages. Everyone noticed the first one, not the other, which she had folded and palmed in her hand.

Seeing the exchange, Saephira paused her discussion with Yhmim and asked, "Anything of importance?"

"A moment please." While Menarbat read it, Preaverca slipped the second one into his pocket. "It seems Falein Village is running short on supplies. No major concerns. They probably encountered a lean fishing season. I will check into it later when we complete your little sightseeing excursion."

Although Saephira felt the disdain in his comment, she decided to ignore it. "Thank you, Tracker, please keep me advised." She turned to finish her conversation with Yhmim. "I should be back in two cycles, perhaps more if we stay longer exploring the ruins. You are the pro tempore leader now for Beayama and the entire southern province. Oversee matters as I would and be careful. We have reports of assassins running loose."

"I'll be watchful, my Lady. You can trust me to run things until you—"

"Excuse me," Menarbat interrupted, exhibiting his usual tendency for rudeness and impatience. "If we plan to make the ruins by midcycle, we must leave soon." He nodded his respects to Lady Yhmim, winked an eye at Preaverca, then instructed everybody to mount up and follow him.

The expedition party traversed a dusty trail that wound west out of Beayama before turning south toward the Mnnie Mountains. The outfit numbered ten people and seven kacks in single file formation. Menarbat had chosen the riding order. As Tracker, he rode point. Next in line was a security escort, one of the two militia, then Melmandus and Annabelle, followed by Saephira and Jesse. The second escort traveled in front of Narleen with Max and Seth taking the end spot. Jesse couldn't see why a particular riding position mattered, other than having the most experienced person in the lead.

As they traveled along, Saephira assumed the role of tour guide, sharing various items of interest with Jesse. "This is where the trail gets steeper and rockier. Fortunately, our kacks are fairly surefooted on the loose shale in these mountain passes." She pointed to high cliffs on the right. "On those exposed ridges, there are small veins of tin and copper ore we use to make bronze."

"This passage with its rugged red cliffs reminds me of the Grand Canyon where I . . ." Jesse caught his blunder. "I mean, it's a grand-looking canyon." Trying to keep their mission confidential until he felt safe to reveal it, he changed the subject. "I don't see rivers or streams below us. Is there water at the ruins?"

"Yes, there is a spring nearby. In fact, it's the only one I know of in Eskaonus with fresh clean water, not the silty mineral water we normally drink. It has the sweetest flavor you've ever tasted."

Ahead, the momentum slowed as the Tracker raised his hand to halt the riders. He yelled to those in the rear, "Nasty rockslide. I better scope it out before we try to cross. Watch for my signal if it's safe to proceed."

As Menarbat jockeyed across the rocky shale, his kack's hooves unearthed pieces, which fell into the steep canyon below. When he reached the end of slide zone, he surveyed the ridges for potential movement, mindful of Eddnok's message. "Looks passable." He motioned for the party to cross. "Go slow and be careful. I don't want anybody to slip or get hurt."

A span later, the ruins came into view. "Before you guys go exploring," Menarbat advised, "release your kacks at the springs, so they can hydrate. No need to hobble them since they'll stay close by and graze."

"Don't you care to see the ruins with us?" asked Saephira.

"Nothing of interest here for me, just old worthless rocks." The Tracker hopped off his mount and began unloading their gear. "Melmandus, you and the militiamen will assist me in erecting shelters for the night." He indicated three locations: "Lady Saephira and her lady-in-waiting by the springs, Jesse and his crew near the rocky ledge, and ours by the trail. We can water our kacks later." Menarbat glanced at the horizon. "Still plenty of light left. Let's make the most of it."

While the four-cornered tents were being erected, Saephira, who was shadowed by Narleen, gave the newcomers a short tour around the ruins, stopping first for a drink at the springs. "See, I told you, delicious, even sweeter than yarm berries." After quenching their thirst and refilling their waterskins, she led them to a collapsed building. Jesse wondered if an earthquake or similar disaster had destroyed it.

Next, she showed them two rock foundations. One contained a mound of fallen rocks in the middle. "Hold on a minute," Jesse said, "I wanna inspect this area a little closer." He searched through the rubble, turning over several of the smaller stones. "You know, these might be pieces of a broken altar."

"You mean a place to sacrifice animals in some ritual?" Saephira asked.

"Perhaps. Hey, take a gander at these." Jesse pointed to a

collapsed section with two symbols carved into the stones: ☡

ᔭ . "One is similar to the letter Z and the other a backwards F. Both have short lines dissecting the middle."

"I've noticed these designs before, assuming they were simply artwork. There are more scattered about, except they're only fragments. Do you have any ideas what they represent?"

"Not a clue." Jesse didn't really know, other than they appeared similar to the mysterious letters on his bedroom ceiling in heaven. *I sure wish Lundy was here.*

"Sir, come see this formation." Max stood in front of two flat stones—one large, the other small—with a crack separating them. "Could be a capstone." Before Jesse could respond, Max pulled out his Gladius and wedged it into the crack.

"Gonna break your blade in two, bro."

"Don't think so, recruit. I was told this sword is practically indestructible." Using brute strength, Max wedged his blade halfway in and lifted with all his might. The smaller stone slid away, revealing an empty chamber.

Anna peered inside and pulled out a small, sealed scroll. "Well now, what do we have here?" She snapped the seal, unrolled it, studied it for a moment, and then gave it to Jesse who in turn handed to it Saephira.

Saephira rubbed the paper between her fingers. "It feels brand new, yet it's been sealed in there for eons."

Hearing the excitement, Melmandus rushed over to see what had caused the commotion. "May I see the scroll, my Lady?" He turned it over a couple times, comparing both sides before returning the document to Saephira. "Strange symbols . . . never encountered anything like them. The paper and ink aren't even cracked or aged. How is that—"

"A message in a bottle, dudes."

Narleen looked puzzled. "A what?"

"Oh, nothing." Seth shrugged his shoulders. "Just a nifty saying I've heard a few times."

"Lady Saephira," Jesse whispered so only she could hear. "Hang on to this scroll until we find someone who can translate it. The message, if it is a message, may explain what happened here and what these ruins represent. Guard it as if the welfare of

Eskaonus depended on it, which it might." *I need to tell her about Lundy and see if she can help find him.*

With the shelters erected and provisions unloaded, Menarbat built a fire next to a downed cottlepine and set up torches to prepare for the approaching darkness. "Dinner's ready, better come and get it before it gets cold." Menarbat's attempt at humor impressed no one. Almost everything on the trip involved dried rations. "I have many duties in this province: master tracker, chief scout, Overseer of Provisions, and I'm not a bad cook either." He laughed as he dished out the meal, knowing he hadn't cooked a thing. The women sat on nearby rocks while the rest of the party sat on the ground around the glowing fire. The warmth kept most of the cold at bay.

Dinner rations consisted of smoked fish, kin bread, slices of antaloop jerky, and dried mushrooms. Narleen picked several handfuls of clover lettuce growing around the springs, and Menarbat added dried herbs to make a tasty salad. Boiled tea and dried yarm berries finished out the meal. Max declined the berries, as did his companions, but asked for more mushrooms, of which he consumed three extra servings.

Once they finished dinner, most of the expedition members retired to their tents, all except Max and Seth who stayed up a little longer to watch the night sky. Max threw a couple more cottlepine logs into the firepit and poked at the embers with his Gladius to keep the fire going.

Narleen noticed them still tending the fire and wandered over. "What are you two doing? It's going to be darkout soon."

"We are waiting for the stars to come out," Seth answered.

"Stars, what are those?"

"The twinkling lights in the nighttime sky. They're totally cool to watch."

"We don't have such things here. Only dayrise, nightrise, and the cold during darkout."

"No moons, no distant suns, no planets? What a bummer."

"Your words are strange to me, but no, not those either."

Narleen moved closer to the firepit and sat by Max. "I wanted to inquire about your sword, Sir Max. It didn't break when you pried off that heavy rock."

Max handed his Gladius to her. "Be careful, ma'am, it's a tempered blade, needle sharp. A supply dealer who lives in a distant land gave it to me."

"A land across the Nae Wilderness or was it farther away?"

"Yes ma'am, farther away."

"Maximus doesn't talk much about his former home or soldiering days," Seth explained. "He mostly chills out about such stuff."

Narleen returned the sword and slid a tad closer to Max. "I see. Certain matters are best kept private, I guess. May I ask you another question?"

"Yes ma'am. Go ahead."

"I noticed you ate several helpings of mushrooms. Do you like them?"

"Yes ma'am. Always have." He continued to stoke the fire with his sword, moving the embers around, trying to appear busy.

"I know where there's a patch of dallups, the best eating mushrooms in our province. It's a short walk from our city. Would you help me gather some after we get back to Beayama? I have a wonderful recipe. My neighbors love it."

"Yes ma'am, glad to assist."

"Good. Thank you for visiting with me. I'll take my leave now." Narleen smiled and trotted off to Lady Saephira's campsite.

"Dude, I think she likes you."

"Merely being respectful, kid; besides, we're their invited guests. It pays to be nice."

"Yeah, sure, whatever. Oh, I forgot to tell you that JW called for a meeting before lights out. We better book it over there and find out what's happening." Max rose, took one last peek at the night sky, hoping at least one star would come out. Nothing there, not even a faint flicker. He sheathed his weapon and followed Seth over to their assigned camping spot.

Nightrise brought the darkness and a chilling cold. As

soon as the partners had gathered inside the shelter, Jesse pulled out his candle lamp and flipped the lid to ignite the flame. The flame glowed with light and radiated warmth. The gang huddled around it.

Jesse started the conversation. "I think this entire area was a temple complex centuries ago. It was either leveled by a natural disaster or destroyed on purpose."

"Who would do such a horrible thing?" Anna asked.

"Perhaps an evil ruler who wanted to end all knowledge of religion. I believe this is one reason we're here, to find out what happened." Changing the topic, Jesse continued, "What did you think about the hidden scroll?"

"Although I'm no expert, I'd say it was a type of Hebrew text. During Sabbath services, I had occasion to view the temple's Torah. The scroll we discovered today had a similar pattern. The letters, however, were cruder, more ancient. If Lundy MacBain were here, he could probably translate it. I feel horrible about—"

"His disappearance was not your fault, Annie, or anyone else's. As the mission leader, I own it. Maybe Lady Saephira can help us locate him. I'll talk privately with her tomorrow on our way home." Having built a rapport, Jesse hoped he could trust her. "What about the two symbols we found near the presumed altar? Any ideas?"

"If there were four of them." Anna traced the shapes in the air, going from left to right. "And if those symbols were Hebrew-type letters, they might represent the name of God, transliterated YHWH, or Yahweh as believers pronounce it. Again, Reverend Lundy would know for sure." She took in a deep breath, exhaling it slowly, frustration showing on her face. "I hope we can find him soon."

"We will, Annie." The frown on his face, however, left more doubt than assurance. "Does anybody have anything to add before lights out?"

Seth spoke up, "I think it's your turn to tell us more about yourself. How about it, JW?"

Jesse went silent. His cheeks turned white. Explaining his failures is what he'd been dreading. "Um . . ."

"Let me go first," Max offered. "You can share next time.

Besides, my story won't take long." Relieved, feeling the blood return to his face, Jesse agreed.

"Thank you, sir." Max fiddled around with his scabbard as he talked. "I was a Roman soldier, Maximus Gallius, a centurion, in charge of about ninety men. I worshiped the false god of war, Mars. While away on an eastern campaign, barbarians raided my hometown. They killed everyone, the whole village. They raped my beloved, Cassia, before they murdered her. Our plans for marriage and children ended. I grew distraught, bitter, and angrier by the season. Then one day I met a fisherman who told me about the one true God. Me and several of my legionnaires accepted His Son as Savior and were baptized. Later, Caesar discovered our new allegiance to the Christ and put us all to the sword. I closed my eyes as they drove the blade into my chest. I awoke in heaven, and I've been there ever since . . . until now."

"I told you it was a sad story," Seth added. "It slams me in the gut every time."

"Ah Maxie, you've sure been through a lot. We love you." Anna wiped the steady stream of tears flowing from her eyes.

Several moments of silence passed before Jesse responded, "I never knew, Max. Your testimony is . . . I mean . . . you remind me of those faithful martyrs we read about in the Bible." He waited to see if more accolades would be shared. When none were, he added, "Well, guys, I really hate to put a damper on things, but we need our sleep. Big day tomorrow."

"Jess, do you mind if I play my glifstring for a while? I'll be quiet."

"Sure, I think a bit of music would do us all good." While Max and Seth laid out their sleeping blankets, Anna began picking the strings on her instrument. A deep calm spread among them, the music sweet and soothing, and soon the circle of friends were sleeping soundly, including Anna. Jesse's eyes also grew tired. Before he bundled up in his blanket, he pulled out his journal:

Entry Six

Really sleepy, so I'll make this entry short; lots happened today. Discovered a buried scroll, must be old, yet it looks new, like the ones in heaven. The ruins are probably an old temple.

How or why destroyed, I don't know. The answers might explain why there's no knowledge of God or religion here. Uncovered two carved symbols. They seem familiar to me. Starting to trust Saephira. Plan to tell her more about our purpose here, just waiting for the right opportunity. Preaverca hiding something. Lundy still missing. The rest of us are doing okay.

A misty cloud floated unnoticed through the ruins, hovering over the group's campsite, long after the four of them had fallen asleep.

At firstlight, the expedition team finished off the dried rations to break their fast and prepared to leave. While the Tracker packed his side carrier, Jesse asked him, "Why is the sky red this morning instead of the normal yellow light?"

"We get this change every few yarns, usually right before a windstorm. Therefore, we better get going soon. Getting caught on a ridge if a windblower develops is risky." The party hurried to complete their packing, mounted up, and started down the trail.

The wind began gusting by the time they arrived at the slide area, where again, Menarbat halted the group to check it for stability. "I will signal you if it's safe to cross." He examined the ridge and noticed movement on the overhang. Once Menarbat reached the other side, he motioned the riders to proceed. The men on the ridge saw his signal, too, and readied their ambush.

They crossed the slide zone in single file, and like the first time through, their kacks stumbled over loose shale and rocks, causing debris to cascade down the slope. As Saephira steered her kack past the unstable areas, Jesse, who was sitting behind her, confessed, "Lady Saephira, I know an individual who can translate the scroll for you."

Turning around to stare him in the eyes, she demanded, "Who might that be?"

"His name is Lundy MacBain. He traveled with us, the fifth member of our collective. We were separated shortly after arriving in your province."

"And you are only mentioning this now?"

"I wanted to make sure whom we could trust before I said more. Lundy has been missing for cycles now, and I fear his life is in peril. Could you help us locate him?"

"Oh, so now you trust me? Fine, I'll consider it, but I will need his description."

"He is an older man with white hair, medium stature, brownish eyes I think, and he has a unique accent."

"Your description would fit hundreds of people. Concerning distinctive accents, your little collective would likewise qualify."

"You're probably right, except Lundy is the only person on Eskaonus who calls everybody laddie or lassie."

"Alright, I'll have Preaverca send homing flyers to our cities and villages. Maybe residents have seen him or know of his whereabouts." She faced forward again to watch those crossing the slide area ahead of them.

"Much appreciated. Can you also dispatch riders to search for him? I'm not sure Preaverca's flyer messages are reliable."

She jerked her head back around. "Why would you say that? She is one of my most trusted advisers."

"It's just a hunch, insight perhaps, possibly unfounded, but I think she's being deceptive about certain things." Jesse's time as a police investigator trained him to recognize red flags and Preaverca had a whole bunch of them. Instead of explaining his rationale to Saephira, he recanted, "Sorry for being presumptuous. I didn't mean to offend. I'll try to be more forthcoming in these matters."

"That would be a helpful change. Okay, when we arrive in Beayama, I will—" A rumble stopped her in mid-sentence. The noise grew louder. Then shale and boulders came crashing down upon them.

CHAPTER 14
AMBUSHED

The raiding party unleashed boulder after boulder from the top of the ridge. Gelr had prepped five landslide starting positions, spaced about fifty paces apart, one for each man under his command. On his cue, they released the starting boulders and watched as the avalanche of rocks and shale hit the expedition members below. A huge dust cloud arose as the slide increased with intensity. "I think we got them all, except for Menarbat, of course. The Tracker kept a safe distance away once he signaled us."

"Shouldn't we wait to see the final outcome?" inquired one raider.

"No, we did our job. Nothing to see other than dead bodies. You guys mount up and get out of here." With a worried frown, Gelr scanned the reddish skyline. "It seems a storm is brewing, which is another good reason to get off this mountain top. Don't wanna hang around if a windblower hits."

"Commander Gelr, aren't you returning with us?" another one asked as he climbed upon his kack.

"I'll follow after I get rid of any evidence identifying us as being the cause. It needs to appear as an accident in case someone checks the ridgetop later."

"Alright, we're out of here. We'll meet you in Briacap and hoist a couple drinks to celebrate."

"Yeah, sure. Now get going. Report to Lord Eddnok about his successful ambush. No doubt he'll be pleased. To play it safe, take the trail around the backside of the mountain. Stay hidden until you enter the Blighte. From then on you should be in the clear."

Gelr watched his men leave and waved them a hearty farewell. When they were out of listening range, he yelled, "You'll never see me again. I've done my last dirty deed for that blasted Lord Eddnok." Instead of disguising the ambush site, he loaded his gear and departed, taking a different route, heading east to the Cali River. His eyes were full of tears.

As the rockslide barreled downward, Max grabbed Seth by his arm and tossed him about twenty feet to the rear. "Run, kid, run, and don't look back!" The whole hillside started to collapse, boulders flying everywhere, the noise deafening. Sliding debris followed in its wake, covering everything in sight.

Seth raced up the trail, dodging rocks, until he reached a stable area. Only then did he turn around and see two large boulders rolling toward Max as he struggled to control his ride. The animal instinctively bucked when the first stone passed by, tossing Max high into the air. The second one hit a few seconds later, knocking the kack over like a bowling pin. Loose gravel slid over and buried it. "Max, are you okay? Max? Hang on, bro, I'll be there in a minute." Seth rushed over to find Max digging franticly to unearth his mount. He was bleeding from cuts on his arms and legs.

"Seth, try to locate Narleen. She was riding in front of us. I'll be right behind you." Max continued tossing rocks aside until he uncovered his kack. The animal whinnied and pawed at the ground with one of her front legs in a futile effort to rise. "You saved my life, old girl, when you flung me over that boulder." The kack peered at him with pained eyes as he stroked her neck to comfort her. "Sorry gal, I have to leave now and search for survivors. I know you're hurting, but I'll come back. Lay still and rest."

"Max, Narleen is over here, barely hanging on, slipping over the cliff, and I can't reach her. The terrain is too unstable. She's calling for help. Hurry!"

Max scrambled over the sliding rubble to Seth's position. "Quick, give me your rope." Seth untied it from around his waist and handed it to Max. He knotted a loop on the end and tossed it toward Narleen. The rope fell short, so he tried again. His second throw landed within her grasp. "Grab it, Narleen!"

"I can't, my clothing is snagged on a broken tree limb. If I move, I'll fall off into the canyon."

"No, you won't. Take ahold of the rope and I'll pull you out. Don't think about it, just flip over and grab it. Do it now!" Narleen let out a tear-filled sigh, lunged forward with all her might, seized the rope with one hand and then latched on with the other. Hand over hand, Max dragged her away from the edge to secure footing. She stood and clung to his shoulders, crying uncontrollably.

Her clothes were torn, her arms and face cut and bleeding, her auburn hair, tangled in knots. The mount she rode, nowhere in sight. In shock and hyperventilating, tears continued to run down her cheeks. "Narleen, sit here for a moment and catch your breath. Seth and I need to look for survivors. We'll return soon." She only nodded.

"Who was ahead of Narleen?" asked Seth.

"One of the militia escorts. You check for him, and I'll keep hunting for the others. Unless the flow shifted them, Lady Saephira and Jesse were positioned fourth in line." Max tossed the rope to Seth. "Thanks for the loan, recruit. Your *tijvah* was a life saver."

The search for people continued. Seth heard moaning under the next pile of rocks and began rolling the stones aside. He found a dead kack and a militiaman who seemed disoriented, perhaps from a concussion. His left arm was badly broken. "Dude, don't move. Aid is on the way. Right now, I gotta zip off and keep searching. Do you understand me?" Seth got no response. He scanned down the line and spotted Max tearing apart another mound of rocks. Seth yelled, "Hey Max, I found the soldier guy. He'll live. Did you locate anybody else?"

"Yes, Lady Saephira and Jesse. They are sprawled out underneath the torso of a lifeless kack. I hope they're alive. Come help me dig them out." Seth hustled over and they worked feverishly to unearth them, rolling boulders out of the way after

Max pried them loose with his Gladius. The debris they scooped aside with their hands.

Saephira and Jesse were lying with their faces buried in the dusty gravel. "Looks like their mount created a protective barrier, which diverted some of the flow." Max quickly turned them over. Their clothes were shredded, stained with blood. He shook each one by their shoulders, calling out, "Ma'am, Sir, can you hear me?" No response.

"Bro, their faces are turning blue. I don't think they're getting air." Seth inspected their mouths and found them full of dirt. Using his fingers, he removed what he could. Still not breathing. As a surfer, he knew what to do for individuals who drowned. Instinctively, he began administering CPR, blowing into Saephira's mouth and applying chest compressions. "Dude, follow my lead or we're gonna lose JW. Pinch his nose, exhale into his mouth twice, then push on his chest, and keep at it until he responds."

The procedures worked. Soon color returned to their faces and the two sat up, dazed, gasping breaths and coughing. Their eyes opened slowly. Finally, Jesse spoke. "We saw the rocks coming. I don't remember much after that. What happened?"

Max replied, "Massive landside. Your kack's body shielded you guys from the worst of it. Narleen is fine although a bit distraught. One security person has a head injury, concussion I think, and a broken arm. If you two are okay, Seth and I better keep checking the debris field."

"Wait, I'm going with you." Jesse glanced over at Saephira who shook her head in agreement. "I guess we're both going." He rose to walk but winced in pain from what felt like a sprained ankle. Saephira offered him an arm for support, and together they hobbled onward, following Max and Seth. The four of them stopped at the next mound of debris and began digging. "This should be Captain Melmandus and Anna since they were riding ahead of us."

Meanwhile, Menarbat, who was at the head of the line,

began to panic. He heard voices and the sounds of digging behind him. He couldn't believe there were survivors. If he's implicated in Eddnok's plot, they would imprison him for life or worse, execute him. He had to think fast. If his ride survived and he was uninjured, the dubious result might compromise him. Impulsively, he led his mount over to the ledge and swatted it on the rear. It didn't budge. He grabbed a torch from its side carrier and beat the kack until he forced it over the edge to its death. To complete the ruse, he used a jagged slab of shale to make a gash on his forehead. He tore his garments, laid across the trail, face up, and pretended to be unconscious.

It didn't take long to see the results of their digging. They found Captain Melmandus, crushed almost beyond recognition. Saephira covered her mouth and began wailing uncontrollably, her tears relentless. "No, no, no, not him!" Near the captain, Anna lay curled in a ball. Her eye lids blinked repeatedly as if she were waking from a dream. Their mount was half buried in the rubble, dead.

"Annie, are you okay?" Getting no reply, Jesse asked again, "Annabelle, can you hear me?" She wiggled her fingers as if she were grabbing for something. "Do you have any pain?" She turned her head toward Jesse, trying to respond, her words inaudible. He brushed the grime off her face and moved her tousled black hair aside to check for head wounds. "Your cuts are only superficial, so you're gonna be fine."

Still in a state of shock, Anna peered at Melmandus' crumpled body and then stared at their deceased kack. When she glanced back at Jesse, her eyes held a deep sadness. "Jess, I can't feel or move my legs."

"Are you sure? Let me help you stand." As he lifted her, she collapsed, unable to support her weight. "Here, grab on to my neck and I'll carry you to safety. We must get away from this spot."

As the fogginess cleared in her mind, she asked, "Where's my musical instrument?"

"Sorry Anna, your glifstring is probably mashed to bits like the rest of our supplies or pushed over the shelf."

"No, here it is." Max leaned over and cleared away the dirt. "Not damaged either. Somehow it ended up lodged in this hollow. That might have saved it." He dusted the instrument off and handed it to Saephira. With Jesse carrying Anna and Saephira holding on to her glifstring, they walked away leaving the fallen bodies and lifeless animals behind.

With Anna dug free, Max and Seth continued their search for the second militia escort and Menarbat. They found the militiaman, dead, his forehead smashed by a large boulder. His mangled kack was nearby under a pile of shale. Leaving the remains undisturbed, the duo continued on to the end of the rockslide where they discovered the Tracker sprawled on the ground, unresponsive, with a cut on his head. His mount was missing, which Max presumed had been swept into the canyon by the avalanche.

"Seth, see what you can do to aid Menarbat. I gotta check on my injured kack. I'll send everyone this way. It will be safer in case the landslide starts again." Max passed Saephira and Jesse, checked on Anna's condition, and suggested they keep moving until they were out the danger zone. Continuing his trek uphill, he approached the wounded soldier who was now standing with Narleen beside him. Max gave them an update on the situation and directed them downhill to meet with Jesse and Saephira.

He finally arrived where he left his ride. She was in extreme distress, making strange moaning sounds. Max knelt on one knee, stroked her neck, and pulled the mane away from her eyes. The kack lifted her head to look at him as she labored to breathe. "Sorry girl, I don't think you're going to make it. Three of your legs are broken and you're bleeding from your nose. I'm not going to let you suffer any longer." He gently patted and rubbed her neck. "You are a good mount, better than any horse I've ever had. You can travel with me anytime."

As he continued stroking her neck, he pulled out his Gladius. She seemed to know what he planned. "Rest now, old girl, ya done well." And he thrust his sword deep into her ribcage, finding her heart. It was over in a moment. The animal lowered her head and closed her eyes, the pain and suffering over. He stood in silence, wiped the blade off on his clothes and sheathed it. "It's been an honor, old gal." Then he marched down the debris field to the rendezvous location. As Max drew close, he heard the group discussing their current dilemma.

Menarbat, who now had his head bandaged, paced around giving orders. "Without rides, supplies, and only one torch, we must leave now to reach Beayama before darkout. And it's a long walk."

"First we need to gather the personal items from Melmandus and the militiaman who died," Saephira said.

"There's no time for such foolishness; we hafta get going." Menarbat continued to strut about, kicking the ground, acting nervous.

"We will make the time, Tracker, and you know the reason why."

The escort with a broken arm said, "I'll get their personal effects, my Lady, and proudly carry them back to their friends and families. They were my comrades, you know."

"I'm sorry but I don't believe I know your name."

"It's Phauch, my Lady. Served under Captain Melmandus for five yarns."

"Thank you, Phauch. Leave their bodies where they lie. We will send a burial detachment next cycle, assuming we arrive at Beayama by then. If you can break their swords in two, please leave them draped over their bodies."

"Yes, my Lady, I will try. However, with a busted arm, I'm not—"

"I will assist you," offered Max. "My Gladius is made from a superior alloy, and it's sharp enough to slice through almost anything, even bronze." Max led the way to their locations: first the militiaman, then Captain Melmandus. It didn't take much, just one swing from Max's blade to cut their bronze swords in half. They crossed the sections and respectfully placed them on top of their deceased bodies.

"This is how we honor fallen soldiers," Phauch said. "When their lives are cut short, so are their swords, never to be used again." After they finished placing the honors, Max helped Phauch gather the personal effects of his comrades, and together they headed for the rendezvous spot.

At the designated area, the survivors were taking inventory of their remaining supplies. Most of their provisions were destroyed, buried under the avalanche, or swept into the canyon below. Their only resources were a half-full skin of water Max found and one used torch from Menarbat. The Tracker, who seemed to have recovered quickly, led the trek back to Beayama. Gusty winds continued to buffet them as they descended the Passage, slowing their progress, yet they pressed on. Jesse carried Anna for about an hour before he tripped and fell. The second time it happened, Max ran over to intervene.

"Here, sir, let me transport Anna the rest of the way." Max leaned over to make the exchange but Jesse resisted. "Sir, although your efforts are worthy, you're exhausted, and if you keep collapsing or dropping Anna, you may make her condition worse."

"What happened is my fault. I agreed to this fateful expedition, and now people are dead, Anna paralyzed, and Lundy, well, I lost him too. I am supposed to be the leader. I'm responsible."

"Jesse, sir, we are all responsible." Max lifted Anna into his arms and carried her until dayrise changed to twilight. At nightrise, the party entered the city. They passed the watchman on lookout duty and continued on to the mender's house. Captain Waubush of the Safeguards followed behind asking questions about what happened at the ruins. Lady Saephira simply responded, "It was not good."

CHAPTER 15
THE AFTERMATH

The mender organized a triage in her dining room. Since Anna was not in pain, Ottaar asked Max to take her upstairs to rest in her bed while she examined Menarbat and the militiaman. Diagnosing Anna's condition would be more complicated. Those with less-severe injuries, waited.

"Seth, since you don't appear to be hurt, I could use your help with the others. Take my washbasin and fill it with mineral water." She pointed over to the counter. "Use the fresh towels stacked on my shelf and start cleaning out everyone's cuts and scrapes. Then use my Helixzon healing salve, which is next to the towels, and apply it to all the wounds, including any bruises. Start with Narleen. After you finish treating her, she can assist you with the others."

Perturbed at all the noise, Ottaar glared over at the table where Captain Waubush and Saephira were in an intense discussion. "I know you have questions and important matters to discuss, but please keep your voices down. I have much work ahead of me this nightrise, and I don't care to be distracted. And that goes for the rest of you. Quiet please! I'll give you updates on conditions as I go along."

"Alright, Tracker, you're up first. Let me see your head wound." Menarbat slipped into the chair by her table.

"I think I received a bad concussion. I have a serious cut too. Probably needs stiches." He removed the bandage wrapped around his brow and leaned forward so the mender could diagnose his injuries.

"There's no swelling or bruising anywhere, no bleeding from the ears, no bloodshot eyes. No headache, right?" Menarbat shook his head no. "And the cut on your forehead looks more like a scratch." She opened her mender kit and removed a small jar. "Take this healing salve home and apply before you retire for the night. You'll be fine." With a flick of her hand, she shooed the Tracker away. "Phauch, you're next." The militiaman hurried over and sat in her examination chair.

She inspected his arm, moving it in circles, gently bending it. Phauch flinched. "Yep, your arm is broken. Not a bad break. Almost no swelling. I will splint it for the night. On the morrow, I'll set the forearm in a permanent support. The healing salve Narleen applied will do wonders for all your cuts and bruises." The mender padded his left arm with a clean towel, positioned two flat boards on the top and bottom, and wrapped the splints with cloth strips, pulling them tight before tying them off. "Do you require medicine for the pain? I can give you some Netherute."

He flexed his splinted arm, twisting it a few times. "No, I'm fine. It doesn't hurt much at all."

"Good. I'll see you at firstlight. Jesse, your turn, let me see your hobbled foot." Jesse didn't budge. He remained seated at the dining table. Lost in his thoughts, he didn't realize the others had departed after receiving treatment. Menarbat and Phauch went home. Saephira and Narleen walked outside to talk privately with Captain Waubush. Max and Seth retired to their quarters, totally fatigued, and climbed into their beds.

"It's only a sprained ankle, not much swelling, hardly hurts." Jesse wiggled his foot around in a circle trying not to wince. "If you have a support wrap I can borrow for a couple cycles, I'm sure I'll be fine. I would like to wait for your diagnosis of Annie. And while waiting I was wondering . . . hmm . . . do you have anything to drink?"

"Sure, there's Anatora tea I can brew. Also have yarm berry juice and a little kunakk I keep on hand to mix healing remedies."

"I'll try the kunakk."

"Very well, considering all you have been through this cycle, it may help settle your nerves." Ottaar pulled the jar off her shelf and handed it to Jesse with a small cup. "Just sip it, though, it's a strong intoxicant. I'll let you know shortly about Annabelle. She's such a sweet girl. What happened to her is sad." Ottaar grabbed her mender kit and climbed the stairs to Anna's room.

Outside on the street, Saephira and Captain Waubush continued their conversation as Narleen, her trusted lady-in waiting, stood by her side and listened. Saephira kept glancing over her shoulder to make sure no one else was eavesdropping. "Captain, I want flyer messages sent to all our cities and villages, including Tabahir in the Disputed Lands. It concerns a missing fifth member of Jesse's mysterious band of travelers, a man named Lundy MacBain. Give this memo to Preaverca and make sure she gets copies into the air before you leave:"

Missing person, named Lundy, older man, foreign traveler, unusual accent. Contact by rider if seen. Don't use flyers. — Lady S

"Is there concern with Preaverca?"

"Not sure. Maybe not, just using discernment. I'm also honoring a promise made to Jesse."

Waubush tucked the memo into his coat pocket. "We usually don't send homing flyers to settlements in the Disputed Lands."

"This time we will, and please follow up on those messages with riders to each location." Saephira gave him Lundy's full description, which Jesse had provided, to use in the dispatches. "Have the riders leave at firstlight. And one more thing, please arrange memory tables for our two fallen soldiers. Narleen and I are heading to our quarters now. We are both heartbroken and . . ." Saephira couldn't finish or stop the tears from cascading down her cheeks. "We can discuss additional matters on the morrow."

"Yes, my Lady, I understand. It was a trying day for all of you." He bowed and rushed over to the Postal Tower as the two women walked, arm in arm, to Residential Hall.

The captain found Preaverca leaving the mail room, heading to her quarters for the night. "Excuse Preaverca, I need you to send out several dispatches requested by Lady Saephira."

"Sure, I will get to it at firstlight."

Handing the memo to her, Waubush said, "No, they have to go out now before you retire. Lady Saephira asked for copies to be sent to Ritwell, Bayegulf, Falein and Cali fishing villages, Midvill on the boundary line, and Tabahir in the Disputed Lands."

"Aren't sending homing flyers to places above the boundary line, like Tabahir, forbidden since they are controlled by the Upper Realm?"

"Usually. This time, however, we will. Besides, Tabahir is supposed to be a neutral city. I will stay and assist you." Preaverca frowned and kept asserting she could handle it, but Waubush insisted. "If I write the messages and you attach them to the flyers, it will speed things along for both of us." After all six homing flyers were airborne, he thanked Preaverca for staying late. Having completed his errand, Waubush descended the steps to exit the tower.

When she was sure he had gone, she wrote two more dispatches, both to Briacap in the Upper Realm:

1. Ambush killed captain, 1 militia. Lady S, Narleen, travelers, and 2 others survived. Suspect my involvement. Tracker may be implicated. —P

2. Lady S looking for 5th traveler, named Lundy. If you have, suggest concealment, intern to mines, or eliminate him. —P

Jesse poured a half-full cup of kunakk and sipped it slowly. The soothing effects warmed his insides. The longer he waited for Ottaar's report on Anna, the more he worried. *What's taking her so long?* He refilled his cup and started to drink it when the mender returned.

Jesse stood as soon as Ottaar descended the steps. "What's the diagnosis?"

The mender pulled up a stool and sat at the table across from Jesse. "It's not good, sir. Annabelle has paralysis in both her legs."

Jesse slid into his chair. "Yes, I know. She had no feeling there after the accident, but it's temporary, right?"

"No, I'm afraid not. It's permanent. When I examined her, I discovered a deep gash in the lower section of her back. I pulled out several rock fragments and cleaned the wound. The damage was extensive. I think a larger piece of shale cut her spinal cord. It's severed, the vertebra, central nerve, everything. Sadly, she will never walk again. There is nothing I can do for her loss of feeling or the paralysis. I applied healing salve to her cuts, which will heal quickly. Her back, unfortunately, will not." Ottaar's clinical update held little emotion. Still, he could tell the mender had been crying because of the dried tear streaks on her cheeks.

Jesse shook his head, biting his lower lip. He appeared as if he were ready to say something yet remained silent. He reached for his cup and took a few more sips of kunakk.

"Annabelle has no pain, so that's fortunate. She's a resilient woman, kind, even thanked me for the diagnosis. Before I came downstairs, I gave her a dose of Netherute medication to help her sleep and placed her instrument close to the bed in case she decides to play it later. I'm sorry, Jesse, I really am. All we can do is to make her comfortable."

"Okay, thank you for . . ." His voice grew hushed as if it had dropped into a deep void.

Ottaar waited for him to finish. When he didn't, she continued, "It's been a long cycle, Jesse. I am heading to my room now. I suggest you do likewise and get some rest." The mender pushed her stool away from the table, rose, and started toward the upstairs hallway.

"I'm gonna sit here for a while, consider my options, perhaps write in my journal. I know you did your best for Annie."

She turned around to face Jesse. "I wish I could have done more for her." Jesse wanted to respond, say he understood her frustration. Instead, he remained silent. "Since you are staying up, I will throw a couple more logs into the hearth. It gets cold in this room during darkout. Again, I am sorry about your friend. Good nightrise, Jesse." With a distraught face and tired eyes, Ottaar shuffled off to her room.

Jesse gulped down the rest of his second cup of kunakk and then poured a third. The intoxicating properties dulled his senses, while emotions of remorse plagued his mind, dragging up past memories and failures from his life on earth:

He remembered taking medications to deal with his aching, injured knee. When the doctors quit prescribing them, he turned to alcohol to numb the pain. First it was beer, then hard liquor, but only on the weekends. Soon he was bringing a fifth of scotch to work. One night, while driving drunk in his patrol car, he hit a woman in a crosswalk, leaving her paralyzed. He lost his job, lost his friends, even lost a coworker. *As police chief, I was supposed to be a responsible community leader and make wise decisions. I didn't.*

Jesse feared the tragic scenario was repeating itself, but this time with Anna and Lundy: a second woman paralyzed, another friend lost. And now he's getting stoned again, just like before. On earth, he failed as a leader and on Eskaonus, nothing had changed. Jesse believed the angels made a mistake asking him to lead. Maximus should be the group leader, not him.

He opened his satchel, pulled out his candle lamp, flicked on the flame, blew it out again, and stuffed it back into its pouch. That's how Jesse felt in his heart—his light extinguished, snuffed out by circumstances. *Maybe if I focus on something else.* He took out his journal and quill pen to write an entry. Dizziness and blurry vision made finding the right page difficult. The pen kept slipping out of his fingers. His handwriting looked sloppy.

Entry Seven

Massive rockslide at ruins, many injuries, Anna paralyzed, townspeople dead, Lundy lost. It's all my fault. Guess I'm still a failure. I'm not gonna . . .

Discouraged, intoxicated, and blaming himself for all the mishaps, he closed the cover and crammed his journal and pen into the satchel. He stood, staggered over to the hearth and tossed his satchel into the flames. *I quit.* He wobbled back to the table, dropped into his chair, and emptied the last of the kunakk into his cup. He swallowed it in one gulp. A few moments later, he passed out, sprawled face down over the table.

THE DAY AFTER ALWAYS

CHAPTER 16
UZZIEL AND CHESEDEL

The Fountain of Living Water was one of the more popular venues in heaven. Centrally located, this eternal wellspring sprayed twelve jets of water high into the air, which drifted back down as a refreshing mist. Clusters of saints had gathered around the fountain to drink from the life-giving waters. A few waded in the pool surrounding it. Others splashed water at one another, reveling in the festive spirit always present. Some sat nearby on one of the many benches, visiting and laughing. Uzziel, the Cherubim, stood off to the side, watching as the saints enjoyed the blessings of the waters of life, freely given by God.

"I apologize for the delay," Chesedel said as he materialized in front of Uzziel. "I was over at the Hall of Records reading incoming scroll messages."

"Apology unneeded, no such things as delays in a timeless eternity." Uzziel glanced around the perimeter looking for a quiet spot. "Since the fountain is crowded, I suggest we try a more secluded area. The Garden of Supplication should work." In a flash, they both disappeared.

Heaven contained an endless number of prayer gardens. The supplication garden sat near the junction of Charity Street and Narrow Way. It contained two-person altars, spaced in between trees and bushes to offer solitude as people prayed. The angels moved inside the gazebo, seeing it was unoccupied at the

96

moment. "Yes, this is much better," Uzziel remarked. "What have you learned about the mission in Eskaonus?"

"We've received seven transfer messages from Jesse's journal. I wrote the second entry before he left. He logged the rest. The last five come from Eskaonus. I constructed his diary from heavenly scroll paper, so anything written thereon is simultaneously recorded in the Hall of Records."

"Does he know we see his log entries?" Uzziel asked.

"No, I didn't tell him beforehand because I didn't want him to feel restricted about the things he recorded. His journal has been our only source of information about the assignment in Eskaonus. Since Jesse traveled to a different time and space, I no longer hear his thoughts or prayers."

"Not unusual. It happens with most outer-realm communications. What do his entries reveal?" Realizing Chesedel seldom gave short updates, Uzziel strolled over to the nearest bench to find a comfortable seat.

"Jesse wrote that Reverend MacBain did not arrive with the group. He is still missing. Archive scrolls that document recent deaths do not indicate his, so I assume he's alive somewhere on Eskaonus. The other four members came down with a sickness soon after arriving due to eating poisonous berries. We almost lost our team on the first day. Fortunately, a local leader found their bodies before they succumbed and took them to a healer. Their souls of course, being eternal, were never in jeopardy."

"Not a great start, Chesedel, is it?"

"No, not at all, but matters got worse. Assassins attacked Jesse and the southern province leader. Later, when visiting one of our ancient temples, which is now in ruins, Jesse encountered a massive rockslide that injured most of his party, paralyzed Annabelle, and killed several of the locals who were part of the expedition."

"Wickedness has spread faster than we anticipated." Uzziel frowned. "Hmm . . . is there any information about their current situation?"

"Yes, the last journal entry. It was brief, incomplete, and concerns me the most." Chesedel walked over and sat on the bench by the cherub. "Jesse blames himself for all the setbacks and feels like a failure. I think he is ready to give up."

"Quit?" Uzziel stood and began pacing around the gazebo. "This would be disastrous for the inhabitants of Eskaonus, not to mention our emissaries and their outreach. You were Jesse's guardian angel and know how he reacts better than most. How do you suggest we proceed?"

"I need to visit Eskaonus, check on the conditions of Annabelle and Jesse, and see if I can locate Lundy." Chesedel arose, tightened his sash and checked the sword at his side. "It cannot wait a moment longer."

"Agreed. You have permission for interdimensional realm travel. Use the White Pearl Gate portal. In the meantime, I will request more prayer cover. I wish you Godspeed."

Chesedel transported to the main gate, pictured Eskaonus in his mind, and then walked past the white column. A flash of light appeared, and he was gone. Moments later, he appeared in the night skyline over Eskaonus. It was past midnight, what the Eskaonites called darkout. He flew unseen to Beayama and located Annabelle's room at the mender's house. He popped into her quarters and found Anna sound asleep, lying on her side.

Knowing he had to materialize to administer God's healing power, he allowed his visible shape to take form. He slipped over to her bed and placed his hand on Anna's middle back. His fingers began to glow with a bright golden light. Anna's body relaxed as healing poured into her spine. After he repaired the damage and restored feeling in her legs, he whispered into her ear, "You'll be okay, Annie." In a dreamlike state, she looked up, smiled, and watched as Chesedel stepped silently out her door, his blue sash and sword visible at his side.

He found Jesse downstairs, passed out, an empty liquor bottle tipped over on the table beside him. "Oh Jesse, drinking away the pain and frustration won't help, but maybe this will." He reached over and touched Jesse on his right shoulder. Again, the angel's fingers glowed. Instead of physical healing, Chesedel released spiritual encouragement into his soul, something more expedient right now. He noticed Jesse's satchel in the fireplace yet left it where it lay. The angel became invisible again and popped away into the night.

Chesedel flew by Briacap. He could sense the evil there.

He entered the fortress unseen and found Lundy MacBain's room. Although they had imprisoned him, he was safe for now. Having completed his tasks, he pictured heaven in his mind and returned to his home dimension, arriving at the White Pearl Gate. He gave his update to Uzziel who was waiting for his return.

CHAPTER 17
LUNDY TRANSLATES SCROLL

Looking outside his window, Lundy noticed the morning light had turned reddish brown, not the normal hue he'd grown accustomed to seeing. The change in the horizon also brought a hot, dry wind that gusted through the streets, swirling up the ground, creating little twisters. Several times during the day a tower bell rang out, warning people to stay inside as a windblower approached their area. Thus far, none of them breached the city. Still, he decided to stay inside in relative safety and work on the translation of the ancient scroll.

Lundy was an avid reader who enjoyed studying different languages. As a minister and linguist, he already understood five dialects from his time on earth. He learned several more while reading various texts in heaven. Eddnok's scroll was similar to the earliest script of heaven, which he referred to as the God text. Lundy had seen it on heaven's copy of the original Ten Commandments, written by God Himself. Eddnok's scroll matched certain Hebrew and Aramaic characters, although the form was different, older.

Using a specialized decryption code, he finished translating the words, guessing at a few of their meanings. He folded the translation into quarters and stuffed it into his boot beside the Gospel of John. Lundy assumed Eddnok's guards searched his room when he left to wander around the city, yet for whatever reason they never checked his shoes. He chuckled to himself; *even a blind Scotsman is more adept than those fellows.*

The scroll turned out to be a directional word map, written

in strange rhyming prose that revealed the location of a treasure containing wisdom and power:

> If treasure is what you seek
> Then don't be meek
> Nor forgo the rift
> Near the highest cliff
>
> Buried deep within lies a secret twin
> Of the richest gift
> Known to gods or men
>
> Take an uphill pace to seek a taste
> Of wisdom sublime
> And power divine
>
> So follow the trail to the mountains red
> Through the forest dead
> Past water's shed
> And peaks that grow during daylight glow
>
> Past ancient grave lays hidden cave
> Where treasure awaits
> For a ruler of fate

The reverend had never encountered such a map before. It seemed like a crossword puzzle with some of the answers filled in. He hadn't decided if he would give Eddnok the translation but not doing so would be deceitful on his part, and Lundy detested lying. To play it safe, he planned to make an extra copy for himself. It might come in handy in case of attempted skullduggery by Eddnok's stooges. He'd save the duplicate project for later. Right now, he wanted to go outside and stretch his legs. Tomorrow he would try to depart Briacap.

The sky stayed red for a second day. The wind gusts had

died down overnight, even though the heat remained unabated. Lundy decided to take Eddnok up on his promise to let him explore the countryside. As he approached the tower gate, Sub-Commander Brappt stopped him. "Where to you think you're going Master Lundy?"

"I have your lordship's permission to leave. I'm his honored guest, you know, and the only one who can translate his wee little manuscript."

"The man's right," stated Bolgog as he listened to the conversation. "He can go. However, our guest needs an escort to make sure he stays out of trouble. And guess what, commander, you're the escort."

"I can't. I have guard duty all cycle."

Bolgog ignored his concern. "Requisition a kack from the stables and take him out for a couple spans, except don't let him interact with anyone."

"But sir—"

"Get going and I'll cover the tower gate while you're out being tour guide." Bolgog leaned backwards and laughed, followed by a bout of guffawing. "At the first sign of windblowers, I suggest a hasty retreat." More snickering ensued. "You don't want to get swept away or put our esteemed visitor in danger."

Angry, Brappt stomped off. In a quarter span, he returned with a mount. As they rode double out the gate, the sub-commander hollered, "Where do you wanna go, old fella?"

Lundy surveyed the mostly barren landscape. "Have any towns nearby?"

"The closest one is Tabahir. It's inside the Disputed Lands. Since we control the commerce there, I guess it'll be okay. If we encounter locals, I'll do the talking. You got it!"

"Aye laddie, that'll be just dandy with me." *In a pig's eye.*

As they drew near Tabahir, a windblower arose in the south and approached the city, twirling a huge dust cloud in its wake. Moments later, the tower bell rang out a warning. Brappt rushed to find shelter in the nearest building, which happened to be a tavern. "Good place to wait it out. You stay outside with our kack and make sure it doesn't run off while I hoist a drink or two. After the danger passes, we can finish your little outing and return to Briacap."

"You want me to stay out here and face gale-force winds while you wet your whistle?"

"Better you than me. You'll be fine. Make sure you tie our ride to the hitching post. If it gets too windy, you can take shelter on the porch. I'll see you after a few cups."

Brappt had just ordered his first kunakk when Lundy burst through the door. "Greetings laddies, I'm Lundy MacBain, and I'm searching for me four companions, three lads and one lass. Anybody seen them?"

"Alright Lundy, I've had it with you. We're going back now, windstorm or not." He downed the rest of his drink, then grabbed Lundy by the scruff of the neck and dragged him outside. "Get on the kack! Now! We're leaving! Lord Eddnok will not be pleased, nor will Commander Bolgog."

In the rear of the tavern, two merchants sat at an oval table enjoying a drink together while they planned their next stop. They watched the confrontation between the elder and younger man escalate to the point of yelling. "I think he's the person the Lower Realm is searching for, the older guy."

"He sure matches the description we received. I wonder if Lady Saephira is offering a reward."

"I don't expect one. Never much cared for the Upper Realm or the way they treat their people. Besides, there's no love lost between Lord Eddnok and me. He's cheated us on prices too many times over the yarns. You handle the rest of our trades this cycle. I'm riding south as soon the all-clear bell rings."

CHAPTER 18
A DAY IN THE LIFE

The reddish glow of dayrise prevailed for a second cycle. The winds had tapered off to moderate gusts. During the previous night, though, a warning bell rang out indicating an approaching windblower, yet it never touched ground or caused storm damage in Beayama. In the common room, Jesse lay face down, asleep on the dining table. A tipped over kunakk jar by his hand suggested he had overindulged. Realizing Jesse was hungover, Ottaar put on a pot of Azollie tea for him and left it to simmer on her woodstove before she and her houseguests went outside to visit the memory tables erected in the city square. As was the custom, relatives had invited the citizens to drop by and remember their deceased soldiers as heroes.

After paying his respects to Captain Melmandus and his militiaman at the tables, Max returned to the mender's house. He wanted to speak privately with Jesse. He was still slumped over in an apparent stupor. Max approached and stood across the table from him. "Sir, you have to get up now." Getting no response, he spoke a little louder, "Sir, wake up!" When that didn't work, he kicked his chair a couple times and pounded his fist on the tabletop. Jesse finally stirred and glanced around the room. His eyes were bloodshot, his clothes in disarray. Max let him adjust to his surroundings for a few moments before continuing. "Sir, we need to talk."

Jesse righted himself in his chair and blinked his eyes trying to focus. "Max, I'm . . ."

"So, tell me, sir, what happened last night? As I recall, you were waiting for the mender to diagnose Miss Anna's condition."

"I'm not really sure where to start."

"At the beginning is usually best." Max pulled a chair over and sat facing Jesse.

"Alright, here it is, the whole ugly story:" Jesse told Max about injuring his knee in the Navy, losing a law-enforcement partner during a robbery shootout, getting hooked on pain meds and alcohol, driving drunk, causing a woman to be paralyzed for life, and being fired from his position as police chief. "It's déjà vu all over again. What happened on earth now repeats itself. Except this time, Anna is paralyzed, Lundy is missing or dead, and it's my fault. My leadership failures caused them all. The truth of the matter is . . . I have no business being in charge of this group or any group. You should take over."

"I'm not going to do that, sir. You are the chosen leader, picked by the angels and by us. If you struggle, your colleagues will support you. No matter what transpires, we will not discount your leadership or take matters into our own hands. As my commander, I will follow you through the fiery abyss and back. The others in our squad will do likewise. And now if I may, I have something important to share."

"Another one of your famous teachings I suppose. Rule Number Three, right?"

"Correct. This one, however, is for you, not Seth, and I didn't receive it from my elders. I heard it from a disciple named Saul. He was a leader, not unlike you, who struggled with many circumstances and in the process learned a valuable lesson."

"What lesson?"

"Not to let weariness or disappointments dictate our actions because in due season we shall reap the good, if we don't quit, give up, or lose heart."

"Sounds like a Bible verse."

"Indeed, it's found in an epistle to the Galatians, and if you recall it's the same advice the Cherubim gave us before we left heaven for our assignment in Eskaonus: don't quit or lose heart." Jesse exhaled deeply and gave a sorrowful nod. "And now, moving on to the reaping part, I have two confirmations. Here's the first one." Max reached into his coat pocket, pulled out Jesse's satchel and tossed it to him.

"What? No way! I threw it into the fireplace last night. It should be fried to a crisp. Where did—"

"The mender found it this morning and gave it to me. She assumed you made a mistake."

"How did it survive intact?"

"Let me tell you about things made in heaven. They are eternal. I've lived there longer than the rest of you, over 2000 years in earth time, and that's the way of it. There may be exceptions, but none that I've encountered. Take my sword for example." Max pulled it out of its scabbard and held it high over his head. "It's unbreakable and will never lose its sharpness." He sheathed it again. "Remember Anna's musical instrument?" Jesse bobbed his head yes. "Not luck that it survived. It was providence. Her anointed glifstring cannot be harmed or crushed, even by a rockslide. Regarding Seth's thin rope, it's enduring. Even if sections are cut off, the cord retains its original length and strength. The same goes for your satchel. It cannot be destroyed nor anything in it, including your journal or candle lamp. Go ahead, check it out. It's all there, untouched."

Jesse turned his satchel over in his hands, inspected it, and peeked inside. "Wow, I never knew."

"And there's something else you don't know. Here's your second confirmation. You have a message from Miss Anna. She told me to let you know she's out window shopping."

Jesse's eyes opened wide, causing his eyebrows to rise on his forehead. "What? How can she be okay?"

"The mender said her paralysis must of have been temporary."

Surprised and shocked, Jesse knocked over his chair trying to rise. "You mean she can walk again?"

Max stood. "Yes sir," grinning at Jesse's reaction. "I saw her skipping down the steps this morning. Annabelle said she would catch you later at the memory tables."

Jesse rushed over to Max and the two embraced, arm to arm. "I can hardly believe it."

"Like I said, you will reap in due season if you don't quit or lose heart."

"Max, I don't know how to . . ." The emotion of the

moment took his breath away.

"A pot of dark tea is simmering on the stove. I think a cup or two will help clear your head. The mender also put out a change of clothes on your bed. Saephira is waiting for you at the memory tables. I would imagine Miss Anna is there by now, too. It would be good if you honored the fallen expedition members, which Seth and I have already done. You'll find their customs interesting."

Feeling renewed in his position as team leader, he asked, "What about you and Seth. What's happening with you guys?"

"Seth has gone fishing with a couple of the town youth, and Narleen asked me to help her pick dallups for dinner. We both figured the more we interacted with the locals, the more it would help with our mission. The recruit and I will meet you for dinner later to plan our next moves."

"Okay, sounds good. Again, I don't know how to thank you for helping me come to my senses."

"Sir, nothing more needs to be said. Therefore, I take my leave." Max gave a short salute across the chest and left the room.

Jesse poured himself a cup of steaming hot Azollie tea and sipped it slowly, pondering everything Max had spoken. Afterwards, he went upstairs, cleaned up, and put on a set of new clothes. He felt encouraged for the first time in days. Before going outside, he drank another cup of brewed Azollie. As he approached the city square, he could see it was crowded with people. Two large rectangular tables were placed in the middle of the street where most of the mourners had gathered. The first table was empty; the second contained one item.

"Shalom Jess, over here." Anna waved at him to join her at the table where she and Saephira were talking. As he got closer, Anna ran over to him, put her arms around his neck, and gave him a kiss on the cheek. "Look at me, I can walk." She twirled around as if dancing, her curvy black hair flowing across her shoulders. "The mender said my paralysis wasn't permanent, even the gash on my back is healing. No scars either."

"Wonderful, Annie, I can hardly—"

She pulled him closer and whispered in his ear. "Last night I had a dream that Chesedel came by my room, and in the morning, I could move my legs. I think it was a miracle." Jesse just listened, unsure how to respond. "I've already honored the fallen soldiers and now I'm off to do some window shopping."

"How are you gonna shop? We didn't bring money with us."

"Lady Saephira gave me a purse of credits. I may even buy gifts for you and Max to say thanks for saving me on the mountain." She offered a quick curtsy to Saephira and then departed, dancing down the street.

"She sure was lucky," Saephira remarked. "I am happy for her and your group. The mender assumed she would never walk again." With all the chatter going on around the tables, their conversation was being drowned out by the crowd, so Jesse stepped closer to hear Saephira's comments. "It's as if her injury never occurred."

"Annie thinks it was a miracle."

"Not sure I believe in such things. Whatever the explanation, it's a good report, and it seems as though she made a full recovery." Changing the conversation to the memorial, Saephira reiterated, "Here are the displays I mentioned last cycle." She pointed at the two tables in front of them. "This is how we honor those who die in service to the Lower Realm. There is no ceremony, only a memory table. Friends and family pick one personal item from the deceased as a keepsake. This is why we carried those items back with us from Onnie Passage. As for our fallen soldiers, they will be buried where they fell. I already dispatched a detail to the Passage to handle it. The swords we cut in half will be buried with them, crossed over their bodies to honor their lives."

"Why is one table is empty and the other only has a single item on it?" Jesse asked.

"The tables were put out at firstlight, and the keepsakes go quickly. The one left is from Captain Melmandus."

"Why did no one take it? Isn't it a valuable fighting staff?"

"Indeed, except it's more than an effective weapon, it's a

leadership staff, which I awarded him when he became Captain of the Militia. You know, he respected you as a leader and wanted you to have it in the event of his death."

"No, no, no, I can't. I'm not a very good—"

"I disagree." Saephira reached over and removed the staff from the table. "Everyone knows you're a leader. They can sense, and I can as well. I know you struggled last cycle; most good leaders do." She placed the staff into his hands.

"I don't . . . umm . . . deserve his staff, especially after last night."

"It is settled." Saephira continued pressing the staff into his hands. When he realized her resolve, he quit resisting and accepted it. "Since you don't carry a sword, use it as defensive weapon. It also makes a good walking stick."

Their conversation was interrupted when Menarbat rode by. "You sent for me, my Lady."

"Yes, I did. Excuse me for a moment, Jesse, while I talk to the Tracker." She turned to face him. "I see you have recovered quickly from your injuries." Remaining seated on his mount, Menarbat brushed aside his long wavy hair to show her his healed forehead. "Good, I need you to follow up on the flyer message from Falein Village about their supply shortages."

"Exactly where I'm going now. Stopping by Cali first, then on to Falein. I'll make a report once I know more." He leaned forward on his mount, clearing his throat as if his mouth were dry.

"Please see you do. We haven't heard anything from Falein, either by flyer or rider. Their silence causes me concern." She dismissed him with a gentle wave of her hand. "Be watchful in your travels. We have reports of lingering windblowers in the region."

"I will, my Lady." Kicking his kack hard in the sides, the Tracker galloped away, heading for the western egress. Once outside the gate, instead of turning left on the trail to the fishing villages, he veered right toward the Disputed Lands and Briacap. Under suspicion as a traitor and feeling implicated in the rockslide attack, he had no intention of ever returning to the Lower Realm.

Saephira watched until Menarbat exited the gate before

she continued her conversation with Jesse. "I know Anna is visiting our shops right now, and later she plans to return to her room and compose a few songs. I hope she'll sing one for us sometime. Before we part, I'm curious what Maximus and Seth are doing this cycle."

"Seth has been invited to go fishing at Mista Lake. I think he already left with two youths from town. And Max told me he is helping Narleen pick dallups for dinner." Upon hearing the news, Saephira tried to muffle a series of giggles with her hands. "What's so funny?" Jesse asked.

Saephira stopped chuckling, replacing it was a grin. "Here in Eskaonus, picking mushrooms with a young lady is a courting ritual."

"Oh, I'm sorry, I didn't know. I can probably stop Max."

"No, let them go. It'll be fine."

The crowds began to disperse, leaving a handful of people around the memory tables. "Jesse, I'm finished here myself. Feel free to stay until you're done meditating. I have realm business to attend." She studied Jesse's bloodshot eyes. "Please don't take this the wrong way, but you still look tired from the last darkout. Try to get some rest this cycle. I'm hosting a leadership banquet later, and you and your fellow companions are invited." The grin reformed on her face. "No doubt, mushrooms will be one of the dishes." She started giggling again as she strolled toward the Great Hall.

CHAPTER 19
FISHING AND MUSHROOMS

Hoping to glean more information about Eskaonus, Seth accepted an invitation to go fishing at Mista Lake with Calrin and Raydoo who were two teenagers close to his age. Even though the lake was only a couple span hike from Beayama, the boys decided to bring two mounts with side carriers in case they caught any tarkkies for tonight's banquet. Since Seth had not mastered the leg movements necessary for steering kacks, he rode double behind Calrin. Two harpoons and a sack of bait were tied to their side carriers. As the teens approached Mista, they noticed several large uprooted cottlepines and piles of broken branches and debris spread across the trail.

"Probably from the windblower that bypassed our city," remarked Raydoo.

"No doubt," Calrin replied. "We were lucky this time. Don't worry Seth, I think the danger has passed for now. These storms normally last two or three cycles at the most. Even so, we should keep an eye out for lingering gusts."

"Hey dudes, this lake looks pretty deep."

"It is," confirmed Raydoo. "Mista's waters are deeper than Falein Lake and the fishing is usually good all yarn. The village keeps several boats moored to their dock. We'll use one of those to paddle out to the middle where the bigger ones are harpooned." Seth felt a nauseous twitch arise in his gut. The idea of going out on the water, especially deep water, still terrified him.

"I wonder if we can fish from the shore." Seth didn't want to tell his new friends he was deathly afraid of water since his traumatic encounter at Malibu.

"Yes, but we will have better luck farther out. Why?" Raydoo asked.

"I'm not too psyched about going out into the water. I had a bad rap once, and I try to avoid it if I can."

"Sure, we can try from the jetty and see how our luck goes. Grab one of the harpoons and I'll show you how we prep it." Seth watched as Raydoo unwrapped the line connected to the harpoon and looped it in loose circles around his feet. He then stepped clear of the line. Holding the knotted end in his right hand and the harpoon in his left, Raydoo hoisted it over his shoulder. "Once you have it balanced, uncork the barbed point before you cast. Those are the safety procedures we use before each throw. Here, you try setting it up while I get the bait."

Seth practiced with the harpoon a few times until he mastered the routine. "What do you use for bait?"

"Yarm berries." Raydoo opened the sack Calrin had unloaded from his side carrier. "All tarkks are predators, flesh eaters, but the juvenile ones, called tarkkies, prefer the sweet taste of yarm berries, so we use it as chum to attract them. When they swim close enough, we harpoon them."

Calrin tossed a handful of berries as far as he could into the lake from the dock. "This would work better if we used a boat, faster too." They chummed the shoreline for about a span before the first tarkkie arrived. Its dorsal fin cut the surface, moving fast, leaving a wake behind it.

"Hey, dudes, looks a like a shark to me. An eight-footer."

"What's a shark?" both boys asked in unison.

"Him!" Seth pointed at the tarkkie. "It sure ain't Flipper." The fish, seemingly unaware of the danger, came within range and began gobbling down all the floating berries.

Calrin set his harpoon and tossed first, followed by Raydoo. Both hit their marks. After a gallant struggle, they managed to haul the fish to shore. "At least ten stones. Good size. One more of these should do it." Raydoo pulled both harpoons out and laid them aside. He handed Seth an extra knife and together they gutted and skinned the tarkkie, throwing the entrails into the lake for the eels.

Calrin sliced their prized catch into smaller sections and loaded the fillets into his side carrier. "The next one is yours, Seth. Here, use this harpoon. It's my dad's favorite. It never misses." The boys repeated the process, seeding the water with yarm berries until another tarkkie approached. "Okay, you're up. Do what Raydoo showed you."

Seth prepared his harpoon, aimed, and tossed it high into the air. With all the excitement, he forgot to maintain a firm grip on the knotted end of the line, so it slipped loose. The harpoon kept going and splashed into the water about a hundred feet out. It spooked the fish, which dove under the wake and swam away. "I'm sorry dude. Where can I buy a replacement?"

"Arrgh! My father's lucky harpoon. I better swim out and retrieve it before it sinks."

"What about the adult tarkks?" Raydoo asked.

"Shouldn't be a problem; they don't come out to hunt until after twilight." Before they could persuade him otherwise, Calrin removed his clothes, jumped into water, and began swimming. As he neared the still floating harpoon, a huge dorsal fin broke the surface and started circling.

"Seth yelled, "Shark! Calrin! Get back here!"

"He can't," cautioned Raydoo. "If he moves or makes one little ripple, the tarkk will attack. Maybe it will leave if he remains motionless." It didn't. Instead, two more monsters breached and started circling. One was over thirty feet long.

To Seth, the tarkks were similar to great whites, like the one that attacked him while surfing in Malibu, except these were much bigger. "I thought Calrin said the adults didn't come out till later."

"They usually don't. Maybe the dark red glow in the sky appeared as nightrise to them."

"What are we going to do? What about one of those?" Seth indicated the boats at the front of the dock.

Raydoo just shook his head. "We would need a bigger boat. Those on the landing are too small, more like canoes. The tarkks would sink us with one bite. Besides, it would take time to remove the weather cover, ready it, and paddle out there. Calrin doesn't have a span to spare."

With his adrenaline pumping, Seth shouted out, "Rule Number One: always expect the unexpected." Almost instinctively, he started prying off an old wooden plank on the dock. Glancing over at Raydoo, he yelled, "Help me get this loose." They tore it off the crossbeam in seconds. "Rule Number Two: face your fears to overcome them." Seth grabbed the torn section and dove into the water, using it like a surfboard.

He skimmed through the gentle swells, paddling hard and fast, as if he was chasing an oncoming wave. He glided right into the middle of the circling tarkks. *Rule Number Two.* "Dude, climb on my board and let's book it out of here." Calrin tried to pull himself up but kept slipping off. "Kick your feet to give yourself some momentum." Seth offered his hand and with one final tug, slid Calrin aboard. The kicking attracted the smaller tarkk, and it lunged at them, jaws wide open. *Rule Number One.* Seth grabbed the half-submerged harpoon nearby and stabbed the monster in the snout. "Carlin, take this gaff and if more sharks get close, poke them in the nose or eyes. I'll keep paddling." Before they reached the dock, the largest tarkk sped forward to intercept. Seth turned his makeshift surfboard around to face it. *Rule One.* He stood, doing a hang-ten on the board's edge. The fish breached the surface to attack. *Rule Two.* Seth kicked it as hard as he could between its eyes. The tarkk, being stunned, turned away and dove out of sight.

Seth tried to keep his balance; however, with all the commotion, the plank bobbled and flipped over, tossing both of them into the water. They swam the rest of the way to the dock with Calrin holding on to his dad's lucky harpoon, and Seth following behind him, keeping an eye out for more tarkks. Raydoo leaned over and lifted them to safety. "Whew! You two were almost fish food."

"I don't know about you guys. I've had enough fishing for a yarn." Calrin checked to see if he had any bite marks. He only found a few splinters from Seth's paddleboard, which he proceeded to pull out. He slipped into his clothes without drying off. "Let's load our gear and return to town." They all agreed and mounted up to leave.

Seth asked, "Can I steer the kack this time?"

"I thought you were afraid of them." Calrin jumped down

and climbed on behind as Seth slid forward.

"Not anymore."

Seth rode the kack all the way to Beayama. His friend only helped with the steering motions a couple times. "So, tell me," Raydoo asked as he trotted his mount beside them, "where did you hear those two rules you keep quoting?"

"Maximus Gallius."

"This way Maximus, they're over here." Narleen pointed to a patch of mushrooms growing under a large cottlepine. She had suggested they share a ride today since most of Beayama's animals were reserved to search for Lundy. Max did the steering while Narleen, who sat behind him, snuggled her hands around his waist. "You don't mind if I call you Maxie, do you?"

"No, ma'am, that's fine."

"You know, most people call me Narleen."

"Yes ma'am, I'll try to remember." Since they were riding double, Max couldn't see her smiling at his response.

After deciding on the best spot, they dismounted, pulled out two sacks from the left side carrier, and began gathering mushrooms. "Leave the big dallups alone. Those are the seed spreaders that keep the patch full. Just pick the middle-sized ones."

"You mean these mushrooms grow by seeds, not spores?"

"Not sure how the ones where you live grow. These sprout by seeds. So where is it you hail?"

"I've lived many places. Most recently in a high country called Heaven."

"Ask a silly question, get a silly answer." She stared at his face, expecting a response or at least a grin. "Well, I guess it doesn't really matter where a person's from if they have a good heart. That's all that's important, and I feel you are such a soul."

"I hope so, ma'am, I mean Narleen." Her smile brightened, as did her eyes.

It didn't take long to fill two bags with dallups since the ones they collected were the size of serving pitchers. Their caps were oval with a Christmas tree shape, jagged at the top with green gills around the undersides. Max tied the bags and readied them for loading on their kack. "Daylight is fading, and we didn't bring torches. Maybe we should head back."

"Right now? I was hoping we could sit underneath the cottlepine and visit a bit before riding home." The low-toned reply revealed her disappointment. "Alright, if we are leaving, let me help you load the side carrier." As Max bent over to lift one of the bags, Narleen kissed him on the cheek. Startled, Max dropped the bag and stood, squaring his shoulders. "Oh, I'm sorry, I didn't mean to—"

"Embarrass me? You didn't. In fact, it has been a long time since a woman has shown any interest. I kind of . . ." His voice trailed off. Narleen waited for him to finish his statement, but he never did. Instead, Max eyed the hillside. "There's smoke rising above those hills."

"We keep our seasonal stores over there. We better ride over and investigate."

"No, please, you stay here. It might be dangerous. I'll check it out."

Max climbed on his mount and galloped toward the location. When he got closer, he saw a group of men setting fire to the storage area. In an apparent delay maneuver, one of them charged him with a spear. Max pulled out his sword and with one swing, cut the assailant down. The feint tactic succeeded in buying extra time for the other marauders to escape. They raced away, hauling loaded kacks behind them, which Max assumed contained the raided provisions. A scan of the area revealed the food huts were either burning or destroyed. Believing the immediate threat had ended, he dismounted and retrieved the fallen man's spear, then returned to where he left Narleen. She was nowhere in sight, the dallup patch trampled, footprints everywhere. "Narleen, where are you? Narleen!" No answer.

Searching for signs, Max spotted hoofprints leading north along the Cali River. He tracked them until the dimming twilight made their trail difficult to see. Out of options, he turned around and rode back to Beayama, making it just before nightrise. He raced past the entry tower, not answering the sentry's hail, only stopping after he reached the Great Hall where he found

Saephira and Captain Waubush overseeing the kitchen staff as they readied a dinner feast.

Max bowed, not waiting for Saephira to bid his welcome. "My Lady, a gang of mounted men raided your food storage area. I asked Narleen to hide while I rode over to investigate and when I returned, she was gone. There were indications of a struggle. It appears the marauders kidnapped her. I discovered their trail and followed it until the light faded. They were traveling north along the river."

Max held up a red and black long-handled spear with a bronze point. "I took this from the person who attacked me, which I was forced to kill in self-defense. I hope somebody can identify who uses this type of weapon." In frustration, he tossed the spear down. The clanging noise echoed through the hall as it slid across the floor. All activity stopped; the people stared in silence. "We must rescue her! Who will go with me?"

CHAPTER 20
RESCUE PLANS

Waubush rushed over to inspect the spear Max had tossed on the floor. He recognized it as soon as he picked it up. "This is a long-handled weapon used by guardsmen in the Upper Realm. It has their unique red on black striping, and the bronze spearhead comes from their forges, not ours."

"Good enough for me. Let's go there and get Narleen back." Max fiddled with his Gladius, pulling it halfway out of his scabbard, then sheathing it again. His eyes looked stern, angry.

Waubush watched Max's reactions. "I understand. It infuriates me too. If Eddnok's raiders abducted her and she's still alive, unharmed, they probably transported her to their fortress. Speculation aside, before you race off to a place you know nothing about, you should allow those who also share the same concern to join the rescue efforts. Consequently, a strategy is warranted."

"Yes, sir, but her life is at stake. It can't wait!"

"The circumstances are indeed urgent. However, with darkout approaching, wouldn't it be wiser to wait until firstlight? I suggest we discuss our options before attempting any rescue. You appear to have military experience, Max. I'm sure you realize the advantage of planning."

"I wholeheartedly agree." Saephira interrupted the exchange and moved over to hold Max by the hand. "Narleen is my lady-in-waiting, and I'm heartbroken. She's a close friend, like a sister, and I empathize with you. For her sake, we must consider the wisest course of action. Therefore, I'm postponing the banquet, so we can meet in my conference hall to discuss this matter. I have maps there. Captain Waubush, since our militia captain is no longer with us, I need you to cover his command. Maximus and Jesse, please join us."

"What about Annabelle?" Jesse asked. "Her insights may be helpful." As Saephira contemplated her reply, Anna hurried over to Max and whispered into his ear.

"Ma'am, can Seth attend? He's young yet very brave." Max glanced in Seth's direction. "Anna says you saved a boy's life on the lake today."

"Agreed, your friends may participate." After Saephira dismissed the servants, the group walked over to the conference hall, and she unrolled the map of Eskaonus across her desk table. "Alright, Max, show us your exact location, where Narleen disappeared, and the route the marauders took."

"Yes, ma'am. We were picking mushrooms in this area when we noticed smoke in the hills." Max placed his finger west of Beayama on a path that turns south toward the Cali River. "After I dispatched the raider who attacked me, I returned to the spot where I left Narleen and found her missing. I tracked the trail made by her abductors upriver to a lake where I lost it." Max ran his finger along the map ending at Mista Lake. "According to the hoofprints, they were traveling north toward the next lake." He slid his finger over to Falein.

"It appears they were riding to the place marked Disputed Lands," Jesse offered.

"I concur," added Waubush. "We can assume they're heading to Lord Eddnok's fortress at Briacap."

Saephira leaned in to examine the map. Using compass tweezers from her top drawer, she measured the distance between Beayama and Briacap. "It's a two-cycle trip. Well, Captain Waubush, what are our options?"

"A direct assault is out. Their walled citadel is nearly impregnable, and our city militia only has twenty men, most of whom are volunteers from farming and fishing villages. We are vastly outnumbered." Waubush studied the map and pointed to the Disputed Lands, running his finger along the boundary line between Midvill and Tabahir. "This area is fairly desolate and mostly uninhabited. Perhaps we could enter from here and somehow approach the fortress unseen, take out the tower sentinels, scale the wall, locate her prison cell, and get out before the general alarm sounds. More likely, though, they would see us coming from leagues away and annihilate us."

"What about a night raid?" inquired Jesse.

"A raid during darkout would require torches, which would give away our position, resulting in an ambush or worse."

"What if I told you I have a lamp that can provide enough light for us, but not attract the attention of the tower sentries."

"You have such a device?" the captain wondered.

"I do." Jesse pulled out the candle lamp from his satchel and demonstrated it. The flame provided a gentle glow. "I've used it several times, even after nightfall."

"Hmm, interesting. I suppose if one person led a small band, single file, and kept the light shielded in front, it might work during darkout. Weapons are another issue. Ours have limited-range. Any confrontation is unlikely to be successful."

"What weapons do you have?" Max asked.

"Just swords, spears, and throwing knives. As you already know, swords are close combat weapons. Most of our spears can only be tossed fifteen paces accurately, knives even less, and once thrown, they are no longer available for skirmishing. Besides, a couple dozen paces aren't far enough to reach their battlements, let alone, take out the guards stationed there."

"I know of several weapons that can hit their targets from over a hundred paces away, and I can have a few ready by firstlight." Max stepped back from the table and observed Waubush, waiting for his reaction.

"Then I would say we might have a chance."

"Interesting ideas," Saephira said. "Let's meet at firstlight on the practice field and see these new weapons demonstrated, and if they work, perhaps a rescue could be attempted. If Captain Waubush recommends the mission, we could leave by midcycle. However, only he and I will choose the members for the party. I suggest we all get a good night's rest." She dismissed everyone. Most of them stopped by the kitchen to grab a bite to eat before returning to their quarters, all except Max and Seth, who took torches and searched outside the city for the nearest cottlepine tree. Max used his Gladius to cut seven branches for his weapon project.

"Hey bro, what are these for?"

"Five will be Celtic longbows and the other two, fighting staffs. The wood is green and pliable and should retain its shape without breaking. Due to the urgency, we don't have time to season it." They gathered the branches and returned to the mender's house.

While Max trimmed and shaped the limbs into long sections, Seth used a knife given to him by Raydoo to cut five strands from his rope to use as bowstrings. Jesse and Anna watched for a while and then retired to their rooms. Interested in their project, Ottaar stayed downstairs to observe. "Let me put out some antaloop jerky and kin to snack on as you work. There's fresh tea brewed too."

"Thank you, ma'am. We both missed dinner." The mender organized a food platter and placed on the table, along with pot of Azollie tea. "Okay recruit, tie little loops on both ends of those cords while I notch out the bows." When they finished, Max strung one up, drew the bowstring and released. *Twang!* "Perfect, all we lack now are arrows. For those we will definitely need dried or seasoned wood."

"Maybe these will work." The mender unhooked the long wooden rod used to open and close her shutters and handed it to Max to examine. "If you can shape this handle into a tiny spear that works with your bow contraption, then I have dozens more on my shutters upstairs. I can get the woodsmith to make replacements for me later. I'll go fetch them."

Ottaar returned with twelve rods. Max cut them in half, whittled a sharp point on one end, and notched the other, making twenty-four arrow shafts. "No time to make fletchings to steady their flight, but a tail will work well enough for our purposes."

"What kind of tail, bro?"

"The kind a person ties on the end of a kite to stabilize it."

"A kite? An interesting word, what is that?" the mender asked.

"A triangular-shaped device, covered with paper that's flown in the air at the end of a long string. The tail helps it fly straight. The concept is over two thousand years old. I'll show you how to build one sometime." Max held one of the shafts and eyed it down the length. "Nice! Not warped either. Now, I only had a boring tool or miniature drill and a spool of yarn, I could rig these arrows to fly true."

"I have both tools and lots of yarn. I use a drill on certain surgeries, fixing rotted teeth and such, and the small punch for various household tasks." She grabbed the drill out her mender kit and a spool of yarn from her knitting basket and handed them to Max. He drilled a small hole ahead of each notched end, strung yarn through it and tied it off, leaving two dangling runners. Max explained how the tails would stabilize the projectiles from behind, keeping them on course as they flew.

Working together with Seth, they completed two dozen arrows to use with their five longbows. "Although metal points would make these arrows more penetrative," Max noted, "a sharpened wood tip will be just as deadly at short range." After sorting their arrows into five plies on the table, he asked the mender, "Do you have a couple strips of dried leather you can donate to our project?"

"Yes, I have several in my desk drawer I use as ink blotters. What are you making now?"

"A sling." Max stretched the leather she handed him to test its strength. "This will work."

"I know how to make those," replied Seth. "I built them when I was a kid." Using Ottaar's boring tool, Seth punched holes into the ends of the leather strips. Next, he cut four more strands from his special corded rope, which never seemed to get shorter in spite of how much was trimmed off. He strung the pieces through the holes and tied them tight. He gave one completed sling to Max for inspection, and the other he twirled around his head in a circle. "All I need are five smooth stones like David, and I'll slay a few giants."

"I don't understand your terms or references," the mender commented, "and I've never seen such weapons before. Nonetheless, they appear to be sound."

"And effective," Max added. To finish up, he turned the last two branches into battlestaffs. He scraped away the bark with his sword and leaned them against the wall by the hearth. "Seth, let's rise early and test these things out before the spectators arrive. Help me clean up our mess before we get a bit of shuteye. Early comes early around here." Looking at Ottaar, he inquired, "Can we leave the weapons downstairs until firstlight?"

"Sure, fine with me. You guys have earned a good night's rest. I'll tidy up. Good nightrise." Max and Seth returned the greeting, smiled, and scurried upstairs to their rooms.

About thirty minutes later, Jesse wandered by the bedroom doors of his team members. Anna had stopped playing her glifstring. Max was snoring. Seth mumbled in his sleep. With everybody settled in for the night, Jesse returned to his room and opened his journal. Embarrassed about his recent actions but feeling the need to put his thoughts into words, he wrote:

Entry Eight

Second day of red sky. Fewer windstorms. I imagine all of heaven knows about my failures from last night. Everyone in my group does, yet they continue to support me as leader. Not sure I would do the same. If someone is listening, all I can say is I'm sorry. I tried to erase my last entry, except for some reason, the ink is permanent. Couldn't tear out the page either. Max said things made in heaven are eternal. Apparently, this goes for my journal, the ink written thereon, as well as the satchel itself. Chesedel told me heaven is the place of second chances. I pray there's a third one for me. I sure blew my first two.

Annie feels we will receive word on Lundy soon. I hope so. She exhibits an uncanny discernment in these matters. Annie also mentioned Chesedel visited her room last night. If so, that's wonderful. Miracle or otherwise, she's fully recovered. We are planning a rescue mission for Narleen who was abducted by the Upper Realm. Our answers lay there, I think, including the evil we were sent here to confront. Well, time for bed.

As Annabelle slept, she dreamed of a barren land between two boundary lines. Nearby, a man with a crooked index finger sat by a firepit, roasting a varmint on his sword. It was late afternoon. He seemed sad. She noticed tears in his eyes.

CHAPTER 21
BROKEN PROMISES

Lord Eddnok read the two messages from Preaverca at first light. The one about Menarbat didn't concern him. The Tracker had played his deception well over the yarns and Eddnok figured his spy would be implicated at some point. The other message about Lundy, though, bothered him. He sent word to the tower gate to stop him from leaving the city. He was too late. Lundy and his escort, Brappt, had already departed.

If Lady Saephira was searching for him, he needed to keep Lundy under wraps from here on out. Maybe he'd put him to work in the mines as Preaverca suggested, but not until he finished the translation for the ancient manuscript. Eddnok was obsessed with finding out what the document revealed. The spans passed slowly as he waited for Lundy and Brappt's return. "Where are those fools?"

Finally, twilight moved in, bringing an end to the second cycle of red light and the wild weather it generated. A few isolated windblowers continued to ravish the area. Most of those, however, arose south of Briacap or in the Disputed Lands. The gusty winds had died down for the evening but not the heat. Never the heat! It remained the only constant in the Upper Realm, which seemed to have only two seasons: hot and hotter.

"Rider coming in," shouted the tower sentential. "It's Sub-Commander Brappt returning with Lundy."

Bolgog, who had been covering Brappt's duty station while he played tour guide, shuffled over to the wall to hear his report. "So how did your little outing with Master Lundy go?"

"Other than running into a windblower and the old fool yapping to the locals, telling everyone who he was, it went just fine. Next time, you should take him out sightseeing."

"Not likely! Oh yeah, Lord Eddnok wants him back in his room to finish the scroll translation. Said he would visit later to pick it up, and it better be ready."

"It's too early to be locked in my room," Lundy complained. "It's not dusk yet."

"Sorry, we all have our obligations to meet. You have yours, and I have mine." Brappt kicked him off his kack. "Get going. Finish what you promised, and when you do, I'm sure Lord Eddnok will allow you to leave our city permanently. And good riddance as far as I'm concerned."

As soon as Lundy entered his room, the bolt slid shut locking him inside. Lundy yelled through the closed door, "Aye, that's the way it works, is it? You laddies will be lucky if you get the correct translation." No one responded. *So typical.* Taking inventory, he glanced around his room and noticed things had been displaced. *Searched again, eh?* Sitting at his table, Lundy pulled the translation from his boot and made a duplicate for himself. He laid Eddnok's copy aside, folded the duplicate and hid it inside his boot. *May need this later.* After he returned the ancient scroll to Eddnok, along with his translation, he would skedaddle out of here and never look back.

Atop the tower gate, a sentinel yelled out his second alert,

"More riders coming in."

"Busy cycle I guess." Bolgog pulled out his magnifier to sharpen the images. "It's Commander Rennard and his raiding party with more confiscated stores." As they drew closer, he hollered, "Better hurry you guys. I want everything unloaded before nightrise."

Rennard dismounted from his kack holding on to a prisoner. "We lost one military asset in the raid but captured a more valuable one, Narleen, Saephira's lady-in-waiting."

"Lord Eddnok will be pleased, and I imagine he'll offer you and your men a hefty bounty. You should take her over to him right off. You know how Eddnok hates to find out the news secondhand. I'll send down a crew to help offload the provisions." Rennard waved his acknowledgement and then made his way to Eddnok's quarters, dragging his prisoner behind him.

"Ah-ha," Eddnok jeered, "if it's not Narleen, the lady-in-waiting, herself." The smirk on his face, telling. "I haven't seen you in yarns." The commander pushed her forward, still gagged and restrained. "Tell me, Commander Rennard, how did you capture her?"

"During the raid west of Beayama, we found her hiding behind a cottlepine. Her escort, a huge soldier with a sword, gave chase. Our guard distracted him while the rest of us doubled back and abducted her. Although we lost a man, we confiscated several kack-loads of provisions. They're being offloaded now."

"Good, good. A job well done and a surprise bonus. My compliments. Give triple portions to all your men. Take off her gag and let's hear what the lady has to say." Rennard slipped the cloth off her mouth, leaving her hand restraints intact.

"You'll pay for this. Lady Saephira will—" Eddnok clicked his fingers and the commander pulled the gag up to silence her again.

"Hmm, what to do with you?" As Narleen struggled to free herself, Eddnok paced around the room thinking. "You would bring a nice ransom or perhaps you would like to be one of my concubines?" He chuckled as he considered his options. "Until I decide, I'll lock you in the stockade. Take her away!"

Eddnok waited until twilight faded into nightrise before he

made way down the hall to Lundy's room. He slid the bolt open and entered. "Good nightrise, Master Lundy."

Lundy expected the visit. The manuscript and translation lay waiting on the tabletop. "I suppose you are going to apologize for me treatment today."

"I am." Eddnok wandered closer, eyeing the table where Lundy sat. "Also to let you know your escort guard has been harshly disciplined. Again, I'm sorry for all the misunderstandings."

"Yeah, right. Your tune is getting old."

"I assume you have my translation ready."

"Aye, laddie, I do." Lundy handed over the original manuscript and his translation. "It appears to be a word map, giving directional clues to a hidden treasure of sorts. I had to guess at certain unfamiliar terms, including how to rhyme the words. At any rate, this is the best I could do. I wish you good fortune on your search. And now, what about your promise?"

Eddnok unrolled the translation and started to read it. "What promise is that?"

"To let me leave after I finished the translation."

"Yes, yes, of course." He clicked his fingers and two warders rushed in. "Master Lundy is free to go. Free to go work in our mines, I mean. Take him to the stockade for the night, and then at firstlight, transport him to one of our mines in the Narnj Mountains. He will fit right in with our captives from the Lower Realm."

"But you prom—"

He interrupted Lundy's reply by pulling out a knife and pointing it at him. "I only promised you could leave the city, which you will. Guards!"

The warders bound Lundy, hand and foot. "Which mine, the Dig or the Pit?"

"Whichever one needs more workers." Eddnok bent over laughing hysterically. It was a wicked laugh.

Lundy struggled and screamed as they carried him out of the room. "You laddies are pure evil, and when I find my friends . . ." The rest of his words were garbled when one of the jailers yanked a cloth across his mouth, gagging him.

As darkout replaced nightrise, Eddnok returned to his

study and took out his boundary map of the Upper Realm. He put the original scroll away for safekeeping and read Lundy's translation several times, comparing map locations and passages. He pondered the references of *mountains red, forest dead,* and *hidden cave.* Some phrases made sense, others did not. He would sleep on it and make plans for an expedition come dayrise. He believed he was the *ruler of fate* for whom the *treasure awaits,* but what kind of treasure was it? He had to find out.

CHAPTER 22
WEAPONS AND DEMONSTRATIONS

Max and Seth rose before firstlight, skipped breakfast
and went outside, carrying the weapons they made during
darkout. The reddish daylight from the previous two cycles had
diminished somewhat, shifting to an orangish glow. The wild
windstorms had also moved on, leaving only a few gentle
breezes blowing from the east. Visibility remained clear.

Max borrowed a tote bag from the mender to haul the
longbows and arrows to the militia's practice field for testing.
Seth brought the fighting staffs and slings. Since targets were
already set up for spear and knife throwing, they only needed to
move two of them. They positioned one a hundred feet away and
the other at two hundred. Max, an experienced archer, notched
an arrow, pulled the bowstring, aimed and released: *whish*. The
arrow sped toward the farthest target, hitting a tad below center.

"Nice one, bro. You wanna try a couple more?"

"No, not necessary, these bows and arrows will work fine,
at least for our purposes. See if you can sling a rock and hit the
closer target." Seth grabbed a handful of small stones, chose a
rounded one, placed it in the sling, and began circling it above
his head. At the right moment, he released the rock. It skimmed
the side of the target.

"Not bad, kid, try another toss. See if you can get closer
this time." Seth's next launch hit left of center, rotating the target
sideways. "Now, that's more like it. With a little practice, you'll
be able to put a dent in someone's plans or make a good
impression on them." Max grinned at Seth.

129

"Hey bro, those are puns. I didn't know you had it in you."
Seth smiled back.

"There are a lot of things you don't know about me, recruit." They laughed together, enjoying their playful banter.

The teasing stopped when Lady Saephira, Captain Waubush, and five militia arrived at the field. Jesse and Anna followed behind them. The group watched with keen interest as Max fired off a volley of arrows and Seth demonstrated his sling. Jesse's collective already knew about such weapons. The Eskaonites did not—and were impressed by their range and effectiveness. Max was in the middle of explaining the weapon's dynamics when a messenger approached Lady Saephira.

"Excuse me, my Lady. You said you wanted to be informed as soon as the Lundy search parties returned."

"Yes, I did. What did they find out?"

"I'm sorry. There's no word on Lundy's whereabouts, although one rider reported Falein Village was raided five cycles ago. The raiders killed three town elders, raped their wives, and wounded villagers. Some of the injured have since died. Before the assailants left, they plundered their stores and set fire to several lodges. The village postal clerk sent a homing flyer to ask us for help yet never received a reply."

"Really, I guess Jesse was right about not receiving all our messages. Summon Preaverca immediately. Take militiamen with you."

"Not possible, my Lady. The stable master reported she requisitioned a mount before firstlight and rode off on an urgent matter."

"I see. I doubt she'll be returning to Beayama, but if she does, please notify the vice-leader in my absence. Lady Yhmim will know what to do. I will be unavailable for four cycles, perhaps longer. I'm overseeing the search for my lady-in-waiting who we think has been abducted by northern raiders."

After the messenger departed, Max continued his weapon demonstration by describing basic quarterstaff techniques, both offensive and defensive. "Jesse sir, I require your help with this part. Attack me with your leadership staff." Jesse clutched his staff with a two-handed grip and swung it at Max's left side. Max blocked the swing and then spun around to increase momentum as he swiped at Jesse's knees, which buckled, landing him flat on his back. He finished with a mock thrust to the chest. "See how easy it is to defend yourself with just a stick. Now let's try a sword attack. He stared at Captain Waubush and said, "Your turn."

"I don't want to hurt you, Max. A walking stick is a poor choice against an experienced swordsman with a sharp two-edged blade."

"It's more than a cane, sir. I call it *the persuader*. In any event, we shall see. Pull your weapon, captain, and attack me like I'm your worst enemy." Waubush relented, rushed forward and the duel began. As they circled, Max parried or blocked all sword maneuvers with his persuader. Each strike by the captain was met with a counter strike, dodge, or fake. Waubush never even got close. With a final spin and strike, Max knocked the blade from his opponent's hand and swept his feet, causing Waubush to tumble backwards onto the ground. He finished with a mock hit to his forehead. "Would you care to change your view on the effectiveness of quarterstaffs?"

"Indeed, I would. Where did you learn those moves?"

"Doesn't matter. What does matter is that I can teach these same skills and many more, assuming anyone's interested." Max scanned the spectators for responses.

"Hey bro, I'll take one of those persuaders."

"Me too!" Anna shouted. "I'm not keen on hurting people, but I would love to learn how to defend myself." Four militia raised their hands, indicating they were also interested.

"Sorry guys, I only made two. It's first come, first served." Max tossed the battlestaff he used in the demonstration to Seth and handed the second to Anna. "They're yours. Start practicing so you're prepared for the rescue attempt. We can make more for every member of the rescue team. Cottlepines are a solid hardwood, perfect for creating these long-handled weapons."

"Perhaps I should have said this beforehand." Everyone grew silent as Saephira looked at Anna and Seth. "Only nine were chosen for the rescue attempt: three militiamen, the militia lead, a militia chief, Jesse, Maximus, Captain Waubush, and myself. You two will have to stay here."

"Not fair. We both—"

"Our decision is final. We feel a small team will have the best chance of success." As intense arguments ensued, mostly from Seth and Anna, an individual dressed as a merchant approached and asked for an audience. Following normal protocol for unfamiliar people wishing to see the province leader, an armed militiaman escorted the person. Saephira studied the man's face for a few moments prior to introducing herself. "I am Lady Saephira. May I inquire as to your name and your purpose for an audience?"

"I know who you are, my Lady, almost everybody does." He dismounted from his kack and checked on his other animal that was loaded down with bundled packages. "Folks call me the Unnamed Merchant. For the most part, we merchants don't use names for anonymity reasons. Since we trade between the Lower and Upper Realms, we must use discretion. We don't want to be accused of trading contraband."

"I see. So what is your request?"

"Let me explain first. My normal route runs between Midvill and Tabahir, and sometimes to the port city of Bayegulf. I trade in additional places, too, wherever the deals are good and the profits fair."

Saephira crossed her arms, looking impatient, annoyed. "Go on."

"Last cycle, I stopped over at Tabahir to plan my next trade call. While hoisting cups at the local tavern with a fellow merchant, I overheard an argument between two men. I recognized one as a guard from the Upper Realm. The other said his name was Lundy MacBain." At the mention of that name, Jesse, Max, Seth, and Anna stopped what they were doing and moved closer to listen to the conversation. "He was an older man who called all the patrons in the tavern, laddie. According to a recent homing flyer message, I understand you are searching for him."

Jesse interjected, "Yes, we are. Was Lundy okay?" Anna stayed silent, attentive, hoping for a good report.

The merchant paused for a moment, then continued with his story. "The guard was furious with Lundy, wrestled him out the door, and said Lord Eddnok would not be happy he had talked. I think they were riding back to Briacap. He appeared to be a prisoner."

With a stern face and determined eyes, Anna interrupted the merchant and spoke directly to Saephira. "I respectfully request I be allowed to participate in the upcoming rescue operation. You said Narleen is your closest friend. Well, Lundy is mine, and if he's there in Briacap, I'm not staying behind."

"Nor am I," Seth added.

"Obviously, this new information changes things." She glanced at Waubush who nodded his approval. "Very well, we will allow two more to join the team."

"If you are going to attempt a rescue," the merchant added, "you may need a place to hide out. I recommend staying at the Copper Rail Tavern, southeast of town. It has lodging upstairs and boarding stables in the rear. A close relative runs the place and it's discrete, safe, and they don't care for Eddnok nor have allegiance to the Upper Realm. Tell the proprietor the Unnamed Merchant sent you."

"You have been most helpful, nameless one. Are you seeking a reward for your troubles?"

"Nope, simply doing what I feel is right. However, I do have merchandise to sell, and if I have your permission, I would like to conduct business in your city."

"You are welcome to trade here anytime. Again, thank you for the information." The merchant bowed, turned his two animals around and trotted off, riding one, leading the second.

Saephira watched the merchant to see which direction he rode. After he rounded the corner leading to city square, she motioned for her security escort to tail him. "This is sure a busy place this cycle." Before more disruptions could sidetrack her, she explained the rescue mission as a four-day excursion, a two-cycle trip each way if all went as planned. They would make camp outside of Falein and the following cycle, cross the boundary into the Disputed Lands, south of Tabahir. From there, they would attempt a night raid on Briacap and rescue Narleen and Lundy.

"We can divvy up the bows and make weapon assignments once we're underway," Waubush said. "Go gather what you require for the trip and meet here in one span. And just so you know, we are all riding kacks."

"Anna and I are not competent steering them, not yet anyway." Seth's voice cracked as he spoke. "Can't we ride double?"

"I understand you've had difficulty, but you both received initial riding lessons. It will have to suffice. We will give you two gentle mounts. Out of instinct, they'll follow the lead kack, giving you an opportunity to master the guiding motions prior to arriving at Falein. Besides, we need all the side carriers for provisions and supplies. A portion of those will be dropped off at the raided village to replenish their stores. Therefore, the answer is no." Seth and Anna could hardly disagree with Waubush's reasoning.

Max retrieved the arrows from the target and packed them into the mender's tote bag, along with the longbows. Anna and Seth, carrying their new long-handled bludgeons, walked over to watch as Max sorted the weapons. She waited for him to finish before inquiring about the slings. "Since Seth made them and wants to keep his, I wondered if I could have the extra one. I would prefer it to a bow. Seth said he would teach me the technique."

"As far as I'm concerned, yes, it's yours. Slings and fighting staffs complement one another, and from what I observed, the recruit can sling a stone well, so he'll be a good instructor. Here, take this one, Miss Anna. It may save your life one day or somebody else's." Max threw the tote of weapons over his shoulder, and together the three of them rushed back to their rooms to pack their belongings. Jesse said his goodbyes to Captain Waubush and Lady Saephira and hurried off to join his colleagues.

A span later, the rescue party departed Beayama, turning right on the trail leading to Falein Lake. The team consisted of eleven members—Jesse, Maximus, Seth, Annabelle, Captain Waubush, Lady Saephira, and five militia—all riding kacks. Their side carriers were filled with supplies. They wanted to arrive south of the boundary line by postcycle. That would allow them time to plan the rescue in detail and practice with the new weapons before using them.

Preaverca's late night activities were not discovered until dayrise. While most city residents were still asleep, she visited Yhmim's residence and slipped a note under her door:

Dear Vice-leader,

Lady Saephira suspects my treachery and will undoubtedly summon me to answer questions. As you well know, this would be detrimental. Therefore, I am leaving at firstlight. The Tracker fled the city last cycle. When they find out about the northern raids to plunder their stores, the ambush at the ruins, and Lord Eddnok's plans, we will both be facing arrest, imprisonment, or perhaps the death sentence. Your ruse is safe. No one suspects you. Just play your part until the time comes.

Take care,

Preaverca

From there, Preaverca returned to her quarters in the mail tower, packed her clothes and personal items, and then snuck out to the stables. Finding the stable master asleep, she roused him and ordered him to strap a side carrier on her favorite kack. Creating a deceptive alibi, she told the man she had important business to attend and needed an early start. After she loaded up the carrier, she rode out of the city as first light dawned, avoiding trails, moving cross-country through the farmlands, heading to Briacap via Tabahir.

CHAPTER 23
SEARCHING FOR TREASURE

Lord Eddnok hardly slept during nightrise. At firstlight, he arose from bed and dismissed his concubines. He dressed quickly and walked outside. Staring at the horizon, he noticed the bands of red daylight had changed to shades of orange, which meant the windstorms had ended for another yarn. As he made his way to his study, he could not stop thinking about the rhymes and clues in Lundy's translation. *What was this treasure? And where was it?* He needed to organize an expedition to start searching, and for help he would turn to his most experienced and knowledgeable subordinate, Senior Commander Bolgog.

He called to the sentry stationed outside his study. The man entered and bowed. "Yes, Lord, how can I be of service? Do you desire to break your fast here? I can have food sent over from the kitchens."

"No! Summon my senior commander and be quick about it." The man bowed again and raced out to locate Bolgog who had gone off duty at the tower gate a span earlier. Once the sentry departed, Eddnok moved over to his tabletop desk to study the boundary map of Eskaonus. He hoped the treasure lay in the northern lands, not the southern ones, because he didn't want his rival, Saephira, snooping around and making his search more difficult. While he waited for the commander to appear, he wrote down a few questions to ask him.

After working two shifts in the tower, Bolgog had retired to his sleeping quarters. Covering Brappt's duty and then his own left him exhausted. He had just fallen asleep when someone knocked at his quarters. "Arrgh, go away!" But the voice shouted that Lord Eddnok had summoned him. Bolgog realized it was unwise to keep the impetuous ruler waiting, so he climbed back out of bed, threw on his clothes, and hurried over to Eddnok's office.

"Good dayrise, Lord Eddnok. What did you need to see me about this early span?"

Eddnok motioned for him to come over to the desk. "Take a look at this translation and tell me what you think."

If treasure is what you seek
Then don't be meek
Nor forgo the rift
Near the highest cliff

Buried deep within lies a secret twin
Of the richest gift
Known to gods or men

Take an uphill pace to seek a taste
Of wisdom sublime
And power divine

So follow the trail to the mountains red
Through the forest dead
Past waters shed
And peaks that grow during daylight glow

Past ancient grave lays hidden cave
Where treasure awaits
For a ruler of fate

Bolgog read it several times, scratching his graying beard while mumbling to himself.

"Well, I'm waiting. Any thoughts?"

The commander pointed to the words *uphill* and *mountain*. "We have three mountainous areas in Eskaonus: Mnnie in the south, Narnj in the east, and Colrath in the west. Perhaps this mysterious treasure is buried in a cave somewhere among those rugged slopes."

"I'm aware we have mountain ranges. Don't give me the obvious. Tell me something I don't know."

He glanced again at the document, this time touching the words *red* and *highest cliff.* "These descriptions sound like Gaulmore Peak or Birgo Summit. They are the two highest areas on Eskaonus. And both have reddish shale."

"Hmm, and what about this *forest* reference on the fourth stanza?"

"As you already know, we have two forested areas: Lost and Narmoot. The Lost Forest earned its reputation from hunters and miners who vanished in the dense interior. They're presumed dead. Even now, most people avoid this grove of timber. Maybe *forest dead* refers to all those who perished there."

"Perhaps. Seems like a stretch on the meaning. What about the other woodland?"

"The Narmoot? It never recovered after the fireball hit ten yarns ago. Half the trees died out and the ones that survived are strangely deformed. On second thought, if I were choosing a *forest dead* to search, it would be the Narmoot. And it's closer."

"Alright, we'll start our search in the Narmoot Forest, then follow the old trail up the mountain range. I want you to organize an expedition, staffed with experienced trackers, porters, and a crew of miners with excavating equipment. We can run supply lines from Briacap to the search area and water runs from Trobell Springs. Prepare for an extended stay. Bring two homing flyers for communications. And tell no one about this translation or the purpose for the outing."

"Yes Lord, I can arrange everything and have a team ready by next cycle."

"No, this cycle. We're leaving in two spans and you're

going with me."

"But sir, I just finished two shifts of guard duty. I'm beat."

"You can rest later. I require you by my side for this excursion." Bolgog just stared at Eddnok in silence, rubbing his tired eyes. "And a couple more things. Concerning *waters shed*, have you heard if there's a watershed source or hidden spring in this area?" He shook his head no. "How about an *ancient grave?*"

"Sorry sir, I'm not aware of either one."

"I guess you're not as knowledgeable as I assumed. No matter, I'll figure out those references later. Oh yeah, before we leave, make sure Lundy is removed from the stockade and escorted to the mines."

"What about Narleen?"

"Leave her in jail!" Bolgog bowed and left Eddnok's office without further comment. As the commander shuffled down the hallway, he frowned, shrugged his shoulders, and cursed under his breath. Two spans later, however, the team was equipped and ready to leave.

Since the Narmoot was only a short ride from Briacap, the search party arrived there in less than a span and continued searching it until twilight. They looked around trees, examined drainage areas, dug up varmint holes, and scrutinized every dead stump—finding no clues or much of anything else. With dayrise ending soon, they decided to make camp for the night and try again at firstlight. The expedition turned right and took a side trail to the base of Gaulmore Peak, which would provide a level area to set their campsite. Halfway up the ridge, one of the kacks stumbled and knocked loose several rocks. Moments later, water came bubbling from the depression.

Eddnok slid off his mount and rushed over to the spot. "Look, commander, water!" He dipped his cupped palm into the bubbling liquid and lifted it to his face. He sniffed it, took a sip, smiled, and reached down for another handful. "It's mineral spring water, much better tasting than our silty wells."

"I think you've discovered *waters shed*," offered Bolgog.

"Apparently so." Eddnok raised his hand over the spot and proclaimed, "I hereby name this water source Hidden Springs." He turned back around to face his commander. "Have two men refill all the waterskins. I will lead the rest of the group to the base of Gaulmore. I've got a feeling the morrow will be a good day for discovering more clues. Now get going! We don't want to get stuck in this dying forest during darkout."

CHAPTER 24
RESCUE TEAM

The three-day storm event passed by midcycle, allowing the familiar yellow daylight glow to return. The weather changed as the group traveled north. The cool, moisture-laden temperatures of the southlands became arid and hot. They shed their coats and tucked them away into their side carriers and continued on, only stopping to fill their waterskins and let the kacks drink their fill at the occasional spring. Although the animals could go days between water stops, Captain Waubush wanted to make sure their mounts were well hydrated before entering the barren landscape of the Disputed Lands where water was scarce.

The farmlands they rode past were unaffected by the drier weather conditions since the crops drew moisture from a shallow underground water table. Saephira explained to the newcomers that their farms produced several varieties of gourds and melons, starchy roots similar to yams, various vine-grown vegetables, and stalks of orange and brown-kernelled maize, used to make kin. Concerning yarm berries, they were not planted this far north and grew better by the Gemous River where the vines could be irrigated on a regular basis.

It was late postcycle as the team drew near to Falein Village. The captain sent two militiamen on ahead to drop off supplies and obtain permission to pick two days of maize rations from the nearby fields, which they purchased for two credits. While waiting for the men to return, the remaining partners set up camp east of the village, just south of the boundary line. After unloading their kacks and erecting a tent for the two women, they dug a firepit for cooking. To save time breaking camp on the morrow, Waubush decided the men would sleep around the fire and forgo using shelters.

With the campsite organized, Waubush, Max, and Jesse sat around the firepit and discussed how best to distribute the weapons among their rescue party. They considered each person's expertise and preferences as well as the items they already carried. Jesse pulled out his journal and wrote down everything as they talked:

Me	leadership staff, oil lamp
Max	gladius, bow (6 arrows)
Seth	sling, fighting staff, hand knife, thin corded rope
Anna	sling, fighting staff, glifstring
Capt. Waubush	bronze sword, throwing knives
Lady Saephira	dagger, bow (6 arrows)
Militia Lead	bronze sword, spear, throwing knives
Militia Chief	bronze sword, spear
Militiamen	3 swords, 3 spears, 3 bows (4 arrows each)

Since he had his journal open, Jesse added a short entry:

Entry Nine

Attempting a rescue mission tomorrow night. Hope to find Lundy and Narleen who are being held as prisoners and break them out of jail. Saephira hasn't pressed me on our purpose in Eskaonus, how we got here, or where we came from. I will probably share what I can tonight. Lord, grant me wisdom in this. Right now, however, everyone is focused on the night raid at Briacap. Praying for success and safety.

They scarfed down an early dinner of dried fish, kin, fresh maize, which Anna and Seth picked from the local field, and quenched their thirst with hot tea. With a span left before twilight, the group split up to practice with their new weapons.

Max filled a large tote bag with dirt and leaned it against a dead stump as a target. Those given bows and slings gathered nearby and watched as Max stepped off ten paces, loaded an arrow in his bow, and shot at the target. It struck dead center. "I want you four archers to do the same, step off ten paces and shoot, trying to hit as close to center as you can."

Max walked over and removed his arrow, tucking it away into a small circular tote bag strapped to his belt. "After you are proficient at this range, move back twenty paces and shoot again, practicing your accuracy. When you're satisfied, drop back another ten paces. Each time you hit the mark, your skill level improves, and you'll gain more confidence. Continue adding more distance from the target until you start missing. Then stop and return to the previous pacing mark. This is your effective range. At fifty paces, you should be able to take out a tower guard. If you're accurate at a hundred paces, you are hired as a legionnaire, I mean, bowman." Max grinned at his Roman reference yet made no effort to explain it.

"Same routine for the slingers. Practice, practice! Tomorrow is the real thing. You bowmen have four arrows and Lady Saephira, six. Try not to break or lose one on a wild shot. We will need every arrow tomorrow. I only have a few extras, so be careful with your aim. This does not apply to our slingers. You can lose all the stones you desire, just don't run out during the rescue operation."

"What about us two knife throwers?" asked the mulita lead.

"Follow me," replied Captain Waubush. "Let's go toss a couple blades at a different target so we don't interfere with the others." He pointed to a cottlepine tree nearby. "This one will work."

"For you three with staffs," Max continued, "I can you show you more tactics tomorrow before we break camp."

The teams practiced until the light began to fade. Afterwards, everybody gathered around the campfire to discuss their training results. Saephira excelled with the bow. Of the three militiamen, Chepho had the best archery distance and accuracy. Seth's rock slinging was outstanding. When the comparisons and playful bragging ended, Captain Waubush highlighted the plans for the morrow. The militia lead and Jesse offered suggestions while the rest listened and nodded their approval. They would finalize the details next cycle and make changes as warranted. Saephira passed around dried yarm berries for dessert. Jesse's bunch declined. Everyone else enjoyed serval handfuls as they warmed themselves around the fire.

"Annabelle, why don't you play us a song?" Saephira asked. "You mentioned you were composing a few. Before Narleen's abduction, I had planned on asking you to sing at the banquet. How about now?"

"Yeah Annie, let's hear one. It would be way cool."

While living on earth, Anna seldom received the recognition she deserved for her musical talent. A few neighbors and close friends loved her songs and believed she should embrace a career as a recording artist or lead guitarist in a band, but for whatever reason, those opportunities never presented themselves.

Anna smiled at Saephira and Seth. "Thank you for asking." Removing her glifstring, Anna began picking a tune. "This song is called *The Unseen One*. I wrote it the day after my miraculous recovery from being paralyzed."

Her music sounded wonderful, soothing tired bodies and troubled hearts. She picked the melody through once and then started strumming chords as she sang the verses, her voice sweet and tender, the notes harmonious like a stringed quartet:

Every time you watch the night flyer soar,
have you not wondered if there could be more?
Or felt the hand of a presence unseen,
offering a shoulder upon which you can lean?

Have you not considered what dwells high above,
or He who created all things in His love?
The divine One who is eternal and true,
can redeem a lost soul by making it new.

As she played, a misty cloud formed above the campsite. This time, the entire party noticed it. "Strange, it's not usually foggy this far north," Waubush noted.

"Not fog, dudes, it's something else."

Saephira glared at Seth. "And what would that be?" She stood and tried to touch the mist floating just above her fingers.

After several attempts to reach it, she stopped and looked at Anna with a puzzled face. "Okay, that's different." Sitting down again, she asked, "So who is this unseen one who created all things in his love?"

Anna replied, "He is the ruler of all rulers."

In apparent frustration, Saephira threw her palms upward, as if pleading for a better answer. "What ruler is that?"

Jesse jumped in, realizing the time had come for a little clarification. "A sovereign who hails from a different kingdom."

"Well, that much is obvious. You possess mystical objects unfamiliar to us. Maximus has a sword stronger than any we can forge, seemingly unbreakable. Seth carries a small, corded rope, and amazingly, it remains the same length no matter how much is trimmed off. The design of Annabelle's musical instrument is unusual, and when she plays it, a mysterious cloud forms overhead. And you, Jesse, own a lamp that lights without a striking stone and never runs out of oil. These things are either magic or sorcery. Moreover, you construct shooting weapons never before imagined. I've been tolerant enough, and now I need answers."

"You have been . . . and I agree." Jesse bit down on his lower lip as he carefully considered his reply. "These items are not magic or sorcery. They're divine gifts from a distant place. Concerning us, we were sent here to help overcome an evil trying to destroy your realm."

"Distant place . . . sent here . . . divine gifts? Do you represent a god?"

"If you mean a demigod, then no, but we are envoys for an eternal One, a creator of all things who rules a boundless realm."

"Most Eskaonites discount such concepts. They are considered fables. Still, I've often contemplated if it might be otherwise. Our archives mention ancestors who embraced a religious dogma and worshiped a deity. All traces of their creed are gone now, lost eons ago. Before his untimely death on Onnie Passage, Captain Melmandus and I debated these same matters. We wondered if an ancient conflict may have ended their beliefs."

"I suspect you are correct. I believe your ruins were once a temple for their religion, the altar too. Apparently, a catastrophic event or an unsympathetic regime destroyed both. The scroll we uncovered at the ruins may reveal more once Lundy translates it."

"All this is very interesting." Captain Waubush rose to address the group. "And no doubt it deserves further discussion and consideration. With darkout approaching, however, we should retire for the night and get some sleep. We can debate these religious matters later." Waubush threw two more logs on the fire for warmth. "We have an early start next cycle and much to accomplish before we leave, not to mention a long day and night thereafter. Good nightrise."

Saephira and Jesse stayed up a while longer and talked. She seemed open to these new revelations, which surprised him because he felt the Eskaonus leader would reject the spiritual aspects. Instead, Saephira pondered their significance and how they correlated with her recent premonitions about confronting an ancient wickedness. In those dreams, she observed a man with a tarnished crown, an unnatural plague burning anything it touched, northern raiders who plundered villages, and band of foreign travelers. It seemed as if parts of what she envisioned had come true.

Jesse responded by sharing his dream about a woman with long braided hair, which he thought could be Lady Saephira. He also observed a man with a tarnished crown who seemed to fit the description of Lord Eddnok. Additional images included temple ruins similar to the ones they explored, burning fields, mysterious fruit, a hidden cave, and various images of violence.

Both their dreams were puzzling and certain symbols seemed to foreshadow current happenings or were at least connected to them. Although they wanted to continue their conversation, they agreed the captain was right about being rested for the rescue attempt. Jesse said his goodbyes and settled around the fire. Saephira went to her tent. The anointed cloud stayed all night, hovering over the campsite. At firstlight it was gone.

CHAPTER 25
PREPARATIONS AND SURPRISES

Puffy auburn clouds spread across the northern skyline at firstlight, an event that often occurred following a windstorm. After the group broke their fast on dried fish and kin, Max gathered those with battlestaff weapons to demonstrate offensive and defensive skills. "There are four basic moves: *Lunge*, *Strike*, *Block*, and *Sweep*," Max explained. "Don't worry legionnaires; there are no live-action drills this morning." He glanced in Jesse's direction. "Sir, let me borrow your leadership staff." Jesse handed it over to Maximus, relieved he wasn't drafted for another weapon presentation. Last time he didn't fare too well.

Holding Jesse's staff, Max outlined the four techniques, expounded on their effectiveness, and followed up by going through the appropriate stances and deliveries for each. "A *Lunge* is a thrust forward, hitting a vital area like the chest, arm, or thigh. There are vulnerable targets on the face as well. Poking an eye or smashing a nose will stun your opponent, at least temporarily. Also consider a lunge below the ribcage." He used his fist to indicate the best spot. "It will knock the air out of a person's lungs, allowing an opportunity to escape or respond with a different move."

"*Strikes* come in various forms: reverse, counter, and spin around. The spin adds momentum to your strike. A hit to the neck will daze opponents. With more force, it can damage their spinal cord, permanently disabling them. Striking at an arm or leg will injure a person's limb, and if delivered hard enough, can

147

break bones. I hope you'll never be forced to employ these more lethal methods but keep them in mind."

"*Blocks*, also called deflects, can counter whatever action an assailant tries, whether they're using a spear, sword, or another staff in their attack. Likewise, fakes and dodges are helpful in confusing the attacker, giving you a slight advantage. All these are great defensive strategies. Use them."

"For a *Sweep* or reverse sweep, hit behind the knees or ankles to drop your enemy to the ground. This will facilitate the next three options: escape, immobilize, or apply a lethal blow. One of the most effective sweeps is an upward swing between the legs to the groin area. It works well, especially if the adversary is a man. Remember, a quarterstaff is primarily a defensive weapon and if used as such, can save a life. You only need to disable an opponent in order to get away. It is not necessary to kill, but if using deadly force is your only option to survive, then take it."

When Max finished his training session, the team split into smaller clusters to practice with their various weapons, honing their skills until it was time to pack and leave. A span later, the rescue party crossed the boundary line and entered the Disputed Lands. As they traveled, Anna rode up alongside Jesse. "Jess, can I talk with you for a minute?"

"Sure, go ahead Annie, what is it?"

"Two nights ago, I dreamed about a barren area between two boundary lines. It looked similar to the land we're riding through right now. In my dream, I saw a man with a crooked index finger, sitting by an open firepit, roasting a large rodent on his sword. It resembled an overgrown rabbit. Anyway, it was late afternoon and he appeared sad, even crying. I believe my dream was prophetic, and somehow, we are going to meet him out here."

"Hmm, interesting. Would you recognize the guy if we run across him?"

"I think so. I saw his face and everything. I got the impression he wants to help us free Lundy and Narleen. I just had to tell someone."

"Thanks Annie, maybe your dream was a premonition. If so, we may have to act on it. Let us know if you see him again . .

. I mean in person." With the burden lifted, she thanked Jesse for listening and retook her position in line behind the militia lead.

By midcycle, the group approached Tabahir and stopped about a half league outside the city in a deserted area where they were unlikely to be noticed or disturbed. According to the agreed plan, Saephira and Jesse would enter the city, locate the Copper Rail Tavern and inquire about lodging arrangements for later nightrise. Whether the rescue attempt was successful or not, they would require a safe place to hide out until firstlight.

As their comrades waited, Jesse and Saephira rode into Tabahir and with a little searching, found the tavern southwest of the main square. Saephira pinned her long-braided hair into a bun and slipped a hood over her head to help conceal her identity. No one, however, seemed to be paying them any mind. "These boundary settlements are that way," she mentioned to Jesse, "especially the ones near the Upper Realm. They can be treacherous places. For the most part, though, people keep to their own affairs, some of which are questionable at best."

The tavern had a covered front porch with a table and benches for dining outside. The building was rundown yet freshly painted. The lobby and dining hall were empty. A man stood behind the counter, shuffling papers. He stopped as they entered. "Good dayrise, folks. My name is Nanlon." He gave a short bow. "You seem like a nice couple. Need a room for nightrise? We have the best rates in town."

"What's the going price?" Jesse asked.

"We charge one credit per person, paid in advance. If you have kacks, we can put them in our stables for an additional credit. Feed is included."

Jesse wandered up to the counter and leaned against it. "How many does each room sleep?"

"Planning a party, are ya? Fine with me. We make no judgments around here. You can sleep four per room. It'll be four credits. Dinner provided."

"Alright, fair enough," Jesse replied. "Book us three places for the night and reserve stable space for eleven kacks."

"Big party, huh? Fourteen credits then: twelve for the lodging and two for the boy who'll see to your mounts. Signing a register is unnecessary. We ask no names, make no judgments."

"We were told to say the Unnamed Merchant recommended you," Saephira added.

"Ahh, if that's the case, only ten credits total." Saephira reached into her script purse to take out coins out to pay the man, and as she did, her hood slipped back revealing her face.

Nanlon's eyes grew large. He bowed and stepped around the counter to take a knee in front of her. "Lady Saephira, I didn't know it was you. It's been yarns since you traveled north. You were younger in those days and courting that Eddnok fellow. You made the right decision to dump the scoundrel." He arose, bowed again, and stepped behind the counter. "There's no charge for the rooms, my Lady, other than paying the stable boy for his services." She handed him two credits for the stablehand, plus fifteen more. He tried to refuse it, but she pushed the coin across the counter, insisting he take it. "Okay, much appreciated. Your business in Tabahir is confidential with me." He fiddled with the coins in his hand as if he were contemplating his next statement. "If it concerns the Lundy matter, though, you have my full support." Jesse and Saephira glanced at one another at the mention of his name yet said nothing.

"My cousin and I, along with his merchant friend, were enjoying a cup at one of the front street taverns a few spans ago. We saw an Upper Realm guard drag off an old man named Lundy MacBain. Probably took him to Briacap. Don't care for those soldiers, never did." His frown slowly changed into a wide smile. "At any rate, I'm happy you chose the Copper Rail. The rooms will be ready whenever your business is complete, whatever it is."

After a moment or two of awkward silence, Jesse thanked Nanlon for the reservations. "It may be past darkout before we arrive."

"No problem, we'll leave a light out for ya. Dinner will be waiting in your rooms. Nobody will know you were ever here. We take no names and make no judgments." He waved a friendly farewell. As soon as they left, he stashed the seventeen credits into his pocket.

Jesse and Saephira returned during aftercycle and rendezvoused with the others. They conveyed what happened in town, including confirmation on Lundy's whereabouts and securing their lodging. With the first part of the plan accomplished, the collective mounted up and rode to the upper boundary line to wait for twilight to begin. "We have several spans before we leave," Waubush advised. "You guys can rest, work on your weapon skills, or take a walk to stretch your legs. Either way, stay alert."

Anna decided to stroll around and see the area. The landscape seemed familiar. Wandering past a nearby ridge, she noticed smoke rising and felt led to investigate. And there he sat, cooking a skinned animal over the fire, the same person in her dream. She approached him, stepping within five paces. The man, however, was lost in his thoughts and didn't see her until she spoke, "Sir, may I ask you a question?"

Startled, the man dropped his half-roasted bush varmint into the ashes, stood, and grabbed for his dagger. Seeing only a young woman with a hiking stick, he sat down and tried to salvage his meal from the fire. "What do you mean by sneaking up on a person like that? You could get knifed or something."

"Sorry sir, I simply wanted to ask if you need comfort."

"Nope, I'm not in the mood for your services. Go back to town and try clients there. Besides, I don't have the credits to pay you."

"You misunderstand me, sir. I'm not here for carnal considerations. I've sought you out to offer encouragement. I had a dream where I saw you at this same campfire, cooking your dinner, looking sad with tears in your eyes. I assume you are troubled about a certain matter. I can sympathize. Not long ago, I became distraught after I was paralyzed in a rockslide at Onnie Passage." At the mention of the rockslide, the man let out a mournful groan, covered his face with his hands and began to cry.

"Does it ever end?" He continued weeping and wiping

away the tears. "You were at Onnie the day of the rockslide?"

"Yes, except I survived and was given a second chance at life. I received a healing, not just in my body, but in my heart as well. And I believe you can too. This is the kind of comfort you really need."

"It's too late for me. I've done horrible things for Lord Eddnok, more than I dare to count. It would be better if I were dead."

"I know you may feel this way, except now you have an opportunity to change your destiny."

"How do I accomplish that?"

"By doing good. Eddnok kidnapped my friends and imprisoned them. My outfit is raiding his fortress tonight, and we seek a guide who can locate their prison cells and help us liberate them."

"Impossible! Briacap is nearly impregnable. It has sturdy ramparts, high battlements, guarded parapets, and numerous squads of armed soldiers. I know because I was one of them."

"Will you not try?" She moved closer and stared straight into his eyes. "You can stand up against this wicked ruler. Make things right, and if you die in the process, you will die for good, not evil."

"You would trust me?"

"I would!"

"What about the companions in your little raiding posse?"

"I hope once they hear your story, they'll be supportive."

"I'm not so sure. If you only knew what I've done, how many—"

"I know enough, and I feel you're an honorable man at heart."

"Really! Did you know I was involved with the ambush at Onnie Passage where you were injured, and people died?"

"No, I did not." The unexpected news did not deter her. "If you participated, it was because you were following orders, malicious orders, and the person who gave them to you is the one accountable, not you. I am not saying there aren't consequences for our actions, but you no longer have to face them alone. I have forgiven you. Will you not forgive yourself?"

"Maybe, I don't know . . . I feel sick in my gut about what

happened, my choices, who I am and what I've become."

"And who are you if I may ask? What's your name, good sir? Mine is Annabelle."

"I'm Gelr, former commander of the Upper Realm, and I am not a good sir at all."

Anna leaned over and put her hand on his shoulder. "Would you at least hear us out, and if you decline, so be it. Meeting you here this afternoon was not by chance. I believe providence played a part. Besides, our little alliance needs your help. I need your help."

Gelr arose, wiping the last few tears from his eyes. He tossed his burnt meal into the fire and sheathed his sword. "Okay, young lady, I'll go talk to your cohorts, except I make no promises." He followed Anna over the ridge, leading his kack behind him.

From a distance, Jesse spotted her returning and shouted, "Annie, where have you been? Everyone's been worried sick, wondering if you were . . ." He stopped mid-sentence when he noticed the stranger following behind her. "Who is this guy?" Two militiamen positioned their spears, ready to deploy.

"It's all right gentlemen. I'm safe, put your spears away." She motioned for them to come closer. "Let me introduce Gelr, former commander from the Upper Realm, the one I told you about, Jess, the man I saw in my dream. I've asked him to assist us with the rescue mission."

Gelr scanned the band of individuals and considered turning around to leave but paused when he recognized one of them. He dropped to his knees in front of Lady Saephira. Tears began welling up in his eyes again. "My Lady, I don't know how to . . . Ahh . . . I mean . . . Sorry for—"

Anna interrupted before he mentioned the ambush or other confession that might further complicate the situation. "The commander told me he regrets working for Lord Eddnok who ordered him to do terrible things. He no longer serves him and wants to support us in our quest to free the prisoners, if we give him a chance."

"What terrible things were those?" Waubush asked.

"Does it really matter? The past is the past and he laments his former actions." Anna stepped nearer to stand by his side. "If he can aid in our attempt to save Lundy and Narleen, would not forgiveness be better than condemnation? We all deserve a second chance, an opportunity to make amends." Jesse nodded his agreement, having recently faced a similar dilemma. Instead of being judged for his failures, he received mercy and understanding from his colleagues.

"Stand up, sir, and face me. Is this true, Commander Gelr? You would avail yourself and join us?"

"Umm, I'm thinking on it." He rubbed his stubbed finger across his chin. "I know the citadel better than most, having lived there all of my life. The garrison has several weak spots in their defenses. The western lookout tower on backside by the Narmoot Forest is not heavily fortified and only guarded by three or four sentinels who are not too attentive, especially if they're drinking kunakk during their duty shift. It might be our best location to breach the fortress. You will probably all die in the process, including me. However, if you can somehow eliminate the sentries, scale the rampart wall undetected, enter the plaza without sounding the general alarm, then I can direct you to the main stockade where most prisoners are kept before being transferred elsewhere. Getting out, though, is another matter."

"Alright commander, if you will assist us, I will pardon you for all past wrongs committed against the Lower Realm. Gather your weapons and gear; you are now part of our strike force." It was as if an unseen weight had lifted off his chest. He bowed to Saephira and hurried back to his ride. Anna followed and helped Gelr sort and repack his side carrier. To lighten the load, he tossed all unnecessary items and kept only those required for the mission.

After the surprise appearance of Gelr and the following confrontation, Captain Waubush approached Maximus about a concern. "Can I have a word with you?"

"Yes sir, what is it?"

"Lady Saephira asked me to meet with you, Commander Gelr, and Jesse to go over our plans and make changes if warranted."

"Sure, I'll be glad to offer my input. Right now?"

"No, later."

Sensing an undercurrent to their conversation, Max asked,

"Is there anything else? You seem bothered."

"I'm just wondering what you think about Gelr. I'm not certain I trust him."

"No doubt, we'll find out more once the fighting starts. Still, from what I know, Miss Anna is a good discerner of people, and if she trusts Gelr, I think we should go with it." Waubush thanked Max for his advice and decided to let the matter drop for now.

While Seth distributed early dinner rations, Waubush and Gelr met together, along with Jesse and Max, to discuss the upcoming night raid and rescue attempt. Max showed the commander their new weapons, detailing their long-range capability and relative silent operation. After careful consideration of all the options, they agreed upon a modified plan and different timeline, believing it was a better strategy.

Prior to sharing the amended plan with the entire outfit, Captain Waubush discussed it with Saephira and received her approval. The team would cross the boundary line and head north into Upper Realm territory during the current postcycle instead of waiting for twilight. They'd leave their kacks in the Kunakk Vineyards, which should be unattended at that span, and travel on foot to the Narmoot Forest, pausing until the cover of darkness to begin their raid.

With the new tactics outlined, the liberators mounted their rides and moved out. Waubush cautioned, "Stay alert and keep your bows, slings, and other weapons at the ready."

Seth checked his quarterstaff to see if it was tied down securely. He placed a stone into his sling and tucked it under his belt for easy access. "I hope there are no freaking patrols out there. It could get real gnarly."

"If they show up, we will deal with them. Besides, we have the advantage. Their patrols don't expect us." Max patted the Gladius at his side. "Just remember Rule Number One, kid, and you will do well." Sporting a half-grin, he reached into his tote bag, drew out an arrow, and notched it into his longbow.

The rescue party arrived at the Kunakk Vineyards prior to latecycle. All the workers had departed for the day, heading to their homes in Nakk Village. The group concealed their mounts among the trellises and left the militia lead and Anna behind to guard them. Under the guidance of Gelr, they followed a dry riverbed, staying low, using its banks as cover, and took positions at the leading edge of the forest, hiding behind large cottlepines and dead tree stumps. The assault team could see the western battlement from their location. And then, they waited.

CHAPTER 26
TREASURE FOUND

Lord Eddnok arose early that morning. While most expedition members slumbered in their tents, he walked around the camp thinking about his treasure, wondering why the translation called it *the richest gift*. He stopped to take in the view as firstlight emerged over the Colrath peaks, revealing bands of auburn clouds floating high above the northern skyline. The cycle after a windstorm was always a beautiful sight.

Bolgog lumbered by as Eddnok stared upward, studying the horizon. "Good dayrise, Lord. What are you gazing at so early this span?"

"Gaulmore Peak. It appears different somehow as if I could almost reach out and touch it. I don't know if it's our proximity to the mountains, the light reflecting off them, or if the puffy clouds have created an illusion. Nevertheless, at firstlight, these peaks seemed taller."

"Lundy's document said to look for *peaks that grow during daylight glow*. Perhaps it's another clue, a confirmation we are on the right track."

"I believe you are correct, commander. Wake the men, feed them, and let's get going. Lots of places to explore this cycle."

"What's the heading?"

"The scroll says to *follow the trail*. Therefore, it's what we're gonna do. Search the uphill areas for *the mountains red* mentioned in the translation."

"Actually sir, all these mountaintops have reddish shale

157

and rock. There is, however, an area not far from here called Red Drop where a rockslide halted a mining project."

"I didn't realize we still had operations in these hills."

"We don't. About fifty yarns ago, prospectors searched these ridges for tin and copper. Past records indicate they dug three mines. Not finding sufficient quantities of ore, they shuttered them and moved over to the Narnj range."

"Yes, yes, I know. The active digs at Narnj are good mineral producers, especially with plenty of prisoners to work them. These abandoned ones, though, interest me. They might be worth checking out."

"No one has been this way in yarns. The trails are precarious and the excavations in ruins."

"No matter. We will inspect all three, starting with Red Drop. Perhaps one of them is the *hidden cave* described in the text. I'm going to break my fast now and when I'm done, you better have the outfit packed and ready to depart. I hafta to find the treasure before nightrise." Bolgog bowed and hurried off to carry out Eddnok's instructions, scowling as he left.

The expedition labored up the rugged trail and its seemingly endless switchbacks. The route was steep and difficult to traverse. Some sections were covered by rock and debris. In other places, entire portions had dropped off into the canyon below. Forward progress required careful navigating, but they finally arrived at the Red Drop rockslide area.

"It would take a yarn to clear out this decrepit mine, assuming we could find the entrance under all that rock," Bolgog noted. "The cave-in was one reason miners abandoned this area and continued their search elsewhere. In fact, all the mineworkers inside at the time of the massive slide were buried alive. It became sort of a shrine. After the accident, family members made a seasonal trek to leave keepsakes or written messages. The pilgrimages ended ages ago when the trail fell into disrepair."

"Then it's an old gravesite, right? Why didn't you mention these facts to me last cycle?" *You're such an idiot.*

"I never considered them relevant." replied Bolgog, his face turning red with embarrassment. Eddnok shook his head in mock disgust.

Eddnok pulled out the manuscript to study the exact wording. "It says the treasure awaits in a *hidden cave* past an *ancient grave.* I would bet this slide is the ancient grave, which means my treasure lies ahead in one of the two abandoned mines we haven't located yet." He returned the document to his pocket. "Tell me commander, can you find the remaining ones?"

"I could try, but I'm only aware of the area's history, not the actual locations of—"

"You better figure it out if you expect a share of the loot." Eddnok waved him away. "Go check with our mining team. Maybe one of them was around back then."

Eddnok's obsession with his treasure hunt was getting out of hand. Even so, the senior commander went ahead and made a few inquiries. Joelurt, the seventy-yarn-old crew chief, told Bolgog he had worked in two of those digs and felt with a little luck he could locate one, maybe both.

Joelurt took the lead, and the group continued their ascent, with the elder prospector stopping every half span to hunt for discarded equipment and leftover tailings. Seeing several promising signs, he turned left down a side path and discovered an open lateral mineshaft. Although the support timbers were missing, the passageway was intact. "Over here! I found one."

Eddnok rushed over and peered inside but couldn't see past fifteen paces. "Bring me a lighted torch." He walked in, following a long tunnel until he came to an excavated cavern. It was empty. He decided to leave half the porters there to poke around and see if they could uncover anything of value. If they caused a cave-in, no big loss, they were expendable. "Well, old man, where's the third mine?"

"As I recall, we dug one on the next ridge, near an overhang with a large fissure running across it."

"Sounds findable to me, lead on, Joe or Lurt or whatever your name is."

The party loaded up and the mining crew chief escorted them onward. The higher they climbed the more the trail deteriorated. Even their sure-footed kacks were slipping on the loose shale. By midcycle, they reached a fork in the trail: one led uphill into a closed canyon and the other downhill into the Blighte wilderness. They followed the canyon route until it ended in a pile of rocks and debris. Joelurt climbed off his mount to study the elevated rock formations, focusing on its steep bluff face. "I think this is it, but it appears as if the overhang gave way and buried the entrance."

Eddnok wondered if the crack crossing the rock face was *the rift* and the elevated bluff was the *highest cliff* described in the translation. "Start digging and see if you can uncover the opening."

Using picks and shovels, the miners removed piles of rock and shale. They used ropes harnessed to kacks to pull the larger boulders free. Finally, a small hole emerged. "Looks pretty unstable in there," Joelurt said. "I'm not sure we should keep going. Could trigger a collapse."

"Continue the dig and stop complaining," Eddnok screamed. Each passing span he yelled at them again. At twilight, the men broke through. The entrance was wide enough for one person to squeeze in. Eddnok grabbed a torch and crawled past the entry on his hands and knees. Once inside, he used a striking stone to light the torch. The jagged tunnel curved to the left, ending in a wide-open area. Halfway back, he saw a large, silhouetted shape. As he crept closer, he could tell it was tree, a living tree, growing in total darkness without a one speck of light. *How is this possible?* It was twelve paces tall or higher with its top touching the cavern ceiling. The branches spread out wider than a cottlepine and contained whitish fruit on all the limbs.

Remembering the words *to seek a taste,* he pulled off a fruit and took a bite. Sweet juice trickled down his throat. Instantly, a wealth of knowledge flooded his mind. He became aware of the divine wisdom in goodness and the powerful knowledge of evil. With such delicious thoughts, he became giddy and danced about the tree, spinning around, laughing, until the dizziness overwhelmed him. Never had he felt so delighted. At that moment, Eddnok made a choice. He dismissed the good and embraced the evil. With such knowledge, he could finally destroy Saephira and the Lower Realm or anyone else who got in his way. Every wicked deed, every foul thought, and every vulgar act would be his arsenal—and he would use them all. He was the *ruler of fate* after all.

Eddnok climbed out the entrance and called to Bolgog. "Set the camp. We are staying here through nightrise. We will feast tonight. And break out the kunakk, we celebrate."

"Did you find the treasure?" Bolgog asked.

"Yes, it's inside."

"What is it?"

"It's beyond anything one could imagine. The richest treasure of all. And it's mine."

"How shall we split up the expedition's share of the bounty?"

"We don't." Bolgog looked bewildered and wanted to ask why—yet didn't. Not stopping to explain his rationale, Eddnok added, "I need the entry enlarged by firstlight and a security detail posted at all spans. No one is to enter. And I mean no one! Those who try will face the sword, along with their entire family. Do I make myself clear?"

"Yes Lord, very clear."

"Send flyer messages to Briacap. I want a company of warders to prepare for extended duty at the cave with enough provisions for a yarn. Have the metalsmith start building a locking bronze door for the entrance. I'll provide the specs later. Also notify my woodsmith and alchemist to expect new project assignments."

"Alright, I'll send off those messages after firstlight."

"No, send them now." When Eddnok finished relaying his orders, he grabbed an extra torch and crawled back inside the cave to savor his newfound knowledge: *wisdom sublime and power divine.*

Sadly, wickedness had found a foothold. It usually does in wicked hearts.

CHAPTER 27
RESCUE ATTEMPT

Anna wanted to participate in the actual rescue, but someone had to stay behind with the animals. Captain Waubush chose her for corral duty, along with the militia lead. After their colleagues departed for the Narmoot Forest, Anna and the lead started hobbling their twelve mounts so they wouldn't wander off. The kacks didn't seem to mind being tied near an endless supply of grainy vines to nibble on. They were about to unpack the food rations Seth handed out earlier when Anna heard people talking in the distance, growing louder as they approached. She and the lead ducked behind the vines, hiding the best they could, and watched. Three individuals appeared. The men, armed with black and red striped spears, were marching down a path from Nakk Village. "They're Upper Realm guardsmen," the lead confirmed.

"Maybe if we stay hidden, they will pass by," Anna whispered. The three guards walked within paces of their location yet never noticed them or their rides. They just trudged on, talking, laughing, and sharing a jar of kunakk between themselves. "Whew, a little too close for comfort." As soon as she spoke, one their mounts whinnied, followed by a chorus of neighing from the herd. The men turned around to see where the noise originated and spotted kacks in the vineyard. They also sighted Anna and the militiaman.

"Hey, what are you two doing in our vineyard with all those animals?" No answer. "Not talking huh?" Silence. "Did you two guys steal them?" More silence. "Alright, we'll make you talk." And the detachment rushed them, spears at the ready.

"Get your sling out, Anna, and see if you hit one." The militia lead assumed his throwing stance and aimed his spear. He waited for the attackers to get within range and launched it at the closest one. The spear impaled the man in the belly; he moaned, falling sideways to the ground. Anna twirled her sling around, preparing for a toss, while the lead pulled out his knife and drew back for a throw. He flung his blade toward the second assailant at the same moment the guy launched his spear. Both weapons flew past each other. The spear penetrated the lead's chest; the knife pierced the neck of the guardsman. Both staggered and crumbled to the ground. Distracted by watching her partner fall, Anna's first toss missed. Trying to stay focused, she loaded a second stone into her sling and began whirling it, building momentum for another throw.

The third man stopped to check on his two fallen comrades. They were dead. He posted up and launched his spear at Anna, which she dodged at the last moment. She reset the stone in her sling, spun it around several times and released. The rock smacked into the man's cheek, causing only a scratch. "Ouch! That hurt. Now you're gonna pay." The man raced ahead, sword drawn. Anna grabbed her persuader and stood ready to defend herself.

She blocked the first sword swing and dodged the second. She tried a thrust to the man's chest to knock the air out of his lungs, but he parried and swung his curved blade at her hand, attempting to knock the staff loose. She evaded. Stepping forward, she faked a lunge maneuver to his face. When he ducked to avoid it, she followed through with an upward sweep between his legs, smacking his groin. The guard staggered backwards, shocked and in pain, barely holding on to his weapon. Before he could use it again, she spun around and struck his neck as hard as she could. She heard a cracking sound before he fell. Afterwards, he never moved. Anna didn't pause to rationalize her actions or how she felt; instead, she hurried over to the injured militia lead.

He lay flat, legs stretched out, barely breathing, blood oozed from his wound. Although the spear shaft had broken off, the point remained stuck in his chest.

"I'm not gonna make it, Anna."

"Yes, you will. I'll go fetch the mender kit and bandage your wound."

He shook his head no. "Please don't leave."

"Only for a moment. I'll be right back with the . . ." The lead just kept shaking his head no. Feeling helpless, she knelt and took his right hand into hers. His breath grew labored, and his eyelids flickered as he tried to keep them open.

"Your song about the unseen one . . ." His voice faltered so she leaned in closer to hear him. "Do you think he's here now, cares about me, knows . . ."

"Yes, Yeshua is always present." She tenderly squeezed his hand. "And He knows."

"I would like to visit his kingdom someday, if he'll have me."

"He will." The militia lead smiled, closed his eyes, and exhaled a final breath. Anna knelt at his side for the longest time with tears streaking down her cheeks. Before twilight faded into darkness, she located his coat in a side carrier and covered him with it. After uttering a short prayer, she sat beside his body, leaned against a vine trellis, exhausted, and closed her eyes.

While the team hid in the forest waiting for the approach of nightrise, they discussed the raid and rehearsed their roles. They could not afford mistakes—unknown factors were a different matter—those could hinder even the best-laid plans. Waubush, who had been keeping a close eye on the horizon, tapped Jesse's shoulder. "It's time. Get your lamp out." He reminded everyone to use hand signals as much as possible and keep their talking to a minimum. With Jesse at point, the band of liberators snuck out of the woods under the cover of darkness. He flipped on his candle lamp, shielded it behind him, and led them onward. The lamp gave off a faint glow, allowing the rescuers to see where they walked. They stepped off three paces, stopped, then three more, trying to avoid any continuous movement that might alert the lookouts to their presence. The group continued this pattern until they were within bow range of the western battlement.

Torches were spaced at intervals behind the parapet, which illuminated the entire walled area, including the battlement tower. At fifty paces away, Jesse stowed his lamp because the torches from the fortress provided enough residual light to silhouette their surroundings.

The strike unit spread out and stayed low. Max, Saephira, and three militia archers maneuvered into position and notched arrows to their longbows. Seth pulled out his sling and prepared for a toss. Since Waubush, Gelr, and the militia chief didn't have long-range weapons, they positioned themselves behind the rest as spotters. Jesse slipped to the rear and joined them.

"I can see three sentinels," Gelr advised. "There might be more behind the merlons. Every time one passes in front of a torch, it casts a shadow."

"This makes them the perfect target." Max acknowledged Gelr's observations and whispered orders to his four archers. "With three known sentries, we will launch our arrows in succession. I will draw down on the first one." He pointed to the two-person unit on the right. "Chepho and Lady Saephira, I want you to aim for the second man." He motioned to the unit on his left. "You other two hit the third sentry." Max took careful aim and released the first arrow: *whish*. Two more volleys followed: *whish – whish, whish – whish.*

Max achieved a solid hit on the first man, and he disappeared below the parapet. The second lookout was pierced by one arrow; the second shot fell short. The last two arrows flew wide, hitting the merlon with loud snaps. Hearing the noises, the third watchman glanced over to find his two comrades lying on the alure. He yelled "I need some—" As he spoke, a stone from Seth's sling smacked him in the forehead, silencing him. He crumpled sideways against an exposed barrier. Two additional sentinels, patrolling the rampart, heard the cry and dashed over to investigate.

Max and Saephira launched again. Both arrows connected. The two soldiers groaned in pain and plummeted out of site.

"Okay Seth, you're up," Jesse said. "Show us your free climbing expertise." Seth stuffed his sling into his pocket and handed Jesse his quarterstaff before he sprinted over to the rampart. The wall had a sheer façade. It contained plenty of cracks and protruding stones to use as holds. As he had done many times on challenges at climbing gyms on earth, he scaled the wall in a matter of moments. Once he gained the top, Seth pulled himself over the parapet and dropped onto the wallwalk. First, he checked to see if any of the fallen sentries were moving. They weren't. Next, he scanned the cobblestone walkway in both directions for more patrols. No hidden insurgents. *Cool, nailed it.* Working quickly, he unwound his corded rope, tied one end to a merlon, and tossed it over the edge to Jesse. "It's clear. Come on."

Jesse tied the slack end around their two fighting staffs, and Seth hauled them up. He leaned Jesse's staff against the bulwark and tucked his quarterstaff under his arm. He knotted the rope every three feet for handgrips and lowered it. One by one, Max, Jesse, Waubush, Gelr, and the militia chief climbed the rope, followed by two militiamen with bows. Seth helped pull them through the crenels to reach the parapet. Saephira and Chepho stayed below to watch for intruders, their arrows notched, bows at their sides. Seth and one of the bowmen remained atop the battlement tower and monitored the courtyard below. They stood ready to launch projectiles as cover fire if the six-person strike force confronted stiff resistance.

Rushing down the tower steps, the squad shadowed Gelr as he led them across the dimly-lit courtyard to the stockade. Thus far, the plaza was empty, no alarm bells. Gelr and Waubush pushed open the stockade's main entry door and encountered a jailer on night duty.

"Hey, what's going on here? Is that you Commander Gelr?" The jailer, who had been sitting at the desk, stood and approached him. "Where have you been?" Getting no answers, he drew his sword. "Better answer me!" When Gelr didn't reply, he peered over his shoulder and yelled toward the backroom, "Intruders, ring the alarm!" As the bell sounded, four more warders scurried out.

The assault squad had two options: either retreat or fight. Captain Waubush and Commander Gelr looked at each other, drew their swords and advanced, leading their militia. Max and

Jesse protected the rear flanks. Metal crashed against metal. Spears and throwing knives whizzed by in the air. Both militiamen fought well, but two enemy javelins hit their marks, dropping one comrade to the floor. The other nicked the militia chief, causing a deep gash to his shoulder. Ignoring the blood dripping down his arm, he kept fighting until he dispatched the warder who wounded him. As soon as the man collapsed on the floor, another guardsman stepped over his dead body and continued the fight. The rescue mission had stalled.

Max, who had been waiting in reserve, notched an arrow and released it: *whish*. The person stared at the strange shaft sticking in his chest. He tugged at the projectile and tried to pull it free as he crashed to the floor. Deciding to save his three remaining arrows, Max slung the bow over his shoulder, drew out his Gladius, and charged into the melee. Although Gelr and Waubush exchanged blow for blow with the warders, they were not gaining the advantage. The hallway was still blocked. Max battled past their defensive line, dropping all who opposed him. Jesse tailed him, swinging his staff in all directions. In the distance, the alarm bell kept ringing.

From their tower position, Seth and his cohort could see soldiers filing out of the barracks and entering the courtyard. The bowman aimed and launched his last three arrows. All of them hit their targets, dropping men to the ground. Seth slung stone after stone, taking out several more. "I am out of arrows, Seth, so I'm going below to face them head on."

"I'll bring my persuader and join you."

"No, stay at your post and keep slinging stones. If sentinels try to access the alure, you'll be needed here. Don't let them retake the tower area." The militiaman leaned his longbow against the bulwark, grabbed his spear, unsheathed his sword, and descended the steps to engage the enemy.

Meanwhile, Max went up one cellblock, Jesse the other, calling out for Narleen and Lundy as they searched the chambers. Max checked a block of empty cells, finding a locked one. He sliced off the bolt with one swing of his Gladius and pushed the door open. Narleen, who had been crouched in the corner, ran over and hugged him. He held her for a moment, then clutched her hand and led her out of the cell into the hallway.

"Are you okay?" With tears flowing, she nodded yes. "Have you seen an older man named Lundy?"

Gaining her composure, she wiped away her tears. "I overheard a few warders say they were taking him to the mines."

Jesse returned from his search and found Max and Narleen talking in the hall. "Great, you found her. What about Lundy? I didn't see him anywhere."

"Narleen said he was transferred to the mines."

Turning to Narleen, he asked, "Where are those?"

"In the mountains past—"

"We can worry about the location later. Right now, we have to get out of here." With his sword in one hand and Narleen in his other, Max led them around to the entry. "Sir, if you see any undamaged arrows, seize them. Our supply is limited." Passing through the entry hall, they noticed six fighters lying on the floor, including one of their own. Jesse bent over to check his pulse: none, not breathing either. Reluctantly, he took the extra arrows and slung the militiaman's bow over his shoulder. They rendezvoused with Waubush, Gelr, and the wounded militia chief who had repositioned to the entrance to watch for combatants.

Together, the retreating party hurried out into the courtyard. However, before they could reach the tower to make their escape, they encountered a squad of four guardsmen with spears. Max fired his last three arrows in rapid succession. The first shot missed, the second and third hit, dropping two assailants. Gelr, who still carried his spear, launched it at the third guardsman. The spear pierced the man's side, causing him to double over. Waubush tossed his throwing knife at the last one before the guy could launch his spear. A direct hit stopped the fourth guard in his tracks. The way seemed clear for the moment.

"Quick, to the tower everyone," Waubush yelled. "I'll cover our retreat." The liberators raced across the plaza, jumping over bodies, steering for the tower steps. They discovered another militiaman lying face down with a spear in his back, dead. He had been on the battlement with Seth. Sadly, they had to leave him where he fell. Max retrieved what arrows he could find on the way, pulling them from deceased bodies, knowing they would be useful deterrents if ambushed again.

Behind the parapet, Seth continued to sling rocks. One by one, the liberators arrived at the wallwalk and slid down the rope. Max rappelled first, holding on to Narleen. The militia chief went next. Jesse tossed their two fighting staffs over the edge to Max. Seeing an extra longbow leaning against the bulwark, he seized it and slung it over his shoulder with the first bow. He was about to descend the rope when Gelr yelled, "Waubush never came up. I'm going back to find him."

"Wait a minute, I'll come help you."

"No, I can handle it. That's why you invited me on this little adventure." Gelr laughed, turned, and hustled down the steps. Seth continued to lob stones at the soldiers in the plaza, trying to stop them from approaching the tower stairway. Gelr conducted a quick search and found the captain cornered against a side barrier by two warders who were holding spears to his throat. He charged them, swinging his curved blade in circles above his head, yelling like a wounded kack. Surprised by his sudden appearance and the noise, the warders cowered backwards. It was all Gelr needed. He rushed forward and dispatched them in mere moments. "Let's go captain, before more arrive and we're surrounded."

"Gelr, I'm sorry for not—"

"We can talk later. Let's leave this sickening place and get these people to safety." Together, they ascended the stairway and escaped down the rope. Seth rappelled off the rampart last. Once on the ground, he flicked his rope and it came loose from the merlon, dropping into his hands.

While the raid played out inside the fortress, a squad of ten soldiers deployed outside and began searching for intruders. They found two suspicious persons below the western battlement. Assuming they were the reason for the warning bell, the squad advanced with spears in hand. When the guardsmen got into range, Saephira and Chepho launched several volleys of arrows, taking out four attackers. The ones who survived the onslaught of strange-looking projectiles kept advancing. With all their arrows gone, Saephira switched to her dagger and Chepho to his spear. They were outnumbered three to one and losing ground.

After descending the wall, the collective noticed their two companions in peril and darted over to join the battle, easily defeating two guards and routing their squad. With the skirmish ended, Max and Seth yanked all salvageable arrows from dead bodies and added them to their hip totes for later distribution. "No need for stealth now," Jesse remarked. "They already know we were here."

"And they'll be sending searchers at firstlight, if not before," Gelr added.

It was late nightrise as the rescue team, now two members less, scrambled back to the forest, gathered their torches, and made a hasty retreat, heading for the vineyards.

CHAPTER 28
ESCAPE TO TABAHIR

Torches made it easier for the group to traverse the unfamiliar landscape in the dark, but like little beacons, using them gave away their location. Jesse had little doubt that Upper Realm pursuers would soon be tracking them. Although they may wait until firstlight, they surely would follow. Realizing the urgency, the team kept a steady pace until they reached the Kunakk Vineyards.

At the vineyards, Anna had fallen asleep sitting by the deceased militia lead. She was physically and emotionally drained. The sound of muffled footsteps and talking awakened her. She arose, peeked over the grain vines into the darkness and saw nine torches coming from the north, approaching fast. Assuming the worse, she pulled out her sling and checked her stone carrier. Empty. With no time to search for more rocks to use as projectiles, she clenched her fighting staff, saying to herself, "I'm not going down without a fight."

"Annie, it's us!" She recognized Jesse's voice.

"Over here, Jess." she said, relieved, allowing a smile to form on her lips. Since last night only sorrow had prevailed. The confrontation with the three guardsmen at twilight, watching the militia lead sacrifice his life, and killing one of the attackers had left little joy in her heart. She never imagined herself capable of hurting or causing someone's death.

Anna waited until everyone entered the vineyards, then ran

171

over to Jesse and threw her arms around his shoulders. "Oh Jess, it was terrible. We were attacked after you left." He shined his torch around and noticed four bodies lying nearby, one covered with a coat. "The lead is dead. He forfeited his life to save mine. Even worse, I had to kill a person to protect myself. I feel horrible."

"Sometimes we have to do the hard thing during a battle, Miss Anna." Max tried his best to reassure her. "As a centurion, I carried out my duty to protect my men. All too often, valuable lives are lost."

"We lost good people as well, Annabelle." Captain Waubush added. "We had to leave two militiamen behind who were killed in action." He went over to inspect the covered body of his militia lead and sighed. "I guess we lost three."

"Did you guys rescue Lundy and Narleen?" Anna asked Jesse, still clinging to his shoulders.

"No, not the Reverend. Last cycle, Eddnok relocated him to his prison labor camp inside their Narnj mines. However, we did save the lady-in-waiting."

"That's wonderful news about Narleen, it really is." When Anna released her hold on Jesse, she noticed Narleen and Saephira leaning against a vineyard trellis, trying to catch their breath from all the running. She hurried over and gave Narleen a big hug. The three women shared a few private thoughts with each other. As soon as their visiting ended, Anna turned around and locked her eyes on the captain, "So tell me sir, how do we free Lundy?"

"Not sure," Waubush replied. "Right now, though, we need to depart for Tabahir. No doubt, we are being pursued or will be at firstlight when they can track our trail better. Once we arrive at the Copper Rail Tavern, we can make plans on what to do next."

"What about the militia lead?" Anna pressed. "Shouldn't we gather his personal affects for a memory table?"

"Sadly, we have to forgo those protocols. Time is not on our side." Waubush glanced over at Lady Saephira who nodded her agreement. "Besides, we are not going to bury him here in enemy territory." The captain wrapped the militia lead in his coat, carried him over to his own kack, and secured the body for travel. Out of instinct, the lead's unridden animal would follow behind the herd as the alliance made their escape. Because they only required eleven mounts, Waubush left one hobbled in the vineyard, knowing laborers would discover it on the morrow. "Mount up and grab a torch. If we ride hard, we can make Tabahir in a span or two, long before dayrise."

The streets appeared empty as they neared the town. During darkout, most businesses close for the night, except those with taverns and brothels. The group entered from the southwest and approached the Copper Rail, and just as Nanlon had said, he left a lighted torch out for them. They rode around to the rear. The stable boy stood outside waiting. "I'z ben expetin ya."

Saephira dismounted and walked over to the stable attendant, "Good nightrise, young sir, my name is—"

"I'z knows whos ya'r. Da says you be the Great Lady. It'l be honr to tak care of yur kacks."

"Your father runs this establishment?"

"He be the ownr. And he no care for northrn relm, me neithr."

"We have a fallen comrade secured to the side carrier on one our mounts. Can you attend to him for me? He is wrapped in his coat. We have weapons, too, and supplies. Don't want them to be stolen during nightrise."

"Me be spectful of yur falln comrad. And I'z guard yur wepons rel good." The stable boy hoisted his pitchfork and jabbed it like a spear. "Me stick any woo trys to take um."

"You are very brave, young sir." Saephira grinned as she dug into her purse and pulled out two credits.

"I'z paid by my da alredy to feed, water, and brsh dwn yur amimls. Treat um nice. Watch til ya leav." He shuffled over to pet Saephira's white-striped kack and offered it a handful of yarm berries. "Ya rooms ar ready. Take the bak steps frm the stable." The boy pointed to an entryway behind one of the stalls, leading upstairs. "Dinner in ya rooms waitin for ya, Great Lady."

Saephira curtsied to the young boy and motioned to her

entourage to dismount and follow her through the passageway. Halfway up, she turned around and tossed him two credits, which he snatched in one hand while holding the pitchfork in the other. "Thanks for your service, young master." He pocketed the coin, gave her a wide, toothless smile, and then bowed so deeply he almost fell over.

The party ascended the stairs and found three rooms with the doors propped open. The adjacent unit was marked occupied, and the door closed. Saephira, Narleen, and Anna claimed the first one; Jesse, Max, Seth, and Gelr moved into the second; and Waubush, the militia chief, and Chepho settled into the third. In each bedroom, Nanlon had laid out a cold dinner of smoked fish, kin, baked maize, and antaloop jerky. Since the rooms contained washbasins and towels, the weary travelers cleaned up before devouring the food. With their hunger satisfied, they headed downstairs to the dining area to have a discussion. Nanlon, the proprietor, cook, and sole barkeep, was milling around behind the bar. He hurried over. "Good nightrise ladies and gentlemen. I put on some Azollie tea to brew when I saw you ride in. It should be ready to serve." He stepped into to the kitchen and came back a moment later with two tea kettles and a tray of cups.

"Thank you, good sir," Saephira said. "The meal was wonderful, and the hot drinks are appreciated." She began passing the cups around the table. "Oh, just wondering, I noticed a spare ride in the stables. Do you have an extra guest?"

"Yes, the fourth room was taken by a woman before you arrived. She won't disturb you. Said she'd be leaving at firstlight." Nanlon left the dining hall, assuming his guests coveted their privacy, and moved to the front desk. In an apparent attempt to appear busy, he began sorting ledgers.

"I realize it's late and everybody is tired. I sure am. Nonetheless, we need to make plans for the morrow. Who's gonna speak first?" Waubush asked.

"I will." Narleen stood to address her colleagues. "No suggestions for next cycle, but I wanted to thank the rescue team for saving me from that cruel Eddnok. I realize lives were put in jeopardy and three good men were lost. It makes me . . ." She stopped, unable to finish her words as tears began streaming down her face. Saephira reached over to hold her hand, trying to console her. Soon both women were weeping.

"I'm sorry to bring this up again." Anna paused until Narleen and Saephira finished their grieving. "What about Lundy?"

Seth rose from his chair. "Yeah, dudes, what about the Rev? We cannot leave him imprisoned in the mines while we all go our merry way. That would be uncool."

Waubush paused to consider how best to respond. "Perhaps we can arrange a different rescue mission at a later date. My first duty, however, is to return Lady Saephira and Narleen to our territory. Since the Disputed Lands are a dangerous place to tarry and because our ladies' welfare is my utmost priority, we are leaving at firstlight for Falein Village. My militiamen and I will serve as their security escorts. Falein is the closest Lower Realm settlement, and we should be safe there. Besides, my militia chief received a severe wound in his shoulder, which requires surgery, and they have an experienced mender in their village. Afterwards, I will venture on to Midvill and enlist more militia for our cause. We will honor and bury our militia lead in their city."

"Annie, I've been talking with Commander Gelr, and we think there's a way to break Lundy out from jail without more fighting," offered Jesse. "Since most of the guards know Gelr, we might be able to talk our way in, using somebody who pretends to be captured."

"I'm willing to play that ruse." Chepho rose to his feet. "Captain Waubush, sir, please release me from escort duty so I can participate in their rescue mission. And if what Gelr told me is true concerning Lower Realm captives imprisoned there, and if one of them is my brother, Bonarb, who went missing half a yarn ago, then I gotta find out. Whether he's there or not, I feel compelled to help secure the release of those who are."

"This will leave us shorthanded on security. However, I see you feel strongly about it. Alright, I'll authorize it. You're hereby reassigned to Jesse and his crew. May your ploy find success."

Max slid over and gave Chepho a hard slap on the back to show his appreciation for volunteering. "Decent swordsman. Not a bad archer either."

Waubush poured himself a second cup of tea and took a few sips while he formulated a question for Gelr. "You have earned my respect, commander, and my trust too. You honored your pledge to help rescue Narleen, and our Lady has pardoned you for past crimes. Considering that you can leave here a free citizen, why volunteer for another dangerous raid against your former cohorts?"

"It's simple. I desire to change my destiny." He pointed at Anna. "And it's all because of her. She trusted me. Asked me to embrace good and shun evil, which I'm trying to do."

Anna beamed, pride showing in her eyes. "I just offered him a little encouragement, along with my prayers."

Saephira, who had mostly listened thus far, replied, "Thank you, Annabelle. Your support sure made a difference for Narleen. In fact, I appreciate everyone's efforts." She stood and walked over to where Anna sat and placed her hand on her shoulder. "I think you should travel to Falein with Narleen and me. It would be much safer with a security escort. A secondary rescue in enemy territory sounds risky, even with the best laid plans."

"Your concern is appreciated, my Lady, except I'm not leaving until we find Lundy. I'm going with Jess, Gelr, and their outfit."

"I don't agree but understand. Let me know if you change your mind. On the morrow, I'll reserve rooms so your party has a safe place to return after securing Lundy's release. Right now, I suggest we all get some rest. It will be a long cycle for all of us, and we only have a couple spans until firstlight."

At firstlight, Max distributed the remaining arrows. He gave three to Saephira knowing she still had her bow. He handed Commander Gelr two arrows and a longbow because he wanted to learn archery, having seen its effectiveness as a weapon. Chepho took three arrows. Max kept six to use or allocate as needed. Seth strapped the extra bow to his side carrier for safekeeping.

Before the two parties departed, one for Falein and the other to Narnj, Saephira paid for an additional night at the Copper Rail. She gave the owner twenty credits to cover lodging and stable space, also reserving the now vacant fourth room. The person staying there had left early before the partners arose. After spying on the group as they discussed their plans in the dining hall, Preaverca entered the stables a span before firstlight, checked out her mount from the stable boy, lit a torch, and rode for Briacap.

CHAPTER 29
PRISONER RELEASE

As firstlight gave way to dayrise, the puffy layers of auburn clouds from last cycle began to fade. Everyone hoped it was a good omen. With Commander Gelr in the lead, Jesse, Max, Seth, Anna, and Chepho rode out of Tabahir, leading an extra kack behind them. Even early in the morning, the heat beat down upon them, causing both rider and mount to sweat profusely.

After last night's raid on Briacap, the group assumed Upper Realm soldiers would track their trail to the Kunakk Vineyards and then cross the boundary line into the Disputed Lands. They would probably search the area west of Tabahir first, looking for signs before they stalked into the city limits to question or threaten residents for information.

Hoping to avoid any search parties, Jesse's little band of rescuers traveled east along the boundary line until they approached the Lost Forest. The team turned north and followed the western edge of the woods to reach the foothills of the Narnj Mountains where they encountered a steep draw that crossed the main trail. One direction led to the mines; the other way skirted northern side of the forest and entered the Nae Wilderness. The Nae was an arid, desolate, mostly unexplored wasteland. It had no flowing water except in the southern part where the Gemous River intersected the Heill Void.

They took the left fork and approached the mining area from the backside, hoping the sentries were only monitoring the main route from Briacap, not the seldom-used rear trail. The liberators stopped behind a ridge, dismounted, and studied the mining camp. White smoke from an unattended campfire climbed upward, drifting east in the gentle breeze. A cooking pot hung from a tripod over the fire. Several spears leaned against a boulder. "I see three kacks hobbled out front, so I assume there are at least two warders and one sentinel on duty," Gelr advised.

"Where are the prisoner dudes being kept?"

"Here in the Dig, their copper mine. There's a holding cell about halfway down the shaft where they are shackled during the nights. Every few cycles, the watch transports the prisoners uphill to the Pit to dig tin. They could be at either place."

Keeping low, Anna crept forward to take a closer look. "I hope they are at this one, Lundy too."

"Okay guys," Gelr said, "let's put our little plan into action." While Jesse, Max, Seth, and Anna spread out across the ridge, Gelr tied Chepho's hands in front, using slipknots in case their scheme didn't work and he needed to free himself. He dragged his mock hostage along behind him, holding on to a rope as Chepho pretended to struggle against it. When Gelr got within thirty paces of the mine entrance, he stopped and yelled out, "Ho there in the camp! Can I approach?"

A sentinel sub-commander holding a spear, leaned out of the entrance and replied, "And who are you?"

"Commander Gelr."

"Well now, I haven't seen you in a yarn." He wandered over to the firepit and stoked the coals with the butt of his spear. "Where have you been all this time, commander?"

"Lord Eddnok commissioned me for a special mission. Kept me busy for a couple cycles." Gelr shuffled a little closer to the firepit, leading Chepho behind him. "I just captured a rebel who was fleeing Briacap. I'm bringing him to work in the mines."

"Yeah, we got flyer messages at firstlight about a rebel attack on our fortress, including a follow up dispatch saying magical flying sticks and floating rocks killed dozens of guards. Weird, huh? At any rate, I'm glad you caught one of the assailants." The officer bent over, took a cup, and filled it with steaming liquid from the pot. "We are always shorthanded for labor. As you know, captives don't last long, maybe a half yarn

179

at the most. Only have nine now. It's hard work digging minerals. Better them dying than us, though." He gave out a hearty chuckle, laughing so hard he spilled some of his drink into the fire.

"Then this one will come in handy. Should I take him to the tin mine?"

"No, we'll use him here. Our chain gang is mining copper today. Moving them to the Pit on the morrow."

"He's all yours." Gelr advanced five more paces, extending the rope.

"Oh, I meant to tell you, Commander Gelr. The third flyer message said you were spotted helping armed insurgents break a woman out of the stockade during darkout." He snapped his fingers and two warders appeared in the entrance. "You're under arrest for high treason to the realm." The soldiers drew their swords and rushed forward. "Don't kill them, you fools. We need more laborers for the mines. Put your blades away and get the shackles."

"Wait, you are mistaken about—"

"Nope, I'm not. Thanks for volunteering, commander. You'll enjoy digging copper and tin ore. He watched his men approach, carrying two sets of chain shackles. "Bind these traitors and march them to our lockup."

On the rise, Max notched and released two arrows in rapid succession: w*hish, whish.* One warder fell before he could take three more steps. His comrade dropped beside him. Seth and Anna began twilling their slings to take down the sentinel, who seemed bewildered, turning around in circles and scanning the sky. "Hold off a minute you guys," Jesse advised. "Let's see what he does."

"Surrender now and you'll live," Gelr shouted. "It's your choice." The sub-commander released his spear and unstrapped his scabbard, tossing both on the ground. He put his hands behind his head and knelt on his knees. Chepho slipped free of his rope ties and hurried forward to confiscate his curved blade and long spear. Gelr moved to within a pace of the man, drew his sword, and pointed it at his chest. "Don't twitch one muscle." After searching him for throwing knives, Chepho sprinted to the mine entry holding on to the officer's spear and peeked inside, checking for additional sentinels. None were spotted, no movement either.

The rest of the crew charged ahead, leaving their rides hobbled behind on the ridge. Max arrived first, trailed by Seth and Anna who both had their slings in hand. Jesse brought up the rear with his leadership staff poised for a strike. As Gelr waited for the group to assemble, he bound the officer's hands with ropes. "Show me were the detainees are held," he ordered as he yanked the man to his feet.

At the entrance, Chepho stationed himself as lookout while the other four followed Gelr and his prisoner into the mine. Grabbing nearby torches, the party entered the tunnel and traveled down the passageway to where they heard muted voices. The chatter came from a carved-out section in the mineshaft with metal bars across the opening. A slatted wooden door secured the holding cell. The prisoners were huddled against the rear wall.

The men were chained at the ankles to one another. Most wore the remains of tattered clothing. Their faces were dirty and their bodies so emaciated that bones protruded under the skin. "Well, laddies, it's about time you showed. It's a wee bit cramped in here."

"It's Lundy MacBain. He's alive!" Anna stepped closer to peer through the bars. Lundy's face was grimy, his hands bruised and bloodied. His clothing, however, appeared in better condition than his fellow captives.

"Aye, Annabel, it's the old Scotsman in person, along with me new clan."

"Open the blasted door and take off those darn chains," Gelr commanded. "Afterwards, put a pair on your own legs. You have new living quarters now." Gelr, always cautious, scanned the passageway, keeping an eye peeled for concealed guardsmen. "And be quick about it. We don't have all dayrise."

The sentinel used his master key to open the door and a second set of smaller ones to unlock the shackles. When he finished releasing the nine hostages, he chained his own ankles. "Aye, good job. Me thinks you won't be needing these." Lundy grabbed his keys, locked the cell entry, and tossed the key ring into the darkness of the tunnel. "Since we're not uncivilized, here's a half skin of water in case you get thirsty. A little kindness goes a long way. Something you never much cared about in our cases." He gathered the freed laborers around him and said, "Lads, it's time to leave this fine establishment."

As soon as the party returned to the entrance, Chepho noticed Bonarb among the detainees. He hardly recognized his brother sporting a full, unkempt beard and being thinner than a stalk of maize. He ran to him, and they embraced, spinning in half circles like dancing partners. "Hey little bro, our family wondered if you were still alive, and here you are." Chepho's smile beamed from ear to ear. "I'm happy you survived." Both brothers were overcome with emotion and neither wanted to release their hold. "We gotta leave this varmint hole before more troops show." He grabbed Bonarb by the arm, and together they staggered toward the ridge. Due to a lack of nourishment and overexertion, his brother stumbled three times and had to be carried the rest of the way.

Max retrieved one spent arrow. Since the other was broken, he tossed it into the fire. He loaded a fresh arrow in his bow and tarried behind to keep watch as Seth helped the oldest captive climb the crest. Six prisoners rode double to the ridgetop using the seized animals from the Dig. Anna held Lundy by the hand and pulled him along. When everybody reached the top, the rescue team mounted up and together with the released hostages, galloped down the trail, returning the same way they approached. The collective had grown to fifteen individuals. Chepho and Bonarb rode double. Lundy and the other seven prisoners did likewise, sharing the three kacks commandeered at the mine and the extra ride they brought from Tabahir. Max Jesse, Seth, Anna, and Gelr steered their own mounts.

The escapees raced forward, turned a corner and ran into a company of Upper Realm guards blocking their path, at least twenty of them, all riding kacks. They were outnumbered and to make matters worse, also outarmed, since the liberated captives carried no weapons.

"Commander Gelr, we know you're there," Brappt yelled out. "Out of respect for our friendship and years of service together as commanders, I will give you a half span to surrender. If not, we will attack."

"I think they are trying to delay us until reinforcements arrive," Gelr advised. "We better decide what to do soon, or we'll run out of options."

"I don't know how they would know our plans unless someone betrayed us," Anna whispered as she clutched her sling and loaded up a small rock. Seth placed a stone in his as well and began to twirl it around.

Gelr noticed their slings. "If you fight them, we will undoubtedly incur heavy losses, and the men we freed will either be killed or imprisoned at the mines again. I suggest you put those things away."

"If you think it's best." Anna tucked her sling into her pocket. "Won't they surround us if we wait and do nothing?"

"Probably."

Seth kept his sling at the ready but lowered it out of sight. "Hey commander, what do you suggest we do about these turkeys?"

"Make a run for the Lost Forest. However, this creates a whole new set of issues, ones even more dangerous."

"As for me," Bonarb said, "I'm not going back to their filthy mine and die there. I'd rather take my chances in the cottlepine grove." All the captives voiced the same sentiments.

"I don't mean to second guess you, commander, and I know we don't have a lot of time for discussion. But maybe you should explain what you mean by more dangerous issues." Jesse chewed on his lower lip as he waited for clarification.

"The Lost Forest is so dense you need torches to see your way through it, even during dayrise. It's like darkout all the time, especially in the interior. Many have entered these woods, including loggers, explorers, miners, soldiers, and merchants. All were lost, which is how the forest earned its name. It is said to be haunted, filled with large carnivorous plants or creatures. No one who enters is ever seen again."

"Sounds squirrely, yet better than facing a school of hungry tarkks. Maybe we should employ Rule Number Two and dip outta here."

"What rule is that?" asked Chepho.

"Face your fears to overcome them." Max replied, smiling at Seth. "I agree with the former captives and the recruit. Let's try it."

"Aye lads, sounds decent to me, considering the alternatives. Time to skedaddle."

"I don't think they will follow us in there," Gelr said. "Most are afraid to enter this strange grove of timber, including me, but I'm not surrendering either. I say we proceed. If we want to survive and return these relatives to their families, the only option is escape, not fight." Each person affirmed with a nod or an uplifted hand.

"Okay, we're all agreed. On the count of three, we'll ride hard for the forest. Let's hope Brappt and his soldiers will be caught off guard, giving us a head start." Jesse closed his eyes for a moment of silent prayer and then counted, "One, Two, Three . . ."

CHAPTER 30
EDDNOK'S EVIL PLANS

Eddnok spent the night in the old mine, dreaming about hidden caves, treasures, and magical trees. Scraping sounds from picks and shovels awakened him. Since his torch had gone out during the night, all he could see was a small ray of light coming from the hole he had crawled through to access the main cavern. He relit his torch with a striking stone. The tree was still there. *Not a dream after all.* He reached up to the nearest branch and picked a fruit. Immediately, another one grew in its place. He devoured it bite by bite, savoring the sweetness, swallowing the little seeds whole, wiping the excess white juice off his chin with his shirtsleeve. With each mouthful, more and more knowledge filled his mind. The evil knowledge interested him the most. He picked one more, tucked it into his pocket, and crawled out of the entrance. When the miners saw him, they stopped digging. "Sorry sir," Joelurt, the mining chief said, "I didn't realize you stayed in there last night. Your orders from yestercycle were to enlarge the opening, so we started on the project at firstlight."

Lord Eddnok stood and stretched his back. Sleeping on a hard rock floor had stiffened his muscles. He glanced around the campsite and observed puffs of gray smoke drifting upward from the firepit. Bolgog was tending it, stirring the embers into flames and adding more kindling. Getting no response from Eddnok, the chief added, "Excuse me, sir, just wondering, do you want us to stop the dig?"

"No, no, no, don't stop. This access must be enlarged as

soon as possible. Make it two paces wide by three paces high. Concerning supports, I noticed several scraggly cottlepines down the trail. Cut and trim them for beams to reinforce the approach. I'm having our metalsmith build a bronzed locking cover for those exact measurements. After you expand the entry as specified, you and two miners will stay here and keep watch. No one is to enter under pain of death. Understand?"

"Yes Lord, understood. What about supplies?"

"I'll leave three kacks to haul timbers. The tents and all the provisions are staying here for the time being. The rest of the expedition team is leaving with me. You will secure this area until you are relieved."

"But sir, we have no weapons. What if—"

"You won't need any." He leaned over and retrieved a shovel. "No one's gonna bother you. Few people travel this abandoned trail anymore. In the event you are attacked, use this shovel to defend yourselves." He tossed it to the ground, nearly hitting one of the miners. "Once I return to Briacap, I'll dispatch a company of warders to replace your crew. They should arrive in two or three cycles. If your tunnel enlargement is completed by then, you can return to your homes." Eddnok paused to take in the northern skyline. The auburn clouds from the day before had mostly faded, which indicated the approach of a new season, one without windblowers. "That's all, chief. Now continue your work."

Senior Commander Bolgog waited for Eddnok to finish talking with Joelurt before he walked over to offer greetings and report the upsetting news. "Good dayrise, Lord. We received two homing flyer replies from Briacap before firstlight."

"What did they say?"

"Our fortress was attacked during darkout. There are reports about magical flying sticks and floating rocks."

"Pure foolishness."

"Perhaps, except those strange weapons killed a couple dozen soldiers."

"They're replaceable."

"Their families may not think so." Bolgog hesitated a moment before reading the second dispatch. "In addition to our losses, a band of assailants broke Narleen out of the stockade."

"What? How is this possible? Don't answer that! I assume some of the attackers were captured for interrogation."

"No, none captured. Two were killed. They appear to be Lower Realm militiamen. All the others escaped heading south, probably across the boundary line into the Disputed Lands."

"What a bunch of incompetents!" Eddnok spit on the ground and smeared it around with his foot. "Since our two homing flyers have returned, I want messages sent to Briacap immediately. These perpetrators must be located. Instruct the duty commander to dispatch a squad of guards to track them. Also have Briacap send flyers to our Narnj mines and alert the warders of possible attacks. These militia rebels may try to free those prisoners as well. If they make an attempt, have an ambush ready. Twenty men in two mounted contingents should suffice. And rouse the porters, we're leaving."

"What about all the gear?"

"Leave it for the miners. They're staying until armed reinforcements arrive. Now get going. We will break fast on the way off this mountain."

Eddnok dashed over to their hobbled animals and located his mount. He unstrapped a small wooden chest from his side carrier and hurried back to the treasure cave. The miners had already opened a small walk-in passage and were busy chiseling it out to specifications. He dismissed them to break their fast, then grabbed a torch and entered the cavern. He picked ten fruits from the tree, placed them carefully inside the chest, and locked the lid. He carried it over to his kack and strapped it onto his side carrier. Several porters offered to help, but he declined and cussed at them. "You blasted sloggers, mount up. We have to make Briacap before postcycle."

Lord Eddnok didn't wait for the rest of his outfit; he started down the pass by himself. The stragglers closed the gap by the time they reached Gaulmore Peak where the entire party stopped to break their fast. The expedition increased the pace as they trekked downhill, pushing their kacks at a full run through the lower sections. Two spans later, they entered Briacap, arriving during aftercycle.

Eddnok dismounted and unlatched the chest from his animal. He called out to Bolgog who was talking with a band of sentinels near the watchtower. "See me before you dismiss the crew." The commander slid off his ride and hurried over. "Two more things are expedient: First, summon Deamonn, the alchemist, and have him meet me in my office. Second, arrange for a company of ten warders to protect the hidden cave. I anticipate at least a yarn deployment. Set a rotation schedule for replacements, every thirty spans." Bolgog didn't question anything; he just bowed and rushed off to carry out Eddnok's orders. The sentinels heard their commander cursing as he left.

Eddnok ignored the two concubines who had been waiting for his return and instead entered his private office with the chest under his arm, placing it atop his desk. He closed the office door behind him and opened the lid to inspect his fruit. Remembering the one in his pocket, he pulled it out and added it to the chest. He sat in his chair and poured himself a cup of kunakk. As he sipped it, he pondered how to implement the wealth of wisdom this unique fruit mysteriously imparted.

Besides evil, the properties of the fruit contained good knowledge—ways to help people live better lives, increase crop yields, expand farmlands, improve fishing techniques, clean silty water, developed new medicines, use effective medical procedures, and a myriad of virtuous ideas—yet those things might also benefit his enemies. He couldn't allow that. Eddnok took out two scrolls of paper and began making notes, listing compounds and drawing designs. Knowledge he never understood before flowed into his thoughts. Eddnok disregarded most of the good aspects and concentrated on the evil attributes: new forms of wickedness and ways to destroy the Lower Realm. His malicious heart provided fertile ground for this immoral knowledge to sprout and grow. Instead of rejecting it, Eddnok lusted for more.

A knock at the door startled him. He jumped out of his seat and slammed the chest shut. "Enter."

Preaverca sauntered in and curtsied. "Good to see you, my Lord. I hope all is well."

"Oh, it's you, Preaverca. I was expecting the alchemist. Yes, yes, everything's wonderful. I'm glad you're back with us now. What did you find out in Tabahir?"

"As you suspected, Saephira organized a raid to rescue her lady-in-waiting. Somehow, during nightrise, her team succeeded in breaching our fortress. They freed Narleen from the stockade and escaped, causing heavy losses to our forces. You were away on a secret undertaking during the attack."

"Yes, yes, I know, go on."

"The returning raiders arrived in Tabahir after darkout. Those four cryptic outsiders were involved in the attack. Their group also included a handful of militia, Lady Saephira, Captain Waubush, and our own Commander Gelr who is a collaborator now. An informant told me they would be staying at the Copper Rail Tavern. Therefore, I rented a room and waited. Sure enough, they showed up. I snuck into the hallway and listened to their plans."

"And what are they?"

"The rebels decided to split into two parties and leave at firstlight. Saephira and Narleen are traveling to Falein Village with two militiamen, one who is wounded and needs surgery. I assume they will wait in Falein a couple cycles until he recovers before moving on to Midvill. The second party, led by Gelr and Jesse, plans to attack the mines and free Lundy and our prison laborers. I suppose they'll return to the Copper Rail thereafter."

"Okay, thank you my dear. You have been most helpful. I have a surprise for traitor Gelr and his friends. An ambush will be waiting for them in the Narnj Mountains. Sub-Commander Brappt and two armed contingents will handle that. And I already have spies in Falein. They'll keep an eye out for Saephira and Narleen. Perhaps we can capture them before they reach Midvill. To cover all possible outcomes, I'll assign a squad of sentinels to watch the Copper Rail in case the rebels return there." Moving around to the front of his desk, he asked, "What about Yhmim, Saephira's vice-leader?"

"She's waiting for your signal."

"Good, good. I will see you are well rewarded for your efforts. Right now, I have important matters to plan. You're dismissed." He gave her a lingering kiss on the lips. "If the alchemist is waiting, send him in."

Preaverca curtsied, adding a sultry wink. "As you wish, my Lord." She passed Deamonn on her way out. "Lord Eddnok is ready to see you now."

"Ah, Deamonn, my brilliant and faithful alchemist. Your assistance is enjoined."

He bowed, not exactly sure how to respond to the compliment. "How may I be of service, my Lord?"

"Tell me about the alchemy skill you specialize in. Does it include the study of chemistry?" The concept of chemistry was part of the new knowledge Eddnok gained from eating the fruit.

"Chemistry? I have never heard this term before. As for alchemy, it involves converting base metals into precious ones by transforming matter. Alchemists also combine ingredients to make universal elixirs or other useful compounds. However, I've quit trying to manipulate the structure of minerals or develop potions to prolong life. Now, I only mix common substances and record their reactions."

"Perfect, I have two mixing experiments for you. Here's the first one." Eddnok pulled out a whitish fruit out of his chest and handed it to the alchemist. "This fruit has two unique properties. I expect you to extract one and leave the other. Under no circumstances are you to taste the fruit or any concoction you make. It will kill you or cause you to go horribly mad." Deamonn frowned as he turned the fruit around in his hand to examine it. *The idiot doesn't even know I'm lying to him.*

"How will I know which property to remove?"

"Practice on bush varmints. If they act crazy, you're getting close to the elixir I desire. If they seem calm, try another formula or distilling method. This research is confidential, and if I find out you told anyone, you'll be sent to work in the mines as a prisoner. Consider this a friendly warning. As my noble and trusted servant, though, I'm sure you'll do the right thing."

Eddnok's threats and additional accolades worried Deamonn. His hand trembled as he placed the fruit into his lab coat pocket. "You said two experiments, sir."

"Ah yes, the second one, should be easier, less experimenting involved. Give it priority." He handed him a list of chemicals, the mixing directions, and the amounts required.

"You'll combine these substances, some of which you may have in your lab, and make a compound I call liquid fire. It is highly combustible. Be careful not to drop it. It will ignite on impact and burn whatever it touches. Fill three half barrels with the liquid and seal the lids. These devices must be ready in two cycles for a test."

The alchemist reviewed the list and directions. "I don't know how you conceived this mixture, but I keep all these ingredients in my stores. I can probably have your three barrel devices ready on the morrow."

"Good, good. Keep me posted on your progress." Eddnok dismissed him. After the alchemist left, Eddnok locked his chest, placed it in his secret compartment, and drew the curtain to hide it. He grabbed his drawings and left his office, bolting the door behind him.

Next, he visited the master woodsmith at his shop. Not bothering with the usual greeting, he asked the man, "Can you build this?" He showed him designs for a small prototype catapult, supported on a tripod base. It had a long arm with a counterweight on top and a bucket on the end. "It should be attached to wheels, so it can be pulled by a team of kacks."

"Wheels, what are those?"

"They're in the sketches. Logs cut in thin slices, rounded smooth, with a hole drilled in the middle for an axle." When the woodsmith asked concerning axles, Eddnok impatiently cut him off. "Those are outlined in the sketches, too. My catapult will be able to launch firebombs hundreds of paces. The alchemist is creating three of those weapons for testing." Eddnok scanned the room, scrutinizing the timber bins for materials. "You'll have a mockup of the launcher ready by two cycles, right?"

"Yeah, I can build it alright, although two cycles is pushing it."

"Then push it. Work day and night. Enlist apprentices to help you. Either way, I require a functioning mechanism for testing. It doesn't have to be fancy, just work."

"Fine, I'll start construction this span. One way or the other, sir, it will be finished on time."

"Nice! Don't let me down." Eddnok exited the woodshop and walked next door to the foundry. He gave the metalsmith specifications and measurements for a bronze cover to secure his hidden cave entry. With those concerns off his mind, he could now concentrate on more intimate matters. He returned to his private quarters and summoned Bovi and Seirlai.

Eddnok planned to test the catapult and his three liquid-fire weapons on Falein. One would be launched at the village center to see how many huts it could burn. The second aimed at a nearby farm to incinerate crops and the third against fishing operations on the lake. If the trials went well, which he assumed they would, he would have more fire weapons built and begin burning Saephira's Lower Realm, city by city, village by village, farm by farm, until it all turned into cinders.

Moreover, if his alchemist could produce an elixir from the knowledge fruit, figure out how to leach out the good properties, leaving only the evil ones, then Eddnok would make enough batches to pollute the minds of everyone in the Lower Realm with every form of wickedness. He would sneak the mixture into their yarm berry drinks and contaminate their water sources. And that would only be the beginning.

CHAPTER 31
THE LOST FOREST

Sub-Commander Brappt assumed Gelr's party would surrender. He had them surrounded, outnumbered, and more reinforcements were on the way from Briacap. He could afford to wait them out. Suddenly, ten kacks bolted toward the forest. Fifteen people, half of them riding double, jumped the trail and raced their mounts off the ridge. Brappt and several of his men launched their spears, except their throws were hurried and not well aimed. Each spear missed or fell short. His two mounted contingents pursued them, but when they realized the escapees planned to enter the northern edge of the woods, the guardsmen halted. None of the soldiers wanted to approach this haunted grove of timber, nor did Brappt. They knew the rumors all too well. The Lost Forest kept even the bravest men at bay.

Max, who rode behind all the others with an arrow notched in his bow, glanced to the rear a few times to determine if the patrol was following them into the forest. Seeing they chose otherwise, he called out to Gelr and Jesse, "Sirs, they've stopped. I think we can slow our pace now."

The group threaded their way around the dense cottlepine trees. Their green branches and oak-shaped leaves spread across the canopy, blocking out the light of dayrise. The deeper they traveled into the interior, the darker it became, and soon torches were required to see. The fleeing comrades paused to light them. However, with only six torches, they needed to pair up: one individual carried a torch while the other person kept an eye out for danger. The fugitives urged their mounts forward at a slower clip until the trees became too dense and the canopy too low, forcing everyone to dismount and proceed on foot. By instinct, their animals followed them bunched together in herd formation.

Unnatural hissing penetrated the silence, which seemed to be coming from all directions at once. The kacks started to whinny, bothered by the noise or something they saw.

"Hey recruit, can you check on our rides to see what's spooking them?"

"Sure Max, let me borrow your torch. I'll be back in a flash." Seth conducted a quick inspection, and everything seemed secure. He petted one of the kacks. "Easy girl, there's nothing to be nervous about." As an afterthought he decided to do a count. Two were missing. He shined the torch around yet didn't see them anywhere. He returned to the front, worry lines showing on his forehead. "Hey dudes, we're missing a couple animals."

"Maybe they are simply lagging behind the herd," Chepho suggested.

"No, they're gone. Zippo!" Seth raised his left hand making the zero sign with his thumb and index finger. "Only eight following us now."

The hissing continued, sounding like a coiled viper before it strikes. A kack moaned in torment. Then silence. Max, Gelr, and Jesse sprinted to the rear just in time to see a large vine disappear into the canopy, holding a kack between two jaw-shaped pods. To Jesse, the plant looked like huge Venus flytrap, black as night, with two matching petals for a mouth measuring at least twelve feet wide. Sharp thorny stems, similar to fags, protruded from the pods. They were dripping blood.

Dins of *sissssss, sissssss* echoed, growing louder. This time, though, they came from the front where the liberated prisoners huddled together, afraid to move. One of them yelled, "He's got me. Help!" Max, Gelr, and Jesse darted back to the front of the line. The plant held the oldest captive in its grip as it rose into the canopy. Max pulled out his Gladius, jumped as high as he could, and cut the vine above the mouth. It fell to the ground with the person still inside it. Jesse and Gelr pried its jaws open and pulled the man out. He was covered with a green acidic substance. It had dissolved his clothes and scalded his arms and legs. Anna searched for a mender kit but was unable to locate one, so she opened a waterskin and doused him, trying to wash off the slime. Seth helped the guy stand to his feet.

The shrieking noises were unrelenting. "We need to keep moving. In fact, we better run!" Jesse screamed. With only three swords to defend themselves, Max scrambled out ahead and swung at anything that slithered above him in the canopy. Commander Gelr and Chepho drifted to the rear and did the same thing with their blades. Seth and Anne held their persuaders, doublehanded, like short pikes. Bunched together for safety, the collective ran for their lives. Jesse hoped the remaining kacks could evade the flesh-eating plants. Notwithstanding, keeping the people safe became his top priority.

As they neared the grove's edge, light began to filter through the tree branches. No longer needing their torches, they extinguished them and kept running. Faint hissing sounds resonated behind them. As they exited the woodlands, Jesse took a head count. All of them made it to safety. Concerning their animals, seven of the ten survived the attack from the carnivorous plants. Seth's mount disappeared, along with various supplies and the extra bow in his side carrier. Fortunately, they still had three longbows and ten arrows: Gelr's bow with two, Chepho's with three, and Max's with five. The plants devoured Anna's kack, including everything in her side carrier, but since she always kept her glifstring strapped to her back, it remained intact. They also lost one of the mounts belonging to the mine.

The refugees cleared the forest near the boundary line about a league from Tabahir. Concerned about another ambush or more guard detachments, Gelr scanned the immediate area for threats. Seeing nothing obvious, he turned his attention to their transportation dilemma. "We have fifteen individuals and only seven rides. Doubling up will leave one person out. Somebody has to walk."

"I'll do it," Max offered. "Marching in adverse conditions is nothing new for me."

"Sorry Mr. Maximum. Let the young dude handle it. Besides, I've run two marathons before. Clocked a decent time. I'll probably beat the rest of you there." Seth grabbed a skin of water, waved a farewell, and took off at fast jog, carrying his fighting staff with him.

"Okay, it's settled. The rest of you mount up and stay alert. There may be pursuers out there." Gelr kept a moderate pace so Seth wouldn't fall too far behind. The riders only stopped once to let him rest and catch his breath. A couple spans later, the group approached the eastern outskirts of Tabahir. They circled around the southern end of the city and arrived at the Copper Rail by latecycle. The stable boy had stalls ready with feed and water.

"I'z knows you'd be back. My da has yur rooms ready for ya. Varmint stew tonite, my favorite. Be cookd soon."

"Thank you, young master. Is your father at the front desk?" Jesse asked.

"He be there, be glad to see ya." The boy hobbled around the stable, frowning as he counted with his fingers. "I sees 15 peple but only 7 kacks."

"Yeah, we're short a few rides. You know where we can purchase a couple more."

"Tlk to da. He'll kno ere to get um."

"Much appreciated."

The boy beamed with his toothless grin and began putting their animals into stalls for the evening as the tired party climbed the stairway to the lobby.

"Good dayrise, what's left of it," Nanlon offered. "All the rooms are yours. Hot dinner tonight in the dining hall, varmint stew with all the fixings. Be ready in a couple spans."

"Your son said to ask about buying two extra mounts. We lost several on our . . ." Jesse paused to consider his wording, "our scouting trip."

"No need to explain. We take no names, make no judgments here." He smiled, knowing Jesse had heard his refrain before. "Sure, I can have two rides delivered to the stables by next cycle."

"How much do we owe?"

"Nothing, my compliments, a gift for the Great Lady. Hope she's all right." Jesse started to respond. "Don't answer that. The less I know the better." Nanlon reached underneath the counter and pulled out an old trunk. "I see a number of your scouts are poorly dressed. I have an assortment of old clothes in here. Most were left by guests. The others are mine before I outgrew them." He grabbed his rounded belly and tried to push it under his belt. "See what I mean. At any rate, you are welcome to them. Take the chest upstairs with ya." He slid it across the counter to Jesse. "Well, I got your meal cooking on my stove. Gotta tend it." The owner started to walk toward the kitchen entrance but turned around. "My tavern is being watched by two men around the corner. Thus far, they haven't done much but look. Thought you should know."

"Thank you for the warning, sir." Max glanced out the window. "Hmm, they're gone now. For how long, who knows? I'll keep watch for a while." He motioned for everybody to settle into their guestrooms. "Get some rest. I'll catch ya later for dinner." Max checked his Gladius, leaned his bow against the windowsill, sorted his five remaining arrows, and reclined on a nearby settee.

The freed prisoners were overjoyed to have a basin of water and decent clothes. After washing and changing into fresh garments, they crashed into their beds, and along with everyone else, slept until the dinner bell rang. Starving for a home-cooked meal, the group hustled downstairs and joined Max in the dining hall. Being the only guests at the Copper Rail, the collective had the entire dining hall to themselves. They enjoyed a hot dinner, the first one the captives had eaten in many cycles. Afterwards, the fugitives rehashed their harrowing escape and began discussing upcoming plans. Gelr spoke first. "Chepho and I have decided to leave on the morrow before firstlight and see these men safely to their homes. Most lived in Beayama before being captured and forced to work in the Narnj mines. One wants to return to Cali Village, the other to Bayegulf."

"That makes ten people. Can you get by with five kacks?" Jesse asked. "This will leave two for us, but the owner says he can have a couple more mounts delivered to the stables tomorrow."

"Five works for us. Besides, we can ride double. What about your party, any plans?"

"Before you lads make any hasty decisions, maybe you should see this translation. I made a copy Eddnok didn't know about. It comes from a scroll he discovered in his archives. It's written in an ancient text, similar to Hebrew, except much older. Using a rhyming pattern, it gives clues to the location of a hidden cave and mysterious treasure." Lundy pulled the folded document out of his boot and spread it on the table. "Eddnok planned to search for it before he imprisoned me. I say we oughta discover what this treasure be or represents. Sounds a wee bit ominous for my liking."

Jesse leaned over to get closer look at the wording. "Reads like a poem or song." He passed it over to Gelr. "Commander, you know Eskaonus better than the rest of us. What do you make of this?"

Gelr studied the manuscript for the longest time. "Hmm, I think the *forest dead* is the Narmoot, and the *mountains red* are in the Colrath range. Those hills have a lot of reddish shale and rocks, and the *hidden cave* could be one of the old, abandoned mines near Gaulmore Peak. If you add in the references of *uphill, trail, highest cleft,* and *peaks,* I would say they are describing the rugged wilderness areas northwest of Briacap."

"How long to get there from here?" Jesse asked.

"If you mean the old mining areas? It would be a two-cycle trip, both ways, through hostile territory. And if Eddnok is searching for this mysterious treasure as well, he will have trackers hunting everywhere, not to mention armed guards. It would be a suicide mission."

"Aye. Me thinks we must find out one way or the other. It might be what we came here to find, right Jesse?"

"Maybe. Let's sleep on it and decide in the morning. Oh, one more thing Rev. Can I borrow your manuscript to copy into my journal? I'll return it tomorrow."

"A dandy idea. With another copy, I won't dinna fash if I lose mine."

As soon as the discussion broke up, they retired to their quarters. Everybody was exhausted. Gelr, Chepho, and the freed comrades shared three rooms. Jesse's crew took the fourth one. Since sleeping five in a four-person unit would be a bit cramped, Max offered to stay in the lobby and snooze by the front window where he could keep eye out for anyone spying on them. With all the busyness, raids and rescues, Jesse hadn't written in his journal for a while, so he pulled it out and flipped to a blank page:

Entry Ten

Busy few cycles, I mean days, so I haven't been recording entries. Good news. We found and rescued Lundy, along with eight other prisoners who were being held captive by Lord Eddnok. He's as wicked as they come. I suspect Eddnok is behind the evil influence here.

Lundy translated an ancient manuscript that reveals a hidden cave with a mysterious treasure (attachment below). It might hold the answers we are seeking. He thinks we should focus on finding it. Me too. Except getting there is another matter. We'll decide in the morning.

Attachment

If treasure is what you seek then don't be meek, nor forgo the rift near the highest cliff. Buried deep within lies a secret twin of the richest gift known to gods or men. Take an uphill pace to seek a taste of wisdom sublime and power divine. So follow the trail to the mountains red, through the forest dead, past waters shed, and peaks that grow during daylight glow. Past ancient grave lays hidden cave where treasure awaits for a ruler of fate.

As firstlight dawned, Commander Gelr, Chepho, and the eight former captives arose and gathered their belongings, which included two swords, two bows, and the dinner leftovers the owner had packed for them. They crept into the lobby. Seeing Max asleep on the settee by the window, they slipped past, trying not to disturb him, and entered the passage to the stables. The stable boy had five of the seven mounts standing in a line and ready to go. "Ba guys out ther, two of thm. Been watchin stables al nightrise. Be carful."

"We will." Gelr peered around the corner and didn't see any adversaries. The route appeared clear, so his outfit mounted up and rode out. No sooner had they left the stables then a gruff voice shouted, "Halt where you are, commander traitor! We are taking those prisoners off your hands. Drop your weapons!" Two sentinels popped out of doorway with spears in hand, holding two more at the ready.

Gelr and Chepho eyed one another and nodded. "Okay, we'll throw down our weapons. The others here are unarmed." Gelr turned and whispered to the men, "Get ready to ride hard." The commander and militiaman unstrapped their bows from their side carriers. Instead of surrendering the weapons, they each notched an arrow and let it fly: *whish, whish.* Before the two sentries could aim their spears, they dropped to the ground, surprised, grunting in pain with arrows sticking in their chests. Assuming more combatants were on the way, Gelr and Chepho didn't stop to retrieve their spent arrows. They turned south and galloped away. Their fellow escapees rallied their mounts and rode beside them, not looking back.

All the commotion outside awakened Max. He peeked out the window and spotted Gelr's bunch riding out of town, leaving a trail of dust in the air. Two men lay in the road, pierced with arrows. Across the street, a handful of soldiers were heading for the front door of the tavern. Nanlon came out of his bedroom, half dressed. "What's happening?"

"We've been compromised," Max replied. "Try to stall them while I alert my friends." He rushed upstairs to the fourth room and bolted the door behind him. "Get up guys, we're about to be captured." He unsheathed his sword.

Downstairs, a squad of sentinels pushed the doors open and stomped around the foyer and dining hall. "Good dayrise gentlemen. Anxious for lodging are ya? We have vacancies. One credit per person, four in a unit, meals included."

"Let me see your register," ordered the squad leader.

"We don't keep one. We take no names, make no judgments here."

"Where are the tenants from last night?"

"They left early. How many places do you require?"

"Don't mess with me. There are two kacks in the stables. Whose are they?"

"Mine, payment for overdue rents."

"Guards, check all the apartments." The squad leader grabbed the owner by arm, pinned his right hand to the counter, and pulled out his dagger. "If I find out you lied to me, you're gonna be sorry in more ways than one." After one last eye to eye glare at Nanlon, the lead released his grip, sheathed the knife, and joined his men searching the rooms. Three doors were open, the quarters vacant, beds made. The fourth was latched.

The sentinels pounded on the locked door. "Open up! We know you're in there!"

Anna whispered, "What do we do?"

"Not sure, Annie, we are cut off, surrounded." Jesse bit his lower lip and paced in circles, trying to think. "No windows, no side door. I'm open for suggestions."

"Too bad we can't transport to a different location like we did in heaven."

"Has anybody tried it?" asked Seth.

"I attempted it when I was Eddnok's guest, I mean jailbird. Tried several times. Didn't work. I surely wish it had. Really wanted to get away from that bampot."

"Since all five of us are together again, maybe it will now. It did for us to get to Eskaonus." Anna swung her musical instrument over her shoulder and went to stand by Lundy.

"Open up in there! We hear people whispering. If you don't release the door, we're going to break it in." Not waiting, they started to pry at the hinges with their spears.

"What's the exact phrasing you use for transporting?" Jessie asked the reverend. "You mentioned it once, the first time we met in heaven."

"Aye, in the meditation garden it was." Using his index finger, Lundy made a tapping motion on the side of his forehead. "Just think where you want to be and you're there."

"Squares with me," Seth added. "We better skitty out of here before these turkeys catch us."

The little band of advocates snatched their belongings and formed a circle. Jesse pulled the scroll translation out his satchel and handed it to Lundy who quickly stuffed it into boot. Anna whispered a prayer, then reached over and squeezed the reverend's hand, gripping it tightly in hers. She would not lose him again. Seth mouthed *Rule Number One, Rule Number Two*. Max returned the Gladius to his scabbard. Each hand grasped another. They were ready.

"So where do we want to be?" Jesse asked.

"The hidden cave," Lundy replied. A moment later, the soldiers broke down the door and stared inside. The room was empty.

CHAPTER 32
CONCERNING NEWS

Chesedel popped into Jesse's room in heaven after requesting a consultation with Uzziel. As he waited for the cherub to arrive, he sat down at the desk and opened a scroll containing the last three transfer messages from Jesse's journal, which usually arrived at the Hall of Records as soon as he posted an entry. The angel read and reread the recent logs, pondering the implications with heartfelt concern. A bright light flashed, and Uzziel appeared in the entryway. Chesedel rose and bowed to show his respect for a senior-ranking angel. "Thank you for meeting with me. I thought Jesse's room would be less crowded and more private."

"Good idea. The Fountain of Living Water is a popular gathering place and always packed with saints. It will be a little quieter here." Uzziel embraced Chesedel, arm to arm, in the typical gesture of appreciation among fellow angelic servants. "I assume you have updates from Eskaonus?"

"Yes, we have received three more journal reports. Entry eight was about Annabelle being fully recovered and Jesse's new resolve as the group's leader."

"No doubt we have you to thank for her healing and his change of heart. Visiting Eskaonus was the right decision. What about the other entries?"

"The next two, entries nine and ten, involve rescue attempts and results. They located and freed Lundy MacBain from jail. The team was also instrumental in securing the release of several captives from the southern province who were wrongly imprisoned by Eddnok."

"All sounds most encouraging."

"I concur, except this attachment bothers me." Chesedel pointed to entry ten, which included Lundy's translation of an ancient scroll describing a mysterious treasure. "Tell me what you think about this wording."

The Cherubim walked over to the desk and studied the document, frowned, shook his head a few times, and frowned some more. "This is not good. The references of *seek a taste*, *wisdom divine*, and *gift known to gods* sounds like the tree of the knowledge of good and evil."

"How is that possible? Didn't that tree disappear from the garden ages ago? No one knows what happened to it."

"Well, God does, assuming the tree exists in the same form it did."

"Exists? Isn't everything in heaven eternal?"

"Yes, so we presume. However, God sets those parameters and there may be exceptions. Either way, most of us believe if the tree survived then God hid it somewhere safe where the wisdom of good and evil would be protected. Such insights are powerful, too powerful for humanity, even for us angels, and in the wrongs hands it could be devastating."

"My concern likewise and why I wanted to bring Jesse's last journal entry to your attention."

"I'm glad you did. As you well know, elChesed, I was on earth during those early days. After Eve and Adam ate from the knowledge tree, God sent a detachment of cherubim with flaming swords to guard the way into Eden's garden. No one was allowed access to either the Tree of Life or the knowledge tree. God removed the Tree of Life later and took it to heaven, where it remains. The tree of the knowledge of good and evil disappeared. I have no idea where it ended up; none of us angels do, although I seriously doubt God replanted it in Eskaonus." Uzziel started pacing around the room as he pondered the situation. "The fruit from this tree released understanding, both good and evil, yet the tree itself was not evil, nor was the fruit. God designed it as a test for humanity."

"A test humanity failed."

"Sadly, that's true. God allowed the first man and woman

to eat of every tree in the garden, even the Tree of Life. Only the fruit from the knowledge tree was forbidden. Humanity did not need such understanding to live, only the awareness of God and a simple faith in Him."

Chesedel rolled up the journal's transfer messages and tucked them into his sash. "I wept when Satan, one of our own, disguised himself as a serpent and tricked Eve in to believing his half-truths. Most of heaven felt the sorrow." Tears formed in Chesedel's eyes as he spoke. "We watched in silence as God's first created humans partook of the forbidden fruit, disobeying Him and thereby releasing sin into the world."

"The fruit was prohibited for this very reason. We all know what happened in a few generations. Wickedness became so widespread that people's thoughts were only evil continually. Corruption multiplied on the earth and evil hearts begat more evil. I wonder if Satan stole one of those fruits before God rebuked him in Eden." Uzziel's wings unfolded as he walked back and forth, the glowing white tips almost touching the ceiling. "If so, he has access to hundreds of seeds, maybe thousands. Our sly devil may have planted one of those seeds in a hidden cave on Eskaonus. If he did, this news is indeed grave."

"I'm sorry, Uzziel, maybe I should have notified you before now. It does sound deadly serious."

"Lundy's translation says the treasure is a *secret twin*, which I'm now convinced is a knowledge tree, not the original tree, but a clone of something that should not exist. If a person on Eskaonus were to eat its fruit, he or she would have unlimited comprehension not meant for humanity or anyone else. Moreover, if any had corrupted hearts, they could spread wickedness and chaos everywhere. Perhaps Satan's plan was to use the same temptations on Eskaonus he tried on earth in some hateful attempt to get even with God. And if Lucifer planted more seeds in other worlds . . . that would be even more devastating."

"What do we do about Eskaonus?"

"Trust God. He chose our five-member group for several reasons. The main ones involve restoring the knowledge of God and saving the Eskaonites from evil. Beyond those, He wants our emissaries to experience the freedom of choice, provide second chances to redeem past failures, and allow them to mature in the ways of God. In fact, He redeems all believers for a divine purpose and it's not to play harps or float around on celestial clouds. Yes, I know, I used a human stereotype." A brief grin formed on his face before turning solemn again. "This overused expectation is not even close to God's intention for the redeemed. His greatest hope is for them to have opportunities to minister, use their giftings, and if willing, to sacrifice their lives for the benefit of others just as His Son did."

"I don't mean to interrupt your line of thought because I enjoy listening to your insights."

"And I yours. Speak freely, elChesed."

"Should I travel to Eskaonus again?"

"Yes, I believe it would be prudent but only to observe. Find out more about this treasure and see if our concerns are warranted. However, allow the individuals we sent there to accomplish their task and conclude it. We must trust them as God does. The items our envoys took with them will help towards that end."

"Agreed. I won't interfere. Can I still minster encouragement if deemed expedient?" Chesedel asked for clarification.

"Of course. Are we not all ministering spirits sent forth to minister?"

"Indeed we are." After the conversation ended, the angels held hands, prayed for each team member, the inhabitants of Eskaonus and for rising evil to be defeated. Then in a flash, they were gone.

CHAPTER 33
HIDDEN CAVE

A bright light flashed, followed by the sound of distant thunder, and five people appeared out of nowhere. The three miners, who had been setting timber support beams near the opening, froze when they saw the strange sight. Reacting in fear, two of them seized their picks, the other a shovel, and they charged forward. Jesse swung his leadership staff, swiping at the feet of the closest man who fell backwards, dropping his pick. Max drew his Gladius but kept it at his side. Seth and Anna set up in defensive stances, holding their persuaders at the ready. Seeing Joelurt, their crew chief, lying on the ground, the two advancing miners stopped in their tracks and released their tools.

"Lads, there is no need for violence here. We only want to take a wee peek inside this dig of yours."

Joelurt retorted, "We cannot allow. Lord Eddnok forbids it under pain of death, namely ours, if we let anyone enter."

"I understand your concern," Jesse replied. "Orders from rulers are important. We have orders from a ruler, too, someone with higher authority than Eddnok. Therefore, we are going to conduct a search." Jesse helped the older man sit upright against a boulder and motioned to his coworkers to join him. "Seth, please cut off three sections from your rope and bind these fine gentlemen while we investigate this cave." After Seth secured the men's hands and feet, Jesse added, "Rest assured, you will be released unharmed once we're finished."

Lundy, Max and Jesse grabbed torches at the entrance and struck them aflame. They led the group into the mineshaft.

About twenty paces in, the tunnel opened up into a main cavern where a large dark shape came into view. At first, the object appeared silhouetted. As they approached, the more distinct it became. "Dudes, it's a tree, a big one! Runs all the way to the ceiling."

"How can a tree grow in complete darkness?" Anna asked. "Makes no sense."

Lundy moved to within ten feet and raised his torch high over his head. "It's not just any tree, laddies. Looks like the tree of the knowledge of good and evil."

Anna followed behind Lundy. "You mean from the story in Genesis."

"Aye, could be. As a minister, I spent a lot of time reading the early accounts of creation during my stay in heaven. The scroll room keeps a record on all events. There are references to a knowledge tree, including several drawings and a description. I'm telling you, that's it . . . or one similar."

"How is that possible?" challenged Jesse. "Why would God replant it here?"

"I don't think He did. The original knowledge tree disappeared from the garden, and there's no written record of its whereabouts. Eddnok's ancient manuscript described the treasure as *a secret twin*, and if this tree is the aforementioned find, it must be a duplicate or counterfeit." Lundy wandered underneath for a closer view. The limbs were massive, the foliage covered with a whitish fruit. He reached up and picked one from a lower branch. Instantly, another fruit grew in the same exact spot.

"Jeepers Preach, you shouldn't handle the forbidden fruit if you catch my drift."

"Eve added the touching part, Seth, not God. It was not the touching of the fruit God forbid, it's the eating of it." To put Seth at ease, Lundy dropped his piece and tried to squash into the ground, yet the fruit remained whole, undamaged. "Hmm, apparently not a fake. All this hoopla makes more sense now. The clues about *known to gods*, *tasting wisdom*, and *receiving power* all point to the tree of the knowledge of good and evil. If Eddnok ate some of this fruit, we are in a wee bit of trouble, as are the people of Eskaonus. The knowledge tree was forbidden because the fruit released knowledge not meant for mortals."

"Wasn't the tree a radical test for those two dudes in the garden?"

"Aye, it was for sure, except more. Remember what occurred when they partook of the fruit, and later, what happened to their descendants. Wickedness spread, uncontrolled. Every imaginable thought embraced evil. I'm not saying the tree caused all those results. Human nature played a big part. Still, this tree, even if it's only a copy, cannot stay on this world. It was forbidden then, and I don't think God has changed His mind. We must remove or eliminate it. No doubt, it's one reason we're here, right Jesse?"

"Apparently, so how do we do get rid of the tree?" Jesse asked. "Aren't things from heaven supposed to be eternal? My satchel, which contains my lamp and journal, couldn't be burned, nor Anna's musical instrument crushed, nor Max's sword damaged. Even Seth's corded rope can't break or be shortened. Not sure how your pocket version of John's gospel fits in, but I assume it's probably indestructible as well."

"Concerning those items, there's something I've been wondering about." Anna unstrapped her glifstring and using two hands extended it in front of her. "What if these objects were more than our choices, but rather ordained gifts to help us succeed? If so, each one could be part of the solution."

"Man, that's heavy! Let me try my rope. The angel called it a *tikvah*, a cord of hope and possibilities." Seth uncoiled it, snapped like a whip and knocked off a fruit on a lower branch. Before it landed on the ground, the fruit vanished and none grew back to replace it. "Cool, it worked."

"Good thinking, recruit. However, there must be thousands. It would take weeks to snap them all off. Time we don't have if Eddnok has evil intent on his mind."

"Yikes, I better start cracking." Seth set his rope for additional strike. "Haste makes—"

Lundy raised both hands. "Hold off a minute, laddie. If we are supposed to use the items we brought with us, allow me to give mine a shot." He pulled out his Gospel of John, unfolded it, and scanned the chapters. "Ah, here it is, John 14:26. The verse says the Spirit of God will bring to remembrance what's important." He refolded the Scripture scroll and stuffed it into his boot. "Alright folks, bow your heads while I say a wee prayer." He pressed his palms together and lifted them upward. "Dear Lord, help us recollect what we need to remember. Amen!"

"Hey Preach, that's gotta be the shortest prayer I ever heard."

"It be true, Seth. Less is more as they say." Anna grinned at their playful exchange. Suddenly, her face took on a serious appearance; her eyes opened wide. "What is it, Annabel?"

"After you prayed, I remembered a truth about praise. It releases the anointing. When Paul and Silas sang hymns, prison doors were opened and chains loosed. Shall we see what an anointed praise song will do? One of my favorites is by Thomas Chisholm." Anna began playing the old familiar tune on her glifstring. Her picking filled the air with sweet, harmonious sounds, and then she added the words:

Great is thy faithfulness, O God my Father,
there is no shadow of turning with thee;
Thou changest not, thy compassions, they fail not;
as thou hast been, thou forever wilt be.

Great is Thy faithfulness!
Great is Thy faithfulness!
Morning by morning new mercies I see;
all I have needed thy hand hath provided.
Great is thy faithfulness, Lord, unto me!

As Anna strummed her instrument and sang each verse of the hymn, a bright misty cloud of anointing filled the interior of the cave. The tree responded and began to glow; even the limbs seemed to sway as if a gentle wind were blowing across the branches. Once the song ended, the tree was noticeably smaller. The top no longer touched the ceiling. The branches were also shorter in length.

"Dudes, did you see what happened?"

"Aye, an interesting development. Maybe we're on the right track, eh?"

"You know, Annie, it's really funny, especially since I don't know the Bible too well, but a thought just popped into my mind as you were singing."

"Like what Jess?"

"If the anointing removes hindrances and if this tree is a yoke upon the necks of the Eskaonites—"

"That spiritual truth comes from Isaiah 10:27," Lundy interjected. "And one translation says the anointing oil destroys those yokes."

"I wonder . . ." Jesse opened his satchel. "My candle lamp smells fragrant and never runs out fuel. Maybe it contains anointed oil." He reached inside and removed his lamp. "Okay guys, here goes my piece of the puzzle." Jesse tossed it at the tree. His vessel shattered into tiny pieces, splattering oil everywhere, releasing the pleasant scent of frankincense. The liquid ran down the trunk, pooled at the roots, and soaked into the ground. As it did, the tree's foliage radiated a silvery light as bright as the sun at high noon. The fruit glimmered, too, sparkling like white glitter. Again, the tree decreased in size, now half as tall as it was before.

"Guess it's my turn." Max raised his heaven-issued weapon, rushed forward and swung with all his might. The blade sliced through the trunk as if it were butter. As the tree fell, the misty cloud dissipated, leaving the walls bathed in a shimmering of rainbow colors. A moment later, Chesedel, the guardian angel appeared. He spoke nothing, simply nodded, then disappeared. The tree vanished, too, as if it were never there. The colorful bow slowly dimmed away.

"Wow! Freaky awesome."

"Aye, the anointing. That was the ticket."

"Praise too," Anna added. "Should I sing another hymn?"

"Later perhaps, right now we have three individuals out front I promised to release." The party followed Jesse to the entrance. Seth untied the prisoners, stuffing the cut pieces of his rope into his pocket. The men stood up, rubbed their wrists to get the blood circulating, and waited to hear their fates. "Like I vowed, you are all free to go."

"Did you steal Lord Eddnok's treasure?"

"No, we did not," replied Jesse. "Nevertheless, it's gone. I suggest you three leave this place and avoid returning to Briacap. If you escape south along the leading edge of the Blighte to Midvill or Cali Village, you will find safety and refuge from Eddnok and his forces. Those decisions, however, are yours to make. As for us, we're departing the way we came."

"Where to JW?" Seth asked.

"I say we transport to the Copper Rail to retrieve our kacks, check on the owner and his son, and then rejoin Saephira in Falein." A short discussion ensued, and everybody agreed with Jesse. "Great, let's join hands and think where we want to . . ." A light flashed, followed by a distant rumble. The five strangers disappeared as the miners watched, blinking their eyes in disbelief. Afterward, all three workers lit torches and raced inside the tunnel to inspect the cavern. They found nothing except a few potsherds.

"The treasure's gone and our necks are on the line. What are we going to do now?" asked one of the crew.

Joelurt, the mining chief replied, "I don't know about you two, but I'm going to follow the advice of those mystics. Besides, waiting here is unwise and retuning to Briacap could be risky." One person agreed with the chief, and together they packed supplies, left their tools where they lay, and rode their animals west, heading for the western edge of the Blighte. The third miner decided to return to Briacap and report in to Lord Eddnok.

In the cave, pieces from the shattered candle lamp miraculously reassembled. Chesedel materialized, recovered the vessel, and faded into thin air.

At the Copper Rail, a slight shaking vibrated the upstairs hallway, followed by a muted rumble. In an instant, the five emissaries were standing in their room, still holding hands. Nanlon felt the movement, heard noises, and hurried upstairs from the lobby to investigate. "So you guys are back. Where did you go? No, don't tell me. It was quite a trick, though. You fooled those chumps big time." The owner glanced around the room. Other than the broken door, everything looked normal.

"What happened after we left?" Jesse asked.

"You mean disappeared?" Nanlon waited a moment,

hoping for telling reveal on their faces. Seeing none, he continued, "Not a whole lot, just more harassment. The squad leader came downstairs and threatened me again, along with my son. I told him everyone had already left, which was the truth since you weren't here. Anyway, the guards stormed out to search elsewhere for ya. I wouldn't stick around too long. They'll probably return in a span or two."

"Understood. How are you and your son faring?"

"We're okay now. Whew!" He feigned wiping sweat from his forehead. "It was a little tense for a bit . . ." He paused, squinted his eyes as if trying to recall an important detail. "There's something else I was supposed to tell ya." He scratched his balding scalp. "Oh yeah, I remember. Those two rides you requested were delivered a span ago. They're in the stables ready to go, and my son has loaded a haversack of provisions into their side carriers." While the visiting continued, Jesse's group followed Nanlon out to the lobby area. "Best if you take the southern route out of town. I hope the Great Lady is safe. Don't answer that. The less I know the better."

"Thank you, sir," Max grunted in a deep voice, followed by a slap on Nanlon's shoulder. "You and the boy covered for us and treated us more than fair, both times."

The tavern proprietor smiled. "Next time you're in town, we'll leave a light out for ya."

Lundy reached into his boot and removed the translated copy of Eddnok's treasure map. He tore the scroll into shreds and handed the pieces to Nanlon. "We don't need this anymore. Please burn these scraps in your fireplace."

Having said their goodbyes, they bounded down the rear steps to the stables. "I'z knew ya be back. I'z tell um northen gurds nothin." The stable boy opened the stalls and led four kacks out into the entry. He peeked around the stable door. "It clear out ther, bettr get goin."

Seth handed the boy his knife. "Take care little dude and thanks for doing us a solid." The boy proudly tucked the blade into his belt, grabbed his rake, and started cleaning out the stalls for the next guests.

The party traveled south until they were out of sight of

Tabahir and then turned west. Since Lundy didn't know how to steer a kack, he sat double behind Annabel. Max, Jesse, and Seth rode their own mounts. Jesse decided to stop at Gelr's old campsite in the Disputed Lands, hoping to avoid detection. They would spend the night there and move on to Falein Village on the morrow.

CHAPTER 34
DESTRUCTION AND DECEIT

Saephira, Narleen, and Captain Waubush enjoyed a restful stay at Falein Village. Their militia chief, who received surgery for his injured shoulder, seemed to be recovering but still needed several more cycles of healing before he was ready to travel again. The captain and Lady Saephira decided to leave him at the mender's aid station and travel on to Midvill where they hoped to recruit more people to serve in their militia. Midvill was a neutral city located on the boundary line, halfway between the upper and lower provinces. Most residents considered it part of the Lower Realm.

Leaving a kack behind so the chief could join them later, Saephira and Narleen, under the protection of Captain Waubush, rode out of Falein Village at firstlight. Unknown to them, spies had been watching their every move since they arrived in the village, keeping Eddnok advised with homing flyers as to their activities. Two ambush units dispatched earlier, waited in reserve by the lake, pretending to be anglers. When the escorted party approached Falein Lake, the guards attacked them.

Two spears flew toward Waubush. One clipped him in the leg and the other pierced the haunches of his kack, which bucked, throwing the captain onto the ground. He rolled over, scrambled to his feet, and drew his sword to face his foes. Saephira dismounted, unstrapped her bow from the side carrier, and unleashed her last three arrows in rapid succession. Two hit their targets; one veered to the left and ricocheted off a rock. The wounded men moaned and fell to the ground, giving her a short reprieve until more guardsmen raced towards her. Saephira tossed her longbow aside, withdrew her dagger, and waited. Not having any weapons to defend herself, Narleen slid off her animal and scanned for an escape route between the lakeshore and trail. From behind, the second unit advanced and blocked her only path. Both women were surrounded.

The captain fought on, dropping four assailants with his sword. Because the guards were unable to subdue Waubush with swordplay, they retreated five paces to stay away from his deadly blade. Instead, they tossed a barrage of throwing knives at him. Although Waubush tried to evade, he couldn't outmaneuver all of them. One knife sliced his neck, hitting an artery. Blood gushed down his shirt. He doubled over and tumbled to the ground, dead.

Saephira watched in horror as her captain fell. She had lost Captain Melmandus in the rockslide on Onnie Passage and now Captain Waubush was gone. She began weeping, overcome with grief, exhausted from all the conflicts and endless struggles. Narleen ran to her side to make their final stand together, expecting they would both be killed next, except the soldiers halted their attack. "Tie the women to their mounts!" the squad leader shouted. "Leave the dead bodies for someone else to bury. And hurry! We must depart Falein before this place burns to cinders."

"Where are you taking us?"

"You'll find out soon enough, ladies." He snapped his fingers and pointed to one of his men. "Make sure to gag them. I don't wanna hear them yapping their tongues at me all cycle."

The ambushers and their women captives arrived at a secret location north of the upper boundary line, where a camouflaged holding tent had been erected in the Kunakk Vineyards. Lady Saephira and her lady-in-waiting were dragged inside, still gagged, and bound hand and foot. Two sentries watched the tent entrance. Two more sat around a firepit drinking kunakk and gaming with gambling stones. After making sure everything was secure at the camp, the squad leader walked over to the nearby village to send off two flyer messages.

To Briacap: Captured Lady S. and Narleen at firstlight. Proceed with tests as planned. —Nakk Village

To Beayama: Yhmim, I'm sorry to inform you that Lady S. and Narleen are dead. You're the leader now. Our condolences to all concerned. —Falein Village

Due to the short distance involved, Briacap received the message from Nakk in less than a quarter span. The catapult, finished ahead of schedule, had already been transported to Nakk Village during the night. At forecycle, the weapon team wheeled the catapult into firing range of Falein. Lord Eddnok arrived a half span later, excited, giddy, his delight almost uncontainable. He could hardly wait to see the results from his liquid fire tests. "Aim for the village square first."

The team loaded the first barrel, raised the counterweight, and let it drop. The projectile flew high into the air, traveling farther than Eddnok imagined. It arched downward and struck Falein Village almost dead center. The barrel burst, igniting the liquid mixture, spreading fire along every path: huts were burned, bodies incinerated, plants and trees scorched. Disoriented, residents ran out of their homes trying to escape the liquefied flames. The firebomb destroyed the village square on impact. Adjacent areas burned out of control. There were few survivors.

"Perfect shot!" Eddnok danced a jig around the launch site, pleased with the results. "Now let's aim for the nearest farm." The next launch hit a large farm of maize. In moments, the crops were devastated, fried to a crisp. The blazes spread to adjacent farmlands. Only burnt stalks remained.

"Good, good. Have the kacks pull the catapult closer to the lake and target the northern docks." The third barrel overshot the docks, landing in the water. Liquid fire spread across the surface, setting any vessel it touched aflame. Those who were fishing, jumped off their boats, only to land in the burning water. The inferno dispersed in a wide circle until it reached the docks, turning them into smoldering scraps of wood.

"Tests successful, good job everyone!" He made the rounds, slapping shoulders and shaking hands. "Okay, okay, enough celebration for now. Wheel my catapult back to Nakk and hide it in the vineyards. I'm returning to Briacap to have more firebombs produced." The weapon team members were sickened by the results and regretted helping Eddnok, yet they still obeyed his orders, fearful he might harm them or their families if they refused.

By midcycle, the fictitious flyer message from Falein Village arrived in Beayama. The postal clerk rushed it over to the vice-leader's residence. Yhmim had expected it. After waiting for yarns, the time had come for Eddnok's planned takeover of Beayama. She wrote an official notification and attached the flyer message. She instructed the clerk to send a shorter version by homing flyer to their villages and cities. Later, she would follow up by dispatching riders to deliver the original declaration to all province destinations.

Official Notification

Dear Citizens:

With a heavy heart, I must report Lady Saephira has died. I just received confirmation she failed in her attempt to rescue Narleen, her lady-in-waiting. They both perished in the endeavor, sacrificing their lives in service of our city and the Lower Realm.

I am declaring two cycles of mourning, after which we will set up memory tables for both women in the city center. As your vice-leader, I have assumed Saephira's positon as leader, and I hope you will honor me as you have honored her. Rest assured, I'll continue to rule with your best interests at heart. There will be changes, of course, but all will be well for those who are law-abiding residents.

By order of Lady Yhmim

She called to her personal attendants who were stationed outside her quarters. Both aides entered, the man bowed, the woman curtsied. "Good dayrise, Vice-leader, how can we be of service?"

"I am no longer the vice-leader. Lady Saephira is dead. I am the *Leader* now." The servants stared at one another, bewildered, not sure how to respond.

A few moments of awkward silence passed before the woman replied, "I am sorry, my Lady. This news must have come as quite a shock."

"It did." She handed the document to the male servant. "Take this notice and post it everywhere in the city. Then I want both of you to clean out Saephira's office and sleeping quarters. Confiscate all items: clothing, personal effects, official documents, and put them into storage. I am moving into her residence immediately." The attendants hurried off, whispering, shaking their heads, wondering why all the rush.

When Ottaar read the notification, she sensed deception. Something wasn't right—the suddenness, the wording, facts left out, and all too convenient—it stunk like a rotted varmint. Angry, she yanked it off her building, stormed inside and tossed the notice on her table. *Better brew some Anatora tea to settle my nerves.*

A knock at the door drew her focus elsewhere. "Excuse me, ma'am. I spotted the mender sign outside your door. I have a couple men here who are in pretty bad shape. Can you help them?"

"Sure, come on in. Tell your men to take a seat and I'll check them over." She retrieved her mender kit from the counter and began her examination, then stopped. "What have you been doing, starving these men? They look as if they haven't eaten anything in a half a yarn."

"Well, they probably haven't, not much anyway. They were prisoners in Eddnok's mining facility for at least that long, maybe longer. A group of us rescued them. Nine were saved, including an older man named Lundy."

"Hmm, Lundy you say. That's interesting. I would like to inquire more about this rescue, but first let me get these men into beds. Later, I'll ask the kitchen cook at the Great Hall to fix a nice dinner for them." She placed her mender kit back on the shelf. "All they need are seven cycles of wholesome food, plenty of sleep, and new clothes. Right now, though, a few spans of rest and a hot meal food will do them good." From a chest on the bottom shelf, Ottaar removed spare clothing she kept on hand for her patients and tucked it under her arm. "Gentlemen, follow me upstairs." As soon as the men were settled into a spare room, she returned to speak to the stranger. She had many questions.

"Please take a seat at my table and tell me about this band of would-be rescuers." She pulled out a chair and joined him. "Who were they, and who are you?"

"My name is Commander Gelr, ma'am. There were six of us on the rescue team: a militiaman named Chepho and four others. Their names were Jesse, Seth, Anna, and a big guy named Maximus who gave me this weapon." He slid the bow across the table to Ottaar. "I'm also interested in obtaining more of these flying sticks." Gelr placed a thin rod with a sharp whittled point on the table. "I only have one left."

Ottaar retrieved the bow and inspected it. "I've seen this design before. Concerning those little sticks, I helped the big guy make them. They're called arrows."

"Yes ma'am, that's the term he used."

"I may be able to help you restock. In the meantime, let me give you an update on our activities. The woodsmith and I have constructed twenty-five more longbows, except they're not as good as your weapon. The bowstring on yours is far superior, practically unbreakable." Before returning the bow to Gelr, she pulled the string halfway taut and released it. *Twang!* "Nice, hang on to this one." Gelr smiled as he slung the longbow over his shoulder.

"We've also made over a hundred of these little wooden projectiles, adding two major improvements." The mender gripped Gelr's arrow, held it up to the light, and pointed to the notched end. "Ours have shaved wood stabilizers instead of these two little flaps of yarn. And the metalsmith added bronze tips, which can pierce through leather armor."

"Notable upgrades. Can I trade my knife for five?"

"You can have them, no charge." The mender returned his arrow and then reached over and picked up a piece of paper.

"You seem like a discerning fellow. Could you take a peek at this recent notification from our vice-leader?" Ottaar pushed the announcement across the table. "These notices are posted all over town."

Gelr read it, threw the paper on the floor, and stomped on it with his foot. "It's a darn lie! They are not dead! I was part of the team who rescued Narleen. So was Lady Saephira. Our raid succeeded. I believe Saephira and Narleen are currently in Falein Village. They had plans to travel to Midvill later to enlist more militia."

"I figured there was treachery going on. Probably involves Eddnok. I'm meeting with the woodsmith later, and I want you to tell him what you told me. I'm thinking we should organize a resistance. Would you be willing to help us?"

"Before I reply, maybe you should know I once served the Upper Realm. However, Lady Saephira pardoned me for my misdeeds. I'm trying to change my destiny now by doing good instead of evil. I've given my allegiance to her and the Lower Realm."

"The pardon aside, if she trusts you enough to enlist your help, then so will I."

"Thank you, ma'am. Then my answer is yes. I will pledge my support, and I know several more people who might join our effort. Chepho, his brother, and the freed captives once their health improves. If Jesse's outfit shows up, I believe they will help as well."

"Of that I have no doubt." Ottaar pushed her chair aside and walked over to the front window to check the street. "Please move your rides around to the rear. I don't want to draw unwelcome attention. And commander, if you don't have lodging for nightrise, you can stay here as my guest." She grabbed her credit purse and headed toward the exit door. "I'm going to the kitchens now for some hot food. Let's keep this resistance thing between us for the time being."

"I will. And yes, ma'am, I would love to stay here."

"Good! In case you're interested, my name isn't ma'am, it's Ottaar. As for Lady Saephira, she is not just the leader of the Lower Realm, she's my friend. We cannot allow Yhmim or Eddnok to steal her city or our province." Concerned there might be spies posted outside her place, Ottaar glanced out her window one more time and then departed.

CHAPTER 35
TREACHERY REVEALED

After the Chesedel appeared in the hidden cave, he remained invisible for the remainder of his time on Eskaonus. His instructions from Uzziel were to observe and not interfere. He didn't consider a brief appearance or nodding at Jesse in the abandoned mine as an infraction. On the other hand, it was hard for him to watch the destruction of Falein and not use his angelic powers to stop it. Although there were certain exceptions, non-interference was the role angels have played through countless wars and holocausts. Only God understands such wisdom. His ways are higher than any celestial or mortal. Chesedel accepted that. As a guardian angel, he stayed focused on his main callings: imparting encouragement, confirming truth, delivering messages, and providing healing. He only took matters into his own hands when directed by the Spirit of God.

Once the devastating fire tests by Eddnok ended, Chesedel popped over to the campsite where Jesse and his associates had stopped the previous night. Their party was exhausted from days and nights of constant traveling, rescue attempts, and escaping pursuers. Dayrise had dawned, yet they were still sound asleep around the firepit. Knowing he would not be discovered, Chesedel materialized to administer healing.

One by one, the angel touched the group members on their shoulders to renew their weary souls. The day ahead for them would be difficult at best, especially when they discovered the wicked acts inflicted on Falein by Eddnok. Anna, sleeping deeply, was the last to receive his ministry. After imparting encouragement, the Holy Spirit quickened him to probe her recent memories. Finding one that might be expedient, Chesedel bent over and whispered into her ear, "Annie, I want you to think about that night in the vineyards. You were all alone. It was dark. You sat by a fallen comrade and fell asleep against a vine trellis. Remember this spot." He didn't believe it was interfering to suggest a memory already hers. She would have to figure out the rest on her own, but Annabelle was quite perceptive in spiritual matters, so he hoped a simple remembrance would help her discern the location where Saephira and Narleen were held captive. Chesedel waited until the five advocates stirred themselves awake, then departed, undetected, moving again into the unseen realm.

"I think we overslept. I had hoped to get moving by firstlight." Jesse rose, grabbed his leadership staff, checked his satchel, and dusted off his clothes. He glanced at the surrounding skyline. "It's mid-morning already. We gotta move out if we want to reach Falein by noontime."

"We are all tired, Jess. We have been running non-stop for days now, ever since we arrived on Eskaonus. It was nice to slow the pace, relax a bit, and sleep in."

"For sure. I needed a good night's rest." Seth completed a set of arm and leg stretches to get his blood flowing. "I feel great, like somebody gave me a shot of adrenaline. I'm totally pumped and ready to hit the ground running. Hungry too. What we got for eats?"

"Varmint stew leftovers, maize, smoked fish, dried yarm berries, and two half loaves of kin." Jesse divvied out the provisions the tavern owner had packed. They scarfed down most of the food, fed the berries to their mounts, and then packed up and rode west toward Falein Village. In the distance, the smell of burning fields drifted in the breeze. Smoke covered the horizon. As the emissaries continued on, they passed a smoldering farm, the soil scorched, crops gone. Nearby farmlands revealed the same barrenness. At the settlement, they found structures in the village center, blackened, as if someone had dropped napalm on them. Huts on the outskirts looked like large bonfires with glowing embers. A few residents were running around trying to put out the flames, their efforts futile. A young woman held a crying child in her arms, trying to comfort him. They noticed another woman on her knees, mender kit beside her, applying ointment and wrapping bandages around the burnt legs of an older man. Thinking she might be the town mender, Jesse asked, "What happened here?"

The mender replied, "Eddnok!"

"Eddnok?"

"According to sources we have in Briacap, he was constructing a massive weapon able to rain fire from the sky. Apparently, he succeeded, and during forecycle it happened. You can see the damage. It's not just here either. Our farmlands were hit, including the lake facilities: boats, docks, everything, gone, burnt to cinders."

"Have you seen the leader of Beayama? She and two realm officials were visiting Falein while their associate received treatment for an injury. Are they okay?"

"If you mean Lady Saephira, her lady-in-waiting, and Captain Waubush, their party lodged here for a couple cycles. I think they left early before the firebombs hit. As for their militia chief, I operated on his shoulder last dayrise. He was recovering in my home, which doubles as our village aid station. It received a direct hit. Everyone staying at the facility is dead, burnt beyond recognition. I was outside gathering supplies at the time, so I guess I'm lucky." She circled her arm in a wide arc pointing at the destruction. "If you call this lucky."

"Is there anything we can do?" Anna asked. "We have two mender kits in our side carriers."

"Yes, I'd appreciate the assistance. Do any of you have mender experience?"

"I took a first aid class in high school," Anna offered.

"And I assisted an apothecary for a week," replied Lundy.

"Since I'm desperate, I'll take both of you. There aren't many of us left. Most who survived are burned, some badly. Use this two-step procedure: Apply Helixzon salve." She held up a blue bottle containing healing lotion. "There's probably several in your mender kits. Next, wrap their burns with bandages. If you run out, use clothes, rags, anything that covers the blisters." When the mender finished treating the older man, she stood and scanned the area for more burn victims. "As you can see, we're overwhelmed here. Up the path you'll find more victims." Lundy mouthed a silent OK, grabbed a mender kit, and hurried off. Anne opened the second kit to check for salve and bandages.

"Do you want me to help you, Annie?"

"No, I got this, Jess. While Lundy and I treat the injured, can you find out what happened to Waubush, Saephira, and Narleen?"

"Let us check," Max offered. "Seth and I will ride out toward the lake and see if we can determine their whereabouts." With his concern covered, Jesse decided to assist with the search for survivors. Maybe some of them knew more about the attack.

As soon as Max and Seth approached the lake, they saw the damage the mender mentioned: docks burnt, walkways gone, fish washed ashore, and the one boat still afloat was smoldering. They dismounted their kacks to walk the perimeter and found signs of a skirmish. Bodies lay sprawled across the ground. "Max, these two have arrows sticking in them."

"This answers one question. Saephira was here. Those were her arrows, two of the three I gave her in Tabahir. Her party must have been ambushed." Seth located four more people, all dead. Nearby they discovered Captain Waubush with his face buried in the dirt. Max turned him over, hoping he had somehow survived. A pale face with rigor mortis indicated the captain had succumbed hours earlier. "Apparently, a knife wound to his neck brought him down. He fought bravely, though, killing those four guards before he fell. His sword is covered with blood, their blood no doubt." Remembering how the Lower Realm honored fallen soldiers, Max pulled out his double-edged Gladius and cut Waubush's copper blade in half with one blow. He crossed the two sections and draped them over the captain's chest. "It's all we can do for now. No time to bury him."

The duo searched the vicinity for clues and found hoof prints leading north. They followed the tracks until they entered rocky terrain and the trail disappeared. Circling around to scan for additional signs, Max discovered a longbow. "It must be Saephira's. Grab it, Seth, and we'll take it with us."

"Okey dokey." Seth slid off his animal, retrieved the bow, and looped it over his shoulder. "I don't see additional bodies; maybe the women survived."

"Let's hope." Max worried about Saephira's safety but even more so for Narleen's, since their relationship had blossomed into one of mutual affection. Having finished their search, they raced back to the village to report in to Jesse.

Jesse found one person who was unscathed by the fire. "Sir, may I ask what you know about this disaster?"

"I really don't feel like talking." Jesse accepted his reply; perhaps it was the wrong time to ask such questions in lieu of what happened. Therefore, he merely smiled and started to walk away. "Alright, I'll tell you."

"Before the fire hit our village, I left to check my fields. It was forecycle, and I wanted to get an early start on dayrise. I was a hundred paces away from my farm when I noticed a tower of sorts in the distance, north of my field in the Disputed Lands. It appeared to be moving, but since it was silhouetted in the background, I couldn't make out much detail." He offered no further clarification.

Jesse waited a few moments as the man stared at him with a blank expression. "Okay, thank you sir, I only—"

"Next, a bright light flashed, and my field erupted in flames. Nothing survived. I ran home and found my hut burning with my wife and two children trapped inside. I heard their screams, then silence. Although I tried to enter, a blast of heat pushed me backwards. I couldn't even get close. A moment later, my home erupted into a ball of fire. It's gone, incinerated. I should have been there with them." The man walked away in a daze, weeping. Jesse wanted to say more to the man, but what?

Max and Seth returned to the village and located their colleagues gathered around a smoldering cottlepine, waiting for the update on their missing friends. "I think Narleen was abducted again, and Lady Saephira captured. Captain Waubush died defending them. The ambushers trekked north." Anger filled Max's eyes. "And I'm gonna track them with or without the rest of you."

"Hold on a minute, Max. I am sure all of us will go with you, and we'll keep searching until we locate them. However, there's another concern. Prior to leaving heaven, I had a dream about fields burning and much violence. Saephira received a similar premonition. And it all came true. If Eddnok has a weapon of mass destruction, a firebomb device, we need to find this thing and eliminate it."

"All righty, lads, north it is, except where?" Lundy asked.

"Maybe it's the wrong time to bring this up, but I keep remembering that terrible night at the Kunakk Vineyards when I was attacked and where the militia lead died defending me."

"Yeah, I know, it was a disturbing event. Such memories often replay in our minds and dreams. They usually stop sooner or later," explained Jesse, trying to reassure her.

"Yes, a bad memory, horrible in fact. Still, what if these remembrances have a prophetic connection? If we're traveling in a northerly direction, maybe we should stop by the vineyards first."

"Are you saying this is where Saephira and Narleen can be found?"

"I don't know. I keep getting the same image in my mind, at least twenty times since this morning."

"Good enough for me," Max replied. "Miss Anna has a discerning heart. I say we go there."

"Aye lads, I agree. As much as I hate the thought of returning to Upper Realm territory, if it's where they be, we have little choice."

"Her dream about finding Gelr was right on," Seth added,

"and we all know how that hunch worked out."

"Fine, it's decided. We'll head back to the vineyards. I will offer our goodbyes to the mender. God help us if we're wrong."

"We're not. And He will help," Anna declared.

They crossed the boundary lines and entered the Kunakk Vineyards without encountering any patrols. It only took a span to get there from Falein. The group dismounted and allowed their kacks to graze among the grain vines, hoping it kept them occupied and quiet. Jesse asked Max and Seth to scope out things while the rest of them hid behind the first row of vineyards and waited. Once the pair returned, Max gave the scouting report: "We counted five guards, two securing the tent. The other three are milling around their campsite. The tent has been camouflaged to blend in with the vines. I suspect their captives are inside, tied up. We also spotted a primitive catapult. They tried to disguise it, yet that's what it is. I've seen similar ones used during my Roman campaigns."

"Should we try to negotiate the release of the ladies?" Lundy asked.

"At this point, we don't know for sure if the ladies are here. Regardless, I don't think the kidnappers would be open for discussion. If they see us or think we are trying to free the women, they'll probably slit their throats before we get close."

"Got a strategy in mind, Maximus?"

"Take down the two sentries. They're the immediate threat. Then we rush the three guards while someone enters the tent to release the women."

"How's our weapon status?" Jesse asked.

"We have two bows with five arrows, two slings, your leadership staff, two persuaders, and my Gladius. They have spears, swords, and perhaps throwing knives, so it's a fairly even match, but we have the element of surprise."

"Max, you're the military expert. How do suggest we proceed?"

"I'll take out those watching the tent with arrows. At the same time, Seth and Anna can sling stones at the three lookouts as a distraction. Two of those men are passing a jar around and probably drunk, which is advantageous for us. I assume the third one, a squad leader, is on watch duty. He may be a problem. After creating some confusion with our slings, at least two people should advance with persuaders and disable them. If they surrender, fine, bind their hands and feet. If not, you'll have to eliminate the threat. Once they're neutralized, I'll sneak over and breach the tent. I hope the ladies are in there. If not . . . well . . . let's just pray they are."

"What am I supposed to do, twiddle me thumbs? Let me have one of those walking sticks. Considering how I've been mistreated, I would love to knock a little sense into their noggins."

"Here Preach, you can borrow mine. Do you know how to use one?"

"Me figure it out as I go."

With the plan organized, they spread out across the first row of vineyards. Max drew an arrow, notched it, and let it fly: *whish.* He aimed again and released his second one: *whish.* Both hit their marks and the two sentries slumped over, screaming in pain. Alerted, the squad leader ran over to investigate, followed by his two inebriated men who wobbled behind him. Stones flew out of nowhere. "What's going on here?" More stones hit, cutting faces. "Ouch, those hurt!" Seth and Anna slung one more volley before stopping.

Jesse and Lundy dashed forward with fighting staffs. "Surrender now and you'll live," Jesse yelled. Two of the men, the drunken ones, dropped their spears and raised their hands to surrender. The squad leader did not. He pulled his sword and charged at Lundy. The reverend waited until the guy got closer and then banged him on the forehead with Seth's persuader, dazing him. Jesse followed up by swiping his feet. The man landed on his back with a thud.

"What will it be laddie, live or die, eh?" The guardsman tossed his weapon aside. "Good choice!"

As the distraction proceeded, Max reached the shelter. Instead entering the front flap, he moved to the rear, raised his sword and sliced it from top to bottom. He stepped in, ready to strike if more combatants were inside. He only found the two ladies. Saephira and Narleen were huddled in the corner, hands and feet bound, both gagged. Max untied them, removed their gags, and lifted them to their feet. Narleen threw her arms around Max and wouldn't let go. "I thought we were gonna die."

"You're both safe now, but we need to hurry. Follow me." They exited the tattered rear opening, and Max led them to the area where their kacks were busy nibbling grain pods. "Stay here. I'll be back. However, if something goes wrong, take two mounts and ride south for Beayama. Don't wait for us. We have alternate transportation we can use."

Looking puzzled at his last comment, Saephira asked, "What are you going to do?"

"Destroy a device being used for evil."

Max returned to the campsite to find Seth binding the three men with strands of corded rope he had previously cut and stuffed into his pocket. "Hey bro, did you find the ladies?"

"I did, and they're safe." Max sheathed his sword. "It appears our little diversion succeeded."

"Aye, nothing like a decent whack on the noggin to get your point across. Let's go check out this wee catapult of theirs."

"You can't have it. It belongs to Lord Eddnok," the squad leader shouted.

"Sorry, laddie, your launcher has come under new ownership. And we may require a bit of firewood."

"Okay gentlemen, it's time to retire to your tent," Jesse said with slight grin. "We'll leave a waterskin for you. You may have a long wait until somebody finds you. Better hope it's not Eddnok. He may not be too happy you've lost your captives again." After securing the kidnappers in the shelter, the rescue party scurried over to the weapon's location about thirty paces away.

"Wow, this thing is taller than I expected." *Rule Number One.* Seth tied a loop onto the end of his rope and lassoed the top. Working together, the five of them yanked it over on its side. Max unsheathed his resilient Gladius and cut the launcher into pieces as easy as slicing a loaf of bread. Soon it was a pile of split logs and shredded kindling.

"This would make a great bonfire." Jesse used a striking stone and set it to blaze. "Sweet justice, don't you think."

"I would love to stay and roast marshmallows, except we better zip out of here before the bad cops show up."

"Agreed, the recruit is right. Time to retreat."

They unhobbled the kacks that the weapon's team had used to pull the catapult and requisitioned them for their own use. The animals could be returned later if deemed appropriate. Right now, though, the group needed them to escape. Everyone had mounts to ride, even Lundy, who decided to try steering one himself. With the catapult in flames, the liberators returned to the cheers of Saephira and Narleen who had been waiting where Max left them. After many hugs and a few kisses, mostly from Narleen to Max, the collective galloped away, heading for Beayama.

CHAPTER 36
OPPOSITION ARISES

Lord Eddnok returned to Briacap pleased with his liquid-fire test. The destruction of Falein was lovely. Now he needed more firebombs, many more. He likewise wondered how the alchemist's experiments with the knowledge fruit were proceeding. Perhaps Deamonn had uncovered a method to leach out the good knowledge and make an elixir to corrupt the minds of those perceived as enemies.

His takeover plans were also proceeding as planned. Yhmim had assumed leadership over Beayama and would soon begin a coup to control the Lower Realm. On the other hand, he could use his vast insights of wickedness and evil to destroy the southern province from within. So many delicious choices. Eddnok would give these matters more thought, but right now he wanted to visit the alchemist. He found him busy at his worktable.

"Ah, Deamonn, how are the tests coming along on my fruit?"

"Oh, just fine. I am making much progress." In truth, the alchemist had stopped the experiments when Eddnok's sample mysteriously disappeared from a locked cabinet in his lab.

"Good, good, keep me posted on the research. In the meantime, I want you to make fifty more barrels of liquid fire."

"I'm sorry Lord Eddnok, I cannot comply."

"Why, are you short on supplies?" Eddnok gave a quick scan of his shelves. They were stocked to the ceiling with various jars and storage boxes.

"No, I have an overstock of the necessary ingredients." He turned off his heating flame, removed the vial of compounds being cooked, and stepped back from his table. "I heard what happened last cycle at Falein and about the three firebombs you launched against the village, farms, and lake. I knew family members who fished that lake. Now they're dead." Deamonn paused to consider if he should say more, then chose to go ahead and speak his heart. "I will not be a part of more destruction. Fifty firebombs will burn the entire Lower Realm. I cannot make them for you if this is your purpose."

"Am I correct to assume you are defying my orders?"

"Yes, your assumption is correct."

"Then you are no longer helpful to me . . . or needed." As Deamonn moved farther away, Eddnok pressed in, pushing him against the rear shelving. He took out his dagger and swiped it across the alchemist's throat. While Deamonn coughed and struggled to inhale, Eddnok added, "I will find others to make my fire weapons and mix my potions. And just so you know, I never liked you much anyway." After Deamonn gasped his last breath, Eddnok wiped his blade off on the alchemist's apron, smiled, and then scurried back to his office. There was a flyer message pinned to the wall outside his entry. The postal clerk must have brought it by while he was out. He wondered why she didn't wait to deliver it in person.

Lord Eddnok: A raid by unknown assailants has freed L. Saephira and Narleen and destroyed your catapult. We're unable to track. —Nakk Village

He ripped the message off the wall and tore it into tiny pieces. "Those incompetent guards! I'll have their heads on spears before nightrise." Without entering his office, he turned around and hurried over to the woodsmith's place. He planned to have him build a replacement catapult, double the size this time. Upon arrival, he discovered the shop was locked. No one responded to his hails either. *Where did that fool go?* He decided to try across the street and see if the metalsmith knew anything. He strode through the entrance, exasperated, and confronted the owner. "Do you know where my woodsmith went? His place isn't open."

"Good dayrise, Lord. The woodwright had a family

emergency and left town. Didn't say how long he'd be gone."

"Yeah right! Like I believe that." Eddnok paced around the premises, looking at various projects, none of which were his. "How is my bronze cover coming along?"

"I'm working on it. Metalwork takes more time than woodwork. Would you care to review the progress?"

"No, just finish it. You have the correct specs, right?"

"I do. Two paces by three. If you check on the morrow, it should be ready."

"It better be." Eddnok stomped out of the building as angry as ever.

The metalsmith waited a couple moments to make sure Eddnok wasn't spying on him before he closed his shop. He had talked to the woodwright earlier in the day and knew why he and his family had gone into hiding. He planned to do the same.

He elected not to build a metal cover for some stupid treasure in a hidden cave. For whatever reason, Lord Eddnok started acting odd after unearthing his secretive find. Now his actions were dangerous, his temperament unpredictable. Both craftsmen wanted nothing to do with him. The alchemist felt the same way. The metalsmith locked up and headed home. His wife and children were waiting, packed and ready to leave Briacap for good.

Eddnok returned to his office and slammed the door shut. He was about to open his concealed compartment and pull out his chest of knowledge fruit when the sentry knocked. "Yes, what is it?"

"One of the mining crew has returned from the Colrath Mountains with a report."

"Good, good, send him in."

The miner entered and bowed. "Good dayrise, Lord."

"Yes, yes, what is it? Did you finish the enlargement for the entry?"

"We did. Then a span later something unfortunate occurred."

"What? Did the tunnel collapse?"

"No." The miner wiped off several beads of sweat forming on his brow. "A group of five people mysteriously appeared and tried to access the dig."

"I assume you stopped them."

"We tried, except they used powerful weapons to subdue us. Although we forbid them, they ignored us. After binding us with ropes, the strangers entered, saying they had higher authority than you."

"Is that so? Go on."

"As soon as their group departed, we raced inside to search around. Their leader said they didn't steal the treasure, yet the cavern was empty."

"Nothing at all?"

"Only a few shattered pieces of pottery."

"Do you remember what I told your crew before I left? You were not to let anybody enter under pain of death."

"Yes." The man began to squirm; sweat soaked his shirt. "But I felt you'd want to know what happened since it wasn't our fault."

"Where are the two digmen who were with you?"

"The chief and his coworker ran away and escaped into the Blighte."

"Maybe you should have gone with them." Eddnok calmly walked over to the man, withdrew the dagger tucked under his belt and made one swift lunge. The miner stumbled backwards two paces and collapsed on the floor. After watching him bleed out, Eddnok called for his sentry. "Remove this body and clean up the mess. And locate this man's family and put them to the sword for treason." The sentry bowed, saying nothing, and departed.

A half span later, two attendants entered to drag the deceased mineworker out and mop the floor. Once they finished, Eddnok shut and bolted his office door. He drew open the curtain to his secret compartment and pulled out his chest. He placed it on his desk and unlocked the latch. The container was empty, all the fruit gone. "Arrgh!" Sounds of rage filled the room. He slung the chest to the floor, breaking the lid, and then grabbed his dagger and jammed it into a nearby countertop. Furious about his missing fruit, destroyed catapult, and failed schemes, he tromped around his office, kicking at potted plants and knocking over furniture. Eddnok slung his door open and yelled out, "No matter what I do, something or someone seems to hinder it. If I am the ruler of fate, why am I not succeeding? And where is my darn treasure?" The guard on duty froze in place, unsure how to respond.

Eddnok wiggled his knife free from the counter, exited his office, and stomped off to the metalsmith's place. *I won't be so nice this time.* His shop, however, was closed and the door fastened tight. His next destination was the watchtower. Cussing under his breath, he trotted over to the eastern battlement, climbed the steps to the top, and found Senior Commander Bolgog talking with two sentinels.

"Good dayrise, Lord. How can we serve you this fine day?"

"Dismiss those men, so we can talk privately." Bolgog waved them way.

"You seem angry, sir. May I ask what's wrong?"

"Spies from the Lower Realm stole my treasure from the cave. Those thieves must be found and punished. Use our torture rack to make them tell you what they did with it." He paced around his commander like a circling tarkk, ready to attack. "Apparently, I no longer need a security detachment. Therefore, notify the warders deployed to the abandoned mine and have them return to Briacap."

"I will get it handled. Is that all, sir?"

"No, it's not all! I also want you to draw up plans for a campaign of war against the Lower Realm, beginning with raids against their villages and cities. You can exempt Beayama since it's now under my control through Yhmim, the former vice-leader. She is eliminating all current leadership and replacing them with individuals sympathetic to my cause."

"I didn't know about Yhmim. Is she a spy?"

"One might say so." Frustration building, Eddnok began tapping his foot. "What about my plans?"

Bolgog walked the alure, scratching his chin. He glanced down the tower steps to see if any comrades were eavesdropping on their conversation. Feeling satisfied they were alone, he replied, "Well sir, military planning this extensive will take at least a week of cycles to draw up and even longer if I raise an additional battlegroup. For such an endeavor, we will have to draft volunteers."

"Get it done in two cycles!"

"Perhaps I can have tentative plans ready in two cycles, but organizing troops, weapons, and supplies will take a least seven." Bolgog agreed to try. In reality, though, he was stalling. He'd find some way to stop this madness before thousands of innocent folks died. "Sir, you do not seem well. May I suggest you see a mender?"

"You may not. I'm fine. Never felt better." Eddnok reached for his blade. Bolgog's remark infuriated him, and he considered relieving him of command, permanently, by ending his life. However, to avoid retribution from fellow officers, their guardsmen, not to mention the citizens who supported and trusted him, he chose to dismiss Bolgog's comments, at least for now. He still required the commander's support for his war.

Seething, Eddnok left the tower and retired to his private quarters. His two concubines approached him, trying to soothe his foul mood. He rebuffed their concern and sincere efforts to comfort him. "You two kacks can get out of here. I never want to see either of your faces again."

His comment hurt deeply yet didn't surprise them. Bovi and Seirlai curtsied and rushed out as Eddnok continued to cuss at them. Without taking time to gather their personal effects, they returned to their homes and families. Instead of being sad, they were overjoyed to be free of servitude unto him. They had always felt more like objects, not respected as women or second wives. Although they cared for him, tried to love him, even take care of his physical needs, they would never allow themselves to be treated that way again, not by him, not by anybody.

Eddnok was all alone now, feeling rejected, vengeful, angry at everything and everyone. Sadly, such is often the outcome of allowing evil to rule one's heart.

CHAPTER 37
RETURNING TO BEAYAMA

Throughout postcycle, Jesse's party, along with Saephira and Narleen, raced south. They crossed the northern boundary line, entered the Disputed Lands, not stopping until they passed the southern boundary and reached Lower Realm territory. Their mounts had run the whole way. Sweat drenched their necks and flew off their long manes into the air. Although kacks are hardy creatures, they were soon showing signs of exhaustion, breathing hard, and dropping their heads halfway to the ground. The animals needed rest. At the first water source, the group encountered, they stopped to take a break. They dismounted to stretch their legs while their rides wandered around, drinking their fill and nibbling on wild field grasses.

Seth passed out the remaining pieces of smoked fish. He decided to save what little kin they had for dinner. Since their provisions were low, Anna and Narleen gathered fourteen ears of maize from a rural farm unscathed by Eddnok's firebombs. Saephira said she would compensate the farmers once they arrived in Beayama.

Before resuming their trek, Lundy filled their five waterskins. Feeling rested and renewed, they turned west at a slower, more moderate pace. The travelers hoped to reach the upper fork of the Cali River during twilight, cross it, and make camp in the Blighte. Not wanting to draw attention to their whereabouts, they avoided the inhabited areas around Falein. Lady Saephira assumed that spies would be keeping an eye out for their location in order to advise Eddnok.

By latecycle, their outfit approached the Cali River. Taking a moment to scan the embankments, Saephira pointed to a bend in the river. "I think we should ford here because it looks shallow. Make sure to hang on tight to your mounts in case the water is deeper than expected. Kacks are good swimmers, but the current is strong, and if you fall off, you'll be swept upstream into the lake."

"Oh yeah," Jesse recalled, "in Eskaonus, water flows upriver, not down."

"Actually, it does both, following the contours of the land. In this location, though, it flows uphill into the lake."

Seth surveyed the current for a few moments. "If water flows upstream, where does it go when it hits the lake?"

"An underground water table returns it to the sea where it begins again."

"Well, campers, I guess we're not in Kansas anymore."

"Kansas? It that where you come from?" Narleen asked.

"Nope, never been there. It's an expression I use for unfamiliar places and circumstances." Narleen looked puzzled; Saephira shrugged her shoulders. Jesse merely smiled, having seen the Oz flick and knowing how Seth liked using movie clichés.

Mindful of Saephira's warning, the riders led their mounts to the riverbank and eased them into the river. At the halfway point, the current started pulling their animals upstream. The kacks swam on, slowly making headway until they reached the far side. With everyone safely across, the party intersected the main trail and continued traveling west, nearing the blighted area before making camp. For dinner, they shared a half loaf of cycle-old kin and the maize picked earlier, two ears apiece. Jesse decided not to build a fire, concerned it might reveal their location. Since only two of them possessed coats, they huddled together for warmth and bedded down for the night.

At firstlight, the team rose early. With all their food provisions gone, breaking their fast was not an option. Instead, they hurried to clear the campsite of any signs indicating their overnight stay, then packed up and rode toward Cali Village. Saephira still had five credits left in her purse, which she had hidden in her undergarment, so they decided to stop in Cali and

240

purchase food provisions and additional coats. The further south they traveled, the colder the weather became. In some ways, the cooler temperatures felt refreshing compared to the dry, arid weather of the northlands.

They followed the leading edge of the Blighte and stopped west of Cali Village around midcycle. Because Saephira and Narleen might be recognized, Jesse and Anna offered to go shop for supplies in Cali. They stopped at the first food stand they encountered and purchased five loaves of kin, two racks of dried fish, and a bag of dallups. Next, they found a trader hut and spent the rest of their credits buying five used coats. On the way out of the village, Narleen paused to read the noticeboard. Prominently posted in the middle was Yhmim's proclamation. "Do you see this, Jess? It says Lady Saephira and—"

"Shush." Jesse put his finger to his mouth and whispered, "We better leave. People are watching us. Let's mosey over to our kacks, load our provisions, and ride off as if we don't have a care in the world." Pretending to have an afterthought, Jesse reached underneath the announcement where a rectangular box held dozens more. He grabbed one and stuffed it into his pocket. "Nice place, however, I'm not sure we want to build a hut here. Let's try Falein." Anne nodded in playacted agreement.

The pair trotted their kacks out of the settlement in the opposite direction. As soon as they passed the village limits, they turned west into the Blighte. Anna glanced behind to see anyone was following them before she spoke up. "It's not true, Jess."

"I know, I know, more treachery. Eddnok, no doubt. Just when you think you're almost finished, more deception arises. We better hurry back. Saephira needs to see this notification right away." The two urged their rides to a full run. As they approached the area where their companions waited, they tugged on the animal's manes to slow them to a walk but forgot to add the correlated leg motions. The kacks responded to the halt command by stopping abruptly, creating a cloud of dust behind them, almost flipping Anna and Jesse over their withers unto the ground.

"Having a pony race? I can dig it." Seth added his two thumbs-up gesture. "Sure hope you brought good eats cause we're starving to death here." Jesse and Anna just stared at one another, the silence telling. Worry etched their faces. "Hey man, what's wrong? Did something go squirrely in town?"

They both dismounted. Anna unpacked the supplies and gave them to Seth. Jesse handed the notice to Saephira. She studied the wording, shaking her head in disgust. Saying nothing, she passed it over to Narleen who became teary-eyed as she read it.

"What does it say?" Max asked.

"That Lady Saephira and I are dead and Yhmim has taken over as leader of Beayama. Next cycle, she's setting up memory tables to honor us. Here, see for yourself." Narleen handed the declaration to Max.

"So, what are we going to do?" inquired Anna.

"For now, keep moving." Saephira helped Seth sort the provisions before they stowed them into side carriers. "It'll be safer to circle around the village and stay away from populated areas. We can rejoin the main trail to cross the river at the forge, then head south. The area below Mista Lake is close to Beayama yet remains somewhat isolated. After we make camp, we can break our fast. Sorry Seth, you'll have to wait a bit longer."

"It's cool. I was only kidding about starving to death."

"I realize that. I'm beginning to understand your cryptic sayings." Seth's freckled cheeks flushed red, revealing his embarrassment. "Let's plan on an early dinner. Not sure about you guys," Saephira said with a grin, "but I think better when I'm not dying from starvation." Everybody laughed, Seth most of all. A moment of merriment lifted their spirits and helped them forget about the disheartening news, at least for a while.

The group endured several more spans of riding and by latecycle made camp along the banks of the Cali River. Seth passed out the food provisions and the entire crew ate a hearty meal. With continued safety concerns, they did not strike a fire or light torches. After discussing their options, they decided to slip into Beayama early to avoid those who might recognize Saephira or Narleen and then sneak over to Ottaar's place. She was one of the few individuals Saephira could trust.

The five extra coats were distributed. Each person had one now, so they could stay warm during the cold of approaching nightrise. They sat around in a circle talking among themselves.

Jesse explained to Saephira and Narleen about the hidden cave, Lundy's translation map, and finding the mysterious fruit tree of knowledge. He assumed Eddnok had already discovered the tree and consumed its fruit, thereby gaining the knowledge to build his destructive firebombs. Jesse didn't go into the theology of good and evil, why the fruit was forbidden, or how a copy of the knowledge tree ended up on Eskaonus. Both the women listened yet didn't raise questions or make comments. Perhaps it was fatigue or information overload, but those matters were dropped.

Instead, the conversation focused on the upcoming cycle, how to confront Yhmim and restore Lady Saephira to rightful leadership. Saephira, who had mostly stayed quiet as the others visited, asked Anna, "Do you have a tune that can inspire confidence, perhaps take our minds off our recent troubles?"

"Yes, I'd love to share a song." Anna took out her glifstring, which she always carried slung across her back, and began picking a melody. The music filtered through the air, having a calming effect on the listeners. "*Blessed Assurance* is a favorite of mine. The words were written by a precious lady named Fanny Crosby."

Perfect submission, all is at rest.
I in my Savior am happy and bless'd,
watching and waiting, looking above,
filled with his goodness, lost in his love.

This is my story, this is my song,
praising my Savior, all the day long.
This is my story, this is my song,
praising my Savior, all the day long.

Annabelle sang all the verses, switching stanzas around for added emphasis. As always, her music was soothing, her voice soft and sweet. While she sang, a misty cloud formed in the sky, except no one gazed upward to notice it. Once the music ended, Narleen said, "You know, Anna, I would love to learn how to play your instrument. Is it difficult?"

"No, it's real easy. I'd be happy to give you lessons on chording. Another time perhaps, it's getting dark now."

Jesse agreed. "Time to call it quits for this evening. We have an early start tomorrow and a lot of unknowns to face." As twilight ended and darkout began, they bundled up in their coats and drifted off to sleep, exhausted. The mist descended and hovered all night over the campers with a gentle warming presence. They slept well and rose early feeling rejuvenated. At firstlight they broke their fast on leftovers.

By forecycle, they entered Beayama to a crowded rush of people coming for the memory table ceremony. Saephira and Narleen covered their heads to hide their identities. The band of allies blended in with the crowds, avoided the city square, and then veered right to the mender's home. They moved their kacks around to the rear of her house to get them off the street. While the others waited in the back, Max returned to the front door and knocked.

CHAPTER 38
THE RESISTANCE

The door opened and Commander Gelr stood in the entry. "I was wondering when you'd show up." He embraced Max in the arm-to-arm welcome often used by comrades. "Where are your friends? Are Lady Saephira and Narleen okay?"

"Yes sir, they're fine. Out back right now waiting to see if it's safe to enter." Max peeked inside and spotted Chepho, Phauch, and Ottaar sitting around her large dining table with a platter of kin and steaming cups of liquid in front of them. However, he noticed someone he didn't recognize. "Who is the older man next to the mender?"

"Oh, that's Membarb, the woodsmith," Gelr replied. "He's part of our resistance team. Come on in and take a seat. I'll let your friends in the backway." Max stepped through the entrance and closed the front door behind him. He remained standing until the rest of his party emerged from the rear entryway.

Overjoyed to see Lady Saephira and Narleen walk through the door, Ottaar arose from the table and rushed over to give them both huge hugs. "I missed you two!" When the mender finally let go, she noticed the others. "Ah, you're all here, the whole group. And you must be Lundy. Wonderful! Come join us." She indicated the empty chairs and her settee adjacent to the table. "If you don't already know, things have taken a turn for the worse. Recent developments are most troubling. The vice-leader has declared Lady Saephira dead, Narleen too, and taken over the city. Their memory tables are already set up in the city square. Travelers have come from all around and the streets are packed with the bereaved. Yhmim plans to offer remarks during midcycle."

"If so, this might be the best time to make our move." Saephira strolled over to the table and sat by Chepho.

"Do you have a plan in mind?" asked Ottaar.

"Yes, a tentative one. Except first, I need to know how many we can count on."

The mender pointed around the table. "The ones you see here, plus Chepho's brother, Bonarb; Seth's two fishing buddies, Calrin and Raydoo, which have been keeping us advised on developments; the freed captives; and a handful of militiamen who are still loyal to you."

Saephira tallied the number of available individuals. "With Jesse's party of five, we have almost twenty allies. It might be enough. Last night, we discussed various ideas but only one seemed plausible." Saephira stood up, went over to the stove, grabbed a pitcher of brewed tea, a tray of cups, and returned to her seat. "Jesse, can you explain our proposed strategy before these loyalists agree to help? Our actions would be considered treason and if our opposition efforts don't succeed, we will all end up in chains or executed."

"We understand the implications," the mender said. "Be assured, none of us are going to sit around and allow our city to be stolen by a deceitful Yhmim or scheming Eddnok. Go ahead Jesse, tell us the plan and how we can assist."

"Alright, here it is in a nutshell: We'll spread out between the memory tables. Lady Saephira and Narleen will filter into the gathering disguised as farm laborers, their faces partially covered with scarves to obscure their faces. Some of us will stand by them as protection. The rest will disperse throughout the square pretending to be mourners. When Yhmim begins speaking, we'll reveal our two ladies as alive and well. They will accuse the vice-leader of lying and sedition in front of all the attendees. If Yhmim's bodyguards or conspirators make a move against either lady, which we assume they will, we must be ready to respond quickly, harshly, and if necessary, with deadly force. I hope the citizens will be shocked after hearing the truth and rally to Saephira's side in support. No matter what happens, do not allow Yhmim to escape. She's to be detained for questioning."

Jesse bit down on his lower lip as he pondered what else to add. "Wear your swords as normal. Those who carry longbows, like Max, Gelr, and Chepho, hide them under your coats as best you can. Also, send messengers to contact all who are involved and ask them to gather here in two spans. Not all at once, though, tell them space it out so they don't draw unwanted attention. I'll go over the final details before we leave for the city square." He looked around the table. "Any questions or suggestions?"

Only the mender spoke. "Not a question. I'm just wondering if those with bows require additional arrows. Membarb and I made a bunch more. We added metal tips for penetration and thin wooden fletchings for flight accuracy."

"I'll take seven of those and a quiver if you have one," requested Max.

"A quiver? Not sure what that is."

"It's a holder for arrows. A small canvas tote bag will work, but a tube-shaped leather pouch is better and more durable."

"Sounds doable. I'll create holders for the three bowmen while we wait for the others to arrive."

"Lady Saephira, did you have anything else to add?" Jesse asked. She shook her head no. "How about you Max?"

"No, not at this point, sir. However, you can only plan for so much. We should assume unknowns will occur."

"Agreed. Final comments?" No one responded. "Okay, our briefing is over. Let's focus on the task at hand. For those who believe in prayer, now is a good time to say one."

"I'll do it," Lundy offered. "God, help us find success in this mission, keep our friends safe as we confront deception, and restore Lady Saephira to her leadership position. Amen!" Most of the assembled repeated Lundy's ending word in spite of knowing little about the God he mentioned or meaning of *amen*.

The spans passed quickly and soon the resistance members began arriving at the mender's home. Calrin and Raydoo stomped in carrying their fishing harpoons. Seth hustled over to greet them. "Awesome, I heard you dudes were part of the opposition efforts."

"You didn't think I would stay away after you saved my life from those tarkks," Carlin replied. "Besides, both Raydoo and I figured it was time to repay the favor."

"You boys won't need those harpoons," Jesse advised.

"They go where we go. The residents expect to see us carrying them. And if we have to, we'll use them to defend our Lady. Rule Number One, right Seth?" Seth nodded. Max acknowledged with a knowing smile.

As midcycle approached, the group fanned out into the streets. Mourners swarmed the memory tables, pushing and shoving to get closer. Everyone wanted a Saephira keepsake, but most of her personal items were already taken. Narleen's table still contained mementos, although it was largely picked over.

Calrin and Raydoo assumed watch positions across the street. Max and Gelr shadowed Saephira as she approached her memory table. Jesse and Seth followed Narleen to hers. Anna and Lundy traversed the perimeter. The mender greeted her friends. Membarb visited with fellow shop owners. The other resistance members, which included loyal militia and former captives, blended in with the crowds, keeping their eyes on Jesse for his signal. Chepho and Bonarb roamed around until they spotted Yhmim within the throng. She had security with her. Her team of guards carried two sets of spears with swords strapped to their belts. The brothers moved within five paces and began stalking them.

Yhmim approached the front area near the memory tables and signaled for her armed detail to drop back a couple paces. After stepping upon the raised platform, she lifted her hands high in the air. "Welcome citizens of Beayama and all those who traveled here to remember Lady Saephira and her lady-in-waiting." The people grew silent. "As you well know, Lady Saephira and Narleen perished in—"

"That is a lie!" Saephira shouted. Max placed her atop her memory table. She slipped off her scarf and revealed her face. Several attendees gasped in shock. Then she yelled again, "It's a lie! Yhmim is a traitor!"

A moment later, Jesse and Seth lifted Narleen onto her table. She removed her headscarf and echoed the same accusations, "It's a lie; it's a lie! An evil deception by Yhmim to take over Beayama for Eddnok. Both Lady Saephira and I are alive as you can see." More shocked faces turned toward

Narleen.

Two spears flew through the air from close range, one aimed toward Saephira, the second at Narleen. Max drew out his Gladius, swung, and knocked aside the first spear. It dropped on the table, barely missing Saephira. Jesse swiped at the second with his leadership staff, smacking it to the ground. Seth took out his corded rope, ready to use it as a whip in case an assailant tossed another spear. Somebody did. Timing his aim, he flipped the rope behind his back and cracked the line, which wrapped around the middle of the shaft. He yanked hard and pulled the spear right out of the air. It dropped, missing Narleen.

Chepho and his brother rushed the two men who had thrown spears and tackled them. Max pulled out his bow and notched an arrow. "If there are more quislings taking issue, please let me know." He drew the bowstring to his chin and held it. "Otherwise, I suggest you surrender." Four more of Yhmim's security guards, disguised as mourners, raised their hands in submission. Six resistance partners darted over and disarmed them.

Yhmim, who had watched it all happen in disbelief, turned and started to run away. Lundy and Anna advanced to block her escape. Anna swiped at the vice-leader's ankles with her persuader and Yhmim stumbled, falling on her face. She scrambled to her feet and continued running, but Anna used a reverse swing to strike at her knees and down she went for a second time, falling backwards, landing hard on the cobblestone pathway. "I wouldn't try fleeing a third time, lassie. Me thinks it's best you stay where you be. Your skullduggery has come to an end."

People rallied to Saephira's side as soon as Max lifted her off the table. Others gathered around Narleen who had climbed down by herself. Many of them had tears in their eyes. The militiamen whom Yhmim had deceived lowered their heads in embarrassment. Most individuals returned their keepsakes to the memory tables. Saephira noticed the ancient scroll discovered at the ruins as one of them, so she retrieved it and placed it in her coat pocket for safekeeping. She hoped Lundy could translate it. According to Jesse, it might be important for the inhabitants of Eskaonus.

After she finished greeting the well-wishers, Saephira addressed her faithful liberators who stood nearby, keeping an eye out for suspicious movements. "Arrest Yhmim and her collaborators. I want all who knowingly participated in this deception interrogated and the results brought to me in the Great Hall." She walked over to where Commander Gelr and Chepho were checking the crowd for additional conspirators. "You two are now in command of our defenses. Please escort Narleen and me to our quarters." Jesse and his group waited for the women leave, scanned the area a few more times while the throngs thinned out, and sensing things were secure, returned to the mender's house.

CHAPTER 39
ENLISTMENT AND PROMOTIONS

Jesse and his party returned to the mender's home. They sat around Ottaar's table, sipping tea and discussing the events from the last several days. The conversation included discovering a clone of the knowledge tree, rescuing captives, surviving the Lost Forest, destroying a weapon of mass destruction, and finding out just how wicked Eddnok had become. A knock at the door interrupted their meeting. The servant entered, bowed, and handed Jesse a note from Saephira:

Please come to the Great Hall. I need to make plans for next cycle and would appreciate your assistance and advice. Banquet at latecycle, planning meeting to follow. Thank you, Lady Saephira

The message was not a summons because Jesse and his companions were only visitors in Beayama, not citizens. Nevertheless, it was urgent, so they agreed to attend. This gave them a few spans to relax before dinner. Jesse found a set of fresh clothes laid out on his bed. His dresser held a washbasin, a water pitcher, and dish of soaproot. Since his old clothes were tattered and a bit grimy, it felt good to wash up and change into clean ones. Afterwards, he opened his satchel and pulled out his journal:

<u>Entry Eleven</u>

We may have discovered why evil has become so widespread. The mysterious treasure appears to be a knowledge tree clone. According to Lundy, it produced forbidden fruit like the tree in Eden and even had a similar appearance. I'm not exactly sure how or why this occurred. Notwithstanding, we think Eddnok consumed the fruit, then ignored the good knowledge and allowed the evil knowledge to spread in his already corrupted heart. If so, many have perished because of his wickedness, including Falein Village, which is now in ruins. In regard to the hidden cave and what became of the knowledge tree, I haven't a clue. Chesedel may have the lowdown since he was present at the end. All we know for sure is the tree miraculously disappeared.

Our group helped rescue Narleen for a second time and restored Saephira to her rightful place as Leader. Most of the conspirators have been rounded up, all except Eddnok. Concerning other news, we were just invited to a planning dinner. I suspect we'll be asked to help participate in an effort to stop Eddnok before more of his wickedness takes root. Countering evil was one reason we came here, right? As for the second part, to bring the truth of God and His ways back to Eskaonus, we're still working on it.

This may be my last entry for a while. It's been a learning experience for all of us, especially me. I wasn't sure I could say this and mean it until recently, but thank you for sending us here. I look forward to finishing our mission, returning to heaven and sipping a cool drink from the Fountain of Life. The water here tastes like mud.

As twilight neared, the party walked over to the hall. They enjoyed the first wholesome dinner in a week of cycles. When her guests had eaten their fill, Saephira addressed the gathering. "First of all, I want to thank my supporters for helping restore order. I owe all of you a bond of gratitude. At the same time, I am saddened by all the destruction and loss of life. I summoned you all here tonight because I need your assistance, but before we get into those details, I will share what we learned from our interrogation of Yhmim. Be assured, no violence or torture methods were used. We simply gave her the option of receiving a death sentence or being incarcerated for ages. If she talked openly and provided the truth, we would spare her life. After considering her two options, she chose the latter, broke down, and revealed all the horrid details of Eddnok's plans."

"Apparently, she had been working with Lord Eddnok for yarns on plans to take over leadership of Beayama and conquer the Lower Realm. As if the raids to steal our provisions were not enough, more recently, Eddnok had accessed certain knowledge to make fire weapons able to burn our cities and villages. Sadly, one place has already been destroyed. Falein, our northern village, its farmlands, and lake facilities have all been decimated."

"Moreover, two individuals I trusted, overseers in our leadership, Menarbat and Preaverca, conspired with him. Eddnok is not the young man I formerly knew, a person I planned to marry one day. His mind has been corrupted with evil and he doesn't care who he hurts. He is power hungry and plans to destroy us all. He has no morals, no decency, and no compassion. Eddnok must be stopped and his co-conspirators, Menarbat and Preaverca, be held accountable."

"Commander Gelr, would you stand please?" The entire hall watched as the commander slowly rose to his feet. "Commander, you once told me you desired to change your destiny by doing good. As I see it, you have succeeded at both endeavors. Therefore, I am giving you a temporary commission as senior officer-at-large. You'll oversee the campaign forces to confront Eddnok in Briacap."

Gelr dropped to his knees. "My Lady, I'm unworthy to—"

"I disagree. You have earned my trust many times over." Overcome with emotion, Gelr tried to raise himself off the floor but faltered. "Would someone help my new officer return to his seat?" Chepho rushed over, lifted Gelr up, and shuffled him back to his chair. The commander had tears running down his face.

"Maximus, you're next. Because of your military experience and expertise, I am also offering you a temporary commission. I need a replacement militia lead, a junior-ranked officer who can train and command an archer squad and assist Commander Gelr with this campaign."

Max stood to his feet and gave his typical soldier salute, his arm across the chest. "You have my sword and my bow, ma'am." Narleen rose beside him, proud, smiling, yet worried about his safety. "And ma'am, I meant to tell you. Seth recovered your longbow outside of Falein. When shall we return it?"

"Thank you, Maximus. It's an effective weapon. Seth can keep it."

Saephira then addressed Chepho and Phauch. "If you accept, you are both promoted to the rank of Militia Chief and assigned to serve under Commander Gelr and Militia Lead Maximus."

Chepho replied, "It will be an honor to fight with the commander and Max. There are few men who are braver." Phauch likewise accepted the promotion, agreeing with Chepho about the bravery and dedication of their new superior officers.

"Narleen, you are no longer the lady-in-waiting. Instead, you'll be Lady Narleen, the new vice-leader of Beayama, having authority to pick the replacement Postal Overseer, Overseer of Provisions, and any leadership position required."

"My Lady, I don't deserve—"

"Yes, you do! More than most."

"Jesse, Anna, and Seth, I'm asking you three to serve on my leadership council of advisors on a provisional basis until I can find citizen replacements."

Jesse glanced at his two colleagues for their responses before replying, "We are in agreement. It's one reason we came here, my Lady."

"As for you Master Lundy, I understand your companions refer to you as Rev and Preach. Others say you pray to an unknown lord and hail from his high kingdom. Although I don't know this god, our ancestors may have worshiped such a deity. Unfortunately, all this knowledge has been lost. Therefore, since we have little information on such matters, I would like you to function as a spiritual advisor and teacher. Please don't force your beliefs on our residents, but if they are interested, explain the truth as you understand it. My first request, however, is for you to focus on translating the ancient scroll we discovered at the ruins." Saephira walked over and handed the manuscript to Lundy. "It may be important for the welfare of all Eskaonites."

"Aye, teaching is right up me alley. I was a scholar and language expert in my land. And I've waited centuries, what you call eons, to fulfill this calling. You have me pledge. Until I leave this place, I will serve you and the people of Eskaonus."

Saephira looked puzzled by the extensive timeframe Lundy mentioned but decided not to press him for an explanation. Instead, she nodded her gratitude.

"Ottaar, my friend, I am creating a position called Mender of the Realm. If you consent, you would no longer be a local mender but rather, the lead mender for all cities and villages. I'll supply you with enough credits to build additional aid stations and train new menders. For your first order of business, I need you to organize a mobile aid station for the campaign: supplies, tents, medicines, everything necessary to treat those wounded in battle."

"As you already know, my Lady, I am honored to serve."

"Membarb, I am told you can deliver twenty-five bows with a hundred arrows that you and the mender have built and hidden in your woodshop."

"We can, my Lady, in fact, even more. Ottaar and I have completed thirty longbows and 140 arrows. All the arrows have bronze metal tips, courtesy of the metalsmith who cut and hammered out the points for us. We are still making the quivers and should have at least half of those completed by dayrise." Saephira again nodded her appreciation. "One more thing, my Lady, even though Ottaar didn't mention it, she and I have also made ten slings patterned after Seth's design. Other than collecting rounded stones as projectiles, they're ready for action."

"My thanks to you both. Bows and slings are long-range weapons our enemies do not possess. They may help us win the day." She scanned around the hall before she continued. "If any of you are declining, which you are free to do, please let me know now." She paused to see if her newly formed alliance had second thoughts about the promotions, assignments, or requests. None did. They all understood the situation and wanted to help. Without prompting, the entire hall stood and began clapping their hands.

"Your support overwhelms me." Her next statement was drowned out by the applause that seemed to grow louder the longer she waited for it to end. Finally, she motioned for the audience to take their seats. "For my last order of business, I want homing flyers sent to all destinations in the Lower Realm, requesting provisions, mounts, or whatever citizens can share for the upcoming campaign. These messages must be airborne by darkout. I will compensate citizens for all contributions in full. Furthermore, I need volunteers who are willing to fight for their province, who are tired of running from Eddnok's raids and losing property to his thefts. In three cycles, we will gather our forces together at Briacap for a final battle or Eddnok's surrender. I hope it's the latter."

"I realize you are all tired, as am I, and that you have listened to a long presentation. However, unless we change our destiny, here and in the northern province, then nothing will ever change. In the end, both realms will be lost, perhaps forever, and evil will prevail." Saephira paused one more time to let her final thought sink in.

"Again, thank you being here this nightrise and for your indulgence in these important matters. While we serve the desserts, I wonder if Anna could sing her song about the night flyer. It has special meaning for me. Perhaps it will for you as well. When she's finished, I would like my new vice-leader, commander, officers, lead mender, and leadership council members to see me before you're dismissed."

Anna stepped to the front and pulled out her glifstring. "This song is actually called *The Unseen One*. I wrote it about a divine One who cares for all people."

Every time you watch the night flyer soar,
have you not wondered if there could be more?
Or felt the hand of a presence unseen,
offering a shoulder upon which you can lean?

Have you not considered what dwells high above,
or He who created all things in His love?
The divine One who is eternal and true,
can redeem a lost soul by making it new.

This time, everyone noticed the misty cloud forming as Anna sang and played her instrument. Instead of rising upward as smoke does, the cloud descended from the ceiling and tarried above their heads. It dissipated as soon as her song ended.

"It's magic!" somebody shouted.

"No," Lundy replied. "It's the anointing."

CHAPTER 40
GATHERING BATTLEGROUPS

Even before first light, people began gathering in the city square. During Saephira's strategy-planning session the previous night, their alliance decided to divide into two detachments with Saephira in charge of one and Narleen the other. The vice-leader's party would travel east to Ritwell Village and then on to Bayegulf to gather volunteers and supplies. Narleen asked Jesse, Militia Lead Maximus, Seth, and Militia Chief Phauch to join her contingent. Saephira would go west to Cali Village and up to Midvill. She recruited Anna, Lundy, Commander Gelr, Ottaar, and Militia Chief Chepho to serve in her complement.

By forecycle, Saephira had departed taking half the assembled battlegroup with her. Some were trained militia, but most were city residents, both men and women who wanted to save their province from Eddnok.

Narleen gathered the second half with her. She was about to leave when Calrin and Raydoo approached carrying their fishing harpoons. "We're enlisting."

"Aren't you two a little young to be fighting a battle?"

"We are the same age as Seth and he's going," Raydoo insisted.

"I think you boys should stay—"

"We are not little boys!" Carlin exclaimed, annoyed by the term.

"Excuse me, Narleen. These young men are right. They are the same age as Seth, perhaps a little older." Seth noticed his

258

friends talking with Max and inched closer to hear the conversion. Max continued, "Why do you fellows want to fight?"

Raydoo responded, "Our homes and families are at stake. It's our battle as much as anyone's."

"Aren't you two afraid?" Narleen asked, concern showing on her face.

"Rule Number Two." Carlin appealed to Max. "If you face your fears you'll overcome them, right?"

"Hmm, think I've heard this rule before. What do you think, Seth, can you train a couple more men to use slings?"

"Easy peasy." Seth reached into his side carrier and handed Calrin and Raydoo each a sling. "You'll have to collect your own pebbles. Can't borrow mine, they're lucky, Rule Number One, remember." Seth watched them frown at his snarky comment, and then he cracked a half smile.

"Quit messing around you, guys." Max wanted to laugh at the playful teasing but maintained a stern look on his face. "Okay recruits, if you two agree to stay away from the frontline and only engage the enemy from slingshot range, you're hired. Mount up, we're leaving now." Feeling vindicated, the pair stowed the fishing harpoons and slipped their kacks into formation alongside Seth. Narleen still had reservations, yet trusted Max's wisdom, knowing he would watch out for their safety.

Once Narleen's detachment reached Ritwell, they noticed a crowd of vinedressers waiting in the village square. The local magistrate hailed Max and Narleen as they came near. "We received the flyer message last cycle and stand ready to defend our lands. We have twenty volunteers, and I'm going as well." Their animals were loaded with yarm berries and various provisions. None of villagers possessed swords or spears because they were not militia, just caretakers for Yarm Vineyards north of their village. They carried sickles, pruning tools, and several long carving knives.

"Thank you, magistrate. Lady Saephira and I appreciate your sacrifice." Narleen pointed to the end of the line. "Please join our caravan. We are heading to Bayegulf next and then through Heill Void to Outlook Point. We will camp there for the night."

A span later, they pulled into the coastal city of Bayegulf. The port chief hailed them. "We received your message during last nightrise. We're ready to join the expedition to save our province." Twenty-seven sailors stood on the docks with harpoons in hand. Their kacks were herded in a circle behind them, side carriers already packed with supplies. Max directed the seamen to join the line behind the band of vinedressers. Together they moved out in a column trekking north, some riding double, others walking. By postcycle, they approached the Yarm Vineyards below Outlook Point.

Jesse spotted a familiar ridge. "Hey Seth, see those cottlepines. We spent a night there once, and as I recall it wasn't a wonderful experience due to all those pink berries we consumed. I don't know about you, but if they're on tonight's menu, I'm not having any."

"Berries, berries!" Seth said with jest. "We don't need no pinkish berries."

Jesse chuckled to himself at another one of Seth's movie reference adaptations.

Instead of stopping at the overlook, the group turned west to Yarm Springs before halting. Lady Narleen scanned the area and picked out a secure campsite for those under her charge. She asked the Bayegulf sailors to erect tents, after which Max took those who were interested in learning the bow and set up practice targets, using the same training methods he'd used in the past. During latecycle, Max taught archery while Seth demonstrated the sling. Since his two friends had already received theirs, Seth passed out the remaining three slings to vinedressers who inquired about them. Both squads practiced with their projectile weapons until twilight. Afterwards, campfires were built, dinner cooked, and yarm berries passed out for dessert. Jesse and his two companions declined on the rations of pinkish treats.

The newly formed militia sat around in small clusters and compared farming methods or told fish stories about giant tarkks that got away. Seth entertained them with a shark story about needing a bigger boat. They all laughed until their sides hurt. While follow comrades visited and told tall tales, Max and Phauch debated battle strategies. Narleen, who was not a military person, simply listened. As darkout approached, those who brought tents settled into them for the night. The remainder bedded down around the firepits.

During the same cycle, Saephira's battlegroup entered Cali Village. Seventeen individuals responded to her flyer message appeal and were waiting in the village center. Most were Mista Lake fishermen and local farmers, but two were miners who recently defected from the Upper Realm. Joelurt, the crew chief, and his digman were equipped with pickaxes and shovels. The farmers carried sickles and rakes; the anglers brought their harpoons. Saephira and Commander Gelr added them to their contingent and moved on, stopping midway between Mista and Falein lakes to make camp. After dinner, Lundy worked on the translation, and Anna handed out five slings, giving the first of several lessons on their usage. Commander Gelr and Chepho discussed battle formations with Saephira. Before the group retired for the night, Anna played her musical instrument and sang another song of encouragement.

The following dayrise, both contingents continued their trek. Saephira's party entered Midvill and enlisted twenty-three people, including four safeguards and a squad of ten militiamen armed with spears and swords. The rest were townsfolk, both women and men, who offered to do what they could.

From Midvill, Saephira traveled to Falein Village to check on the recovery efforts. She left food stores, fishing gear, maize seed, and tools to help the survivors rebuild their settlement. Ottaar resupplied the village mender with medicines and bandages. In Falein, five more joined the campaign. Saephira's outfit continued east, stopping at twilight to make camp in the Disputed Lands. They followed the same routines as the previous night and then retired.

Meanwhile, Narleen's party journeyed across the boundary line into the Disputed Lands, arriving from the south, stopping outside of Tabahir. As sailors and vinedressers organized the camp, Jesse and Seth rode off for the Copper Rail to talk with the proprietor. Max stayed behind to give more archery lessons. Although Tabahir was considered a neutral city, Jesse and Seth approached it with caution and kept a lookout for danger. They stopped at the stables first to drop off their rides.

"Hey little dude, how have things been hanging?"

The stable boy's face beamed with his toothless grin, "I'ze knew you would be comin back. Da wants to see you. Has news."

The two of them bounded upstairs and found Nanlon behind the counter. "Your son says you have news," inquired Jesse. "Hope it's good."

"I do, I do. I heard about the flyer message from the Great Lady, mostly through word of mouth from itinerant merchants. At any rate, I've been talking to my fellow landlords, and we have a handful of folks who decided to volunteer, especially if there's a chance of getting rid of that deceitful ruler. My sources say Lord Eddnok is angry, got a bur in his britches or something. He's been holed up in his room, stewing about a lost treasure. Guards who come here to drink kunakk got a little tipsy and let it slip he's planning a major attack to punish his rivals."

"We figured as much. You said a handful of individuals, how many?"

"About thirty of us. Me included."

Jesse propped his leadership staff against the counter. "Any with weapons?"

"A few carry flat butcher knives. The rest of us have pitchforks and rakes from our stables. Three of us tavern owners arranged for a herd of kacks and enough provisions to feed an entire village for cycles. In fact, they are ready to go now, just say where."

"We are gathering our forces together at firstlight on the outskirts of Briacap,"

"We'll be there. In the meantime, be careful. We still have spies watching our tavern, the whole city in fact." He stopped talking and peeked out the front window to check for any shadowy figures. Seeing none, he continued. "After the big battle, if we survive, you're all invited back to the Copper Rail. I'm fixing my famous varmint stew." Nanlon chuckled as he followed them down the passageway to the stables.

The stable boy had already fed their animals, watered them, and brushed down their long manes. He stood at the entry and held his pitchfork in his hand. "If da let me, I'ze comes fight um northn bad guys, too."

"Little dude, if your father allows it, I'll teach you how to twirl my sling. For now, hang on to it for me and practice. All you need are smooth, rounded stones." Seth tossed the sling to him. The boy dropped his pitchfork and caught it in midair. Excitement showed in boy's eyes, appreciation in his father's. "Well, it's time for us to dip out." Seth and Jesse waved a farewell to the boy and his father, then departed. As they trotted along, their conversation turned into a discussion of tomorrow's tactics.

"You gave your staff to Lundy and now your sling to the stable boy. What are you going to use?"

"I kept Saephira's longbow. Been practicing with the archer squad, and I'm fairly accurate, most of the time." Seth rechecked his side carrier to make the bow hadn't slipped off. "Pretty chill we have thirty more dudes. Do you think our numbers are enough to storm the fortress, slam Eddnok, and waste his superior military?"

"I don't know Seth, I hope so. As Ottaar often says, 'Dayrise will bring what it brings.'"

They arrived at camp prior to twilight and updated Narleen and Max on developments in Tabahir. Similar to Saephira's party, Narleen's outfit followed the same routines as the yestercycle: practice with weapons, serve dinner, and bed down for nightrise.

By the end of the second day of travel, both contingents had doubled in size. Everyone hoped the morrow would change destinies, bring victory, and rid the land of evil.

Before forecycle on the third day, the two battlegroups arrived and surrounded the foreside of Briacap. Max commanded a squad of thirty archers while Anna led a team of ten slingers. Their forces also included twenty-seven mounted sailors with sea harpoons used like lances; thirty militiamen bearing spears and swords; two miners equipped with picks and shovels; and over fifty volunteers holding pitchforks, sickles, lake harpoons, and axes. The Lower Realm had amassed an army numbering 160 strong.

Lady Saephira and Lady Narleen rode in front of their troops, surrounded by Commander Gelr, Max, two militia chiefs, and Jesse, who formed a circle of protection around the two women. Ottaar and Lundy stayed in the rear with the mender tent, ready to offer aid to the wounded. Provisions and supplies were behind the aid station, guarded by a unit of volunteers. The siege on Briacap had begun. The regiment waited for the order to advance.

Suddenly, the main city gate flew open and a small cluster of shapes bolted away at full gallop. "Riders heading out," Max shouted. "Looks like three. Should we launch a volley of arrows to stop them?"

"Can you determine what they're doing, attacking or trying to escape?" Saephira asked.

"Right now, they're turning away from us and moving toward the Nae Wilderness, except they could double back. If we are going to stop them, we must shoot now, or they'll be out of range."

"Send a company of militia to pursue. Try to subdue them. In the meantime, let's began our advance on the fortress."

"They are gaining on us."

"Do we have time to go north and enter the Nae through the Narnj pass?"

"No!"

"How about going south?"

"Too risky. It would put us in Lower Realm territory."

"They are almost in spear range."

"Entering the forest is our only option."

Hesitation, silence.

"What are you afraid of?"

"Aren't those woods haunted?"

"If you believe that foolishness, you two can stay behind. I'm leaving."

More hesitation.

"They're here now. Be captured or escape with me. Make your choice."

"Okay, we'll go with you."

Lord Eddnok, Preaverca, and Menarbat the Tracker entered the Lost Forest. The cottlepines grew dense, the canopy dropped, the light dimmed. Soon, hissing sounds surrounded them.

As the battalion crept forward, the units spread out into their planned formations: longbows on the left, slings on the right. Leaders and officers took positions between both. Lancers and mounted militiamen lined up behind the archers and slingers, and the remaining squads covered the flanks. As soon as the frontline troops reached bow and sling range, they stopped.

Saephira hailed the main tower. "Ho there. I am Lady Saephira of the combined forces of the Lower Realm. We wish to negotiate with Lord Eddnok."

"I'm Senior Commander Bolgog. You can negotiate with me. Lord Eddnok left at dayrise. I'm sure you noticed the three riders leaving our fortress."

"I see. I assume you're the one in charge now."

"That's correct, Lady Saephira. Although I respect you, and I'm impressed with the battlegroup you assembled, it's only half the size of ours. You will never breach our impregnable citadel, which as we speak has over a hundred soldiers stationed on the ramparts and more in reserve. If you approach any closer, we will throw our endless supply of spears until you are all dead or decide to retreat. This is your final warning!"

"And here is your final warning!" Saephira retorted back. "Surrender now and we will spare your city! Perhaps you've noticed our squads of bowmen and slingers. We have an endless quantity of what your guards call magical flying sticks and floating rocks. These weapons can pick off your sentinels, one by one, and we never have to get closer than we are right now."

"I doubt that."

"Perhaps a demonstration is in order." Saephira gave her

prearranged signal by waving a hand toward the tower. Anna stepped forward in plain view of all on the battlement. She twirled her sling to build momentum and hurled a stone. It hit above Commander Bolgog's forehead, causing him to duck to avoid being struck in the face. Next, Max advanced three paces, knelt on one knee, notched an arrow and released it: *whish.* The arrow passed so close to Bolgog's ear that it nearly cut it off. "If we had so chosen, commander," shouted Saephira, "you would already be dead."

On cue, Commander Gelr marched forward to make the final appeal. "Senior Commander Bolgog, you know me. We served together for yarns. Stand down for the sake of the residents who live in your fortress. Eddnok is evil. You know it. I know it. And he's a coward, too, who scurried away like a frightened varmint with his tail tucked between his legs."

"You are a traitor, Gelr. Why should I listen to you?"

"Because I tell you the truth."

"Hah! Your version."

"No! It's not! You are a discerning leader. You know right from wrong. Truth from lies. Can we not discuss this matter before more innocents are killed? At least parlay with us."

"Alright, I will parlay with Lady Saephira, no one else, and I better not see any militia sneaking around or the parley is off." A few moments later, the main gate opened and Bolgog rode out, alone, carrying a blue truce banner.

"Sir, it could be a trap."

"I don't think so, Max. Bolgog always honors his word."

"My Lady, we don't think you should—"

"Hold your positions! I will see what he has to say. If it's a ploy, then . . ." She looked at Narleen, Gelr, and Max with determination in her eyes. "Have our two miners breach the lower rampart and then storm the fortress with our entire regiment." Saephira exited her circle of protectors and galloped away to meet with Bolgog. At the halfway point, he handed her the truce banner. They dismounted, walked a few paces aside, and began talking. After what seemed like spans, she curtsied to the commander and returned his banner. Bolgog bowed to her. She rode back to her frontline. He jumped on his kack and trotted off for his fortress. The entry gate, however, remained open. Ten moments later, truce banners could be seen flying high over the battlements.

Bystanders pressed around Saephira to hear what happened during the parlay. "We agreed to a temporary truce. All hostilities will cease. In thirty cycles, delegations from both realms will meet in Midvill to sign an official peace agreement. We discussed pardons and the idea of a combined province named Middle Realm, where all the cities and villages trade together."

"What about Eddnok?"

"Commander Bolgog said when Eddnok saw our battalion, he panicked and ran off like a wounded kack, abandoning them to their fates. He took Preaverca and Menarbat the Tracker with him. Those were the three riders our militia pursued until they entered the Lost Forest."

"The Lost Forest you say," Jesse pondered out loud. "They may not fare too well."

"Dudes, they're probably plant food by now."

"No doubt. Either way, lost or dead, they're gone, hopefully for good, and so is the evil they embraced."

Saephira glanced upward at the horizon, breathed a sigh of relief, and announced in a loud voice, "We are saved!" The news spread quickly. Cheers rose throughout the assemblage. Families began to celebrate. Some danced about, grabbing anybody for a partner. There were hugs, kisses, and more hugs. Saephira gave the command for the people to return to their cities and villages. The collective gathered necessities, dispersed, and began making the long journey home.

The owner of the Copper Rail galloped by and stopped in front of Saephira. His son sat behind him, holding the sling Seth gave him, grinning with his toothless smile. "If I may have a moment, Great Lady." Nanlon offered a deep bow, which almost caused him to fall off his mount. "You, the vice-leader, and Commander Gelr are invited to dinner at my place. The lead mender, Ottaar, is also welcome. I'll be serving my famous varmint stew with all the fixings. Not gonna take no for an answer." Turning to address Jesse, he continued, "You and your four companions are expected as well. Don't be late, but if you are, I'll leave a torch out for ya." He winked an eye, gave a smirk, turned his animal south, and steered for Tabahir.

CHAPTER 41
TRUTH UNVEILED

The invited group arrived at the Copper Rail Tavern by postcycle. Although it had been a long hard day with many unknowns, it ended well. They avoided a bitter conflict that would have taken numerous lives. For the first time in ages, peace and unity seemed possible in both the southern and northern provinces.

Spirits were high. Laughing filled the dining hall. It was a celebration supreme, and the proprietor had really outdone himself. His tables were set in spectacular fashion. Nanlon was elated to have the two Great Ladies, Saephira and Narleen, attending. A large oil lamp on the center table burned brightly, giving off a sweet smell similar to roses. A blue tablecloth with red stripes ran lengthwise. The pre-dinner fare included trays of candied dallups, tiny rolls of kin, smoked tarkkies, a pudding-textured cheese made from kack milk, hot Azollie tea, and as expected, numerous cups of lightly fermented yarm.

Most were saving their appetites for the main course, the owner's legendary varmint stew, and they were not disappointed when Nanlon brought out two steaming pots and placed them on the table. Everyone ate their fill, and some like Max and Seth, lost count of how many bowls they scarfed down. After the stew, fresh yarm berries desserts were served. Before Jesse could stop him or say otherwise, the reverend devoured a huge helping. "Delicious! And don't worry laddies, we Scotsmen have hardy stomachs." At the urging the mender, Lundy's fellow comrades nibbled on half servings, hoping Ottaar was right about their immunity being sufficiently developed to avoid the harmful effects. Finally, the feasting ended, and the diners pushed their plates aside and waited. They expected Saephira to address the gathering. Instead, it was Lundy.

"I finished the translation of the ancient scroll discovered at the ruins." He reached into his boot and pulled out two documents, the original and his translation, and placed one atop the other on the table in front of him. "I had to fill in a few words I didn't recognize. Even so, got the jest of it:"

When days grow evil and hope fades, five emissaries arrive from distant place. Wickedness they defeat. Old truths they renew. The Word they reveal. Anointed songs they sing. New prayers they pray. An altar uncovered. A temple found. A seed of life. A healing leaf. Five gifts they leave. After victory gained, five emissaries less one. Depart they again, the blessing restored. So it is written.

Lundy read it aloud and then slid both documents across the table to Saephira. The people waited for Saephira to comment, except she didn't. The silence in the room was telling. She read Lundy's translation, paused, read it again, and passed it over to Jesse. The original scroll she folded and tucked into her credit purse for safekeeping.

After several awkward moments of silence, Saephira spoke directly to Jesse. "This scroll, I mean the translation, describes your party of five travelers and the events occurring since you came to Eskaonus, even referring to the five items you brought with you. How is this possible? The scroll was buried eons ago in a small hidden chamber at the ruins. How can it predict your arrival two thousand yarns before it happened?"

"Through divine foreknowledge," Anna replied.

"What kind of knowledge is that? Never mind. Answer me this one thing: are you the five emissaries who hail from a distant land and who were sent here to defeat wickedness?"

"Yes, we are. However, confronting evil was only part of our mission," Jesse responded.

"Only part, then what is the rest?"

"Apparently, it involves leaving five gifts." Anna stood up. "And here's mine." Anna unstrapped her glifstring and handed it to Narleen. "This is yours now. You wanted to play it and now you can. You'll figure out the chords as I did. The instrument is unique, practically indestructible, and never requires tuning. And now, *anointed songs* you will sing."

"No Annie, it's yours. I can't possibly—"

"I always believed the glifstring would find a new owner, just as it found me. This miraculous instrument will help you bring hallowed music and song back to Eskaonus. I couldn't be happier."

"Right on Annie. I'm down with it. Here's my gift." Seth unwound his corded rope and handed it to Commander Gelr. "My *tijvah* is yours now. Some call it a cord of hope and possibilities. This little rope is so strong it can never break, at least I don't think so, and if you cut it, the length remains unaffected. You'll discover it has multiple applications."

Gelr examined the line, stretched it to test its strength, coiled it, and stuffed it into his arrow quiver. "Thank you, Seth. This is an amazing rope, and I'll cherish it."

"Okay lads and lassies, I guess my gift is next." Lundy pulled the Gospel of John he kept hidden inside his boot, unfolded it, and read the first four verses:

In the beginning was the Word, and the Word was with God, and the Word was God. The same was in the beginning with God. All things were made by him; and without him was not any thing made that was made. In him was life; and the life was the light of men.

Lundy handed the Scripture scroll to Lady Saephira. "Interested in knowing more, eh? Well, this little book will enlighten you. Do you remember Annabelle's song about the unseen One? Scripture calls Him the Word. He also has other names and titles. Every spiritual matter you ever wondered about is revealed in John's gospel of good news. It is yours to read and share with all the inhabitants of the land. You will discover the *old truths* and pray *new prayers* to a divine king who made all things, all worlds, and all places, including Eskaonus. Me thinks this represents *the blessing restored*." After Lundy finished, Saephira flipped through the twenty-one chapters, reading certain verses, scanning others. When Narleen motioned to see it, she passed it over to her.

"My turn now," Max said. "I'm leaving my Gladius,

which has an unbreakable blade with a sharpened edge that cannot be dulled." He unsheathed his weapon and laid it on the table. "Except . . . I am staying here with it."

"What?" The unexpected news shocked Jesse. He took a deep breath and held it. When he finally exhaled, he asked, "Why?"

"Because I am the *less one* mentioned in the prophecy. I've felt for a while I was destined to remain. You have all received second chances in one way or the other: Lundy fulfilled his desire to minister again; Seth conquered his fears; Anna is no longer slighted but recognized as a gifted songwriter and anointed prophet; and you, Jesse, were given another opportunity to overcome your failures and succeed as a leader."

"As for me, you all know the story of what happened, how my betrothed was murdered, and my hopes dashed. Love, marriage, raising a family—all lost, stolen by barbarians. And now, like you four, I have my second chance. Even the ancient scroll predicted it." Max returned his Gladius to its scabbard. "I'm not leaving. I've decided to settle in Eskaonus and pick mushrooms again with Narleen. And one day, I hope she'll marry me."

"I will." Her instant response caused Max's face to light up with optimism.

"And raise a family?"

"Yes, perhaps we can start on that after the wedding." She winked, offering a sly grin.

"Wonderful news, Maximus, especially for Narleen. However, this changes things. I have no choice but to withdraw your military appointment. I'm sorry, but serving as my militia lead was only a temporary position during the campaign." Max looked disappointed yet accepted there would be changes if he stayed. "Instead, I'm offering you a fulltime officer's commission. You have just been promoted to Captain of the Militia. You'll command all our forces."

Max never expected such an outcome. He rose from his chair, dropped to one knee, and withdrew his Gladius, holding it high over his head. "I am honored, my Lady, more than you know. You have my life and my sword." Max regained his footing and pointed to Gelr. "What about the commander, should he not be—"

"Yes, he should. Therefore, I am withdrawing his commission as well. Commander Gelr, stand please. You are no longer a commander. You have a new destiny as Captain of the Safeguards." Gelr knelt down and held out his sword to show his allegiance. Max moved over to stand behind him in solidary. A moment later Gelr arose, rubbing the moisture out of his eyelids.

Max and Gelr sheathed their blades and gripped arms in the comrade greeting. Afterwards, Gelr stared at Anna who proudly smiled at him. He mouthed the words: *you were right.* She mouthed back: *as were you.* While they conducted their silent conversation, Narleen left from her spot at the table, rushed over to Max, wrapped her arms around him, and whispered something into his ear.

"Wow, I hate to interrupt the moment," said Jesse, "but I have the fifth gift. At the hidden cave, I broke my candle lamp to release the special oil it contained. Not much left except potsherds. I still have my satchel, though." Jesse removed his journal since it contained his private log entries and slid the satchel across the table to Ottaar. "I want you to have it. There is also a quill pen inside with an unending supply of self-contained ink. Both items are yours. You'll find the carrying bag to be indestructible, waterproof, even fireproof, which I discovered the hard way. It has several pockets to hold things. It would make a great doctor's bag for the new Mender of the Realm. The pen writes well, too."

Ottaar inspected the satchel and opened all the little pockets, finding a hidden flap inside the lining, "What is this?" She held up an old, wrinkled pit.

"Where did you get that?" Jesse inquired.

"Inside the lining at the bottom. I felt a lump underneath and when I pulled back the flap it popped out." She handed it to Jesse.

"Kinda looks familiar. Before I arrived here, I ate a piece of fruit and considered tossing the leftover pit, but a cleric told me all things have a purpose, even an old seed, so I left it on my writing desk. If this is the same one, I wonder how it got into my satchel."

"Who gave you the satchel?" Seth asked.

"Chesedel."

"Wake up and smell the coffee, dude. He probably tucked it in there for a reason."

"Let me see that pip." Jesse handed it over to Lundy for a closer inspection. "Did the fruit have a mango shape with a purple skin?" Jesse nodded. "Where did you get it?"

"From the fruit vender's cart. He had a whole bowl of them. The attendant told me they were his most requested item."

"The fruit vender you say, hmm. Being a new arrival, you probably didn't know what kind of fruit you had eaten. The pip inside this fruit comes from the Tree of Life. I should know. I've been eating the fruit for ages. Best produce in heaven, sweet, refreshing, even invigorating." He appealed to Max and Seth for confirmation. "Isn't this right, lads?" They both indicated yes. "The tree has life properties, as does its fruit, and the leaves promote healing. No doubt about it, laddies, the *seed of life* and *healing leaf* mentioned in the prophecy refer to the life tree. This eternal seed was destined to be planted here for all the people of Eskaonus. Aye, Chesedel is a sly one for sure, smart too. Sneaking it into your bag to get it here."

"Ironic don't you think," Annie added. "One tree needed to be removed, a different one planted."

"Man, totally righteous. A tree to promote life and healing, here, just like in heaven. Freaky cool."

As the realization sank in, Jesse responded by encouraging Ottaar. "After the seed sprouts and grows into a tree, I think you'll find the leaves make a powerful healing tea as well as an effective salve."

"Alas, our ministry assignment is over. I think our new clan brothers and sisters can handle things from here on out."

"I agree with you Lundy. Investigation completed, case solved, things set right, and the truth unveiled. If I were still a police officer, I'd say it's time to clock out."

"Jesse, you and your fellow travelers helped save our realm, both realms in fact. We owe a debt we can never repay." Saephira's eyes misted up. "A simple thank you seems inadequate."

"It's more than enough. We all chose to come here, and I'm glad we did. Now it's time to go home."

"To your high kingdom?" She moved closer and gave Jesse a big hug. "Will I?" She paused to rephrase her question. "I mean, will we see you again?"

"Perhaps." He tenderly touched her face to wipe away a teardrop. "As Ottaar often says, 'Dayrise will bring what it brings.'"

"Alright dudes, it's time to bug out of here. We're burning daylight." Jesse slowly shook his head, chuckling at Seth's constant use of movie clichés.

"If you mean depart, how does one leave this place?" Saephira asked.

"It's fairly simple." The faithful band of advocates placed their no-longer-needed weapons on the table and formed a circle. Jesse glanced at Max with tear-soaked cheeks. "Thanks for everything, centurion, especially Rule Number Three. The leadership staff is yours now." The journal he tucked into his pocket. "Okay, folks, let's join hands. Will you do the honors, Reverend?"

"Aye, just think where you want to be and you're . . ." In a flash, the four of them vanished from the room. Max stared at the place where his friends had been, silent, as if trying to savor a memory before it was lost. After the longest time, he turned away, wrapped his arms around Narleen, gazed into her hazel eyes, and gave her a long overdue kiss.

Moments later, the returning emissaries arrived in front of the White Pearl Gate in heaven. Chesedel was waiting to greet them. One by one, Chesedel hugged each person, then moved aside and leaned against a pillar. He listened patiently as the emissaries talked about the final confrontation with Eddnok, why Max decided to stay, the ways they defeated evil, which captives were saved, finding and translating two ancient manuscripts, and how the Eskaonites responded to the knowledge of God. Chesedel smiled, enjoying their excitement, trying not to interrupt.

"What do you keep grinning about?" Jesse asked.

"Uzziel needs to see you four as soon as possible. He's waiting at the Fountain of Living Water."

"About what?"

"I think you already know."

GLOSSARY

Topical listing of names, locations, and terminology

Note from the Author

We sometimes assume life is the same for all created beings wherever they might exist—that individuals fit into the same mold, follow the same customs and laws, embrace the same plan of salvation, worship the same way, and end up in the same afterlife—or that spiritual warfare and physical conflicts no longer occur in the hereafter. Eternity may reveal this is not the case.

Concerning conflicts, a quick look through the Bible will detail much death and destruction endured by humanity. Some of those struggles are seen in Sodom and Gomorrah and in the violent clashes between Israel and Judah as they sought or rejected God's will. We should never assume that similar scenarios can't repeat elsewhere in God's infinite kingdom. Nor presume immortality merely involves floating on clouds as we play harps or that the final dispensation (Ephesians 1:10) means the Lord has completed His agenda. In regard to the latter, I believe our Creator has more to accomplish. And so do His redeemed.

God is the same yesterday, today, and forever (Hebrews 13:8), but His many worlds and realms, whether known or unknown, will not remain the same. Even our familiar cosmos will change. His new heaven and new earth (Revelation 21:1) will likely be distinctive, present new challenges, and offer opportunities for continued ministry. Redemption, after all, has an ongoing purpose, and eternity, an everlasting timeframe.

Central Heaven

Locations and landmarks in Central Heaven are speculative. Notwithstanding, several are based on Scripture, others inspired by tradition.

"But as it is written, Eye hath not seen, nor ear heard, neither have entered into the heart of man, the things which God hath prepared for them that love him" (1 Corinthians 2:9).

The vast realms of Central Heaven and other only imagined areas have not yet been seen by story characters Jesse Walt and Annabelle Altshuler.

LOCATIONS AND LANDMARKS

Dwelling Places: Housing for the saints.

"In my Father's house are many mansions: if *it were* not *so*, I would have told you. I go to prepare a place for you. And if I go and prepare a place for you, I will come again, and receive you unto myself; that where I am, *there* ye may be also" (John 14:2, 3).

Fountain of Living Water: A wellspring in Central Heaven that disperses the waters of life. Sometimes called the Fountain of Life.

"And he said unto me, It is done. I am Alpha and Omega, the beginning and the end. I will give unto him that is athirst of the fountain of the water of life freely" (Revelation 21:6).

"And the Spirit and the bride say, Come. And let him that heareth say, Come. And let him that is athirst come. And whosoever will, let him take the water of life freely" (Revelation 22:17).

Fruit Cart: Vendor's mobile produce stand on Straight Street.

Hall of Records: A storage facility where all the records and histories from the beginning of time are kept, including the Scroll of Life, scrolls of works, and all other related documents. The Hall of Records also contains a scroll room where residents can access Scripture, prophecies, hymns, poetry, and other writings to study, read, and enjoy. *Note: In biblical times, books were generally in the form of scrolls.*

"And I saw the dead, small and great, stand before God; and the books were opened: and another book was opened, which is *the book* of life: and the dead were judged out of those things which were written in the books, according to their works" (Revelation 20:12).

Heavenly Salutations: Peace to You, Shalom, Blessings, Precious One, Beloved, Favored Ones, Dear Ones, Maranatha, and Godspeed.

Judgment Seat: The place where Christ delivers judgments and hands out rewards.

"For we must all appear before the judgment seat of Christ; that every one may receive the things *done* in *his* body, according to that he hath done, whether *it be* good or bad" (2 Corinthians 5:10).

Orientation: An informational center to help with directions, suggestions, and guidelines for new arrivals. The facility also carries starter kits and offers a wide selection of clothing.

Outreach & Supply: A place to requisition materials, tools, musical instruments, Bibles, Torahs, and other items appropriate for use in heaven.

Patriarch Plaza: The most popular plaza in Central Heaven. It has a lecture podium and unlimited seating.

Paths of the Patriarchs: All interconnecting footpaths in Central Heaven.

Prayer Gardens: Special gathering places set aside for solitude and prayer. Some theologians believe certain biblical references or terms might foreshadow landmarks found in heaven.

GARDEN OF MEDITATION (Philippians 4:8): Located on Straight Street.

GARDEN OF PRAYER (1 Thessalonians 5:17): Junction by Damascus Road and Straight Street.

GARDEN OF SUPPLICATION (Philippians 4:6): Corner of Charity Street and Narrow Way.

Pearl Gates: The pearl gates are traditional names for entries, passageways, or portals into heaven. They are based on descriptions from Revelation 21:12–21, which mention twelve gates made with twelve single pearls. Each gate contains the written name of one of the twelve tribes of Israel. The three gates below are hypothetical.

GOLD PEARL (Matthew 13:45–46): Pearl of great price.

ROSE PEARL (Song of Solomon 2:1): Rose of Sharon.

WHITE PEARL (Isaiah 1:18, Revelation 2:17): White represents purity, newness, and forgiveness.

River of Life: A river with life-giving properties.

"And he shewed me a pure river of water of life, clear as crystal, proceeding out of the throne of God and of the Lamb" (Revelation 22:1).

Everything will live wherever the river goes (see Ezekiel 47:9).

A river went out of Eden and watered the garden (see Genesis 2:10).

Streets and Roads: Thoroughfares to various locations in Central Heaven and elsewhere. Some theologians believe roadways in heaven, like streets, are foreshadowed in Scripture.

DAMASCUS ROAD (Acts 26:12–13).
FAITH AVENUE, HOPE LANE, AND CHARITY STREET (1 Corinthians 13:13).
NARROW WAY (Matthew 7:14).
STRAIGHT STREET (Acts 9:11).

"And the street of the city *was* pure gold, as it were transparent glass" (Revelation 21:21*b*).

Throne Room: The place where the Ancient of Days resides.

"I beheld till the thrones were cast down, and the Ancient of days did sit, whose garment *was* white as snow, and the hair of his head like the pure wool: his throne *was like* the fiery flame, *and* his wheels *as* burning fire" (Daniel 7:9).

"After this I looked, and, behold, a door *was* opened in heaven: and the first voice which I heard *was* as it were of a trumpet talking with me; which said, Come up hither, and I will shew thee things which must be hereafter. And immediately I was in the spirit: and, behold, a throne was set in heaven, and *one* sat on the throne" (Revelation 4:1, 2).

Tree of Life: Ancient tree that grows and flourishes by the River of Life.

"In the midst of the street of it, and on either side of the river, *was there* the tree of life, which bare twelve *manner of* fruits, *and* yielded her fruit every month: and the leaves of the tree *were* for the healing of the nations" (Revelation 22:2).

"And out of the ground made the LORD God to grow every tree that is pleasant to the sight, and good for food; the tree of life also in the midst of the garden, and the tree of knowledge of good and evil" (Genesis 2:9).

The fruit did not fail nor did the leaves wither. Leaves were used for medicine and fruit for food (see Ezekiel 47:12).

Tree of the Knowledge of Good and Evil: Current status and location unknown.

"But of the tree of the knowledge of good and evil, thou shalt not eat of it: for in the day that thou eatest thereof thou shalt surely die" (Genesis 2:17).

"And the serpent said unto the woman, Ye shall not surely die: For God doth know that in the day ye eat thereof, then your eyes shall be opened, and ye shall be as gods, knowing good and evil" (Genesis 3:4, 5).

Waiting Line: An overflow area where people wait to appear before the Judgment Seat.

Walled Terrace: Scenic walkway in Central Heaven adjacent to the River of Life.

CHERUB ANGEL OR CHERUBIM

Cherub or cherubim in the plural form are celestial beings. They serve God and follow His will. The cherubim were first introduced in Genesis: "So he drove out the man; and he placed at the east of the garden of Eden Cherubims, and a flaming sword which turned every way, to keep the way of the tree of life" (Genesis 3:24). Although their biblical descriptions vary, cherubim are thought to have wings and carry fiery swords.

Before his rebellion and fall from heaven, Satan was a cherub (see Ezekiel 28:11–15).

Names and Individuals

Annabelle Altshuler: Also called Anna, Annie, and Annabel. Messianic believer, anointed song writer, musician, raptured saint.

Bolgog (BOWL-gog): Senior Commander in the Upper Realm Guards.

Bonarb (BOW-narb): Whereabouts unknown. Younger brother of Chepho.

Bovi (BO-vee): Lives in Briacap. Concubine in Eddnok's household. Her fraternal twin sister is Seirlai.

Brappt (BRAP't): Sub-Commander in the Upper Realm Guards.

Calrin (cal-RIN): Teenager from Beayama, harpoon angler, friend of Seth.

Chepho (CHE-foe): Militiaman in the Lower Realm.

Chesedel (CHESS-a-del): Official name is *elChesed*. Faithful messenger, Jesse's guardian angel. His name means mercy of God.

Deamonn (DAY-mun): Alchemist in Briacap.

Eddnok (ED-nock): Lord Eddnok, ruler of the Upper Realm, magistrate in Briacap.

Flissae (FLISS-ay): A prostitute who works for Eddnok.

Gelr (GEL-er): Commander in the Upper Realm Guards.

Holley Rossie: Former nurse practitioner, recent resident of heaven.

Jesse Walt: Also called Jess, JW, Sir, and Brother Walt. Served in the Navy, former police officer, chosen as team leader, raptured saint.

Joelurt (JOE-lert): Senior Mining Chief, experienced prospector, crew boss.

Lucifer: Also known as Satan, the devil, and son of the morning.

Lundy MacBain: Also called Reverend, Rev, Preach, and Master Lundy. Scottish minister, Bible scholar, language translator, missionary, martyred saint, resident of heaven.

Maximus Gallius: Known as Max, Maximum, Maxie, and the big guy. Roman soldier who found faith in Christ during the first century, longtime resident of heaven.

Melmandus (mel-MAN-dus): Captain of the Militia in the Lower Realm.

Membarb (MEM-barb): Woodsmith in Beayama.

Menarbat (MEN-ar-bat): Called *the Tracker*. Overseer of Provisions in Beayama, experienced scout, spy.

Nanlon (nan-LAWN): Owner of the Copper Rail Tavern in Tabahir. He is the barkeep, cook, and housekeeper. His son works in the stables.

Narleen (NAR-lean): Lady-in-waiting, assistant to Saephira, supervised the staff at Beayama's two main halls.

Osalawn (O-sau-lawn): A fallen angel.

Ottaar (OH-tarr): Mender in Beayama, medic, physician.

Phauch (PAW'sh): Militiaman in the Lower Realm.

Preaverca (pray-VER-ca): Postal Overseer in Beayama, spy.

Raydoo (RAE-do): Teenager from Beayama, harpoon angler, friend of Seth.

Rennard (REN-nard): Commander in the Upper Realm Guards.

Saephira (sa-FEAR-uh): Leader of the Lower Realm, senior magistrate in Beayama.

Seirlai (ser-LAY): Lives in Briacap. Her fraternal twin sister is Bovi. Both sisters are concubines in Eddnok's household.

Seth Cahir: Known as recruit or the kid. A teenager, athletic, marathon runner, rock climber, loves all outdoor sports except surfing. Accepted Christ as his Savior during the Jesus People Movement in the 1970s, resident of heaven.

Uzziel (use-ZI-el): Called *the Cherubim*, high-ranking cherub angel, carries a flaming sword. His name means strength of God.

Waubush (WAH-bush): Captain of the Safeguards in the Lower Realm. He oversees the tower guards, watchmen, and gatemen. Also holds a secondary command in the Militia.

Yhmim (yah-MIM): Vice-leader in the Lower Realm, assistant magistrate in Beayama.

Eskaonus

Eskaonus is a fictional world or place. However, all tangible worlds and places, whether known or unknown, were made by God.

"Through faith we understand that the worlds were framed by the word of God, so that things which are seen were not made of things which do appear" (Hebrews 11:3).

"Hath in these last days spoken unto us by *his* Son, whom he hath appointed heir of all things, by whom also he made the worlds" (Hebrews 1:2).

"And I saw a new heaven and a new earth: for the first heaven and the first earth were passed away; and there was no more sea" (Revelation 21:1).

"By Christ Jesus throughout all ages, world without end. Amen" (Ephesians 3:21*b*).

OVERVIEW OF ESKAONUS

Eskaonus (Es-KAY-noos) is an offworld planet or place with two provinces: Upper Realm in the north and Lower Realm in the south. It has two seas, one landlocked. Other continents or landmasses, if they exist, are unexplored.

There are no suns or moons. During the day, a glowing light similar to an aurora borealis shines forth until fading into a gloomy twilight. Afterwards, nighttime takes over followed by total darkness. Residents use torches during these darkouts.

The humid southlands have rivers, farmlands, and abundant plant life. The arid northlands are mostly barren with limited resources. Tall exotic trees called cottlepines cover the forests. Most animals are larger than those living on earth. Some have similar sounding names. Predator fish known as tarkks inhabit the lakes and lower tributaries. Slimy eels swim the rivers. Four-footed creatures with long hairy manes are used for riding and pack animals. The locals call them kacks.

Eskaonites harvest berries, maize, root vegetables, squashes, and mushrooms. Their main diet is fish from harpoon angling, but they also hunt for bush varmints and antaloops. Foods are heavily spiced to preserve them. Families generally eat two meals a day: one in the morning and a hearty dinner banquet after twilight. Drinks include various flavors of tea, yarm beverages, and kunakk.

LOCAL GREETINGS AND FORENAMES

Good dayrise:	Good morning
Good nightrise:	Good evening

Although the Eskaonites have forenames and surnames, the latter indicating their family heritage, they prefer using first names only.

TIMES AND SEASONS

Firstlight:	Predawn, also called morning twilight
Twilight:	Time before nightrise
Morrow:	Tomorrow, as in on the morrow
Dayrise:	Daytime or morning time
Nightrise:	Evening or nighttime
Darkout:	Midnight, darkest part of the night
Darkness:	Middle of the night
Dark, the:	Short form for darkout
Day:	Short form for dayrise
Night:	Short from for nightrise

Yestercycle:	Yesterday
Forecycle:	Later morning
Midcycle:	Noon or around noon
Aftercycle:	Afternoon
Postcycle:	Late afternoon
Latecycle:	Later afternoon, nearing twilight

Moments:	Minutes
Span/Spans:	Hour/hours
Cycles:	Days
Periods:	Months, sometimes as undetermined
Yarns:	Years, as in a few or many yarns
Ages:	Long time, many years, long ago
Eons:	Centuries, extensive periods of time,

past eras

DISTANCES AND MEASUREMENTS

Leagues: Distance, approximately 10 miles, sometimes as undetermined

Paces: One pace = 3 feet, thirty paces = 90 feet (height, width, stride, and distance)

Stones: Weight

Hands: One hand = 4 in, eighteen hands = 6 feet (mainly used for height)

Comparison: Tall as a cottlepine
Strong, big, or wide as a kack

MILITARY AND ARMIES

SOTHERN PROVINCE

Militia, the: Lower Realm soldiers (most are volunteers)

Safeguards, the: Lower Realm tower guards, watchmen, and gatemen (also train as militia)

Captains: Senior officers in the Militia or the Safeguards, similar to Colonels

Militia Lead: Junior officer, similar to a Lieutenant

Militia Chief: Commissioned officer with authority like a Sergeant Major

Militiamen: All soldiers, ranked or unranked

Gatemen: Keep or entryway sentries

NORTHERN PROVINCE

Guards, the: Upper Realm soldiers (most are hirelings)

Commanders: Common designations for any officer in the Guards

Senior Commander: Command rank officer, similar to a Colonel

Commander: Middle rank officer, similar to a Major

Sub-Commander: Junior officer, similar to a Lieutenant

Squad Leader: Non-commissioned rank with authority like a Sergeant

Guardsmen: All guards, including officers, sentries, warders, and sentinels

PLANTS AND ROOTS

USED IN TEAS AND MENDER REMEDIES

Anatora: Flowering plant, mild tranquilizer

Azollie: Spiny root, stimulant, similar to caffeine

Helixzon: Oily plant, ground and mashed to make healing salves

Netherute: Root, pain reliever, promotes sleep

Soaproot: White porous root, cut into squares for washing, has antiseptic qualities

Utondra: Thorny bush, leaves are antidote for yarm berry poisoning

VINEYARDS

Kunakk Vineyards (kue-NACK): Trellised vineyards near Nakk Village. The grain pods are cultivated by local vinedressers who grow, harvest, and produce a beverage called kunakk.

Yarm Vineyards (Yah'rm): A farm collective raising yarm

berries. The bushes are tended by vinedressers in nearby Ritwell Village who ship the berries throughout Eskaonus to create juices and fermented drinks as well as fresh desserts.

CITIES AND VILLAGES

Bayegulf (BAY-gulf): Port city, sailors, fishing, shipping center, allegiance to Lower Realm, city mender.

Beayama (bee-YAH-ma): Capital of the Lower Realm, non-fortress, militia headquarters, trading center, commercial shops, woodshop, metalworking, forges, city mender.

Briacap (BRY-uh-cap): Capital of the Upper Realm, fortress, large battalion, nearby mining operations, metalworking, woodshops, forges, alchemist, city mender.

Cali Village (CAL-lee): Lower Realm settlement, fishing at Mista Lake and along the Cali River, village mender.

Falein Village (FAY-leen): Lower Realm settlement, fishing at Falein Lake, farming, bush varmint hunting in the Disputed Lands, village mender.

Midvill (MID-vill): Neutral city, allegiance to Lower Realm, trading center, small militia garrison, city mender. The city straddles the middle of the boundary lines.

Nakk Village (NACK): Upper Realm settlement, vinedressers for Kunakk Vineyards, small garrison, no local mender.

Ritwell Village (RIT-well): Lower Realm settlement, vinedressers for Yarm Vineyards, fishing along the Gemous River, bush varmint and antaloop hunting in the Heill Void, no local mender.

Tabahir (TAB-uh-her): Nonaligned city in the Disputed Lands influenced by Briacap. Commerce comes from taverns, lodging, and brothels. Trading, smuggling, and bush varmint hunting. Lawless vicinity, no local mender.

WILDERNESS AND DESERTS

Blighte, the: Western badlands, barren, deadly hot, dry, no plants, no animals, inhospitable.

Heill Void (he-EL): Also called **the Void.** Arid desert, sand dunes, windy, sparse vegetation, large spiny cactus, herds of antaloop, dens of bush varmints. Located southeast of the Nae Wilderness.

Nae Wilderness (NAY): Also called **the Nae** or **the Wilderness.** Mostly unexplored, dangerous, borders the Lost Forest. Settlements are rumored to exist in the east. Explorers and trackers seldom travel more than a league into the region. Those who do, seldom return. The Nae is lifeless and desolate. It has no flowing water except in the southern part where the Gemous River intersects with the Heill Void.

Northern Expanse: Parched wastelands, scorching temperatures, unexplored.

Southern Expanse: Uninhabited region south of the Gemous River, chilly climate.

MOUNTAINS AND SUMMITS

Birgo Summit (BUR-go): Second highest elevation in Eskaonus.

Colrath Mountains (COAL-rath): Highest mountain range, red rocky shale, three abandoned mines, borders the Blighte on the west and Narmoot Forest in the south. Notable mounts are Gaulmore Peak and Birgo Summit. No minerals.

Gaulmore Peak (GAUL-more): Highest elevation in Eskaonus, south of the Northern Expanse.

Mnnie Mountains (MIN'nee): Southern mountain range, steep cliffs, deep dry canyons, ancient ruins, fresh water spring. Closest rivers are the Cali and Gemous. Veins of tin and copper are scattered among the ridges.

Narnj Mountains (NARN-jay): Second highest mountain range, located north of the Lost Forest and west of the Hallet Sea. It has two working mines with major deposits of tin and copper ore.

Onnie Passage: (ON'nee): A pass through the Mnnie Mountains with steep cliffs and deep canyons.

Outlook Point: An overlook area by the Gemous River that lies east of Yarm Vineyards and south of the Lost Forest. Last familiar landmark before entering the Nae Wilderness and Heill Void.

MINING OPERATIONS

Dig, the: Copper mine in the Narnj Mountains, worked by prison labor.

Pit, the: Tin mine in the Narnj Mountains, worked by prison labor. Ore from both mines are taken to Briacap to be smelted and forged into bronze.

Red Drop: An abandoned mine in the Colrath Mountains. The dig collapsed and buried the miners inside. Later became a graveyard memorial.

Surface Mining: The Mnnie Mountains have small veins of tin and copper on the exposed ridges. The minerals are transported to Beayama for processing.

FORESTS

Lost Forest: A large forest of cottlepines bordering the

Nae Wilderness. It earned its reputation from people who entered the dense interior and were never seen again.

Narmoot Forest (NAR-moot): A sparse forest below the Colrath Mountains. Half the trees are dead or dying. Most of the ones growing in these woods are strangely deformed.

SEAS AND OCEANS

Hallet Sea (HAL-let): Northern landlocked ocean, surrounded by steep mountains and the Northern Expanse wastelands, unexplored.

Nether Sea (NETH-er): Southern ocean, port access, harpoon fishing, costal sailing.

LAKES

Falein Lake (FAY-leen): Shallow waters, docks, boats, harpoon angling, net fishing for eels, water supply for Falein Village.

Mista Lake (MISS-tah): Deep waters, docks, boats, harpoon angling, net fishing for eels, water supply for Cali Village.

RIVERS, SPRINGS, AND WELLS

Cali River (CAL-lee): A tributary of the Gemous River with an upper fork. Supplies water to Mista and Falein lakes. The river is teaming with river eels.

Dry Well: An abandoned well near Briacap, one of many that dried up after the Event.

Gemous, the (GEM-ohus): Main river system of lower Eskaonus. It runs through the Heill Void and into the Nae Wilderness with a lower fork branching from the Nether Sea. The waters contain endless schools of slimy eel and migrating tarkks.

Hidden Springs: Not yet discovered.

High Springs: Artesian spring located in the Mnnie Mountains along Onnie Passage, non-alkaline.

Trobell Springs (TRO-bell): The main water source for Nakk Village and Briacap.

Yarm Springs (Yah'rm): A deep well near the Gemous River. Yarm Springs is the main water source for irrigating the nearby vineyards.

OTHER LOCATIONS

Boundary Lines: Northern and southern borderlines separating the provinces.

Disputed Lands: An area between the Upper and Lower Realms that both sides claim as their own. It's a barren land, lawless, and overrun by bush varmints.

Farmlands: Found entirely in the Lower Realm. They grow maize, varieties of gourds, starchy roots similar to yams, and vegetables.

Ruins, the: An ancient settlement in the Mnnie mountain range, origin unknown.

Items and Information

Alchemy: The forerunner of chemistry based on the supposed transformation of matter. Alchemists attempted to convert base metals into gold, discover universal cures for disease, and develop elixirs to prolong life.

Apothecary: An archaic term for a person who formulated and dispensed medicines. In addition to providing herbs and remedies, apothecaries offered general health advice to their patients. They also sold their ingredients and medications to other practitioners.

Antaloop: Deer-like animal with four horns. Numerous herds inhabit the Heill Void along the Gemous River. They are hunted for their tender, sweet-tasting meat.

Breaking Fast: First meal after fasting through the night, more commonly known as breakfast.

Bush Varmint: A three-legged, hopping creature with one front leg and two hind ones. Similar in size to a large jack rabbit, except the bush varmint has short ears and a long bushy tail. They live in burrows in the Disputed Lands and Heill Void. Cooked or stewed varmints are a popular entrée in the northlands.

Cottlepines: Type of evergreen pine tree with oak-shaped leaves on their branches instead of needles. They grow to a towering height.

Dallups: Mushrooms in Eskaonus. They flourish in the southern lands, propagated by seeds instead of spores. The larger ones keep the patch full by spreading their seeds during darkout. Residents only harvest the middle-sized dallups. The caps are shaped like little Christmas trees, pointed at the top with green gills underneath.

Glifstring: An eight-string musical instrument, half guitar, half harp, which never needs tuning. It comes with a shoulder strap.

Homing Flyers: Fast flying predatory birds able to navigate at night and used to deliver messages. They are the size of a large raven with a smooth underbody and grayish fuzz-covered wings.

Hunting Mushrooms (or dallups): A courting ritual.

Generally employed by women as way to meet interested suitors.

Kacks: Four-footed creatures with long-haired manes used by the locals as mounts and pack animals. They are good swimmers, fast runners, hardy, and can travel for long periods of time without drinking water.

Kin: Crispy baked bread made with maize. Considered a main food stable.

Kunakk: Dark, frothy, liquor produced from vine-ripened grain pods cultivated in the Kunakk Vineyards. The distilling process makes the drink highly intoxicating.

Maize: An orangish-brown vegetable, similar to corn, grown on stalks in the farmlands below the southern boundary line. The dried kernels are ground and used to make kin.

Rule Number One: Always expect the unexpected.

Rule Number Two: Face your fears to overcome them.

Rule Number Three: In due season you will reap if you don't quit or lose heart (see Galatians 6:9).

Sentinels: Upper Realm soldiers who function as lookouts, sentries, or watchmen.

Settee: Two or three-person couch similar to an ancient Roman lectus. Used for reclining and sometimes as a spare bed.

Slimy Eels: Slimy eels, also called river eels, are greenish, non-predator fish that spawn in the seas before they migrate upriver into the lakes where they can grow to over ten feet long. Anglers catch them with hook and line or by netting.

Tarkks: Predator fish found in lakes and the lower forks of rivers, similar in size to great white sharks or killer whales. The sea varieties are huge, growing to over a hundred feet.

Tarkkies: Juvenile tarkks, smaller but still large, about the size of a twelve-foot shark.

Tijvah: A Hebrew word for hope, expectation, and possibilities. It also refers to a rope or cord, which comes from a root word meaning to bind together, collect, expect, or wait upon. Common expression: hope is a rope.

Warders: Upper Realm soldiers who function as security guards, jailors, or stockade custodians.

Yarm: A drink made from the yarm berry, a grape-sized, pinkish berry harvested from bushes in the Yarm Vineyards. Yarm is a lightly fermented drink, which is usually diluted with water for children and adolescents. It's the preferred beverage in both realms.

FORTIFICATIONS

Alure: Access pathway in battlements (see wallwalk).

Battlement: A type of parapet on top of a rampart with spaced gaps that allowed the launching of projectiles from shielded positions (see crenels and merlons).

Citadel: Fortress or strongly fortified building or structure.

Crenels: Gaps between the raised sections (*merlons*) in parapets, battlements, or fortified towers. Defenders were able to observe and deploy weapons through the crenels.

Fortress: Stronghold with a military presence often included in a town or city.

Garrison Quarters: Where soldiers are housed and fed when on active duty.

Merlons: Raised sections between the gaps (*crenels*) of a parapet, battlement wall, or fortified tower. Defenders could hide behind the merlons for protection.

Parapet: Low retaining wall, often part of battlements, offering protection to defenders on the wallwalk behind it. A rampart was the main wall. The parapet was a lesser wall with a height ranging between chest-level and the top of someone's head.

Rampart: The main defensive wall in a citadel or fortified structure. It usually had a broad top with a wallwalk and parapet.

Stockade: Prison, holding area, or jail.

Wallwalk: Walkway running along the interior part of a fortified wall or parapet.

WEAPONS

Dagger: Handheld knife, shorter than a throwing knife, used in combat and for self-defense.

Fighting Staff: Also called a quarterstaff, battlestaff, and according to Max, *the persuader.* Wielded in sparring and combat. Common fighting techniques included lunge, strike (reverse, counter, or spin around), block, parry, sweep, fake, dodge, and deflect.

Gladius, the: A Roman medium length sword, double-edged, with a honed point suitable for cutting, chopping, and thrusting. The iron blade fit into a wooden sheath surrounded by either leather or bronze. Max's heaven-issued sword is patterned after the same basic design but forged with a superior metal of unknown origin. The edge was razor-sharp and the blade practically unbreakable.

Longbow: Although the longbow was commonly associated with the Celts in Wales, various ancient cultures employed them for hunting and warfare. Often made with yew but different woods were also utilized. The bow could shoot arrows over a half mile and were deadly accurate at 200 feet.

Sling: Ancient slings were constructed with a holding pouch connected to two cords. One cord ended in a loop, which slingers would side over their fingers so when the other cord was released, the sling stayed attached to their hand. Rounded stone projectiles flung from slings could reach distances beyond 600 feet and had a high degree of accuracy at 150 feet.

Spears: The Guards used a red and black long-handled spear with a bronze point. It measured eight foot in length. Militia spears were shorter at six feet, unpainted and nondescript. Both types could be tossed like javelins. The accuracy range was between forty and fifty feet. Soldiers often carried two.

Swords: All swords from Eskaonus were bronze forged and tempered. The Guards preferred curved, single-bladed swords while the Militia wielded straight, double-edged ones.

Throwing Knives: Common weapons in both realms and carried in pairs. Depending on a person's expertise, thrown knives had an accuracy range of thirty feet.

BUILDINGS AND HALLS

Archives, the: Both Beayama and Briacap maintained a storage library with ancient documents, detailing their history and cultures, much of it vague and incomplete.

Great Hall, the: A building in Beayama with a large hall for public events such as banquets, exhibitions, and business meetings. It contained conference rooms and two kitchens.

Postal Tower: Also called the mail tower. The structure included a delivery room, residential quarters, a clerk's sorting desk, and roosts for the homing flyers. Cities staffed at least one tower for communications between communities. Villages used postal huts run by volunteers.

Residential Hall: Living quarters for Saephira and other governmental officials.

ABOUT THE AUTHOR

Charles Earl Harrel is a Christian writer with more than 650 published works. His articles, inspirational stories, and devotionals have appeared in various periodicals and in forty-one anthologies. Charles is also a nine-time contributor to Chicken Soup for the Soul. He has written two books: *The Ministry of Divine Healing* and *The Greatest Moment.*

He pastored for thirty years, serving churches in California, Nevada, and Oregon, before stepping aside to pursue writing. Charles holds a doctorate in ministry. He and his wife, Laura, live in Portland, Oregon. They enjoy hiking, community outreach, and teaching from God's Word.